FATED SWIFT

DAVID FARRAR

www.FatedSwift.com
Instagram: @FatedSwift

ISBN: 978-1-7360410-0-0

Cover Art

Alan Lee, AlanLeeDesign.com

This is a work of fiction. The Bronze Age was real – a marvelous, exotic age, the forge of our most enduring myths. Any resemblance to myth or historical events is intentional, any resemblance to real persons is coincidental.

For

Wesley and Geneva

Foreword

Have you ever wandered across an innocuous line in a text and casually thought "I wonder what *that* story was?" I do this often, not because I am particularly erudite, but I am curious – especially about people and the cultures their efforts create.

And so it was with the origin of this story. I was reading about the archaeology of Akrotiri, an advanced Minoan settlement on the Greek island of Santorini, which could boast three story buildings, drainage systems, and beautiful, sophisticated art. It was buried in the massive Theran eruption of 1600 BC, the largest volcanic eruption in the history of mankind.

And here are the lines: **"Only a single gold object has been found, hidden beneath flooring, and no uninterred human skeletal remains have been found. This indicates that an orderly evacuation was performed with little or no loss of life."**

How could this possibly be? A mass exodus – off an island, and they took their valuables? In 1600 BC? How did they know to leave? How did they convince everyone to evacuate a homeland they had inhabited for thousands of years and nurtured into a remote and protected paradise? The amount of planning, logistics and execution are daunting. Little wonder they are identified as the source of the Atlantis legend.

I would like to meet these people. Surely, a race so capable landed on other shores, and we heard from them again under another guise.

Let us find out.

BACKGROUND

The Bronze Age (circa 2800 BC – 1200 BC) was a time of splendor, replete with kings, palaces, gods and wealth – the kind of wealth that is accompanied by invasions, war, pirating, pillaging and socio-political intrigue; an incubator of mankind's activities right up to the present. No dark age, it was an era of rapid advancement and an accompanying rapid decline – a time when civilizations learned how to write and then promptly forgot it in the turmoil which followed, not to be relearned for centuries. Much of this advancement was due to the rapid expansion of international trading networks and the infusion of ideas which cultural contact spawns, much as it would again with the golden age Greeks and later yet again with the Roman Empire.

Bronze, and its supporting infrastructure, became the foundation of a material civilization and the palace economies which went with it. Copper sources and especially tin mines (the ingredient which turns copper into bronze), were coveted resources. Scattered in remote corners about the known world, their locations and trade routes were jealously guarded and sought after. And for good reason; it was the metal around which impressive armories, and empires, could be constructed. Tin acquisition (the rarer of the two) was the cause of more than one trade war. Many believe it was tin, not Helen, which launched a thousand ships at the end of this age. Coined money did not exist, but barter in metal was always acceptable, along with the usual equivalents in barley or grain, made possible by the great store of these commodities in the population trading centers.

But while the land based empires spent much of their time and wealth fighting each other, the inhabitants of the islands of the Aegean - the western world's first seafaring culture - turned their energies to the creation of a trade empire which through its very bureaucratic construction allowed all to benefit from, and share in, the wealth and prosperity – including, of course, the palaces which orchestrated the entire economy.

Considered only a legend for over 3500 years, these people we now call Minoan, preceded the Mycenaean Greeks (Achaeans), and truly stand at the very beginning of western civilization. This culture, unique in antiquity, was a magnificent merchant economy with a fleet that carried the goods of the known world in their bottoms and cleared the seas of piracy, protecting their shores and their way of life, until the war-loving Achaeans - one of their best customers and imitators - usurped their art; their gods; and ultimate mastery of the Aegean and its bounty. And it all happened 300 years before Achilles fought Hector at the gates of Troy and a thousand years before the ultimate inheritors of this legacy – the golden age Greeks – reigned.

But while they still held, the Minoans enjoyed aspects of an enlightened civilization which for many, are not available even today. It was a time and place to enjoy the beautiful things which stability, prosperity, and leisure can supply: art, sports, music, stories, poetry, and beautifully made consumables like perfume, incense, cosmetics, exotic foods, fashions and most important - ideas.

Their highly sophisticated culture delivered social equality not only to the craft and seafaring trades, but also to both genders. Women participated fully in the society via sports, religion, occupations, and freedom of movement, unbarred by any of the social barriers ubiquitous in all the cultures surrounding them.

There was no caste system or any other onerous division of class; slavery is not evident; and the population seemed to be a cosmopolitan mix of races and peoples. The Minoans were the only known civilization where the entire society lived prosperously in their own multi-room homes (as opposed to one room huts) with internal sewer and plumbing systems - that would not be duplicated again for almost 3500 years.

And while their immense wealth still held, they produced not only major technical developments in both land and naval architecture, but they produced art of stunning beauty, reflective of a people at peace with the world, enjoying the bounty not available to those who would instead focus economic resources on war and conquest. But this would ultimately be their undoing, as those more inclined to conquer, would in due course, find them a juicy prize.

But many benefited from the trade relationships for millennia, right up until the time of this saga, circa 1600 BC. On friendly terms with the Minoans, the Egyptians traded extensively with them. So much so that Minoans, recognized by their stylish fashions, are depicted in Egyptian art bringing olive oil, wine, and crafts from the Aegean to be presented to the

Pharaohs. The Egyptians had just overthrown the Hyksos, beginning their New Kingdom, and expanding their frontiers to the northeast where they were skirmishing with the Mitanni and soon to encounter the Hittites, a tough warrior breed, well on their way to creating their own empire based on iron weapons – a new 'black metal' whose secrets they jealously guarded.

The storied Israelites were still enslaved in Egypt, not yet ready to move to the land of Canaan, where there were many walled city-states, including Byblos, Tyre and Ugarit. There, the Phoenicians held sway, trading in beautifully worked gold, ivory and glass, but especially known for their purple dye made from the murex shell, which they used to dye cloth from shades of pink to the deepest purple. Their best customer was Egypt, who bought large quantities of their other famous export - cedar from the heights of Lebanon.

But time was running out for the Minoans. Already on a steep and slippery decline under pressure from the relentless Achaeans, they were just about to suffer a crippling blow from the cataclysmic annihilation of one of their best homeports and the unimaginable devastation rendered to the Aegean. It would be one of the most destructive events in human history.

MAP OF MINOA

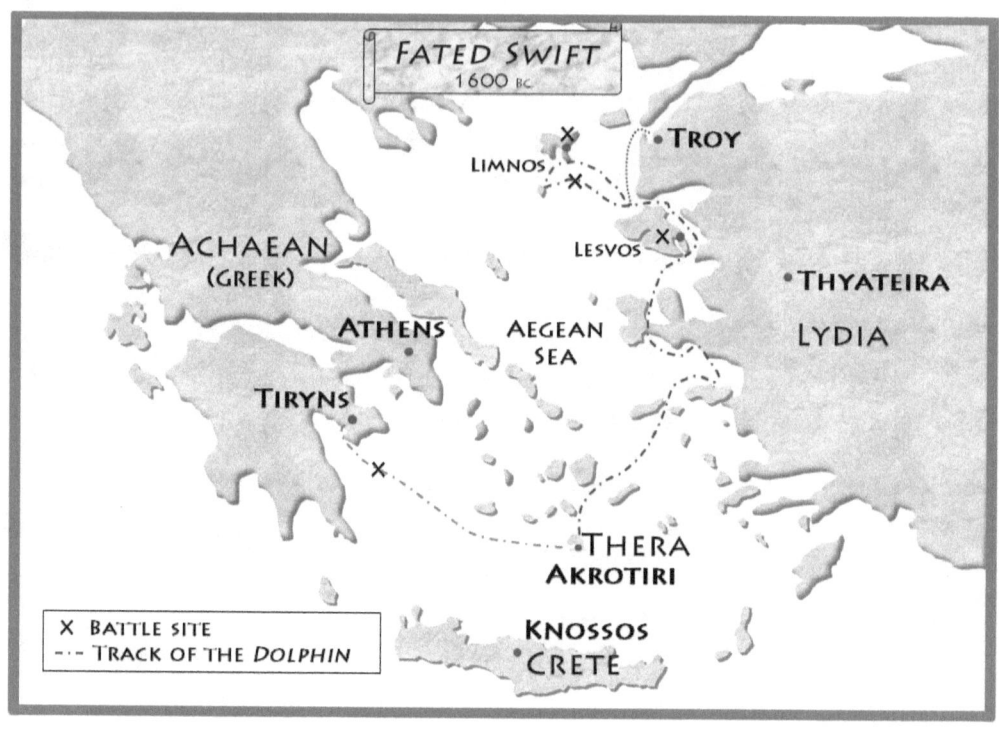

FATED SWIFT
1600 BC

TROY

LIMNOS

LESVOS

ACHAEAN
(GREEK)

THYATEIRA

LYDIA

ATHENS

AEGEAN
SEA

TIRYNS

THERA
AKROTIRI

KNOSSOS
CRETE

X BATTLE SITE
--- TRACK OF THE *DOLPHIN*

MAP OF AKROTIRI

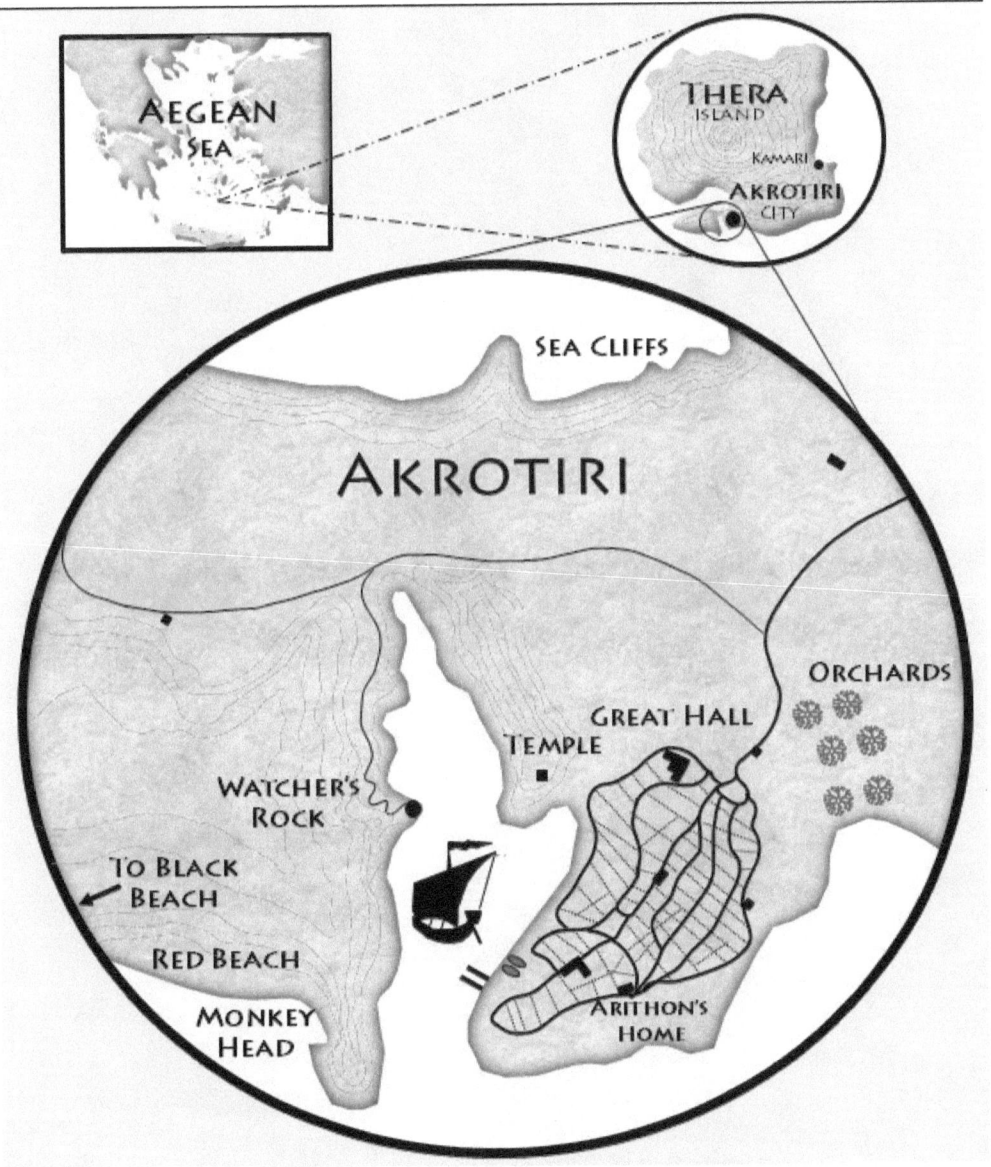

CHAPTER 1 SEA PEOPLES

Nyx, goddess of the night, had protected the lone ship during
her nocturnal reign, but she would soon remove her dark veil and
the mortal's ship would be visible to the hunters who sought her
in the blackness. On board, all had slept, save one, and unto
this mortal Nyx bestowed a foreboding, even as she herself was
forced to withdraw westward from the coming dawn.

Poius, standing on the rear deck, the steering oar thrumming his
calloused hands, suddenly sensed the hunter which stalked him. He
glanced to port, observed the retreat of Nyx, and then to starboard where it
was still too black to reveal the menace which could now see his ship
silhouetted against the backlit horizon of dawn. The mariner twisted his
hands back and forth around the shaft of the tiller, uneasy, and he
wondered why, for he had spent countless nights navigating alone on the
decks of ships, great and small.

But this was no small ship. The *Swallow* was the pride of the Theran
fleet; the largest ship ever launched from the shipyards of Akrotiri with a
thousand years of nautical excellence carved into her sleek hull. Ninety-six
feet in length, she could carry a crew of forty and a prodigious payload
which would establish her as a mainstay of Theran wealth. The entire
island and half of the fleet were in harbor for the festive launch held on
Poseidon's day. After a two-week sea trial, he declared her seaworthy; the
nimblest ship he had ever sailed, ready for her maiden voyage to Crete
carrying copper, textiles, obsidian, pumice, wine, and pottery for the
markets of Knossos. Built for the maritime trades by a peaceable race, she
would be one of their last.

A jolt to the tiller prodded Poius to shift his feet and reset his stance. It
was a common occurrence: the submerged blade striking a fish or roaming
ocean debris; but it jolted Poius' complacency. If only the sail had not been
reefed so short in this steady wind. He peered long into the blackness and
glimpsed, or maybe just felt, something moving with malice and intent – a
savage heart he had encountered once before.

"The dawn has swifter wings," he mumbled to himself. He scanned the west and chewed on his lower lip until he could wait no longer, thinking it better to cut short the watch than their lives.

"Alteron," he called in the direction of the tiny cabin on the aft deck.

"Alteron! To me!"

A tall and powerful man emerged tying back his hair. Deliberate motion; intelligent eyes; his strong features bespoke an intensity for which he was known across all of Minoa, as was his broad, calm smile. He assessed the conditions of ship and sea, glanced skyward at the retreating stars, and stepped to the steering oar.

"What is it, Po?"

"I sense a chaser ... west-northwest."

Alteron did not need to confirm; Po always sensed a pursuer before they became visible – except once – and he lost his wife in the carnage which followed. "Rouse the sheet-men," Alteron said, though his utterance was just a formality: Po and he were of one mind at sea.

Alteron assumed the tiller and held her on a southward course, while Po and the five sheet-men hoisted the ship's one square sail. Alteron kept vigil on the horizon as the muscle-bound Tisander tailed on to the halyard while Po and the other four slackened the sheet and brace lines to facilitate the transference of the rigging. When the yardarm clacked into position Po and Micus tightened the sheet lines of the loose-footed and wildly flapping sail, bringing it to full billow; the ship surging forward as she stretched and flexed her muscles for the coming day.

Po was on the port side adjusting the brace line to stabilize the yardarm and then to the starboard to do the same, planting his foot on the gunnel to heave the tension he needed to satisfy the ship and himself. As he tied off the loose end on the rail next to the fairlead, he looked back at Alteron, caught his eyes, and then cut his own in the direction of the mast. Alteron returned an agreeing nod.

"Micus, tighten that leeward stay!" Po ordered as he stepped forward, his broad gait balanced against the roll of the ship.

Alteron watched Po shinny up the mast, stand on the yardarm and begin his scan, one arm clasped around the foretop. Noticing Po fix his gaze broad-on-the-quarter, he looked back over his shoulder and tried to locate the unseen pursuer but could not detect the disturbance which was agitating Po. A trailing ship in these open waters was not a good omen, especially now during the height of the trading season. The *Swallow* would

2

be a fat prize for any bold enough to try her and Alteron was fully aware of his lone vulnerability. The report from the *Sea Turtle* washed forward in his mind and he gripped the tiller tighter, wondering if he had made a mistake not waiting for the *Coriphenes*.

While the darkness ebbed, he considered their situation and instructed Micus to adjust the sheets when he felt the wind veer round on their quarter. He could not dispel this unaccustomed apprehension he now felt, but he knew its source: there was something aboard he could not lose.

Dawn waxed, and only the brightest stars still held in a bluing sky, when Po broke off and looked down at him.

"Can you make her?" Alteron's voice boomed above the wind and the flapping of the sail.

"Sea Peoples!" cried Poius.

Arithon's eyes snapped open, and he rose on his elbows in his makeshift bed nestled among the coiled ropes stored on the triangular shelf in the forward hold. "Sea Peoples" his mind voiced and a chill shook him. As he began to stir, he could feel the gentle porpoising of the bow and the distinctive sound of the wash against the hull which told him they were running before the wind - at full sail now. It was utterly dark below deck, but he believed he could almost see, amidships at the hatch, something less than the blackness around him. Must be close to dawn.

Others aboard had also heard the alarm, and were rising from where they slept amidst all the jars, boxes, bags and baskets which looked like a random collection from the street markets, poured into the hold and shaken by a curious giant until the contents had settled.

"Up Ari! Poius will require his 'Little Captain'," the lead oarsman said from his bunk high on the inner hull.

"Break surface first," Arithon challenged, as he pivoted over the edge and dropped onto the bolts of yellow and green linen stacked below.

The seamen loved Arithon, the handsome, bright-eyed son of their employer, and treated him as one of the crew. He had grown up in their midst learning the skills of a maritime people, sailing on hundreds of the day-ships which hopped island to island, too small to spend a night at sea. An adept pupil in a community known throughout the Aegean for its nautical excellence, he had already shown enough proficiency for his father to allow him to sail on the 'cruisers', as they called the big ships. He was thrilled, in this his twelfth year, to be part of this voyage. But just as a cyclone begins with a gentle change in the wind, this journey would set in motion the storm which would define Arithon's life.

He stutter-stepped across the tops of the jars to slip past the queue trying to exit the hold; expelling a triumphant chortle as he popped above deck. A torrent of verbal harassment from those he 'corked' chased him aft where Po was just dropping onto the boards on his way to confer with Alteron, who had just relinquished the helm to Tisander.

"Raiders!" said Poius, "In pursuit!"

Arithon joined Poius and his father astern at the starboard rail next to the tiller. A mixture of excitement and fear gripped him as he located the distant sail cycling into view as it crested the swells on the horizon. The crew, without a word from the captain, were busy fitting the stowed oars into their leather-lined locks and taking their positions on the benches nestled in the open, recessed cockpit which ran along both sides of the main hull. Sosius, as strokeman, was ready first, positioned on the aft-most bench, ten feet in front of the steering oar.

"Can we outrun her?" his father asked.

"Do not yet know," replied Poius, still contemplating. "Our load is great. Might need to jettison the marble and jars – or turn and fight."

Arithon turned his gaze from the sea to his father and watched him roll his shoulders as he took in a long breath and held it. Arithon knew this stance and what was coming next. The cargo below contained the best products to be obtained from all points on the Eastern Sea, plus Akrotirian specialties: jewelry, marble-vases, and saffron. The loss would be catastrophic to his family and to the crew, who also held a stake in the profits, but they would lose their lives if the pursuing ship could close on them. Alteron looked at Poius, then at Sosius and his team poised with oars in position, and then back at Poius, who nodded his agreement.

"Pursuit!"

"SQUARE BLADE," Sosius called in a powerful baritone.

The rowers rotated their feathered oars perpendicular to the water in a grand salute.

"REACH," he bellowed.

Starboard and port leaned forward, extending their oars back.

"CATCH, STR———OKE, FINISH," he roared, setting them on the swing.

"STROKE … STROKE … STROKE," he sang.

Each a little faster for the first ten as the ship responded to the additional surge of power before settling into a steady resonance of, "HO! … HO! … HO! … HO!"

The ship had almost doubled her speed as Poius wrapped his bare feet around the girth of the mast and climbed deftly skyward, hand-over-hand on the knotted rope like a spider ascending his setline. His short frame belied the wiry, coordinated strength he possessed; prowess lay hidden under his unassuming and courteous personality. Poius and Arithon's father were old friends, tempered by trials at sea which bonded them in a friendship which required little dialogue. Each knew the other so well they could anticipate each other's needs without a word. They did talk, sometimes long and passionately, but usually at night when others were not near. Arithon would often listen to the murmur of their voices in the courtyard outside his home in Akrotiri, as he drifted off to sleep.

Arithon followed Po up the mast, where the old mariner made room for the boy's feet on the yardarm. There was space only for one, but the boy had yet to fill the frame he had inherited from his father. Arithon looked down through his arms, clasped around the mast, and could see the swaying line of the rowers' heads moving fore and aft. The oars, bristling from the sides like the legs of a giant sea bug, dipped, traveled, and then rose in unison, leaving little whirlpools of froth where they exited the water, propelling the ship forward in a graceful display of speed and power. He loved the view from atop; the billowed sail slapping at the wind, the pole of the mast – amplified by its height – pitching with the swells in a sweeping arc, trying to whip them from its head like an unwanted pair of birds on a windy tree top. It was a grand ride!

But death approached, steady and sure.

"What marks them – the Sea Peoples?" questioned Arithon.

"You know the pirates always have the white sail. But the Sea Peoples have an odd, curved prow," he answered, making a half sweep with his finger.

Arithon looked down at his own sail: head and foot trimmed sky-blue, with broad vertical stripes of white and scarlet; in the center a massive bull's head of black-crimson with horns curving out and across the stripes. It was Poseidon's bull, protector on the seas. Only Minoans had the wherewithal and desire to color their ships. It was their trademark since the faraway age: a declaration that the Aegean belonged to them.

5

Po never took his eyes off the western horizon as he spoke. Arithon knew what he was waiting for. The trailing ship was hull down and Po needed to glimpse the vessel as it topped the swells, but the *Swallow* needed to be cresting at the same time.

"We have a good wind and the angle favors us," said Po, continuing to scan. "There is---"

And then it happened, and Po went silent.

Arithon felt a jab of terror in his stomach as the pursuing ship, with its sail full, heaved to the top of the swell. He thought he saw something else.

"Many oars," breathed Po, and Arithon saw he was right: a score of rowers, slaves no doubt, and their ship would be fast under sail and oar.

"Helios – your beams," summoned Po, looking back to the east, calculating the time to sunrise.

The two ships rolled with the rhythm of the ocean, sometimes in phase with one another, sometimes opposite. The pursuing ship, on a broad reach, was angling to intercept the heavily loaded *Swallow*. Even from that distance, Arithon could see them adjusting their sail to drive her faster. She has run down prey before, he decided, and shivered.

Arithon shook off his reflections and started to count the swells between the two ships, as Po had taught him. He wanted to contribute and after doing the mathematics in his head, decided he had an answer. He ventured another question as Po remained motionless, his eyes fixed on the pirate vessel.

"What do you seek, Po? I have the distance," he said.

Po did not answer. Arithon, watching the ship off his left shoulder, turned to see Po tapping his index finger in a slow rhythm against the mast. Arithon pivoted his head to look off the port side, where the fire of the sun was just breaking the horizon. Wispy morning clouds were glowing orange on their backsides. Moments later the sea was awash with light, and as the dark waters took on a faded gray-blue, Arithon turned back to locate the pirate ship as she again rose to the top of a swell, only a league distant.

"There is another, and she is ..." Po's thought trailed off.

Arithon located the other vessel just rolling over the horizon and knew she was different but could not say why.

Po squinted hard at the next joint cresting, seemed to have the information he wanted, and started his slide down the mast as the *Swallow* slid down into a trough. Arithon followed and jumped the last four feet to the deck and trailed Po over to the rail, where his father stood waiting.

"Two, riding high," he said, "... the distant one is a many-benched black-hull."

"Black-hull?" questioned Alteron looking away to the horizon. "Will we meet?"

"Our wind is better, and their oars may tire, but for now – they gain," Po replied.

"Could we make Crete today?"

"No," said Po, "we will not make nightfall. Hope for mistreated slaves."

"A sad thought with which to console ourselves," said Alteron as he interlocked his fingers, leaned his elbows onto the rail and turned to look at Po and his son.

Arithon knew well his father's views here. Therans, isolated from the empires of the east, had developed a culture of freedom and dignity for both men and women. They had little need of tombs for divine kings or monumental temples built on the backs of slaves. The wealth of their society was more stratified; a system of skilled, independent artisans and traders. Minoans rejected slavery; a cruel practice which required warriors and wars.

After what seemed a long deliberation Alteron made up his mind. "The wolf and the lion hunt together – a foul team. We need to outrun them."

"Agreed," Po replied. "Let us see if they can close."

And so the two men stood at the rail with the boy between them, and watched the pursuing ships with apprehension, as the sun rose and began to warm their backs. Arithon swallowed – his mouth was dryer than he thought it should be. He left Po and his father deliberating at the rail and hopped into the hold, landing on the keel-walk, a board perched above the cargo which allowed travel fore and aft. He located a bulging waterskin swinging from a crossbeam and took a long drink before putting it around his neck. A large roller unbalanced him as he scampered to his cubbyhole in the bow, where he flipped open the round-lidded basket his mother entrusted to him on their city quay. He filled one hand with purple grapes from the family vineyard before rummaging underneath the straw packing to pull out three blocks of goat cheese; each wrapped in a grape leaf and tied with a mother's care using a grass ribbon. He bolted back along the keel-walk to the ladder, popped out of the hatch, bounded to where he had been just moments before, and slipped between the two old friends, handing one of the little packets to each.

"How do you know the wind will hold all day, Po?" asked Arithon.

He bit off a mouthful of grapes and began to spit the seeds into the ocean, wiping his chin with the back of his hand.

"I cannot be sure, Young Captain, but the weather is usually quite predictable during the late spring, and unless the gods have other plans, the wind will hold.

"Look at the swells off the horizons there," Po said, pointing to the east and west.

"Yes," Arithon replied interested. He handed a sprig of grapes to Po.

"Notice their shape; well rounded. And look how each is the same and all are moving south, southwest. Now let us count between them. Start on this swell."

"One, two, three, four, five, six, seven, eight," they counted together, until the *Swallow* again rose to the top.

"Eight," said Po. "That means these waves come from far away and the wind is well established, where they are formed. And those swells on the horizon as far as we can see are not diminishing. The wind will hold, at least until nightfall, but they will either catch us or we will outrun them long before then."

"Who are they? ... The Sea Peoples, I mean."

Silence followed and Arithon waited. He expected his father to answer and was surprised when Po spoke up instead.

"They sail from the North. The Sidetians say they enter our sea via the Pillars; the Lydians think they come from the Black Sea through the spont. Their ways are strange. They began to appear when my years were new, but this is the first time I have seen them in home waters. They must be getting numerous – or bolder. They wreak destruction wherever they go, preying on lone vessels or isolated towns, killing and looting. The Destroyers on the Sea."

Arithon and his young friends knew of the Sea Peoples, and sometimes played games of war and chase with the marauders as their imagined adversary. But he had never discussed them with an adult, and it chilled him to hear Po confirm the image he had built up in his mind. His disquiet lingered and then he asked: "You have fought them before?"

Po did not respond and Alteron looked at his son with a kind but serious look which told him not to pursue an answer.

Po, slowly mouthing the grapes, looked long at the pursuers. "They will catch us if they can maintain that cadence. ... Sooner not later."

"What if they catch us," Arithon asked, his voice rising. "Will —"

"Go," Po interrupted, "and fetch water to the rowers!"

Arithon flinched, gathered himself, and with a nod of respect darted for the hatch.

"Never seen a pirate close so fast," Po said under his breath.

"Nor I."

Arithon, bent at the waist with an armful of waterskins, was using his toes to feel along the planking. His eyes had not yet adjusted to the darkness of the aft hold where the two large water jars stood on either side of the keel; their lids tied shut to prevent sloshing. As he slipped the knot and laid back the lid, he could hear Sosius calling 'Ho' over the creaking of the timbers. As deck-boy, he had fetched water countless times, but never under duress and as he hurried, he dropped a skin down between the frames where the blow popped its cork and the contents gurgled into the bilge.

"BaBai," he whispered, reaching to save what he could and hoping no one had witnessed the waste. He finished filling the eight skins and arranged them around his neck and started a wobbly walk forward, balancing against the rolling yaw of running downwind. The brightness on deck brought a squint, but the fresh air calmed his nerves. He looked back to locate his father, and then moved to each station, squirting a jet into the open mouth of each rower in turn. The crewmen voiced their thanks and then set to, rowing the heavy ship with unremitting endurance.

For the next two hours, Arithon labored to forestall the exhaustion of dehydrated men; their hair already sweat-matted under their headbands. To sustain their strength, he also managed to bring packets of cheese, chickpeas, and raisins.

Po kept watch on the two pirate ships, while Alteron stood with Tisander at the tiller, modifying the ship's angle to the wind and the waves. It was a dangerous game – predator and prey testing each other for a sign of weakness.

But the two pirate ships grew as they closed the distance; rowing to a quicker cadence, they gained with every catch of their oars. Po walked the ship checking the rowers, the *Swallow*'s sail, or her point on the waves. Their interception was now apparent and with a tilt of his head he asked Alteron to join him at the stern.

"The lead ship will catch us," he said, keeping his back to the rowers.

Alteron looked back at the ships weighing his options. His first line of defense was breached.

"Have Arithon dispense the weapons to each station and then come back. I have another need more pressing," Alteron said.

Po did not have to ask. He alone, of those aboard, knew firsthand what awaited captives and he also knew what Alteron was thinking and ground his teeth in his own disquiet.

"Place the axes and spears like this," he instructed Arithon after they emerged from the hold with arms full. "Then put a shield at each station," he finished, pointing to the left of each pair.

"I can do it, Po."

"I know you can," Po said. "Quick and clever now."

On his way back to the steering oar, Po caught the gaze of Sosius, who could not break cadence to talk. "Ho," he cried as he pulled on the timing oar. The eyes of the two mariners met and Po knew what he wanted. He clapped four fingers against the opposing wrist, wobbled both fists and then turned his palms outward. Sosius nodded his understanding and continued to row, never missing a beat.

When Po returned to Alteron, he noticed the pirates had gained even faster than expected, their stroke half again as fast as Sosius, whose team labored against the tonnage in the hold. They could now hear the unsettling Boom, Boom, Boom of the master's drum.

"If they board us, I ask you to defend the boy until it is hopeless," said Alteron.

"Alteron, my place is with the crew," Po tried, though he knew Alteron would not relent.

"No, Po, I cannot, because ..." Po looked Alteron in the eyes, but he cut away.

"I do not want him captured," he continued. "And I am not sure I could ..."

Po placed a hand on Alteron's shoulder and said, "My friend, it is beyond even a god's power to express. If it comes to that, I will do as you wish, though I will earn the wrath of the immortals. He will never feel it, I promise.

"But we are not boarded, yet. I still have a few tricks."

"They will try to rake us. When they ship oars, we will cut to starboard – across his bow – just enough to clear. Theirs is a tough maneuver under sail and they will only get one try. If they miss, I can win through."

Po hurried forward and found Arithon placing the last of the shields.

"Arithon, take two sets of weapons to your father and then get below. Their archers will soon be in range and you cannot be a mark."

Arithon started to protest, but checked by Po's stare, he knew it was a discussion he could not win. He ran the weapons back to his father and then jumped down to the keel-walk, but stayed close to the hatch, unwilling to hide up in his bed.

After ensuring Arithon was below, Po walked down the line of rowers, their backs now pouring sweat and their faces glazed with fatigue. This will end soon enough, he thought, and I will prevail.

"Sheet-men!" he bellowed. "Listen for my orders."

The four men, each manning a sheet or brace line, cast a look of acknowledgement and pulled their shields back up.

Po relieved Tisander of the tiller and instructed him to hold two shields to protect them both: first targets of the archers. He knew these hunters and respected the threat they represented, but he also knew them to be impatient and rash, expending their energy in this sprint. He hoped they would move too soon, and if so, his superior seamanship and trained crew could exploit this weakness. Alteron, gripping his axe, stood furthest aft in the most vulnerable position, the first to repel the inevitable boarders. He could risk himself; assured Po would do for Arithon what he could not.

The closest ship was six ship-lengths away, and the starboard rowers could see the pirate archers taking position: an imposing line the length of the deck, standing above their rowing slaves. Sosius was watching Po but continued the cruise rhythm with a steady cry of, "Ho! Ho!" his voice strong and clear in the sea air. The drums were getting closer and louder, the booms resonating in the chest, seeming to choke each breath in the throat. Fear gathered strength as the menace loomed near and the exposed rowers thought to abandon their station.

"Therans, Lords of the Oar, hold your position!" Po thundered.

When they were one ship-length away, the pirates howled like wolves and released a volley of arrows; two of them making contact on Alteron's shield, and a cry of pain rose from a rower amidships. Time to roll a swell; a reload; and then another volley as the pirate shipped port oars and lay hard over to ram the *Swallow*. But Po had read his mind and gave his order before the pirate committed.

"Starboard, Back Water!" Po cried. He leaned back bracing his bare feet on the deck pulling the tiller with him until it bent like a bow, the fibers strained to their snapping point as he held firm against the resistance of the water, the oar chattering to be released. The ship pivoted smartly with the starboard side in reverse, just missing the careening pirate as the *Swallow* turned across his bow.

"Port Back Water! Slack sheets! Braces!" Po boomed in a torrent of commands as he reversed the tiller and the crew jumped to his orders. The *Swallow* pivoted back on the run, but she was now on the opposite side of the pirate and losing momentum as her sail shed the wind.

"Ship Port Oars! Spears Ready!" Po screamed. The pirate ship, under sail, started to pass the slowing *Swallow*, but unprepared for such a slippery prey she was surprised by such a quick change of sides. The stern of the *Swallow* began to shear off the pirate's starboard oars before her captain could execute a command to his ragtag crew of slave rowers. The oars snapped like dry twigs one after another as the pirate shot past. But Po was not through with them and issued his next order while the oars were breaking on his stern and the pirate was board-on-board with the *Swallow*.

A figure popped from the hold, picked up a spear and hurled it at the pirate ship, where it pierced their sail and arched into the deck. Arithon cried in his boy's voice, "Thera!" before running back to disappear with a jump.

"Port volley!" Po boomed and the port side released their javelins and dropped to their knees. "Starboard volley!"

Darts arched from both ships and men screamed in pain and fear. Arithon could be heard in the hold chanting, "Thera! Thera!" at the top of his lungs. Po turned the *Swallow* to starboard, disengaging from the pirate. "To your oars! Sheet-men: On the run!"

The brace men swung the yardarm around and the sail billowed and flapped as the sail-watch hauled tight the lines. The *Swallow*, a live thing again, surged away from the crippled pirate. Po pivoted around trying to locate the other ship but caught Alteron's stare instead. "Dead astern."

Through the din, Po could hear the cry, "Ερεσσετε!" from the black-hulled ship.

12

Po held up five fingers for Sosius, who responded with the cry, "Ah, Ho!" signaling a change in cadence. The *Swallow* surged to the increased power, but the other ship dropped in behind them before the *Swallow* could recover her momentum. Po watched Arithon slip up on deck and opened his mouth to scream him back when he saw the boy drop to his knees next to a fallen rower.

Po displayed four fingers and Sosius bellowed again, "Ah, Ho!"

The *Swallow* jumped ahead two ship-lengths, but the second ship dug in to continue the pursuit. After a dozen strokes, Po saw the pirate was no longer gaining, but neither was he falling back. He held three fingers for Sosius, and the crew responded to this unsustainable load, their backs fully extended, pulling on each stroke with all the strength left to them. They would not last long.

The crew continued the sprint, but each knew their team limit and there was no more to give. But they were distancing from the crippled ship and dividing their enemy. It would soon be one on one and the pursuer blinked.

Po cried out, "They yield!"

As the distance increased, they felt the exuberant relief of escape from an adversary they all feared. They maintained their sprint, just as a deer keeps running long after it has escaped the lion.

The pirate turned back to his crippled comrade, and it was over.

Alteron rushed forward to where Arithon knelt giving a prone figure a drink.

"It's Kiloutos," Arithon said as he looked up. Tears were streaming down his face, though he seemed unaware of them. "He is in pain."

Alteron could see an arrow lodged near his collarbone, though Arithon had wrapped a piece of cloth around the wound.

"Go back to Po."

Arithon hesitated and then said, "No, I want to help. He is trembling."

Alteron started again to send him away but relented. "Turn his head to port and crush him to you."

Arithon did as instructed and before anyone could even think what Alteron had in mind, he placed his foot on the wounded man's chest and jerked the arrow out of the wound. Kiloutos screamed so loud Arithon released his grip and the crew pivoted their heads.

"Hold the cloth against the wound."

13

Alteron left and returned with some linen, which he used to bind the wound with a practiced dexterity which surprised Arithon.

"Keep pressure here until the bleeding slows," he instructed.

Alteron returned to the tiller carrying the arrow he had just extracted. He handed it to Po with a weighty silence. Po took it, rotating the shaft in both hands, examining its construction.

"Yes," he said, returning it to Alteron. He looked back at the receding ship and then added, "And I could hear their captain calling: 'Ερεσσετε."

"Then it was no coincidence for that pirate to strike us here – he had help from our friends. I sense a sea change. I hope we have the ship to weather it."

"We are not what we once were," Po said.

CHAPTER 2   KNOSSOS

Hypnos and Morpheus, gods of sleep and dream, rode the bow
of the *Swallow* together that night, as anticipation rose and fell
in Arithon's dreams, keeping time through the night with the
swells of the ocean, until all three were pitched awake with the
expectancy of the new day.

Awake now and imagining his first day on Crete, Arithon lay cradled
inside an enormous coil of rope, the edge of which he used for a pillow.
One of the coils had worked its way under his back in the night, leaving a
perfect imprint of alternating white and bronze scrollwork as he peeled it
free from his skin. A morning yawn caused him to stretch and place his
palms against the hull, which vibrated a gentle wash of a sound through
the boards which he could barely hear above the snoring of the crew. They
lay exhausted and strewn about the hold, some in the open, others hidden
away in the dark corners, where only their contribution as a tenor or
perhaps a bass, revealed their presence. Arithon grinned at the thought of
the crew competing at one of the festivals as a chorus of snorers but
dismissed the idea; the crew could sing – and did – but they were not
competition quality.

As soon as his head cleared the deck, he could see Po through the
rigging in his open stance, staring ahead with both hands working the
tiller. Only one of the wanderers, bright in the southern sky, held forth
against the coming dawn and the winds were steady and true. Seagulls
followed their wake, looking down as they bounced in low flight searching
the froth. The cheerful boy dodged and ducked his way through the
topside obstacles, gave a quick salute to Po and softly opened the small
door to the aft cabin, allowing light to flood the darkness. The cabin was an
innovation for the 'Swallow' class of ships. Theran captains had always slept
on the aft deck under a four-post awning, tucked up into the stern, but this
had been improved by enclosing it completely, with space for two sleeping
benches, one now occupied by his father, asleep on his side.

Alteron rolled over to face the door, his eyes squinting against the light and smiled at his only son. "A morning star!" he said swinging his legs over to sit up.

"Excited about Knossos?"

"A little, I guess," Arithon answered, flopping down onto the opposite bench, pinching his shoulders up to his ears with his hands tucked under his thighs.

"You should be. And I have a surprise for you. We are to meet the King of Crete. He wants to meet the grandson of his friend, Tios. Better outfit your festival tunic and best sandals."

His mind racing, Arithon's mouth opened in surprise. Dozens of stories flooded back to him about the Minoan King Selleres. He could picture his grandfather animating one of his many sea tales at the family celebrations. They were old friends he remembered, but why would the King want to meet him? Suddenly his stomach went cold, and his smile closed to a frown, disquieted by a new thought as he looked down at his bare feet and the traveled kilt he wore.

His father looked at him a bit bemused and extracted a trunk from under the bench.

"Such a frown!" he chuckled. "Fear not, your beautiful mother prepares you. Your festival clothes are packed here with my things. Now go bring breakfast for three and we will weigh up our day."

The festival tunic was dress white, the fashionable color for young boys, but his mother had added a stylish saffron hem on the skirt, sleeves and neck, and the soft linen was so lightweight even a young boy was challenged to wrinkle it. As he slipped it over his head, he could smell the scent of his mother, a musky, woody perfume, popular in Egypt which his father had given her; a fragrance he always associated with mother. Even in the scattering years which followed, when time and separation had dimmed her memory, the smell of her on a treasured piece or even on another would always bring her back.

The young mariner hesitated before tying on his sailor's headband – the identifying signature of the Minoan navy. Seafoam white, a crimson bull's head was positioned over the right eye, and for the Therans a black octopus with sinuous tentacles was splayed above the left representing their homeport. To designate their ship, a blue swallow flew on both sides. The sailors wore them continuously and could be singled out in any port by their 'colors.'

16

"Outfitted like a new ship," Po offered, when Arithon appeared from the cabin his cloud-white attire almost blinding in the new day sun.

"Good as the *Swallow*?"

"Almost," teased the proud captain. "You can leave your colors, though."

"Are you sure?" Arithon asked.

"Yes. You will not see any sailors in the Palace," Po said, ruffling the boy's thick black hair and knocking the linen askew.

With the familiar harbor of Amnisos dead ahead and the pirates on yesterday's horizon, Po was relaxed. Only a league out, he could discern a patch of white on the brown hillside which identified the harbormaster's house and served as a landmark for ships seeking anchorage and opportunity. Ships of laden from every point berthed at one of the four main quays just long enough to barter their goods and pay a hefty percentage in tariffs to the customs house of Knossos. Many would leave the same day, but most would remain at anchor or on the beach, the crews given leave to barter for their own needs.

"Are you coming to Knossos?" Arithon asked Po.

"Later, perhaps, if I can make the deals we want."

"Then you will miss the Palace?" Arithon asked, thinking it unfair that Po be left behind.

"Your father has Federation business," he replied.

"Oh," the boy replied, unsure what that meant.

"Do try to have some fun, Po. The crew was saying you need to go with them to the Temple of Aphrodite."

Po raised an eyebrow. "Who said this?"

"Let me see," Arithon tried to remember, "I think it was Micus, but Polus corrected him and said, 'you mean the House of Harlots.'"

Po shook his head and pursed his lips. "Sailors."

"What do you mean, 'Sailors?'"

"Sailors will squander their stake on women and half of them will return home empty handed."

"Are you going to go with them?" Arithon continued, not yet sure of the answer.

"No, Arithon. ... I *will* talk to Micus though."

Arithon looked up at his father's friend. He knew the sailors were going to have sex with the women – they talked about it often enough, chiding each other mercilessly.

17

"Go to the market if you have time," he said.

"I may. Now, hold the tiller. I want you to help me bring this grand ship into her first port-of-call: Amnisos on Crete."

Amnisos was not like the elegant and sophisticated lady, Knossos, cultivated richly in the sanctum of the hills, but was more akin to a woman from the House of Harlots: expensive, dangerous, and not much comfort; accessible but exposed. The north coast of Crete is under constant assault by the winds, pounding ship and shore alike, making landing a harrowing endeavor. The only respite is a rocky spit of land, which curls around to the east in a hook which protects half of a curved, sandy-brown beach, which the Cretans have the effrontery to call a harbor. It is a workable solution on most days when the ships not at quay can find anchorage out of the wind or a place on the beach. But on the days when the wind crackles the flags or the harbor is overfull, it is a tide pool of racking ships and nerves which pulse with the swells. Today would be such a day.

As the *Swallow*, under sail, cleared the spit, Arithon could see the challenge before them. The ships were stacked gunnel-to-gunnel; some so close they bumped those around them; others were tied in rafts of six or more ships, sharing anchor lines; all waiting their turn at the pier. A narrow lead, barely the width of a ship under oar, undulated its way through the lines of ships, as the wind and waves pushed the sterns into and out of the channel.

A battered tender, with a teenage boy at the oars, floated an operative of the harbormaster back and forth across the channel to interrogate the captains. He stood in the back with his knees cycling up and down with the rock of the dinghy, assessing the contents of each ship. It was his job to shark the loads to the docks, where he could net them long enough to disgorge their contents.

But his system was not a first come, first served – that would be wholly inefficient. The Phoenician ship, last in the line, may contain most of the cargo sought by the Achaean ship which was first in line, and what then did the Carian ship seek? Over half of the merchandise was bound for Knossos and would have to be loaded on carts and hauled inland to the markets outside the Palace. There was little room on dock and shore to store all the goods resting in the holds of the ships at anchor, and the cargo needed to be handled as little as possible by the legions of stevedores and crews. All this information had to be shuttled to shore, where brokers set the price for the day and arranged the exchanges. Once at the dock, inspectors working for the brokers would assess the quality and amount, and all this information would be put into play, while the captains haggled, and the prices fluctuated. Scribes kept tally on cumbersome clay tablets which required ranks of young boys to prepare, stack, and file for use throughout the day. It was a complicated business, and for all this coordination the harbor extracted a fat fee.

Not all the ships were stacked at anchor though – there were always vessels in motion; into the channel, out of it, just leaving, just arriving, a few exchanging places with those skidded onto the beach. The beach looked like a seal rookery, where the green-brown hulls, some barnacled, some not, lay shoulder to shoulder in a perfect curve with the surf; the bows hauled up as far as the crews could pull them. Others, small enough or unwilling to wait for the quay, were unloading onto the sand. All eight slots on the stone and timber quays were occupied with ships in different stages of unloading: some still low in the water with the wharf empty, others riding high, the pier piled to overflowing with amphorae, carts, and stevedores, as the loads switched bottoms. Men exited and entered the hold, two on the gangplank, three waiting, and dozens of others on the wharf or on the decks, in an uncoordinated – coordinated affair which mimicked ants carrying food into the mound, or carrying bits of earth out.

Hundreds of ships, attended by thousands, fouled the waters with sewage, ballast, food refuse, and spilled cargoes which foamed the shores and the hulls of the freighters with the sludge of trade. Seagulls attracted by the stench and activity, circled above in great flocks, landing en masse on an untrampled sliver of beach or onto the water where they rafted together like the human fleets around them. One particularly rowdy gull would start the mournful shout, echoed by a thousand others which undoubtedly voiced the same sentiments as the humans swirling around in the same bowl: "Watch your port!" "Make way!" "Careful the line!" "You're afoul!" "Weigh up!" "Backwater!" The drumming of hull striking hull kept the rhythm of the swells while hundreds of stays whistled in the winds. Onshore the burrows bellowed, and the carts clattered on the stones, while stevedores sang their dirges. It was chaos, and Po loved it. The boy at his side was in awe.

"Can we get in there?" Arithon asked.

"If you help. ... Here, hold her steady," Po commanded.

Arithon took the tiller.

"Lower sail! Set oars!"

19

The crew moved in rhythm with the ship. The sail was lowered with practiced perfection; the folds altered fore and aft into a neat bundle on the yardarm and then pivoted about the mast to rest in the stowed position. They were proud of their sleek mistress and wanted her to look her best. The oars were set one at a time from back to front rippling forward like a flag in the wind until all were ready and waiting. They were on display now, and all the harbor was watching.

"Catch oars. Pull!" Po stood behind Arithon, putting his hands on either side of the boy's.

The momentum of the ship never wavered from sail to oar, and continued into the harbor, where mariners on their ships and those ashore stopped what they were doing to watch the magnificent ship enter the scene, a beautiful lady on the plaza.

Several sailors recognized her colors, though not the ship, and so looked for her captain.

"Poius!" a Phoenician called, as she paraded into the channel.

Sosius was chanting a sleepy, "Ho! Ho!" just audible above the squeak of the oars.

"Poius," he repeated, with a point toward the *Swallow*. "Is she the one?"

Poius lifted his arm in a polite salute. Arithon could feel Po smiling, and the joy in his hands on the tiller. Others had heard Poius' name, and so joined in the chorus complimenting him as only sailors can on such a fine new girlfriend. Soon the harbor was celebrating Po and the *Swallow*, cheering or whistling, drumming their gunnels or an amphora, and all clearly enjoying a rare and joyous moment in a tough and demanding trade.

"They know you, Po," Arithon beamed, looking back over his shoulder.

"Steady ahead," he reminded Arithon, who snapped back and gripped tighter.

When they reached the end of the channel there was a bit of open water before the quays. Po bellowed, "Back water!" and the crew reversed their oars, bringing the ship to a stop on center stage.

"Stop and hold," Po ordered.

A tallish man with a square head, richly fed cheeks, and dressed in a shin-length, sky-blue tunic marched down to the end of the quay.

"Poius! So this is your new girl. The *Swallow*, ... hmm. I have heard much about her," he said, while surveying the ship stem to stern. "She is a beauty!"

"Thank you, Marivan," Po answered, as the ship drifted around to starboard, bringing him closer to the conversation.

"It would not do for such a fine-looking lady to have to wait by the well with all of the washerwomen, on this her first outing," Marivan offered with a tilt of his head.

A din arose from the 'washerwomen', protesting Marivan's insult.

"Can you treat her better, Marivan?" Alteron asked, stepping out from the stern.

"Alteron! So, you have come also! Of course! I will have you in the next available berth."

Marivan spoke to the boy at his side, who pivoted and ran as if his job depended on it.

"I appreciate it, as always, Marivan."

"It is nothing! Such a ship deserves to be treated special!"

Marivan was putting on a show for the other ships, but in reality, he was a stakeholder in the *Swallow*'s cargo. He was heavily invested in the merchant fleets of Akrotiri, especially with Alteron's organization, which shipped a profitable percentage of Knossos' luxury items. He had to be careful, though. Accusations of price fixing could be detrimental to his livelihood. He was good at his job, and wealthy because of it; careful, shrewd, and powerful. Alteron and his partners had nourished a relationship with him over the years and it had paid handsomely, so far, for all of them.

The *Swallow* was all-fast against the docks, and stevedores were ascending the gangplank, when Arithon and his father stepped around them onto the pier.

"This is my son, Arithon. It is his first trip to Knossos," Alteron said to Marivan.

"HiHo, Master Arithon! You come on a good day," Marivan said, putting his hand on Arithon's shoulder. "It is the Festival of Zeus. We will have the bulls today!"

Marivan pivoted to walk on the opposite side of Alteron and dropped his voice. "How does it look?"

"Profitable. High quality," Alteron replied. "Almost lost it – we had two pirates chase us yesterday. One of them appeared to be –" Alteron cut off his statement, thinking it something better discussed in the Federation Meeting.

21

"Curse them!" Marivan blasted. "We hear this more and more, just last month ..."

Arithon disconnected to his own thoughts. Marivan had said something about the bulls, but did he mean the bull leapers! Arithon noticed the boy-servant of Marivan's walking beside them.

"Excuse me, but do you know what he meant about the bulls?"

"The bull leapers, of course. You must be from an outer-island," the boy said.

"I am Arithon of Thera," he answered.

"You can't go anyway, so don't bother. Only important rich people can get into the inner yard. You are just a kid and –"

"Prikos, cork your mouth, and get over to Pier Three and tell that self-important Achaean his dock-time is over," Marivan interrupted, before continuing with Alteron on the trek up the hill paralleling the river.

Arithon heard the adults finish their discussion and with a polite farewell Marivan hurried back to the harbor. Alteron stopped at a shrine dedicated to Poseidon, made his obeisance, and continued up. The lane was overflowing with a jumbling mix of needs, wants and anticipations. A line of sweating porters wound out of sight, each bent under their load, trudging the paving stones they had memorized in countless traipses, while marking their progress by the odd crack or dark colored stone toward another paid load. Tourists in festive dress, passengers from one of the ships-a-port, stepped the hills for the first time, taking in the wonders of a new land. Carts clattered by, some human powered, some with donkeys. Countless loads of luxury goods with a price to match were beginning their journey down to a ship, bound for foreign markets. Crates of perfume, incense, cosmetics, exotic foods, fashions, and art were arriving from as far as the Black Sea or Egypt or even Babylon to be consumed by a wealthy populace.

The porters showed deference to Arithon and his father, stepping up on the curb to let them pass; often greeting them with a nod and an 'Honored life' or 'Great Zeus'. Alteron was dressed in a V-necked, saffron tunic with red stripe accents, cinched by a belt of leather with a marvelous dolphin buckle of polished silver. Over this, he wore a fashionable shaggy-wool cloak of sandy white. His wife had just completed it after learning how to make such a garment from one of the ladies in her spinning circle. She was proud of her husband's status in the League and wanted him to look the part.

Arithon had to hurry alongside Alteron who was taking long strides toward the Palace on a road which wrapped itself around the hills, following the contours of the land and taking advantage of the vistas which afforded glimpses of the ocean behind and the city ahead. Tufts of tall brown grass, heavy with seed, growing in the rocky, untilled landscape of the low hills waved them on their way, ever higher. Home to hordes of grasshoppers, whining and whizzing across their path, and the occasional song of a partridge, it soon gave way to tended fields of barley and chickpeas, and as they climbed higher, to mature groves of olives and figs.

The Palace, and the large city which sponsored it, were intermittently visible through the folds of the foothills, even though they were still a half a league distant. Arithon began to get excitedly nervous as it became apparent how genuinely magnificent the structure was, presiding over Crete and indeed all the islands of the Aegean for over two hundred leagues to the north.

The Palace of Knossos was a queen in her own right, sitting on her own throne; a hillock, enclosed by the walls of encircling mountains and roofed by the heavens. Her imposing opulence gathered rivals and allies into a united realm, supplying profit for the patricians, and spiritual reward for the masses.

At the half-way point, the Palace details became clearer – a building varying in height from one to five stories, with large sections stacked and bunched one upon another, until they fused into one colossal structure. The exterior walls were not those of a fortress, but open and airy, pierced with countless verandas supported by colonnades of red columns. Stylized bullhorns serrated the edges of the roof: The Palace of the Bull. It was a building to welcome, not repel, for Knossos was duly protected by her ships, her wealth, and her gods.

As they approached the edge of the city, the road became congested with the traffic of a holiday celebration, slowing their progress, but increasing the pleasant tension of excitement. Opportunistic peddlers, most selling shoddy merchandise, but a few with legitimate goods gotten by illegitimate means, flanked both sides of the road, their wares laid out on blankets for quick display and the quick move, if circumstances required. Most were selling tawdry replicas of what could be found with the established vendors in town, hoping to snare the first-time visitor or the naïve before they could reach the market center.

The blankets began to give way to the edges of the market proper. The family-owned storefronts and workshops were contained in the first story of the buildings that straddled both sides of the main road which paved its way up to the outdoor plaza on the western side of the Palace. Sun awnings of every color hung out from the buildings, covering the tables set up on the small area in front of the shop. White awnings were for the bakers whose bread was stacked chest high in baskets on, under, and around the tables. Cretan bakeries specialized in great round loafs, flat on the bottom and domed on the top with a thick crust cut with patterns from the baker's knife. The loaves in the front even had little designs, like a bull's head or a dolphin, incised into the top. The blue awnings were for the fishmongers who kept up a lively banter with those who walked by. "Only fresh fish in Knossos. ... The King himself eats my fish. ... Cheapest fish in all of Minoa," they bellowed as Arithon and his father nudged past. Arithon's nose told him the fish was at least two days old. He wondered why they would say such a thing and who would be dumb enough to believe them?

The booths with the red awnings harbored a hot meal: a skewer of fish or meat – usually lamb or goat, roasted on portable braziers of fired ceramic. Larger by six than the market on Thera, it was a smoky and crowded place.

Arithon found it impossible to walk beside his father, so he trailed behind him unable to see more than a shaggy-cloaked back. The cloak came to a halt and when Arithon peered around he could see they had stopped at the table of a fruit vendor; a balding man wearing an apron stained with the fruit of many seasons. Arithon squeezed in next to his father; disturbed by the smoldering presence of a muscled man with a strapped dagger who continued past.

"How much for the figs?" his father asked sounding disinterested, but picking up a fat, unblemished one out of a basket wedged in between a basket of pistachios, and another brimming over with dates.

"How many would you like, sir?" he asked, noticing Alteron's expensive jewelry.

"Depends on whether they are good," Alteron said.

The vendor politely took the one from Alteron's hand and peeled it open with his fingernails, revealing a rich, burgundy-colored flesh, moist and fragrant. "For you, sir," he said presenting half to Alteron and the other half to the boy. Arithon took a bite, and smiled at the fresh, figgy taste.

"I will buy the basket, if the price is right and you will hold it for me. You see, I have business with King Selleres and want to pick up the fruit on my return this evening," Alteron said, being sure to drop the King's name.

The tactic worked, and the vendor became more animated, pulling the basket toward him as if keeping someone else from handling it.

"Wonderful, sir, wonderful! I can part with these, to so distinguished a gentleman as yourself, for say a quarter mina." He tilted his head up to look at Alteron to judge his reaction.

Alteron wrinkled his eyebrows a bit, even though he thought it a fair price.

"Throw in a handful of pistachios for me and the boy, and we will call it done," he said.

"Excellent!" beamed the fruit man, dragging the basket from the table and handing it to a skinny, teenage daughter behind him. "Put these in the basement to keep cool," he ordered. "This gentleman is a friend of the King."

Alteron produced a leather purse he kept on his belt and extracted a handful of pea-size bits of raw copper and began to drop them onto the vendor's scales. The fruit man placed two lead disks on the other end, while Alteron plinked the scales level. Satisfied it did indeed look like a quarter mina of copper, Alteron tipped his head in agreement, as did the vendor, and the transaction was done. Alteron grabbed a handful of nuts and taking Arithon's hand, sifted them into his. He did the same for himself and was just pivoting to go, when the vendor reached under the table, extracting a fat fig, and held it out to Alteron.

"For the King. If you will?"

"I will," Alteron said, placing it in his purse.

"And tell him it is from Miltees, if you please," the vendor said.

"Of course," answered Alteron as he squared Arithon's shoulders around and started back into the crowd.

"The figs are for Po," his father said as they merged back into the stream. "It is his only weakness."

Alteron kept one hand on Arithon's shoulder, guiding him ahead through the crowd of backs. "I need to make another stop," he said, moving his head side to side around those in front while getting his bearings. "Turn in here," he said, hooking him out of the press and into an inviting alley off the main road. They walked to the end and through the door of an expensive clothing shop. Alteron backed out for an instant to transfer the rest of his pistachios to Arithon, who remained at the doorway cracking the shells one against another in his cupped hand.

"Alteron! How have you been?" sang the woman in welcome. She smiled and stepped from the high stool where she had been sitting, contemplating how much of her inventory she could move during the festival and wondering for the hundredth time whether her shop was too far off of the main road and whether she was 'too exclusive' in not hiring a crier to work the crowds. No matter, a wealthy customer was in her lair and all those doubts evaporated as she rose to the challenge.

"So far, it has been a good season, Mirina," he replied. "And you?"

"Oh, excellent. Especially when my best customers come to call," she said, putting her arm inside of his and walking toward the counter.

Arithon looked back down the alley toward the moving stream of humanity and saw the dagger-man leaning against the corner of the last building. His occasional glances unsettled Arithon enough that he stepped into the shop out of the stranger's sight.

"Oh, you are a good saleswoman," he heard his father say as he joined them, "but you know it is really my wife who is your best customer."

"How is Raiha?" she asked, letting go of his arm.

"She is healthy, but in great need of the latest fashions, I am afraid."

"Ah, this can be remedied," said Mirina smiling.

"This is my son, Arithon," he introduced. "First time in Knossos."

"Pleased," said Mirina. "You are your father's son – but those are your mother's eyes."

Arithon stammered a yes and looked around at the skirts and bodices, cloaks, tunics, and sandals. He had never been in an exclusive women's shop and he wondered what his father was doing in such a place. He quit eating his nuts and held them tight in his fist.

"So, what does she want? I have all the latest. It is why you come here. I am the best in Crete, as you know."

"As Raiha knows," Alteron corrected.

"I have her size in my head. I could pick a few things out if you would like."

"That would be excellent," Alteron said, relieved to escape the burden of trying to pick them out himself. "But not too much," he beseeched, realizing the trap. "Maybe a mina or two."

"Oh, Alteron, do not worry. I will try not to exceed two, certainly not three," she said, enjoying his dilemma.

Alteron smiled, knowing he would not do as well here as he had with the fruit vendor and resigned himself to the inevitable. He knew it would be closer to four minas. "Yes. Two then," he tried. "I will retrieve the fashions this evening after the festival."

"Excellent. This evening then," she said, flittering back through the shop.

Out in the alley, Alteron breathed a sigh of relief and took a few nuts back from Arithon, who looked to see the man was gone. The good husband could not go back to his wife empty handed, and now with that done he was free to conduct his League business and enjoy the festival.

"We need to get a gift for your sister, Roa, also," he said.

The throng was jammed around the vendor stalls so only the center of the pack was moving. Once in the current, they made their way in short half steps toward the Palace as the southbound road started to push them to the right around the western edge of the Palace. They stopped at a booth, where the Palace cast a shadow across the marketplace.

"A jar of the galbanum incense, and four of the small axe pins," Alteron requested. "One of the middle sizes, too."

They made the transactions quickly and began to pick their way through the edges of the market crowd and out into the open. Alteron took a fork to the right, working his way confidently around an outdoor theater, where hundreds had gathered to listen to a storyteller. They paused on the perimeter of the crowd which had overflowed almost onto the spur and listened briefly, even though they could not see the performer. His voice was strong, and the story must have been captivating, for the crowd was hushed, hanging on his every inflection. Arithon, heard but a few words, something about a pirate battle in a far off and exotic land. His father tapped him to continue.

"What was his story?" Arithon asked.

"It is the story of Akrotiri," Alteron replied thoughtfully. "You've heard it, but you may not remember it. I will see to it we hear the Theran version this winter."

"What's it about," Arithon asked as they continued walking.

They were approaching an overly large outdoor courtyard half shaded by the edifice of the Palace, which was so massive at this point six *Swallows* could be lain end to end along her length. People were already lining its perimeter, reserving the front row for the afternoon's entertainment.

"It is a story of pirates and heroes," his father finally answered, more distracted by their progress than his questions.

"This is the public courtyard," Alteron explained. "The festival has gotten so large over the years that the festivities and ceremonies take place on multiple venues. The largest crowd will be here, where you see them lining up. We will be in the inner courtyard. It is on the other side of this wall."

They continued along the periphery of the court heading for an official looking entrance on the southwest corner when a youth knocked Arithon aside as he dodged through the crowd. Arithon saw him discard something with a toss into the brush. An intimidating man soon followed and caught the youth just ahead of them. It was the muscled stranger, and Arithon's stomach tightened. Before they could arrive, he had removed his dagger from its scabbard and was using the latter to strike the boy about the head and face as he cowered trying to protect himself from the wincing blows. The crowd gave way to avoid the interaction except one, and he strode forward and grabbed the offending arm in mid strike, unbalancing the assailant who turned with ferocious anger.

"Sir! Gather yourself," said Alteron, holding the man's wrist.

The man brought the naked dagger up under Alteron's neck, resting it on the indent of his throat.

"Release me," he said in accented Minoan.

Arithon now knew the man was Achaean and a wary dislike welled up. He stepped forward and slipped into the space between the two. "Please, sir," was all he could think to say.

Startled, Alteron released the wrist as the equally startled man lowered his dagger.

"Do not interfere, Minoan."

"I interfere wherever there is brutality," Alteron replied.

"He ran from me and I shall beat him for it."

Alteron brushed Arithon aside and it appeared the two would soon lock again, but a man ran up out of breath.

"A boy stole some fruit and ran," he accused, pointing at the whipped boy, cowering and in tears. "I think it was him."

All rounded on the boy who opened his palms at his side. Dressed only in a flimsy, tattered tunic, it was clear he was hiding nothing.

Alteron hesitated but stood his ground.

"Excuse me, Sir," started Arithon, "but it was I who took your fruit."

"You?" questioned the vendor.

"Yes. I meant to pay for it, but I lost my father in the crowd and by the time I caught him we were too far away."

The men looked at him doubtfully, and Arithon thought quicker still.

"I slipped it into my father's purse," he insisted.

Alteron, surprised and dull witted by his anger, reached into his purse and extracted the fig he had placed there.

Silence circled until Alteron regained his acumen and took control.

"So. The wrong boy has suffered for your petty crime," he stated, glowering at Arithon. "I will pay you thrice what it is worth," he said to the man's satisfaction, producing a bit of copper from deeper in his purse.

Alteron returned his attention to the other and declared, "You are on Minoan soil, Achaean. Beating boys is not acceptable."

"He is not a boy he is my slave, Alteron of Thera."

Alteron, flinched at the mention of his name, stared expressionless long enough to raise the discomfort level and then grabbed Arithon and guided him away. But as he pivoted Arithon caught the tear-stained eyes of the slave-boy, who communicated a desperate sadness and a heartfelt gratitude.

They began the long descent on the stone-paved ramp and when they were well out of hearing Alteron opened, "So, Arithon. You would lie to save someone. I am surprised."

"I too," he replied as if he had been thinking about it and the full weight was now upon him. "Did I do wrong?"

"Yes," his father exhaled, "but to do something right."

Arithon remained deep in thought as they walked, weighing the right and wrong, but he was unable to arrive at a satisfactory answer for himself. Alteron could feel the boy's internal struggles and finally broke the silence again: "Between the gale and a lee shore."

"I acted without thinking," Arithon answered.

"No, my little Theran, you acted with your heart. … Trust it."

CHAPTER 3 THE LABYRINTH

Ever hungry, ever lurking, the unnatural offspring of Poseidon's wrath lay in wait for the lost and hapless.

At the bottom of the ramp, they stood at the entrance to a colonnaded breezeway of broad steps. A large man, officially dressed in a green, knee-length tunic, was redirecting a herd of tourists trying to gain admittance to the inner courtyard, telling them they would be better off finding a seat on the West Court outside the Palace. One of the ladies in the group was not so easily put off and was trying to gain entry by numerous means and tactics until the gatekeeper saw Alteron waiting his turn.

Alteron extended his right hand, displaying a large signet ring on his index finger with a clever design of a bull's head encircled by the arms of an octopus. The guard stopped mid-sentence and changed his demeanor, standing straighter with a smile now erasing the irritated exhaustion.

"Please enter, Representative of Thera. If you have need, a guide can be assigned to you at the top of the breezeway."

And with a polite, "thank you," the two Therans stepped out of the midday sun and onto the first broad stair. The right side of the breezeway was a stone block wall, but the west side was an ascending colonnade of the same red columns which could be seen supporting the terraces and open portals on the walls above. Arithon counted twenty-four, dragging his hand across the smooth, painted wood of each one. He was modestly delighted to be special enough to gain entry where many could not. At the top, a half-dozen maidens voiced melodic greetings, dressed alike in festive flounce skirts of white and ocean blue with an open-front bodice of deep saffron.

"Would you like an escort?" they invited.

"That will not be necessary," his father replied. "There will be many today who will need help finding their way, so save yourselves for them."

"Thank you," two of them said together and then laughed at their own mimicry.

"We will be busy. So many visitors get lost, even after many trips," said the tall one.

"And then the BULL GETS THEM!" said the mischievous one; putting a finger up on each side of her head and feinting a charge at the handsome young boy. The maiden wished she could escort the two islanders; bored with the gossipy old women she always ended up with, she would have preferred to look smart in front of the youth, barely younger than her.

"We will take our chances," Alteron smiled. He then guided Arithon past the girls and into the portal where the cool, stone-trapped air felt as refreshing as a dip in the ocean. They made a hard right and descended a flight of stairs to arrive at a long, broad hall.

"This is the Processional Corridor," Alteron explained. "The priestess and her entourage will come down this hall, through this pillared room, down that ramp, and then out onto the Center Court."

Arithon nodded as if he were keeping up, but in truth he was already getting confused; there were rooms and hallways everywhere he looked, leading off to hallways and rooms uncountable.

"Do not worry about memorizing all of this. It can be terribly confusing. I came this way because I want to leave you in the museum while I attend to pressing League business."

After a few more lefts and rights, they entered a rectangular room large enough to require internal pillars. It was painted in browns and reds with an astragal pattern in white and yellow which ran the length of all the walls, both top and bottom. But the colors were not what drew Arithon's attention. Displayed around him, on the tables and on the floor were wondrous things; some he had only heard about and others were so exotic he had no idea what they could be or could be called.

He was drawn to an animal skin of orange and white, so tall its neck had been pinned along the length of the wall.

"This is the hide of a giraffe," Alteron said, trying not to disturb the other well-dressed visitors.

"A giraffe! Wow! They are that tall!" Arithon said in a loud voice.

"Apparently. I have never seen one alive," Alteron spoke, even quieter than before.

"I thought you could be entertained here. I will be back for you at midday, but I must go – I am late. Is that all right?"

"Uh, yes," Arithon agreed.

Alteron slipped away from the transfixed youth and disappeared down the hall, unknowingly dismissing the guardianship of his son for the weighty thoughts of a threatened League.

***

"They are in every port now and, if you can believe it, they tell of an Achaean Quarter in Egypt!" insisted the representative from Paros.

Alteron took his assigned pillow under the polite acknowledgement of men already involved in a deep and troubling conversation. Thera was now represented, as was Phaistos and Malia and the Cyclades to the North: Delos, Naxos, Paros, Ios, Amorgos, and yes, Melos now coming in the door. They were men with much to lose and their agitated postures seemed to have been anticipated by the room's designer, who washed the walls in flushes of red and copper. The League members stirred uneasily on their benches in marked contrast to the Sea King, who slouched in pretended repose while his silent eyes stared at each speaker in turn.

"I have seen myself their trading post in Byblos. It is frightening, I tell you," voiced the exasperated representative from Delos.

"Byblos is one thing," corrected the Parosan, "But now in Egypt! Egypt is our oldest trade partner – our most dependent. The Pharaoh knows nothing of deep water. But now! Now this usurper comes!"

"And their arrogance is unbearable," stressed the Iosan.

Alteron watched a murmur of agreement nod around the room and noted their wives had dressed them all in the same saffron-yellow tunic with red stripe accent. He knew them all by name, disposition, homeport, and escutcheon. Delos had her dolphin, Naxos the flying fish, Melos her stag, and so forth around the room to his own ring bearing the octopus of Thera. Ralaki of Melos was agitated, and his temper rose along with the afternoon heat, inflaming the passions to uncomfortable proportions. Alteron, already flushed from his earlier encounter, was beginning to sweat under the confining tunic, which fashion and not common sense had dictated.

"They seek nothing less than total dominion," Ralaki insisted, striking fist to hand.

Opportune refreshments of wine and water appeared as if the Sea King had willed it to cool the tempers which flared. He had indeed willed it, or rather summoned it, though none had witnessed the slight tug to his earlobe: the signal which had set it in motion. He needed the League's loyalty and their minds calmed, especially now with a bold neighbor threatening his rule of the Aegean with guile and brass. Open hostilities versus appeasement rolled over and over in his mind as the argument rolled around the room. Neither seemed a desirable course. Appeasement had been his 'arrangement' of choice, but it had led to steady encroachment and an emboldened competitor. War, on the other hand, was costly and the Achaeans were fond of a warrior's life.

This strange fact – their glorification of violence – had surprised him years ago when he toured the artisan shops of Crete which shipped insatiable quantities of pottery and metal work emblazoned with scenes of heroic belligerence to the wealthy warlords on the Achaean mainland. They had an unnatural taste for blood. His foresight told him even then that the Achaeans would one day be Minoa's master.

"Heretofore, the Achaeans have not been outwardly hostile," offered Alteron who, until yesterday, had been like-minded with the Sea King in policy, though he always shared the views of the other Cycladians about the Achaean temperament. "But I fear that is changing."

The other delegates turned to examine a man they knew to be cautious and temperate.

"Yesterday, a pirate ship of the Sea Peoples attacked us …" the delegation leaned forward, "and a black-hulled vessel accompanied her."

A wild uproar filled the chamber as each delegate tried to speak at once, quieted only when the Delos representative cut through with a reasonable statement: "Perhaps the vessel was seized by the pirates. That would make sense."

"It would," conceded Alteron, "except for this." He pulled the arrow from his cloak and stepped forward to hand it to the King. "And Po heard orders in Achaean from the ship."

If the first disturbance had been an uproar, this was pandemonium as delegates left their seats to be heard; parading around the chamber with arms flying.

"Are we to do nothing, until it is too late? I want my sons to inherit the Aegean," screamed the representative of Naxos.

"What would or could we do?" came a troubled voice.

"I do not believe we could win a war with them – if they joined together."

"We can stand united against them," the Iosan countered. "Otherwise they will blow us over, each in our turn.

"I refused them a trading post on Melos. But I hear others have not been as resolute," grumbled Ralaki, casting an accusing eye at the King.

The King, unperturbed during the outburst, was moved to exert his dominion and he did it with a return stare which left no doubt a line had been crossed. Ralaki assumed a posture of embarrassed defiance and returned to his seat causing an immediate quiet to descend as the others joined him.

"United, yes ..." the King began.

***

Arithon circled the room taking inventory of anything new and exotic. Many of the displays, he discovered, were distinctly Minoan: the seals, faience statues, and marble statuary he had seen before on ship and in Akrotiri workshops, but the precious gems and goldwork were less familiar. He could name the carnelian, lapis lazuli and serpentine stones and give a fair estimate of their value, but was always drawn to blue stones, spreading a delighted smile at a grape-sized sapphire set in a gold necklace.

One display heralded the spoils of a grand naval battle with the shields and banners of the vanquished along with a carved boar's head which decorated the bowsprit of the enemy's flagship. There were also tools of sailing and navigation; maps, sighting instruments, and hull models, along with a tally of the strength of the Minoan navy – almost three hundred ships.

On the farthest wall were the captivating African exhibits with which he had no experience. There were hides of rhinoceros, lion, giraffe, crocodile, ostrich (with an egg), chimpanzee, and products of Egypt such as papyrus, perfumes, linens, tools and inventions of surveying and building. Arithon wondered at so mysterious a place as Africa and all it might contain. His own world of islands, sea, and more sea seemed commonplace and boring in comparison to the unknown lands spread across the massive continent to the south.

He approached the docent, a sharp-eyed woman with a face frozen in a 'do not touch that' look.

"Excuse me, but I need –"

"Out the door, two lefts, a right and then a left," she said.

Arithon hurried along, and noticed a man exiting a room which looked promising and found the toilet but ended up taking longer than expected. When he was done and had poured one of the jars of water down the trench, he exited and turned left, confident of finding his way back.

On his second turn, he was no longer sure of his direction but pressed on when he saw an entrance to a large opening which must be the museum. He strode into a room, where a dozen men and women were lounging on day beds, talking in subdued monotones, while female servants attended the feast-laden table. The diners turned to stare at the young intruder. Arithon pivoted back into the hall, hearing a voice behind him bark, "Someone should clear the Palace of these lost fools. They do not belong on this level."

This scared Arithon, as he did not remember changing levels. He decided to go back to the toilet, and then reverse the docent's directions. He started down the hall, playing back the instructions. Let me see, it was two lefts, a right, and then a left, he remembered. Then I should go right, left, right, right, he reasoned.

"Now the toilet should be about here," he said aloud. But it was not.

He stood in front of a locked door he did not recognize. His throat was beginning to catch as the first ripple of panic washed over him, like a rogue wave on a winter day.

"If you are looking for the toilet," offered a rotund passerby, "it is down this corridor. Then take the first right. You'll see it."

"Thank you," sighed Arithon.

He did as instructed and found the toilet, but he expected it on the right wall, and it was on the left. He walked in to find what he feared was true. It was a toilet, but not the same one. He was hopelessly turned around.

"I will just have to ask someone where the museum is," he mumbled to himself, though there was no one in the corridor now. Unwilling to wait, because movement seemed a better course than standing still, he started to walk down a passage so long he could not see the end of it. As he wandered from opening to opening, the hallway grew darker and darker; the lamps spaced farther and farther apart with no natural light from any of the side rooms. Far down the corridor he could see a room was glowing from a fire within, the light dancing on the wall across. As he approached, he could hear a low drone of voices, moaning or sobbing – he could not tell. His curiosity outweighed his uneasiness: He decided to continue.

He peeked around the opening and was startled by an intimidating woman gazing right through him, her eyes glowing fiercely from the fire at her feet. "Excu –" he started, before he realized it was a full-size statue of Demeter, draped in real clothes. Her eyes were formed from rock crystal, and her painted face completed the appearance of life. Arithon shuddered but remained fixed under the statue's silent will.

At the foot of the dais were baskets of yellow and green, and tall stirrup-handled jars overflowing with the bounty of the harvest: barley, olives, grapes, figs, and Cretan wine. The room was otherwise empty, but there were portals to side chambers on the left and right. A young man with lowered eyes escorted by a priestess crossed from one to the next. With fixed concentration they turned to bow to the statue and as they did so, missed the young boy rooted in the shadow of the door. A throbbing chant, emanating from the room they exited, resonated the cave-like space while thick-clouded incense swirled and boiled from the worshiper's passing. It was disturbing and mesmerizing.

Arithon stole into the room and peered into the chamber they had entered. The man was on his knees, stripped to the waist and bent over, head down, while the priestess hovered over him holding a cup which fit the palm of her hand. In the other she held a wand of serpentine bronze with a knob on the end. She dipped the wand into the jar, extracted it, and with a flick of her wrist shook a spray of oily liquid across the man's bare back, his wetted skin now shiny in the glow of the lamps. She traced the wand along his spinal cord up to his neck, where she brought it down in a feint slicing motion causing his body to shiver. Arithon swallowed, but it stuck in his throat.

The cleansed man rose, and chanting a prayer under his breath, assumed the same position on a low altar at the end of the room. Arithon knew this altar. It was the same as those used in Akrotiri to sacrifice animals. A trench was cut in the right edge to collect the blood from the victim's neck, which then ran into a container on the floor. Arithon could see the container positioned to receive the man's life, his ultimate sacrifice to the goddess of the harvest. The man continued the prayer, his eyes pinched shut and his body trembling in anticipation.

Arithon was trembling also. A human sacrifice! How could this be? Human sacrifice was a savagery of Minoa's past? There were always dark rumors of radical cults which still practiced human butchery in the name of religion, but only under cover of night in a hidden cave, not here in the city! But secreted in this dark recess of the Palace was a cult surfaced and a man about to die. Arithon's legs shook, but they would not obey his heart-pounding desire to flee. His breathing ceased altogether.

The priestess retrieved a stout, bejeweled dagger, and a gold chalice from a shelf on the wall and positioned herself over the man. Arithon could see his face, but the priestess blocked the sacrificial body. She cried out in a shrill and quavering voice, "Blood of life, a sacrifice for Demeter. Favor our harvest!"

Turning slightly, she raised the cup and brought the dagger down to rest against the man's carotid artery. The face of the sacrifice winced, and his head rattled in fright at the touch of the cold blade. He started to rise as if having second thoughts, but two men stepped out from an unseen corner and hogtied the victim after a brief struggle. Arithon was terror-stricken. The priestess reset as if nothing had happened and pulled the knife-edge slowly up across the neck as the man screamed his death. She poured wine down onto the dying face to mix with his blood, the red liquid spattering into the trench and splashing down into the libation jar. The body went limp against the ropes.

Arithon's knees buckled and he caught the edge of the doorjamb to keep from falling, while the priestess raised the chalice and the dagger over her head and chanted 'PU-MA-KU · NE-MI-NA · TA-NE · KU-RO · DE-ME-TE', the ancient language of Cretan past. For Arithon it pulsed to a disturbing unearthly echo. When she had finished her litany, she placed the stained knife on the altar and bent to lift the container, which she also placed on the altar. Demeter's devotee then knelt and prayed with both hands clasping the edge of the stone, her head down. When she stood, the fear which had paralyzed him, now goaded him to retreat into the hall.

He stepped backwards as the priestess emerged into the main chamber carrying the libation container. She placed it before the effigy, knelt again and prayed in a low voice, her robe of sky blue, trimmed in gold, splayed onto the floor. She rose, rustling like winded leaves, and moved back into the room of sacrifice. Arithon hesitated in the shadows of the hall unsure of whether to bolt screaming for help, or just scamper away. Maybe everyone in the Palace was part of this! Lost and alone, maybe he would meet the same fate; a victim of human sacrifice; and no one would ever know what had befallen him.

Taking off his sandals, he bounded on his toes down the dark corridor, turning his head to investigate the chambers as he passed. Most were dark, but a few were lit and contained statues of other gods and goddesses watching the frightened Theran pass the entrance to their sacred abode. Arithon preferred these to the portals blocked with darkness, thinking something could be lurking, poised to reach out and snatch him as he attempted passage. When the hall teed, he slipped to the left, relieved to be out of the area.

But his relief soon turned to fear. It was a dead end.

Reversing to the intersection he continued straight, forced into a series of choices, which he made with little thought. Another dead end! Retrace, turn, and turn again, only to find another dead end. He was trapped. Unable to make any sense of his choices, his fear was mounting to panic: something he had never experienced.

When he arrived at the same dead end for the second time, he knew he should take a more thoughtful approach. Instead, he ran faster, thinking if he kept moving, he could not be captured to have his throat slit.

He chanced upon a narrow down-stairway, and chose to take it, wanting off this level of cult chapels. On the floor below, he found an even greater array of narrow corridors and rooms, some open, others with closed doors. He soon lost the stairs and within seconds felt more trapped than he had before. Where was everyone? Shouldn't he have chanced upon someone by now? But then he became fearful of stumbling into anyone – they could be hunting him. How would he know whom he could trust? Who would help him out of here? He desperately wished for one of the guide girls. Surely, they could be trusted. And where was his father?

Moving slower and working his way back from a false path, he heard something which made the hair on his neck stand. It was the heavy breathing of a large animal. A flush of fear and a rushed memory from long ago; that one-eyed sailor on the docks yarning the tale of the half man, half bull of Crete: a monster with a lust for human blood. The girl was right. He was lost and the bull would get him.

The beast and the cultists were hunting him.

The sound echoed up and down the corridor baffling its true direction. Was it behind or in front? The weighted thud of a powerful battering sent muffled shocks reverberating through the stones. A predator, heavy and powerful, was moving – to get him! Arithon was dripping cold sweat; beads were forming under his hairline and rolling down along his spine. Afraid to go on, afraid to go back, he continued until he could see another fire-lit chamber ahead. He pressed his back against the wall and sidestepped toward the opening, hoping to pass unnoticed. But just as he reached the doorway, the beast screamed, and he tripped.

Inside, blood was erupting from the neck of a massive bull, hogtied on an altar, voicing a nauseous squeal, and struggling to break free. A priestess was deflecting the stream with a small shield down onto the trench where it gurgled into the libation jar. The bull, smelling its own blood, was panicked, and straining against the ropes; one of its legs loose enough to pound the wall in its struggle. Supplicants were splayed prostrate in neat lines on the floor behind the priestess, chanting prayers for Zeus, while the animal's life ebbed away. The priestess looked over her shoulder, made eye contact with Arithon lying on the floor and beckoned him into the room with a tilt of her head.

This was too much for the frantic boy, who stood, turned, and bolted, his bare feet slapping on the stones as he disappeared into the darkness. Arithon ran with no stops or dead ends for longer than usual, and the distance helped to bring down his heart rate, which had been accelerated to frightening proportions. He found a stairway which was larger than the other, and this time he went up and then up again before trotting along another passage. This level supported a clerestory, allowing shafts of natural illumination, which warmed his heart, though he was not yet free. Somehow he had made his way out of the public side of the Palace, which contained the chapels, and rank upon rank of storerooms, containing many harvests of oil, wine and barley; enough to feed the city for a year if needed.

He was now in the living area: the apartments of the Palace residents, though he had no idea of his location, except it was more airy, bright, and inviting. Frescoes of land and sea filled many of the rooms with colors of red, blue, and gold. As he wandered, he heard a girl laughing. This was the first positive sound he had encountered. Outside a well-crafted door painted a deep blue, he paused and listened. The laugh was playful and bright. He felt no harm could come from that voice and so he knocked.

"Bring it in," the girl's voice responded.

Arithon opened the door and his eyes beheld what he did not expect. The girl was a woman, naked, and lying on a daybed with a man between her legs, his face turned away. Arithon was not what she had expected, and she was not what Arithon had hoped to find. The woman squealed, and as the man turned his face to the door, Arithon slammed it shut and ran, the retreating echo of 'Who are you!' following him down the hall.

CHAPTER 4   BULL LEAPERS

Demeter lay sated on her lounge, content with the offerings of
Knossos, but her brother Zeus paced in anticipation of his
spectacle, foreseeing its power, grace, magnificence, and, sadly,
the quickness of its passing.

Would his troubles never end? Lost in a labyrinth of such immense size, harboring all the beauty and malevolence of humanity, was beyond his experience. He would give up all the wonders of Knossos to be back aboard the *Swallow* with Po and laughing at the antics of his shipmates. But despite all his efforts and hopes, he was again retreating into that accursed stone snare. The horror of the spider's victim welled up inside him, but instead of panic he felt resolve. An impulsive passion to face it head-on calmed him. He would find his way out – or fight his way out; the hunters would not ensnare him daunted and pathetic. Arithon slowed to a determined stride, relaxed his breathing, and remembered himself. He would find a weapon and then proceed as Arithon of Thera; ready to meet whatever Knossos could conjure, including the man-eating bull of sailor's tales.

And so, with the shift of his spirit, he was granted a chance. He came upon a large circling stairway with a lightwell in the center supported by those red columns he so admired. On the second level, he found a balcony which looked out onto the inner courtyard and there at long last he rested, sitting in the shade with his feet dangling over the edge.

As he surveyed the courtyard, the sight of sunshine and men at work soothed his heart and he felt safe again. The workers were busy with rakes and shovels spreading earth and sand onto the white paving stones. A line of porters carried the dirt in large baskets slung on their backs, dumping it ahead of the rakes.

The choreographed rhythms of the workmen calmed him, and he began to daydream about the bull leapers who would perform on this quadrangle. What would it be like to leap over the horns of a bull? He started to strap his sandals, so engrossed in his revelry he did not notice a group had entered the yard until he heard their voices.

"The King will sit up there, so we must try and keep the broadside of the bull toward him."

Arithon leaned over the edge to see a dozen people, discussing the performance. Were these the bull leapers? Surely not – two of them were girls, one as young as himself. He stared at the young girl, who seemed so out of place. She wore her hair different than the Minoans; obsidian black, of course, but braided to both sides and draped forward over her chestnut-brown shoulders. Her large brown eyes were the most exotic he had ever seen; and there was something about the way she moved which drew him, though he did not know why. Arithon knew all the races and languages bordering the Aegean, though he was only fluent in his native Minoan and the difficult language of the Achaeans. She fascinated him so much he listened to hear her voice. Even in Minoan he would recognize her accent, as he was sure she was not from his culture for she held herself with a different posture than the island girls. He thought to cry out when a shadow appeared at his side.

"Come, Son, the King wants to meet you," said his father's voice.

"How did you find me," said Arithon jumping up to hug him about the waist.

"I saw you sitting up here from across the courtyard.

"Are you frightened?"

"I got lost," he said.

"Apparently," his father smiled.

"No, no, you do not understand," Arithon began. "I saw a human sacrifice in a dark chapel … somewhere in the Palace."

Arithon then told a brief version of what he had seen, the words spilling from his mouth so fast he slurred half of what he said. But as he talked, understanding came to his father, and when Arithon had finished he put his hands on both shoulders.

"What you witnessed was the Radical Cult of Demeter," began Alteron. "They call themselves the True Believers. It was their ceremony. The members of that sect participate in a ritualized human sacrifice. They believe sometime in the future, the world will be in turmoil and it will be necessary to reinstate the ancient rites to save our race."

"But she cut his throat! He was shaking! I saw it!"

"Was she pouring wine onto him?"

"Yes."

41

"The wine is to symbolize his blood. She drags the blade but does not cut him. He shakes because he is willing to offer himself. The fear is part of the ritual. He believes he may someday be sacrificed and so he 'practices' at the service. It is what draws many to its teachings."

"But he was bleeding. They tied him down." said Arithon.

"They tied him?"

"Yes, he fought with them – when he knew it was real."

"I have never heard that. I will talk to someone, but you need to concentrate on the King now," Alteron said, but his mind was wondering if it could be true. Some of the cults were dangerous. Had they infiltrated the palace?

"I will," Arithon answered, relieved his father would investigate.

Stepping under his father's arm, the two began to walk back into the Palace.

"Answer the King directly but be yourself."

Arithon and his father took the same grand staircase, but it all seemed so different with his father leading the way through a muddle of turns to finally enter a grand room. Thirty feet on a side, its eastern end, supported by three columns, was open, allowing a view of the stream and the tended orchards on the mountain across. Soft light bounced into the room where dolphins leapt over the doorways pursuing flying fish, and monkeys swung through the tops of trees chased by lions on the ground. Birds flew on the ceiling, while the Navy of Minoa fought a sea battle against a pirate king on a choppy ocean.

Near the right wall was the King, a middle-aged man, who wore his flecked-gray hair in a short braid, Minoan style. A powerful man in his youth, he remained hardy and fit, though for the present he sat in a padded wooden chair, in which he was at ease, as was his smile. Dressed regally in a sky-blue tunic, with gold filigree hems, he was barefooted and had his left foot tucked up under his thigh with his sandals dropped casually under the chair. On the fresco behind him, beautiful, topless maidens vaulted through the air over a magnificent bull which pawed the ground and snorted vapor from its nose, its tail curled into the air like a striking cobra. A young man stooping next to the King was finishing a subdued conversation. He glided to a side exit as soon as Arithon and his father approached. The King paused and watched the young man leave.

The King of Knossos had much on his mind these days. The Egyptian ports were taxing his ships and the Levant was becoming a battleground

42

once again, but it was the Achaeans and the mysterious Sea Peoples who clouded his thoughts. Nevertheless, he was still at the helm of Minoa's destiny, and he intended to steer his own course. But for now; now he was going to rest, relax and enjoy his guests and the Festival of the Bulls.

Arithon bowed. "I am Arithon of Thera, friend of Crete."

It was the standard greeting for the Sea King, though Arithon delivered it with the sincerity and pride of a young boy.

The King replied with kind pomp, "Well met, Arithon of Thera, friend of Crete, I am glad to have you here at your father's side. Please sit down."

"How is your Grandfather?" the King asked, rubbing his palms. "He and I have been great friends and allies for many years now."

"He is aged, but wise. He told me you were his friend."

"And I am," the King said. "I have not been to Thera since your fourth year, but I know it well. Do the saffron flowers still bloom the hills between the orchards?"

"Yes, they do."

"Can you smell the jasmine on the sea breeze as you round Monkey Head?"

"Yes. Especially in the evening and early morning," Arithon replied, acknowledging these things as much to himself as to the King.

"On clear days I can hike into the mountains to view the archipelago on my north horizon – the necklace of Minoa and Thera its jewel. You live in paradise, Arithon. Cherish it while you can," he added with a distracted somberness.

The Sea King saw the puzzlement in the bright Theran's face. "Alteron has told you of the festival. Have you ever seen bull leapers?" he asked leaning onto his elbow and closer to the attentive boy.

"No, I have not," replied Arithon, "but I am greatly excited about it."

"You should be, for nowhere else – in no other land – will you find such a spectacle," said the King, wagging his finger to make the point. "It *is* Minoa. The athletes train hard and long to achieve this mighty feat. You shall sit with me.

"Come we will eat something before we go. Hand me my sandals if you would."

In the adjoining room, with the same view to the east, there was a hodgepodge arrangement of daybeds, where the wealthy relaxed while attendants served the meal. The recliners reminded Arithon of his earlier

43

mishap, and it was with trepidation that he sat down on the one the King waved him toward.

"I have asked the chef to prepare beef," said the King. "I suspect it is not something you eat every day."

"No. Fish, usually," Arithon answered.

"Good, then it should be a nice treat for you."

Male servants first brought in three shallow tubs of water and quickly and efficiently washed the feet and hands of the three diners, drying them with beautiful linen towels of the purest white. It tickled Arithon's feet. They had no sooner left the room when female servants appeared with knee-high, three-legged tables stained a wine red, and placed them next to each couch. On each, they placed a matched set of bowls, plates, and cups of precious silver, inlaid with lapis lazuli; all displaying a bull's head in profile, the enormously long horns, curving up to the edges of each piece. They were soon filled with carrots, dates, figs, grapes, olives, wheat bread – a luxury food – and diluted wine. The main course, of brazier prepared beef, seasoned with sesame and salt, arrived after they had eaten as much as anyone could want of the fare before them.

Arithon was not used to being waited on but accepted it as something one does in the company of a king. As they began to get full, a lyre player materialized in the back of the room, briefly drawing Arithon's attention, while his father and the King discussed lighter matters of family and friends. The *Swallow* was a source of great interest to Selleres, who, by the nature of his questions, had been to sea. The King soon began to address Arithon directly, asking him many questions about his life in Akrotiri, and his grandfather, Tios. He told funny stories about their times together, and from his descriptions, Arithon was sure he did indeed know his grandfather intimately. But he spoke gravely about the encounter the *Swallow* had had with the Sea Peoples the day before and asked many questions and details about the event. As they were nearing the end of the meal the King asked Arithon.

"To what do you incline yourself, Arithon: love, war, or business?"

"I know little of love or war, and I am newly learning the business of trade from my father."

"An honest answer, young man," clapped the King. "Though I believe the Fates will take an interest in you."

Arithon started to question this, but at that moment an attendant entered and whispered something to the King who chuckled.

"My wife is complaining about an intruder in her apartment – a young boy she insists."

Arithon froze and felt a flush. His face must be red – red enough to confirm. He hesitated and then resolved himself to admission. The King saw the boy's intentions. He waved his hand as if shooing a fly, popped a fig into his mouth and started fumbling around for the hidden sandals.

"My wife has many to guard her," he said with a wink.

Sandals bestride his feet and his guests in tow, he started down a long corridor, but stopped outside a narrow entry.

"I am going to make use of the toilet; it is a long pageant."

Arithon and his father did the same, Arithon asking to go second, as he was afraid of being left behind; palace toilets had been nothing but trouble for him. The three began a long trek through numerous turns and changes of level, until Arithon was completely bewildered. Along the way, they picked up a train of officials and attendants, until there was a veritable procession making its way through the maze.

The entourage emerged onto a balcony which overlooked the internal courtyard from the west side. How they had arrived at this point, after starting from a dining room on the east, was a source of wonderment to Arithon.

Comfortable chairs were arranged in neat rows, with three in the front directly behind a short wall of balustrades. Two massive red pillars on the corners supported the roof which was adorned along its edges with a continuous rank of stylized stone bull horns. There were no less than a dozen people seated on the King's balcony and a look around the courtyard revealed the same on almost sixty other balconies on three levels. Each was packed with those of Crete who were allowed into the Palace; mostly the first citizens of Knossos and their families, but there were also dignitaries from other lands in attendance. Arithon could pick out Egyptians and Achaeans and some of the Purple People. There was also an auburn-haired race, short and stocky, unknown to Arithon, who spoke a strange language and kept to themselves. Arithon was surprised to see a few Persians and Phrygians, but he was absolutely startled when he spied to his right, and down on another balcony, a man of black skin. He had heard of the Africans but had never seen one. He must have been staring because the King interrupted his gaze and asked, "Have you ever seen one of the Black Ones, Arithon?"

"No. Never. I have heard of them. They say they live in Africa where the sun burns their skin."

The King smiled and replied, "They do indeed live on the continent of Africa, but they are born that color. The one you see below is a Nubian, of the allied empire of Egypt. He is here as my guest as are all the people you see. But you and your father have the most honored spot here with me in the King's balcony. Do you know why?"

"No, I do not," replied Arithon.

"Then you must ask your grandfather for the story, but I will tell you this. It is because I owe him a great debt – my life in fact – and I am honored to have his grandson at my side today."

Arithon looked with renewed interest at the King, and sought his memory for one of grandfather's stories, but could not resurrect one. There was a time before his own, Arithon realized: here he sat; the inheritor of respect and honor generated by events passed.

The King, draped in a scarlet cape his servant had slipped onto his shoulders, stepped forward and raised his hands to the crowd which soon quieted. "The goddesses sing of Zeus, the father of gods and men, and uttering their immortal voices, celebrate in song the revered race of the gods, givers of good things. They chant of the race of men and strong giants, and gladden the heart of Zeus ..."

The King continued to discuss the blessings bestowed upon all of Minoa by the gods, but Arithon's mind wandered and he heard little else the King said. Instead, he was thinking about the cult sacrifice, and he was wondering if any of its participants were in the crowd. He scanned the balconies encircling the courtyard and from his vantage point he could see almost everyone. No one looked 'cultish,' but he felt sure he would recognize the priestess if he saw her again. The next thought unsettled him even more – the woman behind the blue door would be in attendance and she might be looking for him. Her secret, if a secret it was, was not something he wanted to be involved in.

He found himself distracted by the robes of one of the Purple People. The color appeared to both shine and wink out at the same time. He had seen the expensive bolts of purple cloth on the docks in Akrotiri, but he had never seen any one person wearing so much.

He was startled from his reverie by a waft of that acrid incense he encountered in the cult sanctuary. He followed the smell to his right where two immense bulls were standing in an opening to the courtyard, spewing vapor from their nostrils. They were the biggest bulls he had ever seen; their heads alone were the size of a man. But as he stared, he realized they were not real. They were giant incense burners, shaped like charging bulls. It has started, he thought! The bulls will soon be here!

His ears returned to the voice of the King. "DA-RI-DA · KU-PA-NU · KI-RI-TA · DE-ME-TE · DA-QE-RA … Zeus the Cloud Gatherer."

The King backed away from the balustrade to sit in his chair, where a comely young maidservant handed him a golden goblet filled with wine. He took a large drink, upending the chalice to soothe a dry voice, and settled into his pillowed chair as the incense bulls, each propelled by a pair of human legs, began to move into the courtyard, taking a position on either side of the portal. A low throbbing sound, from hidden drums, rumbled the quadrangle, as men with pikes, fully twenty feet long and streaming the flags of Crete, were the first to enter. The flags were a yellow rectangle with the profile of a red bullhead, its horns sweeping up in a double arc, almost to the hem of the material. The carriers were stout men, two abreast and eight deep and they entered in synchronous stride until the last two stopped and then the next two and so on until they spanned the length of the court, then parted to form a channel, each side turning to face the audience; either to the east or the west. They planted the ends into the ground and leaned the flags toward the audience in a salute and stood still as stone.

"My honor guard," the King explained. "All Cretans as custom dictates. They would give their lives for me. Would you do the same, Arithon?"

"Yes," he answered and then added, "to save you."

"Oh," the King replied. "It is conditional."

"Conditional?" questioned Arithon. Alteron leaned forward to look over the King at his son.

"You would do so to save me," said the King, "but would you do so if I but asked?"

Arithon's boyish honesty would save him, where adult subterfuge would have ensnared him. "Why would you ask?" he said.

The Sea King burst forth in a laugh so hearty those on the veranda were drawn away from their own discussions.

"A regal question my fine young Theran. Why would I indeed?" He then continued laughing as if he had been told a colossal joke and the balcony entourage laugh in obsequious participation.

47

The prow of a ship on wheels emerged through the gate with a carved bull's head on the bowsprit, the gunnels ringed with gold double axes. On the deck were statues of Zeus and Demeter, like the ones he had seen in the chapels. It came to rest in the center. A choir of men, singing a repetitive song in time to the throbbing of the drums, entered next and took up a position on the north wall, swaying back and forth, their full-length togas sweeping the ground around their feet. A dozen priestesses followed, each holding a libation jar. Arithon shuddered when he recognized two of them: the cultist, and the one with the bull. He shrank down in his chair mindful she had seen him also.

Behind the priestesses came the offering bearers, carrying baskets or jars representing all the foods known to the Minoans, either caught on the sea or harvested on the islands, including a bull being led by two men. And last, but most riveting of all, a statuesque woman entered wearing a multicolored flounce skirt with pendulous, exposed breasts swiveled out by a tight bodice. She was holding two live snakes, their heads swaying and bobbing as she marched with metered steps, summoning all eyes to her.

"My wife, the High Priestess," Selleres whispered to Arithon.

She then stood swaying as if at sea, hearing some internal song of the sirens. Arithon was mesmerized by her heavy breasts, which rolled back and forth with the unseen waves.

An altar was set, and great pots of incense were lit on either side billowing a gray, sweet smoke. The service continued for almost an hour until the bull was tied and slaughtered, its blood collected and placed on the center of the altar. In the public light of day and with the King and his father beside him, this sacrifice was solemn but not frightening.

The King stood and said his own prayer: "TU-PA-DI-DA · DU-MA-I-NA · DA-NA-SI · PU-MA-KU · DE-ME-TE" and when he had finished, the procession proceeded out.

The festivities continued with songs to the King from a young children's choir. The fare then turned more athletic, with a wrestling match, boxers, and a short foot race – all activities Arithon participated in at home, and in which he took more interest than the religious service. As the race ended, the crowd flowed to the balcony edges and kept looking to the far end at a closed wooden door.

"Pay close attention, Arithon," said the King, "for the thing you have been awaiting is upon you."

A crash of cymbals and the large door was flung open with great force as a bull careened into the enclosure, snorting, and flailing his polished horns as he dashed round the courtyard. The crowd roared their approval. It was a grand, mature bull, solid black, man-high at the shoulders with exceptional brown tipped horns which flared outward in a sinuous curve. Arithon could see him as he came to rest beneath the King's balcony. His proud head was bobbing with his breathing, but as he regained his strength, he surveyed the courtyard as if for the first time.

A troupe of acrobats entered from a side door with deliberate movement, watched by the great animal. He snorted his disapproval. The crowd gave a roar and stamped their feet in a raucous explosion of noise. This disturbed the bull and he trotted a few paces to the right, coming to rest facing the intruders. It was the group Arithon had watched earlier: eight men, a woman, and the young girl. They were all wearing a short kilt skirt of gold trimmed white, a sash belt and naked from the waist up. The two girls had forward curls with one horsetail hanging behind. The men had tied a sailor's headband which matched the gold trim of their kilts.

Their lithe, oiled bodies glistened in the sun and a stylized bull's head was painted on their upper chest. Each wore a pair of curious boots of white felt, which clung to their feet. They formed in the middle of the courtyard, genuflected to the King, and then moved off to the sides.

Arithon's gaze followed the young girl whose movements and poise were out of place in that setting. With her hair done up in the manner of the Minoans, he may have mistaken her for a local girl, but her physical grace set her apart. How could someone so young be a bull leaper?

Two muscle-wrapped men entered, carrying double-headed axes, and marched within a few strides of the bull who showed his horns to them, but did nothing. One of the performers left his spot along the wall sprinting toward the bull's side. He sprang from the ground and placing his hands along the spine of the animal, somersaulted over, landing on his feet in mid-stride and proceeded toward the opposite wall. One after another, the acrobats vaulted the bull, one doing a half twist, landing backwards, and rolling up onto his hands to hand-walk to the wall. At one point the performers ran from both sides, sharing the bull's back in their leap, and tumbling under the approaching runners, the entire troupe swirling in synchronous movement.

Just as the excitement diminished, a lone acrobat moved around to face the bull and charged head-on. As he neared, he sprang up to grab the horns from the inside, curling them around his arm with the polished tips protruding out from his armpits. The bull jerked his lowered head upwards as he felt the load, propelling the man in a sharp acceleration which allowed him to do a somersault, land surefooted onto the animal's back and flip to the ground behind his tail. The crowd stomped and yelled in an ear-splitting roar which thundered out into the valley where the market still pulsating with shoppers, stopped, and looked toward the Palace, knowing what was happening and proud to be Minoan.

Then the girl made her run. She was by far the lightest and the bull propelled her so high she easily completed her maneuver, landing rod straight on the shiny back, drawing a loud 'oooh.'

"The bull is getting irritable," said the King. "He will not be placated much longer. Watch for the final runs, Arithon. They are the best."

Before he finished speaking, the performers changed their tactics and started to rush the bull and then back off. After a number of these feigned charges, the bull met the taunting acrobats with a lowered head allowing the tumbler to jump at the horns and execute a spectacular vault as the bull in his anger propelled them skyward with a frightening snort and a snap of his head. The troupe executed a series of dizzying flips and rotations, all coming off the bull in a different way. Clouds of incense mixed with the dust of exertion swirled about the court.

When the girl started her run, the bull pawed the ground, snorted, and charged through the mist: a weaponed black phantom. He angled his head to sight down one horn, intending to gore. The girl, already committed, realized his intention, and grabbed the horns in reflex, trying to avoid the spike. The off-center movement rolled her torso, causing her legs to spin over the left horn. Thrown like a cloth doll, the point caught her right thigh, slashing through the kilt. She pivoted over at alarming speed, crashing the bull's back before flopping lifeless to the ground.

The bull kicked up his back legs and pivoted on his front, seeking the destruction of the impudent acrobat. As he lowered his head to impale her, a shattering axe-blow to his head caused him to stumble. Two acrobats were dragging the girl by her arms as the second axe man dealt another crushing blow. The magnificent animal reeled and toppled, spraying dust and legs, his bulk rocking to a stop with his tongue lolling out and the horns curling skyward.

The crowd jumped to its feet in one move, eliciting a loud communal groan. Arithon found himself standing next to the King at the balustrades but did not remember ever having left his seat. He could see the girl clear of the bull, lying on her side in the dirt, the bronze skin of her back glistening; blood soaking her skirt and running in rivulets down her thigh onto the sand. She was not responding to the man turning her face to his.

The elder athlete scooped her up and hurried her through the side entrance, blood now streaming down toward the ankle, her body hanging limp.

Ascending notes blasted from unseen horns.

The verandas began to empty, and the King stepped to the side with an attendant.

Was this the end?

"Is she dead, Father?" he asked. They were both standing at the balcony looking over onto the courtyard, where men were butchering the fallen animal, his offal already sloughed onto the sand.

"No, I do not believe so, but she will be badly scarred," he said. "Gather yourself. We have to make our farewells."

Noticing Arithon and his father standing by the railing, the King beckoned them back through the Palace.

"So, before your day ends, I have a request," the King said. "I want you to ride down to the harbor in my chariot. My grey roans, Talos and Minos, need exercise."

Arithon looked at his father, who nodded his agreement.

"That would be regal!" Arithon answered in a widening smile.

At the royal stables Arithon moved to admire and stroke the stallions but noticed the King lean in and talk to his father.

"The Guard has found your large footpad. We believe he was from Tiryns. … He will not report back to Achaea.

"And the boy," he said lowering his voice, "bring him back when he is ready."

"I was thinking his twentieth year."

"I can hold out that long," Selleres said with a wry smile.

"Poius has the tiller," Alteron replied.

"Poius," Selleres nodded with satisfied concurrence.

Arithon spun around the far side and mounted the chariot. The Sea King gripped the gilded rail and met his eyes.

"You come from a long and noble line, Arithon. I sense your great heart. You will be renown among Therans – a leader. I have the gift of prescience from the gods, and I foresee your life will be one of great labors."

51

Arithon gazed at the King, feeling complimented, but wondering at the portent. 'Great labors' sounded like the destiny of a warrior king, yet he was only a merchant seaman: Po's apprentice.

"Your time to be tested will come soon enough," Selleres continued. "Prepare yourself and learn from those around you. Now be off."

Arithon had never been on a chariot and the ride was exhilarating; the horses galloping down the paved road with their clopping hooves and the whir of bronze-rimmed wheels grinding over the fitted stones. He wore an irrepressible grin for the whole journey. Alteron had the driver stop for the basket of figs and the clothes: two skirts, three bodices, and a cloak (he was right – it cost him four minas). It was nearing sunset and the road empty of traffic. At the harbor Arithon jumped to the ground, elated, a perfect ending to an unpredictable day.

The *Swallow* was anchored mid-harbor, waiting in a rolling surf. Alteron hired a skiff to row them out, counting to himself the number of black hulls in harbor.

"How was your day, Arithon?" Po asked, meeting them at the rail. "Did you see the bull leapers?"

He spent the remaining daylight telling Po of his adventures, while they ate barley porridge and figs. When he was full, the length of the day overcame him, and he fell asleep on the deck between the two friends talking on into the night.

CHAPTER 5 DOLPHIN

The forge of Hephaestus burned white hot as the bellows roared and throbbed. Poseidon has need of a new trident, wrought beautifully bright and hammered tough.

Arithon was dreaming about the Sea Peoples when the earthquake began. The motion became part of his dream as the *Swallow* rolled in heavy seas, struggling to out-run swarming pirates. As it intensified, a clay pot on the middle shelf wobble-walked to the edge and stumbled to the floor, crashing to bits, startling him to wakefulness. In the adjoining room, the frightened pitch of his mother's voice was muffled by the roiling booms overtaking their city.

It was black dark, the middle of the night he reckoned; but there was an eerie orange glow flickering shadows on the far wall. It was that accursed mountain erupting again. There had been earthquakes on Thera for as long as anybody could remember and Arithon had rattled through so many he had lost count. But they were frequent now, more severe, and often accompanied by these eruptions. Only two years before, his sister had been trapped in the neighbor's house when a wall of earth and stone buckled and dropped the two upper stories. Roa was removed unscathed after a half day of digging, but it had left a permanent mark on his mother.

He stood from his bed shaking off a muddled head and reached for the breechclout hanging on its peg. Why did it always erupt at night? Was it not enough to scare the island's inhabitants into a collective disquiet – did it have to deprive them of sleep too? His torrent of sailor's blasphemy would not change a thing, but it made him feel better. After adding his short kilt, he pulled the belt tight and then hurried down the stairs to join his parents and sister waiting in the main room on the first floor.

"It hunts us – with malice, Alteron. Just yesterday, while spinning, Mysia told us another story of the death fog," said his mother.

"I have heard the stories too, Raiha," said his father as he probed the house holding a lamp and looking for a cracked wall or shifted beam, "it will not be long now."

"But I do not want to leave Thera," whined Roa. "Where will we go?"

"I do not know," said Alteron with great weight, "but you need not worry, my little dolphin," he now lightened, "I will not let anything happen to you."

Alteron hugged the precious girl and moved toward the door, fixing Arithon with a brief look.

"Raiha, we will meet you at the Council House – no one will sleep anymore tonight."

The young man and his father left their affluent home and walked side by side through the lower city toward the docks: their assigned district to monitor in the event of disaster. It was also the quarter of the less prosperous who lived in and around the commercial district in the Flats, making a living as a stevedore, rock worker, or any of the other hard labor trades. A rapid survey revealed no structural damage to the neighborhood, permitting an uninterrupted trip to the harbor where they would inspect the yards, much as a farmer checks his fields the morning after a heavy rain.

"Arithon," his father began, "your grandfather and the Theran Council have decided to accelerate the evacuation. The mountain *is* killing we Therans – and our losses are mounting. Two potters and a marble worker have already left for Naxos. And Palasii, the bronze worker – he left for Mycenae of all places. But most unsettling is the drop-off in our trade. It is just a matter of time before no one will call here."

"What are they afraid of?" asked Arithon. "Earthquakes will not harm their ships."

"They are afraid of the mountain," Alteron answered. "To them the volcano is a sign the gods are displeased with Thera. They believe the immortals are punishing us and they, too, will be punished if they call here. Many of our own priests believe this, and sacrifice much to Hephaestus.

"We will not be able to continue our idyll on this beloved island. We have three choices. We can scatter across Minoa; but we will lose all that is Theran. We can migrate to a land where no one lives, though none of us knows where that might be. And last, we can fight for a new home."

"The last choice seems the least Theran," Arithon said.

"Once we had the Aegean to ourselves, but no longer. Our time of peace and prosperity is ending after many generations," Alteron sighed. "I would not fear for you, if you could live the life of your grandfathers, but this will not be your destiny."

A brief silence ensued in the eerie light of the volcano. Arithon was as tall as his father now, though he did not yet have the girth or strength of his sire. Arithon could challenge even the fleetest in the foot races and only a handful could best him in wrestling. As for boxing, only adults would venture a bout: he was quick as a cat.

"If I must learn to fight then I will do so."

"You would make a reluctant warrior," replied Alteron as he placed his arm around his son's shoulder, "but it may come to that.

"Tios and the Council are sending explorers and emissaries to all points on the wind. We need men to lead these forays, and you will not be counted a man until you turn twenty this autumn, and they have not asked to send you. But I think our need is great. I …"

Arithon interrupted, "Of course, I will go, Father. I am honored to serve."

His father stopped and looked at his son, though he said nothing before they continued their walk.

"We need someone to take our requests to the Achaeans. We wish to ask for land and help transporting our people off Thera. They have been our allies in the past, but they have their hands full. I do not expect a warm reception, but neither do I expect them to be hostile. The world is a dangerous place and you must prepare for the worst."

The two reached the wharves and took their habitual route over to the shipyards where the Therans had three large ships under construction. They stopped next to one of the great hulls; the largest ship ever built in the Aegean.

"We will name this one *Prados* and her twin over there will be *Polus*," Alteron stated. Arithon smiled at the names.

"I doubt those names were chosen for their speed," he ventured.

"No," grinned his father, "they were chosen because they will aid us, as did their namesakes.

"Po believes they can carry two hundred tons apiece – not bad."

Each ship was over one hundred and fifty feet long, and forty-five amidships. The raw timber had been ferried from Anatolia and formed by the shipwrights into enormous beams to serve as prow and keel, frame and stringer, hull, and deck. The dockyard had been working for two years, joining the strakes edge on edge with mortise and tenon to build the shell. The identical hulls rested side by side in their scaffolding; two enormous wooden gourds now being fitted with the massive close-set frames formed to the curvature of the skin. Soon they would be decked; a mast stepped; and then christened.

"Built for the evacuation," his father said. "They are tubs and slow no doubt, but Great Poseidon what a payload."

They walked past her twin and over to the third and much sleeker hull.

"This will be the fastest ship in the fleet when she is completed," Alteron began. "She is longer than the *Swallow* with a broader beam and sail, but her hull is more nimble."

He started running his hand along the planking as he walked down her length. "She will carry the name, *Dolphin*, like many before her, and she will be your ship, Arithon," he said, turning to look at his son trailing behind him.

This was astounding news. Everyone on the island was monitoring the construction of the new fleet, and the innovative fast-hull was the most magnificent the yards had ever built.

"How can this ship be mine, Father?"

"For the last two years I have planned on building you a sister of the *Swallow*. I even dreamed of you and Po making joint voyages, the decks of both ships packed to the gunnels. Together they could have shipped record loads."

Arithon was staring up at the hull through the scaffolding, listening.

"But the mountain has changed my thinking. She will be built for a new mission. Po has re-lofted her lines for greater speed."

"Why is this not Po's ship?"

"Poius tells me the *Swallow* is his last ship," Alteron said. "He wants you to have the *Dolphin*."

"What do you mean 'last ship'?"

"You know how he loves that lady."

"Yes," Arithon said with a spreading smile.

"He will not part with her. He says when we pull her from the grey sea for the last time, he too will stay ashore."

"Do you believe that?" Arithon asked.

"I believe Poius believes it."

"That would be a sad day. I have never thought of such a thing."

"Life continues, Arithon, and others take our place. Poius says you are ready."

Indeed, Arithon's skills and body had grown since the maiden voyage of the *Swallow*. Throughout Arithon's teenage years, he and Po had been inseparable. Multiple deep-water journeys to every port in the Aegean and twice they had sailed east as far as Byblos in Phoenicia. His size provided him great strength, which he carried in a lithe and coordinated body which hardened as he approached manhood.

But it was his keen intellect that set him apart. He quickly understood the nuances of trade and negotiation, picking up the different languages with surprising ease. The mathematics required for sailing and commerce were now so much a part of him he could hardly remember when he did not know these things. Every day he grew in both mind and body and his spirit was a joy to all around him.

Another matter troubled Arithon though: he had never fought or been tested in battle, and he was keenly aware of it – especially now.

Pa-Boom! Pa-boom! Pa-boom!

The thunders of late autumn crack and rattle in poor imitation of these explosions. The mortals flinched and spun round to stare up the mountain as if expecting its final destruction, but witnessed instead orange flashes, which lit the underside of the belching smoke, flattening on the wind and streaming south. Arithon shuddered at the thought of his home island deserted like a ship with a soft hull, drifting on a shoreless ocean. It saddened him, but also set his resolve.

"What will be the *Dolphin's* mission?" he asked.

"War, no doubt. Tomorrow you and the other young men of Akrotiri will begin battle training. We hired a Cretan. They have great skill in the axe, but it is an old weapon and may not fare well against those we encounter. We will see what he can teach us."

They left the shipyards and stepped the narrow and crowded streets of their ancient city, where their neighbors stood in groups outside their homes, talking loudly while making great sweeping gestures with their hands, often pointing up in the direction of the mountain. As they walked many greeted them or sought solace.

"The mountain, she is getting worse, don't you think, Alteron?" asked one of the carvers from the marble works.

"It cannot be denied, Pindar," he agreed.

"Will we have time, Alteron?" asked the potter on Amorgos street.

"I am sure we will, Cebes. We are moving on our plans now," he answered.

"Has anybody been hurt?" asked their neighbor and Raiha's spinning partner.

"I have encountered none," Alteron answered encouragingly.

"The priests are not doing their job,' said a wizened widow, leaning against her door frame.

"Oh, I am sure they are praying hard, Cybele, but I will look into it," he answered.

Akrotiri was a typical coastal town, built on the hills above the harbor in an unplanned and casual style which created both charm and confinement. The two and three story homes sprang from the edge of the stone-paved roads, the upper stories often hanging over like weeds on the edge of a path. The residents not only knew everyone, but they also knew everything! There was little privacy in such close quarters, but the hodge-podge placement of buildings and the crooked streets did block the incessant winds and provided a sense of community and security. No one could remember the last crime, but everyone knew the last time Erato fought with his wife – and who won.

As they neared the Council House, the press of startled inhabitants descending from the side alleys filled the main road. Their progress slowed and boisterous conversation ceased as everyone began to talk quietly to those walking by their side.

"One other thing, Arithon," started Alteron. "A primary role of the First Family is defense. Generations ago, this was a serious requirement. Many Theran ships were present when the Minoan navy cleared the Aegean of pirates and expanded the Minoan Empire to its present size. Your grandfather fought in a huge campaign with King Selleres against the Carians. And you may remember we cleared out a pirate nest on the coast near Kos after your first trip.

Arithon nodded.

"Poius and I participated in that action."

"I remember. Mother was so worried the month you were gone. I also remember Crito telling us the Legend of Akrotiri before you sailed."

"You do? We should have Crito retell it. It has been years since I have heard it myself.

"My final point, Arithon, is we are entering a different phase. My role and yours will change and we will have to assume our protectorate responsibilities. Understand?"

"Yes."

58

Alteron put his arm around his son and they walked the rest of the way in silence, while the crowd around them bumped and talked its way to the Meeting Ground in front of the Council House.

***

The Cretan was a weapons master for the King's navy, a capable man of few words. When Arithon arrived, he was laying double–headed axes in a row on the sand. Many of the men of Akrotiri were milling about talking in small groups, waiting for the training to begin. Arithon's cousin, Glaxos, was there also. Glaxos was the son of Alteron's brother and in a direct line for the Council Head. Five years older than Arithon, he was a much different person in many ways. Average and not outgoing, he spent most of his time managing the bureaucrats and administrators of Thera. He was an able politician and would have made a capable First Family Magistrate if they had remained on Thera, but he was not up to the tasks of an uprooted culture, much less war. Most of Arithon's friends were present also, including Sestos, and Losius, son of the strokeman Sosius, all of whom he had known since childhood. Hyssos joined them, out of breath, having run the league from his mother's modest home on the far side of the ridge. His father, Crensos, had been the able captain of the *Octopus*, the great ship which made the Crete to Egypt run twice a year. The ship was lost at sea, in the legendary storm of Hyssos' twelfth year. The loss to the community was heartrending and made a big impression on Arithon, who was thirteen at the time. After the seas had abated, two expeditions were launched in search of her, but nothing was ever found. Hyssos' mother moved the family to the small, secluded sheep farm of her father, where they lived off the quality woolens she and her three daughters crafted. Despite all his mother's pleas to remain on land, a sheepherder, Hyssos was determined to go to sea – the son of a Theran Captain, anxious to be all his father had been. Alteron, out of respect for Crensos, employed Hyssos on his ships, much to his mother's consternation. 'He was a great captain and a noble Theran,' he had often said to his widow, 'let the boy accomplish what he may.'

"I am not late, I hope," huffed Hyssos.

"No, you are right on time. The Cretan is assembling us now," explained Losius.

"Line up behind an axe and listen up," the Cretan soon bellowed.

As soon as Arithon took his place behind an axe in the middle of the line, the Cretan told them all to pick it up.

"What's the first thing you notice?" he asked the group.

"It's sharp. It is big. It is old. It's heavy," came many voices.

"It is heavy," echoed the Cretan as soon as he heard it, interrupting others trying to talk.

"As a weapon, it is heavy," he began with a drone, "and this is both its strength and its weakness. It is heavy to carry and wield, but when used with skill and strength it is deadly. You will not find it enjoyable to carry on land for great distances. It is a close combat weapon, ideal for naval battles when you must board the enemy's ship or try to keep from being boarded. On a confined deck, crowded with lines, grappling devices, oars, sails, enemies, it is often more useful than a sword or knife. It has been the weapon of standard issue in the navy for generations.

"We begin with the basic moves."

The Cretan then began to show them a series of moves that involved swinging the axe in graceful arcs, designed to maintain a periphery of protection with the minimum amount of effort, so as not to tire the user.

Arithon concentrated on the task before him and was soon comfortable with the moves he was learning. Two hours later, with the lesson over, his back was sore and his shoulders tight from the repetitive movements. He sat down in the sand next to his friends.

"What did you think of all that?" he ventured.

"I don't know really, the axe seems like such an old weapon, and when would I use it?" replied Sestos. "My father thinks we should all move to Crete and not bother with these other ideas. He says the Sea King has the responsibility to accept us because of all the tribute we paid over the years and that your grandfather should appeal to him."

"Selleres is beleaguered on many fronts. I think we will have to make our own way," Arithon said.

"But we are not fighters, Arithon, we are traders and fishermen and farmers," countered Sestos as he tossed a stone into the surf twenty feet from where they sat. My father wants me to take over our rope making business, and he still has my five sisters to marry off. Besides, who would have us, except the Cretans?"

"There are many who would have your sister, Tazetta," offered Losius.

"Watch it, Losius," retaliated Sestos. "Her only brother might have to smack you."

60

Losius laughed, thoroughly amused, as Sestos feigned a punch.

"I am to be given a commission to seek help from the Achaeans," Arithon said staring out.

"The Achaeans!" gasped Sestos, turning away from Losius. "They are a rough bunch, and care only for themselves. My father said they bicker amongst themselves almost as much as they do with us. But what did you say? … A commission? … What commission?"

"I am to captain the new fast-hull and take a crew with an ambassador to Tiryns or Mycenae. My father told me about it this morning."

"They trust you to do that?" asked Sestos.

"It would appear so – though I think they are short on people to send. Most of the leaders are leaving on their own missions. I heard we are dispatching our ships to Lydia and Rhodos to the east, Lesvos, and Limnos in the north. Others are going to Egypt in the South to seek court with the Pharaoh. Felos is sailing to Cyprus to …"

Arithon's voice trailed off as he thought about the destinations to the north, east and south, but not west. Why not west?

"Are you really going to get the new fast-hull," said Sestos, interrupting his thoughts.

"Yes," began Arithon as he snapped back. "It will be ready in six months and I must be ready to sail and command by then."

"You will be," said Glaxos as he sat down next to Arithon, "you are a natural leader; quick and strong besides."

"I hope you are right," said Arithon, "I have much to learn."

"We all do," replied Glaxos, "I was terrible with the axe just now. You took to it with ease."

"Yes, you really did, Ari," chimed in Sestos. "But you are always the best, though I will challenge you anytime with ropes or dice."

"Dice? … No dice with you, Sestos," laughed Arithon, "I know better."

The Therans lapsed into the easy conversation of young men, punctuated with the jabs and challenges of youth. It was playful fun, and a good respite from the dark talk of the challenges before them. Arithon twiddled a piece of beach grass between his fingers, while Sestos palmed fig-size rocks and continued tossing them into the surf.

"I wonder what Achaean women look like?" ventured Sestos. "I have never seen one. Only the men come here to trade, though they occasionally bring one of their slave women."

"I hear they are comely, but modest, and wear stitched clothing from head to foot," added Hyssos. "I much prefer the Minoan dress with the bared breast and flounce skirt."

"The bared breasts are always good," suggested Sestos with a raise of his eyebrows.

The young men laughed and Arithon thought of the Minoan women dressed in their best fashions. A wave of desire coursed his body as he thought of the pure loveliness of their exposed breast, lifted, and pushed together by the tight, enveloping blouse into a smooth curve, tipped with a brown nipple. He was lost in this thought when Sestos pushed him at the shoulder exclaiming, "And who are you thinking about, my Captain?

"Captain ..." Sestos repeated with afterthought.

"Hey, Arithon, who are you taking with you?" asked Sestos, suddenly getting more serious. "You will need a crew, will you not?"

"He will need men of skill, not dice throwers," interrupted Hyssos.

"Hey, dice throwing is a skill," retorted Sestos. "But I have skills with rope, and I am not a bad sailor at that. I can learn to fight, ... besides, Arithon will need friends along to help."

"Yes, he will," chimed Glaxos. "Maybe you should go with him."

Their conversation was interrupted by one of the Council members who told all the men assembled on the beach to return each morning for four hours of training. They could expect training in a variety of skills until Thera was evacuated.

'Evacuate Thera.'

Chilling words which motivated the group to stand, make their departures, and go their separate ways. Arithon set out to locate his father, and soon discovered he was with Tios and the First Council. Not wanting to interrupt, and not yet feeling their equal, he headed for the docks to locate Po. Along the way his mind wandered from subject to subject in that odd thread of loosely connected thoughts peculiar to the human mind.

I will be prepared. I can go to the Achaeans, he thought. And I will persuade them to help us. What are they like he wondered? How will they receive us? He soon followed the original thread of his conversation with Sestos and Hyssos, and again found himself thinking of Minoan women. He was old enough to be interested in the women of the island, though he had no special relationship with any of them. He had been intimate with three of the girls of his city, but not with Sestos' sisters, of course, he now laughed to himself. Awkward and fumbling, those memories now brought him some embarrassment of thought – and they had risks. As in every culture, the fathers and future husbands of the girls would not be inclined to support a child which was not theirs and arrangements had to be made to compensate. All in all, though, the mores of Thera supported the enjoyment of physical passions. Teenage men and women would engage in the trysts of the young, but care and discretion were expected. Arithon was disappointed to think he would have little time for such events anytime soon. He was armed with this sad thought when he found Po on the deck of the *Swallow*, repairing the rigging.

"Hey, Po," he said. "How's the *Swallow*?"

"The *Swallow* is seaworthy, but you look a little shipwrecked," Po replied. "Did you drop the axe on your toe?" he added, glancing at his feet.

"No. A little self-doubt, I suppose."

"For you? – I have no doubts. Come and help me with this old rigging."

And so, for the rest of the afternoon he worked with Po to replace the worn ropes and pins of the *Swallow*. Po told him of his plans to sail to the larger islands of the North, including Lesvos and Limnos. He expected it to take three months but might be able to return before Arithon could set sail for the Achaean mainland.

"It would be nice to find an island home," Po began. "We have had many generations of peace here in our isolation. As traders, though, we get the best the world has to offer without becoming embroiled in the fighting of the mainlanders. But we need one with a good harbor, and all in the Aegean are taken unless I am much mistaken."

Arithon suddenly remembered the thought which had given him pause on the beach. "Po, why do we not sail west in search of a home?"

"Zephyr's realm is dangerous, and on the edge of the civilized world. There are many tales of the west, some true I suspect, some not."

"Have you ventured further than the *Octopus*?" asked Arithon. "And what are the tales?"

Before Po could answer, Alteron stepped onto the *Swallow* and hailed, "Here you are. I should have known you would be with the Master of the Aegean," he said throwing a wink at Po, who smiled, and resumed his work, threading rope through fittings on the top rail.

"I have something to discuss with you," he added.

Arithon started to put down the coil he was working so he could converse with his father, but instead his father picked up two of the new

63

pins and moved ahead of Po on the rail to help in the work. Arithon resumed threading the sheet lines.

"I have been meeting with the Council," Alteron began. "We want to combine our resources to keep the Therans together, rather than disperse our race to the winds. But this will require more planning, more ships and more wealth."

His father paused momentarily to hammer out an old pin with a large wooden mallet he had picked up from the tools now scattered about the deck. The pounding echoed through the harbor mixing with the cries of a seagull which took flight off the stern of the ship. His father inserted a new pin and began again.

"We intend to trade Thera's best goods for exotics like ivory, incense, and opium if we can get it. We will also try to accumulate as much silver, copper, and tin as possible by selling off our excess inventory, especially the heavy stuff, like the marble.

"So, I have another mission for you, before your journey to the Achaean mainland. I want you to accompany Po to the coast of Africa to trade for ivory. Upon your return, our artisans will create luxury items we can use to hire transport or buy ships."

"My training?"

"We will not be ready for the ivory mission for two more months, as we will need time to sell our expendables to our Minoan allies," his father replied. "You can train in that time with the rest of Akrotiri and then continue your training with Poius."

Po looked up from his work at the two men he loved most in the world and tried not to smile but could not help himself.

"Yes, I can help you, Arithon," Po said as he cinched a line to its pin, "and you will learn fast."

"Do not let him fool you with all his praise, Arithon. Poius was a formidable opponent in his day and still is, I would venture," said Alteron.

Po smiled again and then went back to work on the *Swallow*'s rigging.

***

"Here comes the Cretan," whispered Hyssos out of the corner of his mouth, from his spot on the end of their line. The other three heads pivoted in unison to see the approach of their instructor, walking with something on his mind; and it had to do with them. They had spent the morning

64

training and were now sitting on the beach talking before they headed home.

"Arithon," he began after he pulled up, purposely ignoring the others. "You are skilled. I have taught many and you have ability."

"Thank you," Arithon replied, squinting up into the midday sun, uncomfortable with the attention.

"I hear you are exceptional with the glove, also."

"No one can beat him!" said Sestos.

"Is that so?" questioned the Cretan.

"No, Sestos spoke out of turn," Arithon said.

"A bout?" asked the Cretan. "I would enjoy a challenge."

Arithon did not like the tone.

"Oh, I don't know. It has been a long day already."

"Come. You cannot be beat," he mimicked.

"He has won every bout for the last two years," Sestos jumped in, not liking the tone either, but taking a much different tack than Arithon.

"Another time, perhaps?" said Arithon.

"I have some skill in the glove. It would be … well … interesting. Come."

"Go on, Arithon," said Hyssos, entering the fray.

"I will get the gloves," said Sestos, who sprang up and ran into the city.

A warning wave washed in, but Arithon shook it off. He enjoyed a spirited round – a source of internal confusion to his gentle soul – but few would take him on anymore. It might be fun, he reasoned, and besides, it was good training if not the best of circumstances. He competed at the festivals when the competition was organized and refereed, but he had never fought someone just on the beach.

Sestos soon returned and as Sestos was apt to do, he had told several people on his way and a crowd had gathered by the time Arithon and the Cretan began to put on their glove.

Minoan boxing involved the use of one glove, put on either hand, while the other hand went bare. The object was to land blows to the face with the gloved hand, using the bare one on the body. An intentional bare fist to the face was a foul and could result in disqualification. The winner was determined when one of the combatant's knees touched the ground. Knockouts were rare, except in charged fights, when the opponents were exceptionally pugilistic.

Arithon placed the leather glove, padded with wool felt, on his right hand as was customary. The Cretan, though right-handed, placed his glove on his left. This was curious. Arithon had fought left-handers before, but never a right-hander with his left gloved.

Hyssos agreed to referee and the two men stood facing each other on the beach, just above the wave line, where the red sand was soft and dry but cumbersome.

"Begin," said Hyssos.

Arithon stood with his left forward like a shield, his right tucked and cocked. The Cretan, opposite, did the opposite. It was awkward, but Arithon soon found the wisdom of his unconventional approach; and he found it at the end of the glove in his face. The Cretan landed three blows with his left, jabbing in at a rapid rate, for which Arithon had no classical defense. He staggered from the blows but did not fall as he backed off.

The Cretan grinned wickedly.

On the next series, the Cretan faired just as well and Arithon staggered this time, falling to one knee, his nose bleeding.

Sestos and the others were open-mouthed in dismay: Arithon was their champion and an older and smaller opponent had beaten him easily. Arithon knelt on one knee, surprised also at the swiftness of the outcome. Mad, but in control Arithon said, "You are good. Thank you for the match."

"If you are the best of Thera, then Thera is in trouble," he said.

This stung and Arithon's anger, usually slow to kindle, waxed. He was worried enough about the ability of Thera to transform from traders to adventurers, especially his own role. It was a portentous moment not lost on those gathered in the circle.

Arithon stood and looked down at his hands and then asked, "Again?"

"Of course," the Cretan grinned.

"A moment," said Arithon, taking off his glove. "Sestos, help me."

Sestos helped Arithon tie the glove onto his left hand. The Cretan watched with interest and cocked his arms when Arithon set his left foot in imitation and rotated into the new position.

He looked over at Hyssos who said, "Begin."

The Cretan landed only one of the three blows he fired in rapid succession, and Arithon managed to pop him one to the head. They separated.

When they engaged again, he was able to hold his own, swapping blow for blow. The Therans became agitated and began to cheer for Arithon.

"Fight, Ari! Fight, Ari!" Sestos kept the chant.

The Cretan was wary – a first for him. His unorthodox use of the left had been a distinct advantage for him, and none had picked it up fast enough to challenge him on the same day. And he won his bouts quickly and decisively; he was not in the same physical condition as Arithon and it soon showed. He became winded and moved slower, while Arithon seemed to get faster.

On the next exchange, Arithon delivered a withering series of blows before the Cretan lashed out with his ungloved hand, splitting Arithon's lip; the red blood striping his chin as it flowed.

"Foul," cried Sestos, jumping up and down in the sand.

But it was not about points anymore, the Cretan was heaving for breath, trying to buy a few precious seconds. Arithon waded in, tasting his own salty blood, his fury surging. The Cretan was outmatched and Arithon landed two vicious blows, busting his nose open and staggering the Cretan before he delivered an uppercut which landed squarely on his opponent's chin, knocking him out with a crack. He fell like a dropped rope onto the sand.

It was the first time he had ever punched out an opponent in anger and it felt strangely satisfying. Sestos and the crowd which now numbered in the hundreds cheered as Arithon stood looking over the man who had just provided him a valuable service. The crowd collapsed on Arithon, congratulating him, and talking all at once.

The gathering was interrupted by one of the Council Members who had the Cretan scooped up and taken away. Arithon took advantage of the lull and walked unsteadily down to the salty surf to wash his bloodied face. His lip was beginning to swell and throb.

"Want me to fetch Kyllena?" offered Sestos as he joined him. Arithon winced as if his lip stung, but really, he did not want to endure the ministrations of the city healer, the frequent companion of Chlora, the woman on Kronos street whispered to be the priestess of a Mystery Cult.

"No, I will go home and put a cold rag on it," he answered.

"You were marvelous, Arithon. You give me hope."

"You should always have hope," he said turning up to look at his friend standing beside him in the water.

"Yes, you're right. … Are you coming to the storytelling tonight?"

"Of course. I will see you there."

Arithon walked home alone wondering what kind of man he would be.

"And so, my perfect listeners I will tell you the tale of:

Akrotiri and the Dolphins

"Everyone knows the story of Poseidon and Hephaestus," began Crito, the storyteller, with a sinuous sweep of his arms toward the audience.

He stood at the bottom of Story Hill, as they called the natural amphitheater-like slope on the northwest of the city. Arithon was sitting with his family in the front row, reserved for members of the First Family, the Council, and other dignitaries of the island. Arithon's lip was still swollen, but the throbbing had diminished to a dull itch. His mother had fussed long over it, applying wet rags and a strange poultice of some astringent concoction which made him gag. But she followed it with one of her best honey cakes to kill the taste of the medicine and bring a measure of satisfying goodness to her treasured son.

Raiha sat next to her sister-in-law, quietly discussing their husbands and children, while her daughter, Roa, sat on her father's lap, too big really to be there, but still young enough to want to be. Alteron was more than pleased to hold her, knowing the days when he could were short and precious.

"No! Tell it!" she shouted to the performer.

"Only briefly," he said in a singsong voice, "as it has some bearing on our story of Akrotiri."

He then began in earnest:

"Long ago when the Aegean was yet unsailed, and Poseidon had newly taken it for his home, he gave to his nephew Hephaestus – at Zeus' insistence – a pearl to cast onto the perfect spot in all the seas. And when he had done so, a small round island grew, so Hephaestus could have a home on the sea, as well as on the land. Here he built a mighty forge which billows the smoke of his fire, and the island shakes from the pounding of his hammer."

Crito made a hammering motion, sweeping around the arc of listeners.

"An intrepid race of mariners followed the trail of smoke over the sea and found the Small Round One, and they named it Thera, and the mighty smokestack which sat upon it they named Mt. Thera. And they exclaimed that Thera was in the most perfect place in all the seas; an island fit for the homeport of the world's greatest mariners.

"By and by, they asked leave of Poseidon: 'Could we live on your pearl of an island?' they beseeched. We will make it great, and nurture its lands, which are now bleak and barren. And we will make it the most renown of all the mariners islands, for we are the greatest to ever sail your seas.'

"'It is not mine,' Poseidon replied, 'I have given it to Hephaestus, but since you are the fairest of those who ply my waters, I will ask this for you.'

"And he did, but the cripple, Hephaestus, was in no mood for guests.

"'I will not stop my forge for them, and they would certainly complain of my hammering at all hours of the day and night,' he told his uncle. 'They would aggravate me!'"

Several listeners moved uneasily in their seats, all too conscious of the truth in the bard's story. The storyteller continued.

"In the end Hephaestus agreed, but only begrudgingly, at his uncle's insistence.

"'They are mariners,' explained Poseidon, 'and they will honor your forge and bring much wealth and beauty to the flanks of your smokestack – be glad of them!'

"And so it came to pass our ancestors, the Therans, settled on the Little Round One and did all they had promised: nurtured the slopes, brought art and music to the forge, and built the greatest harbor and the greatest shipyards in the Aegean. But no one knew where the land of the Therans was located, and so they prospered for generations, and Poseidon was glad, even if Hephaestus was not."

The speaker paused.

"There lived among these mariners, a sagacious sailor, one Akrotiri, who sailed to all the points on the wind, aboard the best ships of Thera, and brought back the wealth of kings. Soon his fame sailed before him, and the wicked and the cruel envied his treasure and sought his homeland, which they could not find. For they knew all the islands of the sea, but not Thera, as it was but newly formed and hidden.

"'Where is that sailor, Akrotiri?' they would ask, for they knew his name. Always they sought the homeland of Akrotiri, for they had heard of its riches, and its beauty, and many tried to follow him home, but could never succeed.

"But the ugly and awful pirates of Caria, pillaging on the seas, always seeking for the sailor Akrotiri, saw a smoke one day in the distance and followed its trail, hoping it was a hearth fire in the lost land of the mariners.

"And when they came to Thera, the pirate said knowingly, 'This is the hidden land we seek; the island of Hephaestus, obscured in the smoke of his forge.'

"The great Poseidon saw them also, and he frowned, for he loved the Therans and hated the wicked pirates. He sent a storm against them, which pushed them back to their shores, but their lust for the riches of Thera did not die and so they waited for their chance.

"It came one day when the winds were fair and the sun shone bright, and the Therans held their Festival of Poseidon. The god himself came to watch, pleased as he was by the beauty of Theran pageantry. And so it was even Poseidon did not see the Carian pirates that crept closer and closer, intent on the treasures of Thera.

"All the men had assembled to race to the top of the mountain, for in those days all of the men ran, not just the young as we do now (which was a wise change, as you shall see). For while the men were racing to the top, each trying only to beat the other, pirates sailed into the harbor and stole the young women of Thera, who were waiting at the bottom preparing the feast. The treasures they could not find, though they looked and looted and destroyed.

"'Then we will have their women, and sell them as slaves,' bellowed the pirate captain as he captured as many of Thera's finest as he could put aboard and slew those he could not.

"But Akrotiri spotted them from the top of the Forge, and called to all those still running, to turn and try and save their wives and daughters. The pirates, seeing the pursuit, set fire to the Theran fleets so none could follow.

"Akrotiri was first to the beach, just in time to see the ship slip out the harbor entrance and raise her sail. The other men joined him in the harbor, putting out the fires which raged on the decks of the world's greatest fleet – a sad and wanton destruction. Akrotiri espied the women who had died on the beach protecting their daughters. A rage filled him.

"Unwilling to wait, our hero, grabbed a fishing skiff and began to row after the pirates, intent only on preventing their escape. When he was well offshore, the pirates turned to make sport of their pursuer, and so it was Akrotiri found himself alone, without weapons and now the prey of their hunt.

"The pirate ship bore down on his skiff with all the speed of sail and oar, to crush him under the waves where his body would feed the monsters of the deep. Akrotiri stood in his skiff, unable to outrun them and waited, his rage still unspent.

"The pirates laughed at the man standing on the wave and cursed his impudence in the face of their power. But he showed no fear, nor moved at all as the collision began, but only fingered the blue jewel which hung from his neck. When their bow stood high above him, and he could no longer be seen by those aboard, he leapt up at the mighty sprit and caught it, hanging on like a barnacle, out of their view as they all pivoted, hurrying astern, to watch the destruction which would bob up in their wake.

"And so it was they did not see him, as he clawed around to the port side, his feet hanging in the roll of their bow wave.

"Unable to cling any longer he swung back and forth, back and forth."

The bard imitated this motion for the crowd of hushed listeners.

"And then he released and caught onto the first oar, and quick as quick he was standing upon it, and running down the full length of the ship, stepping lightly on each oar in its turn."

Again, the storyteller mimicked this action, kicking his knees up in an exaggerated manner as he paraded up into the audience. Arithon had to turn to his side, to watch Crito, who now stood ten rows into the crowd. He could see the faces of the islanders, peering intently; smiles on all their faces.

"And reaching the last oar, he jumped upon the deck and flung the first pirate over the rail to crash into the outstretched oars – but only after relieving him of his sword. The pirates looking astern at the wreckage of the skiff, turned with smiles to see what the noise was about, and saw only the fury of a Theran warrior of old.

"He cut and hew and sliced his way through their ranks, while the women cried out in the hold below."

The storyteller waded through the crowd, pretending to hack at the listeners as if he had a sword in his hand. Young children squealed with delight and fear when he did it to them, and more than one jumped into the protective lap of their parent.

"They threw SPEARS!" the bard now cried with loud enthusiasm.

"They shot ARROWS!"

"They chopped with AXES!"

"They sliced back with SWORDS!"

71

"But nnooooo. None could touch him, and none could withstand him," he bellowed with great emphasis.

"Until only one remained – the pirate captain. The wickedest, most horrible man on the seas, and he laughed at Akrotiri, even in the midst of all that destruction.

"'Come,' he invited wickedly. 'Come and let me kill you.'

"But Akrotiri said naught and advanced upon the evil marauder and fought him for hour upon hour, until their swords were only this big," said the bard, measuring a tiny distance with his thumb and forefinger.

The crowd laughed at this absurdity.

"No," he corrected. "They fought until they could lift their swords no more but could only stare at each other across the deck planks. And so, the pirate charged like a bull to knock Akrotiri over the rail, but Akrotiri held on, and they both toppled over and into the water."

The bard fell back onto the ground and started wrestling with an unseen opponent.

"They fought in the water, churning over and over like waves on the shore, as the ship sped away under sail, her decks unmanned and unhelmed.

"And then Akrotiri dived, as if he were a fish, and on his way down he grabbed the pirate's ankle and pulled him down with him.

"Down, down, down, he swam and then, … down, down, down some more, until he thought his lungs would burst.

"He swam so far down it was black as octopus ink and then, he swam, … down, down, down."

The storyteller was quite animated by this point and the audience was fully in his grasp.

"He swam so far down he unknowingly disturbed the lair of the Spirilon, the nastiest creature of the depths.

"And then he let go of the pirate's ankle, and began to swim … up, up, up. And the pirate tried to follow him, but Akrotiri was too fast and outpaced the evil captain.

"So intent on reaching the surface, Akrotiri did not look back, and so he did not see the Spirilon, as it grabbed the pirate in its claws – claws the size of a man."

Crito held his hands open to show the size.

"And the Spirilon squeezed the air from the evil captain's lungs and squeezed and squeezed, and squeezed some more, until his eyes popped."

The storyteller showed bug-eyes, and the children laughed delightedly.

"And then the Spirilon ate him in one gulp," the storyteller gulped loudly.

"Our intrepid Theran, though, pierced the surface and fought for air for minutes upon minutes, waiting for the pirate – if he could make it. But he did not, and Akrotiri, looked on all horizons, until he saw the sail of the ship now a league away. He was too weak to swim, so he prayed to Poseidon to help him in his need.

"But the Spirilon liked the taste of man, and thought maybe he could eat another, and another and maybe a dozen or more. And even though he did not like the sun, he began to rise slowly to the surface, seeking, seeking another morsel for his great appetite.

"Poseidon, who knows all in his realm, saw what was transpiring, and hearing the prayers of the valiant Theran, immediately dispatched the swift, Ficaria, and two of his fastest dolphins. Akrotiri, was spent, and began to slip beneath the waves, where the Spirilon now saw him and began to wag his tail strongly, his mouth opening in anticipation."

The bard bared his teeth and lunged at the children, who buried themselves deeper in their parents' laps.

But Ficaria had found Akrotiri, also, and fluttered above him, so that Akrotiri could see the acrobatic bird tightly spiraling above the water.

"'Poseidon has heard your prayer and sends two to help you. Do not despair. And watch for the Spirilon below – even now he approaches.'"

"Akrotiri, looked down and saw it was true, but saw also that it was too late. He began to slip beneath the waves, exhausted. And just as the teeth began to close around Akrotiri's legs, the two dolphins, Polus and Prados, swam under his outstretched arms and lifted the drowning mariner to the surface, where they sped him away with the Spirilon in pursuit, and Ficaria above them, guiding the dolphins.

"And the monster chased them, league on league, hour on hour, his gaping mouth always snapping at their fins and feet."

Here the storyteller, made a jaw out of his two arms and snapped them at the children.

"But Polus and Prados were strong and Ficaria was wily, and they led the Spirilon all through the night, until the sun rose and the Spirilon found they had led him inside the inner harbor of Thera, just behind these hills. And they swam round and round until the Spirilon was so dizzy he

73

floundered on the rocks of the sheer cliffs, and lay there panting from his effort, the sun milking him of his strength.

"Hephaestus, who had heard the wailing of the Therans in their grief, felt pity for them, and hammered hard on his forge; so hard that the cliffs shook and rained giant boulders down upon the Spirilon, burying him alive in the shallows.

"And there he remains to this day, waiting to emerge and eat again – especially little children who swim too near," he said now with a wicked grin.

"But the ship was still sailing, the women tied in its hold, crying to be saved, as they were blown farther and farther west toward the unknown lands.

"'If you could but carry me once more,' beseeched Akrotiri to Polus and Prados, 'I would save those ladies of Thera from what awaits them in the west.'

"And so once again he grabbed their fins and they sped west in search of the lost ship.

"After days upon days, he saw the ship on the western horizon, sailing headlong for the rocks of the western isles, where all would be crushed and drowned.

"'Greater speed if you have it,' he pleaded, 'for we will not reach them in time.'

"And so the Dolphins of Poseidon, swam with all the speed they had left – and I can tell you it was as fast as the falcon flies. Faster and faster they swam, gaining on the hapless ship. As they approached the stern, Akrotiri stood upon their backs as they knifed through the water, toward the shoals. Our courageous Theran jumped onto the rear rail and bounded to the tiller, just as the bow struck the first rock. Turning with all his might he pivoted the ship with the precious cargo, away and into the open sea.

"He freed the women and with their brave help, they sailed back to a celebratory welcome in our fair city, which was given the name Akrotiri in his honor. He became the most renowned warrior and pirate fighter of Thera and all the seas were swept clear of the marauders by the valiant sailor and the fleets of our homeland.

"And the Therans honored Polus and Prados and all of their descendants, and to this day the dolphins play on the bow wave of our ships in memory of Akrotiri and his brave deeds."

CHAPTER 6 DEFIANCE

Eos, the dawn, cursed to love only the young, thought it not a
terrible jinx, as she watched the one who watched for her.

Thera's spirited songbirds announced the first bluing of the eastern sky, and Arithon rose determined, as he had done for all his teenage years. It was the best time of the day, and not to be squandered. The fanciful dreams of youth were beginning to seek realization in the disciplined mind and body of a passionate man. His test would come – he could feel the events converging around him.

His breechclout in hand, he tiptoed naked past his parent's red door, stopped in the toilet, then slipped down the stairs before getting dressed in the darkness of the hall. His mother heard him as she always did and then wandered back into a decadent morning doze.

In the kitchen, Arithon dipped the earth-red cup – the one with the chip – into the clay vessel mounted against the wall and drank the water in one lift. The liquid was cool and quenched his night thirst, so he repeated the motions twice, anticipating the heat of his run. In a clumsy hurry, he clattered the cup too hard onto the stone shelf and hissed at himself for the unwanted noise. Raiha, her stolen snooze interrupted, shamed herself upright and started the silent bustling which she had mastered, and her good son had not.

Arithon hung the cup back on its peg, instructed by the collected repetitions of his mother's admonishments. She insisted that it hang – in its place! – next to the other six; one for each family member; the newest one with the black dolphin swimming around its girth belonging to his youngest sister. With a bit more restraint, he uncorked a jar and grabbed a handful of raisins, which he popped into his mouth as he walked through the darkness to the front room where his sandals lay in the basket next to the door.

With his gangling legs hanging over the threshold, he chewed his raisins while lacing his sandals to the exact tightness he preferred, and then paused with elbows to thighs and listened to the sounds of the early morning. The songbirds were in voluble chatter now, even though sunrise was an hour away. Someone across town slammed a door – near the baker's kiln perhaps: he would be up early stoking his fire.

A half-moon cast a soft glow on the street in front of their house. It was time to go, but a frantic rustling in the laurel next to the steps caught his attention. Three larks fought their way out onto the paving stones – two on one – a flutter of wings, a few frantic pounces and it was over as a lone bird took flight down the alley. Arithon pursed his lips in a half smile at the amusing display, and then grew more somber. They were fighting over territory – something the Therans would soon know.

An odd gentle breeze was blowing as he tied his long black hair into a horsetail and stood to survey Saffron Street. That Westerly might bring a welcome rain later in the afternoon, but for now it was the best of mornings and not a Theran in sight. Skittering down the steps and turning to his left, he began his usual route up through the city on his way to the ridges above Akrotiri. The sandals made a muffled clap on the stones as he began his run, slowly at first, but with ever increasing speed as his body warmed to the motions. It felt good. The strength was there. And this would be a splendid run; a run where he could push his young body harder, faster, and farther. There were days when he felt as though he were a turtle, carrying extra weight in all his limbs; but this was not one of them. Today he was light and powerful. He would make the second ridge before sunrise – yes that would be the goal this morning – the second ridge.

As he settled into his gait, he forgot about running; the mind wandered to its own thoughts; the senses monitoring the events which would mark the route. There on the left was the home of the old couple, up early as usual lighting their oil lamps. She would be the first to sweep the street in front of her home, as she was every morning. Kalliste's accent was like a hummed melody. She told stories of the neighborhood: the old families, the children, the flowers on Moonrise Ridge. Her oregano swags were a perennial gift. He would miss her settled presence – she would probably not be his neighbor in their new city.

Up on the right, the dog of the scribe's wife was already barking his approach even though Arithon was five houses away. Every time. He could still hear the yapping as he slipped by Sestos' house – dark and quiet – and started the first of the three long stairs. His mental wanderings were interrupted; forced to concentrate just enough on his footfalls to prevent tripping on the treads. At the top he turned right and ran a steady slope which would allow him to catch his breath. His mind could roam again, and he began to muse about Thera. 'Round One' – that is what the Achaeans called her; and she was: a pearl dropped by Poseidon according to the legend. A precious thing nurtured by his ancestors and now to be lost to the descendants. His chest tightened. Oh, how he would miss this secret garden of Minoa – to have one more summer of hot nights playing chase in the olive groves.

He ran faster. Where could they find another harbor where the moon rose on still waters and gentle winds brushed verdant slopes? He cut behind the last house and took the familiar path up the hillside trying to beat the sun to the top of the ridge. The second ridge today; today he would make the second ridge before the sun could break the horizon.

The swift-footed Theran had been running with an unusual intensity and his body was sweating from the exertion; rivulets coursed down his chest and back, soaking the cloth around his waist. He pressed on and made the first ridge with darkness to spare. Concentrating only on his body now, he dug in as he crossed the first summit; his legs beginning to cramp and his lungs burning. He counted ten fast steps – one, two, three, pushing up the hill, then another ten to catch his breath; jump up onto the big boulder and over the scraggly juniper and back onto the trail.

Arithon started to pant out loud, "I can do twenty more steps – yes, I can, and twenty more."

The challenge became greater, his determination greater still. Each time he felt he must slow down or collapse, he would catch a glimpse of the east and those wispy night clouds lit on their undersides by the approaching sun. It spurred him on. He would make the second ridge. He could do it.

Thera's child continued like this for another half league, charging up the switchbacks, dodging fist size rocks which littered the path. This trail predated Akrotiri, laid down by the Old Ones, but Arithon would be one of the last to traverse it. This thought entered his mind just as he caught a glimpse of his goal: the summit of the second ridge. After a sharp turn under an embankment, he was facing the east and could see the dark blue streaks which appear in the seconds before the dawn.

It will be close, he thought, and I want to set the best time ever; the best time anyone has ever done – in all the history of the island.

Arithon sprinted for the top, thinking of nothing but the next footfall and the next and the next. He was breathing so hard it hurt his throat and a dull nausea was creeping in, but he kept on running, thinking only: I can beat the sun, I can beat the sun. I will beat the sun today.

And then he was cresting; the slope tapering to the top where the large rock on the mount's edge awaited him, as it had done for millennia. He jumped – with a reserve of power which surprised him – landing surefooted on the first ledge of the rock, and then two more leaps placed him on the top.

Dizzy with exertion he leaned forward, placed his hands onto his knees and heaved air as he fought the nausea which threatened to sicken him. More breathing and he could feel it subside enough to raise his head and look out to sea, where the sun would rise as it always had.

And then that pinprick of white light pierced the horizon, and cut a slit to allow the top of the orange ball to edge in.

Sunrise!

Arithon looked down, still holding hands to knees, and smiled to himself. He did it. His best time; maybe the best time ever; by anyone. He stood straight and was awed that the sun was already half exposed and rising fast. The young man felt as alive as he ever had; proud to have met his goal, proud of his body and what it could do, proud to be a child of this glorious sea-bred race.

"Theraaaaaaaaaaaah," he screamed, as he rounded on the rock and raised his hand, palm forward at the mountain which he had always both feared and admired, and which would now drive him from his home. His own recklessness surprised him.

"Theraaaaaaaaaah," he screamed again, pumping his arm in defiance of its power.

He stood immobile, arm out, until his anger and adrenalin waned enough for him to lower his challenge, relax, and come back to the mortal's earth. His sweat-drenched hair was plastered to his scalp, beads rolling down the back of his neck and dripping from the tips of his horsetail. A highflying gull wailed overhead and as he cast upward to watch, he shivered. It would not do to cool too fast: he jumped from the rock to start his descent, leaving the mountain to its own deep broodings.

It had been two months since his father had asked him to accompany Po to Africa, and their departure was fast approaching. They were waiting for the last trading ship to return from Rhodos with the balance of goods they would use to barter. It could arrive anytime.

He thought of his upcoming voyage as he took the fork which would bend around to the west and down to Fisherman Beach. The sea birds were flocked on the sand when he arrived and took off en masse, circling around to touch down behind him just above the wash of the breaking waves. The air was cooler down by the water, but he could feel on his face the heat of the coming day. Ahead there were dozens of fishermen making ready their beached boats for a day of angling. The two-man skiffs were propelled by four oars and lacked any sail, as the winds were never accommodating enough to make them worthwhile. At close to seventeen feet they were too heavy to be carried by only one crew. Launch-partnerships had developed over the years, hauling the boats by facing each other, and leaning back to raise the keel just above the round pebbles as they sidestepped their way down.

"Dawn's Day, Arithon," they shouted as he wove through the activities of those going to-and-fro carrying boats, nets, oars, food, and drink from the high-water mark to the push-off. Arithon had fished with the fleet many times when he was younger and knew the toil, frustrations and rewards associated with the profession. Regares, one of the oldest fishing, had taught him much of the patience and art of acquiring sustenance from the sea. He could see him at beach end, loading his boat as it rocked in the surf.

"Still at it I see," he called to the ancient mariner, who had turned as he heard the faster footfalls.

"What else would I do," Regares answered, as Arithon pulled up at the bow of the *Little One*. "I am too old to follow you on your coming journeys."

Arithon combed both hands through his wet hair, adjusted his horsetail and smiled at the simple man. "You are not too old my friend. I would have you on my ship. A man who can fish is never hungry."

"You are kind, Master Arithon. I see you are running. Are you training for the races at Poseidon's Festival? You won last year."

"Training," said Arithon, "but not for the festival. I will be gone. I have a mission in preparation for the migration."

"The migration," echoed Regares, "I do not agree with the Council. I will stay here on Thera until Hermes comes to escort me."

"But what of the mountain," interjected Arithon, "it will drive us away."

"I am afraid of the mountain. I will admit that. But I am more afraid of leaving. Thera is all I have ever known. I do not intend to leave. Most of the others feel as I do," he said with a nod back.

"Besides, the priests are making many offerings and prayers. They will appease her."

"Perhaps, … Perhaps," Arithon said.

"Bring me a big blue jack," he added as he saluted and resumed his run toward the quay.

As he came around the gentle curve of the headland, he scanned the harbor as all the inhabitants of Akrotiri did to assess who was in and who was not. Therans could tell the state of affairs by one glance to the harbor; something they all engaged in many times a day. The *Sea Monkey* was anchored in the channel, having arrived late last night. Mariners did not often arrive at night; scheduling their trips to avoid nighttime landings. But time was running out for Thera and all the crews were taking chances.

'Good,' thought Arithon. 'She is back. We will soon leave for Africa.'

Quickening his stride, he raced home, to find his parents enjoying a childless breakfast. With a hasty, "Good morning," he stooped to remove his sandals, tossed them into the basket and headed for the water room, pulling his breechclout off in mid-stride.

"The *Sea Monkey* is in," he called, as he poured a jar of water over his head, the water splashing onto the tiled floor and running down the drain next to the wall.

"Stop yelling!" his mother called. "Your sister is asleep."

Arithon was still drying himself as he bounded naked up the stairs to dress in a fresh tunic, grabbing it from the folded stack his mother maintained on the shelf next to the window.

"Be quiet," Roa moaned from her room, picking up on her mother's admonishment.

With all the mischief of a big brother, he ignored the plea, bounded down the stairs and entered the kitchen where his father and mother conversed on stools around the family table. He took the empty seat across from his father – the one he always occupied, according to the acknowledged but anonymous rules of a family.

His mother stood, according to other anonymous conventions, and without a word slipped over to the copper pot, spooned porridge into a bowl and set it on the table in front of her son, who was chewing on a mouthful of raisins scooped from the jar on the table.

"When do you think we will sail?" he asked.

"It will take a couple of days to finish loading the *Swallow* now that the *Sea Monkey* has returned," his father said, "I hope they made good deals in Anatolia."

"What did she pick up?" Arithon asked.

80

"Swords. Also, a talent of amber jewelry from Scythia and glass from the Lydians."

"Swords," repeated Arithon looking down at his bowl and then up at his father.

"The Africans are keen for weapons, especially those of good bronze. The Nile-born are particularly fond of them. If you bargain well, you can return with talents of ivory."

"Why not just keep the weapons for trade later as we migrate?" asked Arithon.

"It would not be prudent to supply weapons to those we encounter – would it?" his father replied with a raised eyebrow.

"No, I guess it would not be," Arithon said, feeling foolish.

"Besides, we can triple the value of the ivory," his father said. "We still have our ivory carvers. Pherthos has held that guild together, and good ivory is scarce – it always will be."

"I ran into Regares just now," said Arithon, "and he said he will not leave Thera. He wants the priests to quiet the mountain."

"Ah … Regares," mused his father, "Many think like him, and they are welcome to stay, but he may change his mind when the migration begins. There will not be anything here. The city will be dead, and the mountain will soon finish her despite all the incantations of the priests."

His father said the last few words with enough scorn that it peaked Arithon's interest.

"What's wrong with the priest offering to Hephaestus?" he asked, biting a spoonful of the barley mush.

"Do not excite your father," his mother said, "there has been some ugly talk by the priests at the Council – it serves no purpose to dwell on it here at our table. Change the subject, please. I can hear Roa."

Arithon knew better than to pursue it any further. His mother was quiet about political and religious matters, so her interruption left no doubt this must be a serious matter. He would leave it for another time.

"Shall I go to training or to the *Swallow*, today?" he asked.

"Join Poius. You both will have much to do to prepare. You will need to practice whenever you can, but I am afraid your training from now on will be in the far lands.

Arithon was standing with his family on the large quay of Akrotiri, preparing to leave for Africa, when it struck. It was an earthquake of a size not felt since his sister was trapped, and it shook the island with a force only gods can muster. The shaking made it so hard to stand that those on the dock dropped to their backsides to keep from being thrown down. Raiha clutched Roa to her as the child screamed in fear.

Arithon rounded to the mountain, but there was nothing to see; no more than the average smoke was present at the top of the cone. And that was unusual. With each mighty earthquake there had always been an accompanying eruption, and yet this time there was none. He did not have long to think about it before a severe side jolt caused him to drop down with the others.

"Mother Earth!" he cried as his hands slapped the stones.

The motion rolled him to one side where he braced against a piling staring out to sea. A curious site appeared in the water offshore which engaged his attention until the tremors rocked to a more gentle swaying which allowed him to stand. He shielded his brow with his hand, looked out to the horizon and asked his father, "What do you make of that?"

Alteron stared in the direction of his son's gaze.

"A rogue wave – large and moving out to sea. Half-mast high I would judge and traveling at a Furies' speed."

"I saw it form," Arithon said. "The sea reared up and the wave pushed off."

They watched it race into the distance and when the shaking stopped, Raiha and Roa rolled up onto all fours and then to their feet – uncertain and scared.

"I would rather live in a stranger's land than live in fear of being buried alive in my own home," Raiha said to Alteron, her voice quivering. Roa began to sob seeing her mother's fear.

Alteron conversed with his family, but Arithon did not take his eyes off the wave, which was now just a frothy white line on the horizon. It struck him as something important and he began to believe the wave was connected to the earthquake.

"Shall I stay with you, Father?" Arithon asked. "There will be damage to many of the buildings."

"No, join Poius on the *Swallow*. The Therans will endure. Now go and take care that you return to me. I will need you greatly in all my tomorrows."

Arithon turned to go but stopped as he remembered something. "The mountain did not erupt this time. Why is that?"

"I do not know," replied Alteron, "but it worries me. ... God speed."

Arithon climbed down the ladder into the skiff and was rowed out – the last to board. The anchors were hoisted, and the *Swallow* spun round on her axis as the oars waved in opposite directions. Alteron, standing on the dock, watched the grand ship glide out onto open water with his son and most trusted friend aboard. These were unsettled times, and each day brought more risk to his people, but he believed – with a little luck – they could persevere. He hurried up toward the city.

Once they were well away and the canvas had been set, the oarsmen settled down on the deck playing dice, while the sail crew managed the ship. Arithon found Po on the aft deck watching Thera shrink on the horizon as the *Swallow* rushed away on a blustering north wind.

"Thera's hull is giving way," Po said. "The storm that will finish her is on the horizon."

Arithon looked over at his friend. Po had plotted Thera's course in his mind and knew she was on her final tack. There was only one thing to do before she went down.

"Abandon ship," Po said in answer to the stare.

Arithon looked out onto the froth whipped sea and nodded his head in reluctant acknowledgement.

"You are wiser than our priests," said Po, reading the boy's acceptance. "They want a human sacrifice to appease the volcano."

A moment of sick fright washed over Arithon and drowned Po's last words. His mind spun backward to the fear and horror in the lost darkness: the cold gleam of the blade, the victim rattling in fright, the throbbing chant resonating the cave-like space. He could smell the incense cloud again as it swirled and boiled before his face in the lamp-flickered room. Then blood and pain and death – horrible, ritualized death. Trapped panic, and flight –.

"... does not approve and he is fighting those who do," came Po's voice.

There was a long pause, while the two men stared out over the waves, watching the wheeling seagulls following in their wake.

"Who would they sacrifice?" asked Arithon, noticing with surprise that his skin felt flushed and clammy.

"They would purchase a slave," Po replied.

"Thera ... Thera," repeated Arithon as he gazed back at his beloved home disappearing in the haze.

CHAPTER 7 AFRICAN IVORY

Helios journeyed through the night on his ship of west to east,
soon to mount his chariot-of-four to burn the lands of Libya.

Arithon slept little that night. The serenity of his tranquil life was receding as swiftly as that rogue wave; soon to disappear on yesterday's horizon. Why would they bring back human sacrifice; what damage had occurred during the earthquake; was anyone killed? Would there even be a Thera to return to? Like froth and debris in a whirlpool, his thoughts collided and tumbled as they spun in an ever-tightening circle toward panic and away from sleep. Tired beyond thinking, he drifted off for a few hours, but was rolled awake by the swells of a real ocean growing in intensity. He could hear the vibrating whistle of the rigging as he dressed, thinking about the turmoil brewing at home. The wind plastered his tunic when he stepped out of the lee of the cabin, just as the *Swallow* rolled to port and dipped her rail, spraying a fine mist. The crew will earn their mead today, he thought squinting to the east where the sun, surrounded by a fleet of puffy white clouds, emerged into the blue ocean of sky.

He fidgeted at the rail watching the rollers – all different, all the same – as his mind raced ahead. He decided to relieve the man at the steering oar. The swells were heavy on a following sea, so it was exhausting work to keep the *Swallow* running true as she corkscrewed through the troughs. This was nothing new to Arithon. He had experienced worse with Po and felt confident of the ship and his ability to steer her.

On his second trip to Cyprus, they were caught in a severe *meltemi*, as mariners called the ubiquitous north gale, and took two waves over the stern, the first of which knocked Arithon onto the mid-deck, where he caught a shroud before it could wash him over. He was about fourteen – no, probably fifteen that year. Po launched across the deck and caught him during the next wash over. A worthwhile effort, too, for his grip had slipped and he would not have been saved in those high seas. They were forced to turn into the wind and row for half a day. But today would not be as perilous: they could run before the waves – if they were vigilant.

85

Arithon held the tiller until midday, keeping the ship on course: south-southeast. By the time he gave up the helm, she was running fast before the wind on a calming sea.

He was sitting on the back-rail drinking from a waterskin when Po emerged from the hold, carrying two well-made bronze swords.

"Have you seen our cargo?" engaged Po. "We have much to trade including forty-five of these Phrygian weapons."

Po handed one of the swords to Arithon who took it with genuine interest. He withdrew the two-foot long blade from its red, pebbled-leather scabbard and was surprised at how light it really was. The hilt was a frosted, almost-red bronze, secured to the blade tang by three hardened rivets. It was capped with an egg-size pommel, filigreed with a raised grape vine pattern. The hilt fit the hand perfectly behind the short crossguard into which the blade blended with a sinuous swoop. On the center of the blade, inside the cutting edge, was an etched scene of a bull with lowered head, charging a pouncing leopard, surrounded by a floral motif of leaves and flowers.

"They are beautiful," Arithon said admiringly, turning it over and over in his hand. "Do you know how to use it?" wondered Arithon.

"I have and I can when needed."

"Show me then."

"Grab a pin, you will need a shield," advised Po, as he tossed a belaying pin to Arithon. "And put the sword back in its sheath," he added with a grin.

Po then demonstrated three of the classic maneuvers of defense and offense to the young apprentice, standing face to face on the aft deck, next to Mindares at the tiller. After an hour's time, Po stepped back a pace and said, "Now attack me."

Arithon was fully a head taller than Po who was also more than twice his age. Where Po was small and wiry, Arithon was tall and muscular, fast and powerful. It seemed unfair – almost comic. The young man hesitated.

"Come, try," continued Po. "I doubt you can do as you believe."

Arithon made a quick step forward and thrust the sword at his friend's middle. Po struck the blade with the pin, lunging to the side with a speed not expected of one so old. Arithon had left his shield hand down so that Po was able to thrust his own sword in with amazing ease, poking Arithon rather hard in the gut.

"It is you who are dead, my friend," said Po with no hint of pride or gloating. "Fighting is not about size or strength, it is about skill and using your head. You must gauge the time for offense and the time for defense. I, myself, tend to the defense, for I am small; quick maneuvers are my strength. I wait for my opportunities.

"Never underestimate anyone. And patience, always patience."

Arithon felt stupid and embarrassed by it all, but Po showed no triumph in the exercise and so it made it easy for Arithon to show graciousness in return.

"I am glad it is you who teach me these lessons. They would be hard earned if I had to learn them in battle," replied Arithon.

"Well said, Arithon. You control your pride like a nobleman," complimented Po, "and so you will find pleasure in wisdom. Let us teach each other then."

For the entire afternoon and into early evening, Arithon and Po practiced on the aft deck of the *Swallow*. Po strung ropes knee high athwart ship to create lanes through which he had Arithon maneuver. At first, he would have him moving back and forth in the same lane, but later he would have him fight across the lanes, having to jump over each rope as he moved sideways. Po had not the endurance of Arithon, so others in the crew took turns sparring with the young captain under the guidance of Po.

"Move backwards. Now forwards. Sideways," came the orders and Arithon obeyed, not thinking anymore, just driving his body to develop new stamina and new skills. Twice he caught his foot on the ropes and fell painfully, once skinning his left elbow. On the first fall, his opponent moved on him and Po declared, "Dead! Killed again."

Arithon lay on the deck and listened to the laughter of the crew. It maddened him and he stood to begin again. He looked over at Po, who tilted his head and raised one eyebrow as if to say: remember yourself; this is practice. Po smiled and Arithon's anger promptly evaporated and he composed himself to begin again.

"Throw your sword into the third lane," instructed Po, "but keep your shield."

Arithon did as instructed, but he was puzzled, until Po called, "Begin!"

His partner moved on him swiftly and Arithon made a rash decision to retrieve his sword. Xephonus crossed the lanes as quickly as Arithon and had his sword into Arithon's side as he bent for his sword.

"Dead," cried Arithon, before Po could.

"Try again," came the reply, "and this time protect yourself first."

On the next attempt, Arithon fared much better. He took the onslaught of Xephonus with frantic energy, matching each blow with his shield until his opponent showed signs of tiring. He turned aside the last blow with such force that Xephonus was temporarily off balance. Arithon then leapt the three lanes and retrieved his weapon before Xephonus could bear down on him.

"Better," praised Po, "much better."

An hour later, even Arithon was spent, so he and Po rested on the aft deck and talked and ate, while the crew kept the ship on course.

"Are we to land on Crete?" questioned Arithon. He realized as soon as he spoke that he did not know much about the trip itinerary, always trusting such things to Po. In the future, it would be his responsibility, and he felt remiss for not having been more involved in the planning for this trip.

"No, not on this leg, but we may on the return."

"Where will we put in? Close to Egypt?"

"It is called Marsa Matruh, due southeast of us, but west of Egypt. It exists to avoid the tariffs of Egypt; a rough and dangerous outpost, at the end of a caravan trail from the interior desert."

"Can we get what we need? Is it busy?"

"When the caravans are in, there are many ships. We are not the only ones vying for the ivory and somehow the traders, even those from Phoenicia, know when the goods should arrive."

"Father remarked it is not wise to trade weapons – at times anyway. Are we in danger in Africa, or do you know these people?"

"I know them well enough to know we need to be careful."

Arithon began to imagine their destination and his mind wandered to the places he had already called on. Compared to the Minoans, the outsiders always seemed rough and barbaric to him. He grew more pensive as he thought of having to leave Thera and establish a new home; probably in lands as wild and lawless as this Marsa Matruh. He would never have the time to take a wife or settle a home. He would spend his life struggling for these simple things, and this saddened him.

"Why did you never marry, Po?" asked Arithon, suddenly thinking of Po's solitary life on the ships.

"I did once," came the quiet reply.

Arithon looked now at Po sitting crossed legged on the deck, tying a bronze hook to a coil of fishing line, and wondered to himself why he had never thought to ask Po this question before.

"What happened to her?" he asked.

"I am not sure," said Po as he arose and walked to the aft rail, where he baited the hook with a small sardine, twisting it firmly into the hook with a practiced twist of the wrist.

Arithon joined him at the rail where he was now lowering the weighted line into the frothy wake. "Tell me about it, Po. I have never heard of it."

There was a brief silence, when only the creaking of the ship and the sounds of the wind and the water were to be heard before Po began.

"I had a wife when I was your age. She and I grew up together on Thera and we both always knew we would be together. Her family owned the olive farm on Sunrise Hill."

"I know that farm. Old Mokiri lives there with many of his family."

"Mokiri is Gaesera's brother," continued Po. "He was the eldest son of Pleron, who died about fifteen years ago. Gaesera and I joined when I was seventeen – she was fifteen.

"We had a son, who was not yet one, when for reasons I can no longer remember, they accompanied me on the *Aeolus* on a trip to the west. There is a great island close to the peninsula of the boot, where we intended to trade for gems and silver.

"On our third day out, we were overtaken by two pirate ships of the Sea Peoples. We did not know they were pirates, but we should have, because they overtook us at great speed. When they were near, they began signaling they wanted to talk and that we should come to. I was at the steering oar, when our captain ordered us to turn into the wind and ship our starboard oars to allow them alongside – that proved fatal. I realized our mistake as soon as we shipped, for I saw them dig in, steering for our amidships.

"I yelled to the captain, but he had seen it too, and was busy ordering our oarsmen to reset. I turned my own oar with all my strength willing the ship to turn, but we had lost most of our speed. Our rowers pulled valiantly, and the ship began to move ever so slowly as I tried to place our stern to the pirates; but it was not enough. They struck us dead center.

"The impact hurled me over the rail where I just missed hitting the oars of the pirate as he shipped them. I heard the snapping and cracking of our hull as he careened up our starboard side. It was a terrible sound – one no sailor ever wants to hear. Suddenly, I remembered Gaesera and my son were aboard, and I felt a panic and fear which I would not have believed possible."

Po stopped for a moment, as he experienced those intense emotions again, though now standing on the deck of the *Swallow*, fully twenty years later. Arithon kept silent and watched Po tighten his hands on the line hanging over the rail. He remained quiet as he took deep breaths as if bracing himself for a frightening ordeal. He began again, but his voice was thickening.

"Their warriors were hidden behind the gunnels but leapt up after the impact and loosed their arrows and spears. The captain took an arrow through the chest and many of the oarsmen were killed in the first volley. I was in the water looking for a way to board either ship, when one of the pirates threw a spear at me which missed but caused me to dive under. When I surfaced, they were grappling our ship close enough to board. The sounds of battle were all about, as I tried to swim around the backside of the pirate, thinking I could climb up her stern, while attention was focused on my ship. The second pirate ship came alongside as I pulled free of the water and trained their bows on me. I thought to dive, but they motioned for me to come aboard, which I did.

"No sooner was I on deck, when –"

And then Po's voice broke and he choked up, unable to speak. Arithon dared not look at Po, for he knew eye contact would break him, so he remained motionless with his eyes fixed on the line as it entered the wake curl below them.

At length, Po continued, "I heard Gaesera scream and when I rounded, I saw a pirate ripping our son out of her arms and throwing the child into the sea."

Arithon went rigid – afraid to even breathe.

"My brave wife broke free of the pirates and jumped into the water to rescue him. I also broke from my captors and reached the rail before I was hit from behind and lost consciousness.

"When I awoke, I was on the second pirate ship tied fast in the hold. Seven of the younger men of my ship were also on board, for they had split our crew amongst the two ships. The older men had been slain. I asked of my wife and the men told me she and the baby were brought back aboard the first pirate ship. They did not know anymore, for they were transferred to the ship I was on."

"Po ..." began Arithon in a soft voice, but Po raised his hand to silence him as if to say let me finish or I will not be able to.

"The pirate ships separated, and I never saw Gaesera or my son again, nor do I know their fate. I was sold into slavery at Porgos on the boot peninsula, where I remained for almost two years, until your father was able to locate me. He purchased me from my keepers and brought me home to Thera, where I have worked for him since. Your father is a good and honorable man, Arithon – the best of Theran blood. You are the fruit of a mighty tree and you in your turn will grow to be a man of great worth."

Po finished his story and Arithon thought to talk, but could not, as he himself was choked up by the emotion of Po's story. Instead, Po said one last thing, "I tell you these things not to upset you, but to help you understand. I am glad you have listened though, for it helps me, to have others know my story."

Arithon and Po fished by the stern rail in silence until the sun had gone down and it was time for them to eat before the light failed.

***

Three days later they approached a cliff-edged coast, but were too far west, according to Po, so they rowed eastward for a half day, until they came upon a small protected bay with a beautiful white sand beach and water so clear you could see the bottom in fifty feet of ocean. There was a small village of one story rectangular buildings visible on the west side with a field to the east on which twenty or thirty nomad tents had been pitched; numerous donkeys on stake lines were grazing lazily in and on the periphery of the camp. There was no quay, but two ships were beached, and one other was anchored offshore. Po had the *Swallow* moored as far out as possible, but still under the protection of the bay from the wind and the waves.

"We will stay at a safe distance until we understand who is here and what they are about. The crew can remain aboard, and you and I will go ashore."

With that agreed to, Arithon and Po, rowed the tender ashore, carrying it up the beach above the water line, and walked up the short slope to the village.

"It has been many years, but the brokers used to have shops right up here on the left," said Po, as he and Arithon entered the main street.

The streets were hard-packed earth lined with roughly constructed mud brick buildings, and the whole place smelled of sewage and smoke, which poured from every dwelling. Unsavory looking men of many cultures were standing in the doorways or shuffling along the streets with grim faces. The place made Arithon uncomfortable, not from fear, but for the filth and ugliness which hovered everywhere. Po soon turned into a low doorway on the left and Arithon followed, having to stoop low to clear the frame. The bright sun and heat of the street were a sharp contrast to the dim, stuffy room and it took his eyes a few seconds to adjust. There were five men sitting behind tables negotiating with three other men standing in the room. One of the brokers motioned for Po to come over to his table and he turned slightly to disengage from the conversation.

"What brings you here? I think I remember you – a Theran, yes?" he said in Egyptian.

"Yes, I am. My name is Poius," replied Po, also in Egyptian.

Arithon knew a few phrases in Egyptian, but he was surprised to find them speaking it here, so far west of the Egyptian empire. Po and the broker soon began a dialogue which quickly transcended Arithon's ability in the language. He could pick up the occasional word and he knew the basic context of the conversation, but he could not keep up. At one point he could clearly see Po did not like what he was being told. He also heard something about the Pharaoh of Egypt. They continued for another few exchanges, until the trader pointed to the east, mentioned the name 'Rafar' a couple of times, and then Po ended the session and glanced at Arithon as if to say, 'let's go.' One of the other merchants standing in the room watched them leave, as if sizing them up. Arithon caught his stare and held his eyes as they made their way out.

Po turned left out of the doorway and walked purposefully up to a path which would take them toward the tents to the east of town. Both men were quiet until they were alone and well away from the buildings. Po found a large rock on which they could both sit and grabbed a stem of grass to play with as Arithon sat down beside him.

"The ivory caravan is still many days away," began Po. "And there has not been much ivory through this year. It is going to be expensive."

"I thought it was always expensive," remarked Arithon with a chuckle.

"Yes, it always is, but it's worse," said Po. "We have a wealthy competitor here in port already; an Ashkelonian."

"The one who watched us leave?" offered Arithon.

92

"Yes, the same."

The two were quiet for a moment. Po was thinking, his eyes down, playing with the grass stem, splitting and peeling it with his fingernails. Arithon sat looking out onto the harbor at the *Swallow*. He could see the crew playing dice on the deck and he smiled, knowing all the bantering which must be going on.

"What's the plan then?" asked Arithon.

"I did not tell the broker we were pursuing ivory. I told him I was interested in buying donkeys and he told me to see Rafar," began Po, ...

"Donkeys. Why would you buy donkeys?" interrupted Arithon.

Po looked up at Arithon, "I'm not."

"Then ..." Arithon started to interrupt again, but thought better of it and checked himself.

"I want to hire a couple, not buy, but I did not want the Ashkelonian or the port brokers to know what we are up to."

"What are we up to?" asked Arithon, puzzled now more than ever.

"We can ride out to meet the caravan, make a deal for the ivory and divert it away from this port."

"We can?" questioned Arithon.

"Why not? If we cut out the broker's commissions, we can offer more. I am sure the caravan drivers have no love for the port – always squeezing them for lower prices. They may be willing to deal directly with us."

"Have you ever done anything like this before?" asked Arithon.

"No, but I have not had this kind of need before. I came for ivory and I intend to sail home loaded."

"It sounds brilliant to me," lauded Arithon, "I am just surprised how fast you came up with the idea."

The two Therans sat on a rock on the desolate coast of Africa and formulated a plan. They decided it would be safer to buy the two donkeys after all; to remove any suspicion about their true purpose. They could sell the animals later.

They waited until the day was almost gone, before Po struck out to find Rafar and purchase the pack animals, while Arithon returned to the *Swallow*. Arithon waited until almost midnight and then had the crew quietly raise anchor and slide out of the harbor.

Looking back, he could see no fires on the shore or on the other vessels. Hopefully, no one had seen them leave. They rowed eastward along the coast for close to an hour, aided by a half moon in a clear sky, until they detected an indistinct glow in a protected cove. Po watched with pride as Arithon backed the dark silhouette into the narrow opening and lay oars at the ready for a hasty exit. His hail brought a relieved response, the hustle and thumping of oars, and the splash of the anchor. Mindares and Arithon came ashore.

Arithon had packed four bags: two with provisions, and two with samples of the goods they had on board, including four of the swords.

"Mindares," instructed Po, "sail up the coast and look for a safe anchorage where we can also load. Do not go more than a day's row from here. Try not to be discovered by anyone, but if you are, you know the story. We will return in five to ten days. If we have not returned after ten days, leave for Thera."

Mindares acknowledged his orders and headed back to the *Swallow*. Po kicked sand onto the fire and led Arithon up the shallow slope through a ragged ravine of broken rock and scrub. The night breeze wafted the promise of donkeys long before Arithon caught a gleam of moonlight on those sad but curious eyes sheltered in the darkness of a bramble. When the indistinct shapes took on their daylight forms, he was surprised to see they were held by a human figure sitting on a large rock.

"This is Fassa," explained Po. "Our guide."

The guide rose to his full but diminutive height and Arithon realized he was a boy of ten – maybe more, it was hard to judge. His eyes were a dark reflection, wary beyond their age and he wore a bright toothy smile which evinced a friendly intelligence. He greeted them in Egyptian, handed reins to his employers, turned with his own and started up the ravine.

After an easy hike through rolling terrain, Fassa brought them to a depressed bowl surrounded by scrubby trees on all but one side where an ancient cliff of broken rock banked a soggy depression. Fassa staked the donkeys on the far side, babbling softly into their ears as he scratched their muzzle and relieved them of their burdens with an affectionate pat on the rump.

"Who is he?" asked Arithon after they had found a comfortable place under the branches of a stubby tree.

"He offered to serve as guide after I bought the animals. I made a deal with him: if he would guide us and keep it quiet, I would pay him double. He says he knows a place called Bir Kaida, where the trails cross, about fifteen leagues from here. According to him, the caravan will stop and water there."

"Do you trust him?" asked Arithon, looking over at the boy.

"No reason not to. He seems to be on his own, a child in the wild lands. I do not think he will be missed."

"Po," began Arithon, "I have never ridden a donkey before."

"It has been a long time for me also," chuckled Po, "Get some sleep if you can. I will watch."

Arithon slept uncomfortably until midday when Po woke him. An hour later, Arithon drooped stupidly in the hot afternoon; astonished that Po could sleep. There was always a breeze on the islands to cool the afternoon swelter, but not here. The air, weighted with heat, only stirred when he swatted the biting flies seeking the sweat of his body. How did the natives cope with this heat and these maddening pests? The boy was not around to provide an answer and Arithon wondered where he could be. He briefly considered the little nomad might have gone to collect a troop of hidden accomplices but dismissed the idea after he found the solace of his axe and stuck it in his belt. Hungry, he was just sitting down to eat a fist of barley bread and cheese, when he heard the noise of someone coming through the trees across the clearing. Fassa soon arrived, walking with a sling, which he spun in absent play until he reached the camp.

"Axe," said Fassa in Minoan.

"Do you know Minoan?" asked Arithon.

"Axe," he repeated.

"I guess not," commented Arithon, more to himself than the boy.

"Sling," said Arithon, pointing.

"Yes," he said.

"You know 'yes,' at least."

The two conversed as much as possible through the afternoon; teaching each other words in the other's language. Arithon offered him some of his fare, which he devoured like a hungry child. After they finished a water skin, Arithon watched the desert dweller dig a hole at the edge of the puddle and filter water into the skin through his cupped fingers with skill and reverence.

Late in the day a nervous Arithon roused Po while Fassa readied the donkeys.

"How does this work: the riding?" he asked, unable to hide his apprehension. Arithon preferred a deck under his feet and a wind at his back. Straddling a smelly beast for a slow, jarring bounce through a suffocating landscape was not a pleasing proposition.

95

"Watch me," said Po, who had Fassa hold his donkey while he mounted.

Arithon accomplished a similar maneuver, but he was stiff on its back and his long legs hung to the ground. Fassa furrowed his brows causing Po to burst into laughter. "He doubts your skills ashore."

A good-natured laugh erupted from all three, tapering off as Fassa prodded his donkey forward through the brush. He picked a path through the low hills, making many un-deliberated choices at the intersections they encountered. Arithon soon felt more at ease on the animal's back but could never get comfortable.

Settling into the plodding rhythm, he began to reflect and examine the countryside. Too dry and hot was the obvious and disappointing conclusion. For years he had harbored a romantic image of Africa: jungle and savannah teeming with exotic fauna; ferocious predators and animal giants; home to the venerable Egyptians and the mysterious Nubians. All he could see from this donkey's back was a pitiless desert shimmering oppressive heat.

As they snaked their way out of a deep ravine and crested the adjoining hill, he believed he could make out a wider and flatter path in the valley below. Finally convinced of its existence, he pointed and asked, "Why do we not take the trail below?"

Po questioned Fassa who answered Po with heightened emphasis.

"He says it is dangerous and his way is safer," answered Po.

After mutual shrugs of acquiescence, they clopped along behind their guide in fading light, until Fassa jerked a quick stop and waved a warning to the Therans. Alarmed but composed, the young nomad dismounted and crept bent over the remainder of the way to the top. Po and Arithon followed and on their way Arithon got a whiff of the wood smoke which Fassa had intercepted. They joined Fassa squatting behind a boulder overgrown with stunted brush and peering down into the valley below. He pointed to a clearing at the knee of the ridge they were now spying from. The flames of a well-fed fire centered a dozen figures busy with the preparations of a new encampment. Arithon did not like the look or sound of this gang – their harsh verbal exchanges were crude and ugly, and they acted accordingly.

"Men bad," whispered Fassa in broken Minoan.

He learns quick, thought Arithon, or he knows more Minoan than he admits.

Po had seen enough. He motioned for the two to follow and they started down the spine of the ridge to where their donkeys were tied. With no warning, from the ravine to their right, came the loud crack of dry wood. They dropped to the ground, scooting under the thorny brush which offered precious little coverage on those impoverished hills.

"Crack!"

Someone was gathering firewood and they were working their way up the gulch. If the person belonging to the sounds continued, they would soon discover the donkeys. Two men and a boy would be no match for the gang below.

Arithon lay in the dirt trying to locate the heavy-footed brute in the thickets. He could hear him trail-breaking through the brambles, snapping off dry branches and then continuing up the slope, where he would soon be in sight of the animals. Arithon crawled deeper into the brush, afraid and unthinking, hoping the man would go back. He realized with a deeper pang his indecision would not save them. He could not wish the man away. He reached down to his axe, which he fumbled out of his belt and saw, to his surprise, Fassa untying the donkeys a hundred steps below.

The native boy disappeared down the trail as the man broke clear of the ravine. Inattentive, ambling, a sling of firewood on his back, he soon found the ridge trail and checked up, then down, its visible length. He stepped down it for a short distance and paused at the spot where the donkeys had been only moments before. His posture changed from wearisome drudgery to alert cautiousness as he straightened his stance and checked the trail again.

Arithon held his breath. The gatherer put his sling down, dropped to one knee, and examined the ground. He shouted in an alien language and was answered by a voice so close it startled them. A cold wave rolled Arithon's gut. He would have to kill these two strangers before they could alarm the camp below.

The second man exited the ravine behind where they lay and was marching down to his companion. Arithon gripped the axe, twisting it back and forth. The man would stumble upon them. Arithon started to bring his knees up under him when Po grabbed his forearm to still him.

Then the first man called again; impatiently this time and the second answered just as impatiently as he passed not more than twenty steps to their right.

97

Arithon breathed again, now aware that he had not been. The bandits were hunched together and discussing the tracks in the dirt. Arithon could guess from the gesturing and agitated pitch of their voices that they were trying to decide how fresh the tracks were. He darted his eyes around the scene and hoped the coming darkness would entice them to return to their camp. Sweat beaded his pounding temples when he saw the second man lean in to examine the evidence. He may have found the human tracks, as he turned his gaze up the hill to stare at the location where they lay hiding.

Arithon's heart hammered so hard he could feel it thumping the dusty ground beneath and wondered in further panic if they could hear it. The strangers would follow the tracks. He quit breathing again.

And then the one with the wood sling picked up his bundle as though he had lost his nerve – searching for intruders in the wild dark would pause any man. He spat an unmistakable oath at his companion and then started back toward his camp. The second lingered for a while, looking up the hill toward Po and Arithon, and then down the trail where the donkeys had gone. He stood and hesitated, but his companion was disappearing into the ravine, so he abandoned his position and followed.

Po and Arithon lay dead still until they heard them pass far below in the ravine, talking to each other in retreating voices. Po tapped Arithon on the shoulder and they picked their way down, stepping on stones as they walked to leave no trace of their passing. They hurried with anxious steps in the gathering night until Fassa stepped out onto the trail.

"Men bad," said Fassa in Minoan, before switching to Egyptian, "they kill the ivory caravan."

Arithon understood. These men intended to waylay the caravan along the trail below. Fassa had saved their lives twice over, as he and Po would have taken the main trail and would now be lying dead in the valley below.

"We will have to go as far as we can tonight. They may try and follow us in the morning. Fassa says he can lead us around this area where they are encamped and back to his original trail, but it will take half the night in this darkness."

"He is a resourceful lad," said Arithon.

Po nodded and told Fassa, who smiled and looked down.

For the next three hours, they picked their way carefully over rough ground, up and down the ravines and hills. The brush was stiff and biting, and at times so interwoven that they could not make passage and had to perform a rather tricky and aggravating maneuver to turn the donkeys

98

about and backtrack. Luckily there was enough moonlight for them to negotiate, although at times, especially in the bottom of the ravines, it was so dark they were forced to walk blindly uphill until they could see a clearer way to negotiate. Often Fassa would dash ahead to the top to orient himself. Both Arithon and Po were amazed at the composure of the young boy and wondered aloud how he could possibly find his way in this wilderness.

First light came and went and still they marched until Fassa found the upper trail and led them out of the brush. After midday, Fassa stopped to let the animals graze and rest in the sparse shade of a copse.

"The wood gatherers," began Arithon, "would we have killed them last night?"

"We did not have to," said Po after a long delay.

"That is not a satisfying answer."

"No, it is not," said Po, "but it is the truth. We chose to hide, and we also chose not to kill by that action. It could have turned out differently and we would be telling ourselves we did the right thing to kill them. Or we could be dead."

"Neither of those sounds agreeable, although dead takes last place," said Arithon. "It troubles me to think of killing them. Are those the thoughts of a coward?"

"No. Killing is not brave," said Po, "even in fear. Do what you have to survive, but do not be cruel."

"I could never be cruel," said Arithon.

"It is easier than you think," Po said, and he rose and walked over to the animals.

For the rest of the afternoon they picked their way over the dusty hills of stunted trees and thick brambles. Fassa was leading them steadily down and every time they crested one of the ridges, they could mark their progress toward the main trail, which wound through the broad valley below. Toward early evening they could see the mouth of the gorge, where the trail they were following met up with the main trail, a tan squiggle in the burnt brown landscape.

Fassa said something to Po and pointed out a few black dots in the far distance, changing position on the thin line: the ivory caravan.

They descended out of the hills to the center of a seasonal watercourse, which this late in the year was a dry wash. A well had been dug down to the water table, which supplied a meager amount of water to the caravans.

Po and Arithon worked through to sunset to raise enough water for themselves and the animals, while Fassa staked and fed the donkeys. Later, as the two men talked, Fassa roasted partridges he fell with his sling and served them up as a shared supper.

Before dark, a lone man appeared on the south trail; a forward scout sent ahead of the caravan to investigate the campfire. Fassa went out to meet him when he was still well out of range. Po and Arithon watched him gesturing and pointing back in their direction, explaining what they were about. Arithon watched them turn together, and the two soon walked into their camp, where the scout greeted them in Egyptian. As soon as Po made it known to him that they were there to parley, he left back southwards to report to the main caravan.

Night was well underway as Po, Arithon, and Fassa tended an after-dinner fire and watched the caravan arrive; over a hundred men roped together, each carrying ivory or provisions, and tended by twenty five more which walked on either side of the line. Two of the men were mounted on donkeys and appeared to be the leaders of the expedition. There were also two unusual animals which Arithon knew must be camels, though he had never seen one. These too carried an enormous load of ivory, fastened in an ingenious manner about the great hump which the beast also carried on its back. The new arrivals began a well-rehearsed drill to set up camp: unloading the ivory into a neat stack; starting cooking fires; drawing water; erecting a hide tent. Arithon wanted to go over to look at the camels, but Po advised against it, until a relationship and protocol had been established.

Fassa was gathering more firewood in the brush on the edges of the wadi, when two men slipped into the light, made their greetings, and took seats on the ground to the left of Po; close enough to talk face-to-face without having to look over the fire. Po began an hour-long discussion telling the men, what he was there to do, and why he had ventured inland to meet them rather than wait on the coast. They displayed a keen interest in cutting out the middlemen at Marsa Matruh, especially since they intended to meet an Egyptian customer at this very crossroads to bargain away a portion of the ivory. The two were obviously excited by the Phrygian sword which Po showed them, holding it in their hands, turning it over and over in the firelight and talking between themselves in an unintelligible language of Africa.

Po told them of the men lying in ambush up the trail, and they were grateful for the news. With so many slaves to be guarded, the twenty-five guards would be hard pressed to defend the entire caravan against determined raiders. Their leader, Atura, displayed through a grimace, that he had experienced this before and was not anxious to do so again. Many other details were worked out, before the men relaxed and began to trade news and stories. Po produced a skin of mandilaria wine he had carried from the ship and they spent the next hour talking casually and drinking. Arithon could not understand all that was said, but he got the general drift and asked Po at times to explain. Fassa was asleep long before the adults had broken off and retired for the evening.

Around midmorning of the next day, the Egyptian caravan arrived. The ivory traders had set up a tent out of the sun, comfortably furnished with rugs and refreshments, to which Po, Arithon and the Egyptian customer were invited. At first, they exchanged news, while casually dining on exotic melons and drinks served by the slaves of the ivory men. Po offered up two innocuous stories: the launch of the *Swallow* and the loss of the *Hoopoe* – a cruiser presumed lost in a storm off Karpathos. The traders talked about their troubles in the south, acquiring slaves and ivory, but really saying very little. The Egyptian was more animated.

"We have many problems at home and in the east," began Natrun. "The Mittani have our armies tied up in Canaan and we are hard pressed to repel them. Our generals are clever and well-equipped, but it is a drain on our economy."

"But you Egyptians have always won your wars," Atura said.

"Yes, we have, but there is trouble at home also," said Natrun, lowering his voice as if he did not want to be overheard.

Atura raised an eyebrow at the news, as if he already had rumor of these tidings.

"What would that be?" he asked with feigned ignorance.

"Plagues," whispered Natrun.

Both Po and Atura shifted uncomfortably on the rugs as if they wanted to move away from the Egyptian.

Sensing this the Egyptian quickly added, "But not diseases – not yet anyway."

"Anyway?" questioned Atura.

Natrun leaned forward, "There are others prophesized."

There was a pause in the conversation at these words. Po leaned over to Arithon and quietly told him in Minoan what had been said.

"By whom?" Atura finally ventured, his mouth full of a sweet melon that Arithon had never seen.

"The Israelites," Natrun replied, obviously enjoying the interest in the conversation.

"Who might they be?" asked Po, seeing that Atura was unwilling to carry the conversation alone.

"Our slaves from Canaan. They are *extremely* troublesome," he finally began, satisfied that there was sufficient interest in the subject. "They want to be set free to return to Canaan and they are making our lives miserable. Their leaders claim that the plagues are the doings of their gods and they will not cease until the Israelites are set free."

"Kill them," said Atura, spitting a seed to the far side of the tent.

"Not a bad idea, but there are many of them, and they work well – for slaves," replied Natrun.

"Israelites – a strange name – I have never heard of them," said Atura.

"They are a small peoples, from the Levant, that we enslaved years ago," Natrun explained. "They say that they are children of their founder – some crazy man named Israel. They are all crazy, I think – so strange. They will not worship our gods and they keep themselves apart. I don't know why the Pharaoh puts up with them, but he has troubles elsewhere as I have said."

"How do you know so much about them," asked Po, endeavoring to be polite.

"Oh, I have seven in my charge, and they rail on day after day about the plagues and freedom and their powerful gods. – Actually, it is only one god now I come to think about it. That is something else they go on and on about – their *one* god. As if having one is somehow better than having many. As I said, they are all crazy. Would you like to buy one or see one? I have four here with me today. Some of the women are passable."

"No," laughed Atura, "not after that description. You can keep your Israelites and their plagues to yourself. What are the plagues?"

"Oh, they are awful," said Natrun, punctuating his distaste with a scowl. "Last year, the Nile ran red at flood time and when it receded there was a great nastiness in the fields. The cattle which ate there died and so the planting was delayed. We are still trying to recover from that one. And this year, the insects are multitudinous and bothersome. It is hard to be outside near the fields. I am glad to be on this trade mission and away from there for a while. The slaves claim credit for all of these maladies, but I think they are just a coincidence."

"Well, leave none of them with us – the slaves or the maladies," said Atura. "Let us conduct business."

It was over quickly. Po showed his swords and the Egyptian displayed examples of oils, linen, and perfumes that he said came from the east. Atura, for his part, had examples of the ivory he was offering. Po negotiated for how much he wanted, and the Egyptian did the same. Atura was willing to trade for all the swords, reluctantly acknowledging he could sell them in the South to the Nubians or the southern Egyptians. Po also leveraged the donkeys and the glass and amber jewelry on board the *Swallow* and ended up buying over half of the ivory, the remainder purchased by Natrun. Atura was more than pleased to have two competitors for his merchandise.

"We will sort the goods between you and Natrun. Tomorrow we can start for the coast. But not by the wadi."

"Agreed," Po nodded.

The ivory was laid out on the ground in groups of four that were sorted to include a large and a small tusk with two of middle size. After the lots had been identified as either Egyptian or Minoan, Natrun call for his slaves to move the ivory to their camp. Atura's slaves would carry the Minoan ivory to the ship.

They were all standing over the ivory, when Natrun's slaves came to gather it.

"There is one of the Israelites," said Natrun, pointing at a middle-aged man preparing to pick up two pieces of ivory. "Hey, Reuben, come here."

"No that is quite alright, I do not need to meet him," said Atura as he made his way away from Natrun and over to his own people as if he needed to attend to something.

"Superstitious, isn't he?" grinned Natrun.

Reuben walked over to where Natrun stood and nodded slightly, as if he needed to show deference to Natrun, but no more than necessary.

"See," gestured Natrun, "they are arrogant as always."

Arithon was getting uncomfortable with this exchange and hoped that it would end soon. He wanted to get back to the ship and away from this Egyptian and his slaves.

"My new acquaintances want to know if you are you going to conjure up any plagues any time soon," he said to Reuben but with a wink at Po.

"No, our god only wants the Egyptians to set us free. He has no reason to smite these people," Reuben replied with dignity.

"Are they not as funny as I said?" said Natrun, slapping his thighs. "Are you sure you don't want to buy one of these slaves? They will keep you highly entertained."

"No, thank you," said Po, also anxious to end the spectacle.

"Very well then," Natrun sighed. "Reuben, get back to work then. You can go back and tell your leaders that even the Minoans do not want any of you Israelites.

Natrun turned to Po, "We are departing. Look me up next time you are in Egypt and perhaps we can do business. Those swords would sell well. May the gods see you safely home."

With that, he turned and was gone.

Chapter 8 New Minoans

Artemis stopped quietly at the well she had founded for her
lions, but vanished unseen into the wilds, leaving her bow for the
one who might need it more.

The next morning found Po and Arithon, perched on the sitting rocks of
last night's campfire, watching the ivory traders break camp. The rock was
so hot that Arithon squatted on his, convinced he was being baked like a
loaf in an oven called Africa. Fassa, a child of the desert, retired to a shady
copse of brambles growing under the protection of a low wall. He was
watching his new friends, puzzled that they sat in the hot sun. He liked
them despite their strange ways.

The whole company was active with practiced motions: rolling, folding,
packing, and tying their possessions into bundles of a size and shape,
which fit into one exact spot, be it on a camel's back or a porter's shoulders.
It reminded Arithon of all the activity on a dock when loading a ship; only
this cargo was stowed and un-stowed for usage every night.

Atura's tent came down last so he could sit out of the sun. It fluttered to
the ground like a dropped flag; the signal that prodded each member of the
troop to their assigned position in line. Without a word, the first in line
began the trek, followed by the next and the next, until the column was
moving at the same pace. The caravan made good time on the narrow trail
even though the slaves were roped about the waist in one continuous line
that required a synchronistic locomotion born of cooperation.

They passed an uncomfortable day and an uneventful night and the
caravan was away before sunrise, repeating the drill they had performed
countless times, only this morning there was an anxious edge in the slave
ranks: a foreboding tension bound them as sure as the gang rope. They
were attuned to the signs: the flight of birds, the restlessness of the camels,
a whiff of strangers – close and getting closer; they were expecting an
unwanted misadventure and just before midday it arrived.

The convoy was working its way around the knee of a ridge, when
Arithon heard men crying in alarm from an unseen spot around a bend in

the path. Like an oblique wave hitting the shore, the roped slaves, one by one, starting from somewhere around the turn; dropped their ivory and dived off the path into the brush seeking whatever shelter they could find at the limit of their rope. Atura had already dismounted and was tearing down the trail, pulling his sword in mid-stride. Po and Arithon followed, leaving their donkeys with Fassa, and instructions to get clear. With his heart beating wildly, Arithon raced down the path, high-stepping over the roots, rocks, and tusks that littered the way. He reached down and pulled his axe from waist belt bringing it up into his right hand.

As he made the turn, he realized the bandits had attacked the rear of the caravan; but that was all he could discern. The confusion of men scrambling and fighting in knots of two and three, with no clear distinction of who was who, bewildered him. His overheated mind allotted him a moment to wonder if all battles were like this – confused and unorganized to the point of bedlam. He witnessed Atura's silent charge into the melee, his sword held high over his head, and then his violent chopping at the shoulders of two bandits before they knew he was upon them. Arithon lost track of him as the fight closed around.

A hundred steps ahead of Arithon, four bandits emerged from the undergrowth to collect the ivory discarded by the slaves. They were the 'quick thieves', set to pilfer the spoils while their fighters created a distraction. Po moved on these men but glanced to his right and dove to the ground. Two arrows emerged from the brush, the first off the mark and high, but the second, adjusting to the moving target, struck the ground next to Po and skipped up just missing his back.

Arithon veered into the tangled scrub in pursuit of the covering archers who would dare take aim at Po. Arithon could hear his own pulse – sound and movement slowed down as if it were all happening underwater.

The archers heard him and took aim where they believed he would emerge, and their guess was good. But Arithon saw them at the same instant and threw himself into a thicket. The loosed arrows penetrated the scrub but were deflected by the tangle, lodging short of their mark. Arithon grabbed a melon size rock and emerged as the two men were fitting another arrow. He launched the rock at the first man, hitting him in the chest with a sickening thud and knocking him backwards. Mad with violence he charged the second who panicked, dropped the arrow, and jabbed his bow at Arithon's middle trying to avoid the raised axe. But Arithon altered his stroke to intercept the bow, which broke on contact.

Now unarmed, the archer shrieked, pivoted, and ran out of control down the slope from his towering foe. Arithon started to pursue, then thought of the other, the danger behind. Rounding, he saw him on his knees, wincing in pain, but trying to fit a new arrow. Arithon advanced and raised his axe to kill, but the man dropped his bow, pulled a short knife, and struggled to his feet.

Arithon hesitated.

Both men looked at each other, panting in their fear. Arithon could see the bandit was no older than himself, scared and hurting. The rock must have broken a rib and he was laboring to stand. They stared. Arithon could feel his heart exploding against his chest, and still they stared, poised with their weapons. A shrill cry caused them both to look up the hillside. When they looked at each other again, they both knew somehow for them it was over. Arithon dipped his head to the right and the man understood. The bandit broke off to his left and picked his way down the hill, knife in one hand and clutching his ribs with the other. Arithon grabbed the discarded bow and started up the hill.

He stepped onto the trail to find the last of the bandits retreating down the slope, three carrying tusks, with Atura's men in pursuit. Arithon joined the main group at the end of the line, where he found Po unharmed and glad to see that he was also. Atura soon returned and ordered his men to reorganize the slaves and get an assessment of the losses. The maddening chaos was over and only moments had elapsed since its onset. Perhaps all battles were this unreal.

But it was real: the bandits had killed a slave and two of Atura's men and taken three pieces of ivory in those fleeting moments. Four of the bandits lay dead, and an unknown number were wounded.

"They have what they wanted, though they have paid for it," Atura began. "I do not expect them again, but we will go as soon as my men return."

Atura turned away, barking orders in a foul mood which sent Po and Arithon back up the trail to find Fassa.

"That is a marvelous bow. How did you come by it?" Po asked.

Arithon looked down at the weapon in his hand. "I forgot I had it," he said. "I stripped it from one of the bandits."

"It is beautifully made," Po said as they reached Fassa holding the donkeys.

"Nubian," said Fassa touching the bow.

"Nubian?" echoed Arithon, looking with renewed interest.

The bow was taller than those used by the Minoans – up to his shoulders, stout, and requiring a pull-strength beyond the capability of some. Arithon could draw it, but his hand wavered so that his shot would not be accurate; it would take practice to perfect its use. The ends curved away from the string and were tipped with bronze in the shape of a lion's head. The rest of the weapon was incised with a snake motif that wound its way from both ends to the center, where the snake heads emerged from the wood, mouths open, on either side of the nock.

"Stolen," said Fassa.

"He is right. It is a great bow of a Nubian warrior," said Po. "I have never seen the like of it.

"But come, let us go. It is not safe here and Atura is beginning to move."

For the rest of the day, they made an uneasy and watchful journey, stopping only twice before nightfall. Fassa reckoned that they were approximately four hours from the coast, but the men needed to rest and take a meal, so Atura and Po decided to halt for the remainder of the night.

As before, they were moving before dawn. An hour from the coast, Po rode ahead with Fassa to find Mindares and the *Swallow*. He met the main body again when they arrived at the end of the trail and guided them to the location of the *Swallow*, safely anchored in a small bay east of Marsa Matruh.

Arithon was elated to see the *Swallow* and her crew, and pleasantly surprised to see that the crew had not been idle, and indeed had built a small quay of rock and wood that would allow them to load swiftly. Always careful, Po and Atura arranged for the slaves to carry on the ivory and carry off goods of equal worth so that the exchange would be made fairly and with less anxiety. Many a deal, such as this, made in a lonely cove on a foreign coast, had resulted in murder and robbery.

Tensions were always high in these situations, but Atura's men were especially testy because of their own losses the day before. They treated the slaves with a harsh hand as the loading began, prodding and cursing their every move, untying them to carry a horn up the gangplank and retying them when they returned to the beach. Close to the water a gray-headed slave slipped on the algae and fell with his burden, breaking the tip of the horn on a sea-crusted rock. The guard swore and kicked the fallen man in the ribs and then aimed another blow at his head. But an adjacent slave, who had come to the aid of his fallen companion, blocked his kick. The overseer and the young slave fell in a flailing scuffle, but the overseer, better fed and unencumbered by ropes, reached his feet first and drew his sword. With seething hatred, he aimed a strike at the slave, intending to split his head, but his blade met the haft of Arithon's outstretched axe. The guard wheeled to face Arithon, anger still mastering him. He raised the sword to Arithon, but Po and Atura stepped between the two would be combatants. The crew of the *Swallow* thundered over to the gunnel, and Atura's men pulled their weapons.

"What are you doing?" Po asked. "It is their slave. You should not interfere!"

An awkward pause followed.

"Ask him if we can buy the slave?" said Arithon.

"Why?"

"Just ask them, Po. ... Please."

Po shrugged and did as requested.

"They want to know why you want the Nubian."

Arithon thought and then replied, "Tell them our priests need a human sacrifice to quiet our volcano."

Surprise enveloped Po's face and he hesitated. "Tell them," Arithon hastened.

Po translated Arithon's statement. The Nubian slave seemed to understand Egyptian, as his eyes widened before his face went blank.

The traders laughed and asked if he would suffer.

"Tell them it will be very painful."

The slave was hogtied, taken aboard by laughing men and dropped onto the deck – a piece of merchandise which cost Arithon his bronze dagger: a gift from his grandfather.

The exchange of goods continued, while the slave lay bound on the deck like an animal awaiting slaughter. Arithon stayed close to Po until Atura and the traders vanished into the narrow draw, which led out of the cove. He was glad to see them go, believing himself very apart from them in a way that made him feel guilty – but not so guilty as to disengage from the thought. His romantic notions of Africa had vanished, and he was ready to do the same.

They ascended the gangplank together, and looking back saw Fassa, watching from the foot of the makeshift quay as the men bustled about the ship.

"Did you not pay him?" asked Arithon, half smiling.

"You know I did – half again as much as agreed."

"Then why does he tarry?"

"We do not need any more homeless – we shall be homeless ourselves soon," said Po before he chuckled. "Fassa," he yelled, "do you want to come with us?"

The young boy broke into a wide toothy smile then ran back up the beach to fetch his travel bag – so tattered it had obviously been discarded by its original owner.

"Yes," he said when his feet hit the deck. "I am alone here. I want to be Minoan too!"

The ship slipped out into open water and began its journey north. Arithon looked back to make sure no one was watching from the shore then found the slave crumpled on the aft deck. He cut his ties as Po joined them, handing to each a waterskin and an earthen cup of lentils mixed with chickpeas.

"He understood you back on the beach," Arithon said. "Ask him his name."

The Nubian was silent though he looked at them with an expression which acknowledged he understood the question. Arithon watched the man as he ate his legumes; sometimes looking straight at his captors, sometimes away. He appeared to be about Arithon's age; lighter of build, but long limbed and slightly taller than Arithon, who was tall by anyone's measure. This was the first time he had faced a black man and he thought him beautifully featured. Arithon wondered how fast and far he could run and whether he could best him in such. His skin was shiny black as if it had been newly oiled and his teeth were white as clouds; an elegant contrast to the darkness of his face. He sat erect, dignified.

Arithon became uncomfortable when his mind returned from his musings and still the silence lingered. He looked over at Po and the man read their discomfort.

"I am called Szaba," he spoke.

Arithon brightened and responded with Po translating, "I did not purchase you for sacrifice. I said that to save you. It was the best I could think of in the moment."

Szaba's eyes brightened and then he was stoic again, "Then what is my fate?"

"Your fate is what you choose."

"Choose."

Arithon noticed him fingering the bronze fetter on his left ankle used to chain them together at night.

"Yes. Choose," Arithon said. "You are free. My father and I do not take slaves."

Szaba was quiet again as if he did not comprehend what Po had translated. He harbored much doubt about these men of the sea and their odd sounding language. He had never been on a ship and the ocean was a thing of immense wonder. Perhaps they were taking him to a dark end of the earth from which there was no return. But it did not seem so. The one called Arithon appeared genuine and without guile as he talked quietly with the older man, Po.

"What am I free to do? Am I not captive on this ship?"

"I will put you ashore, up the coast," he pointed, "or on Crete or any of the lands we visit. Or you can stay with us: a free man."

Again, Szaba was silent before he continued. "I would choose to go with you, but I am afraid in this. But I owe you my life – that is clear, for Ista meant to kill me where I lay."

"You owe me no debt. But wait here a moment," Arithon said as he dashed back to the hold. He returned with a collection of tools, including a hammer, anvil, and a chisel.

"Let us have that manacle off. It will hamper you if you have to swim."

Szaba frowned at the translation but watched the seafarer chisel off the binding. It broke free with a ping, and Szaba wrapped his long fingers about his ankle and massaged the skin. Arithon offered his hand and pulled Szaba to his feet and the two went to the aft rail to watch Africa disappear in the distance.

"We can teach you to swim when we get back to Thera," Arithon stumbled out in his best Egyptian. Szaba smiled when he understood and felt a relief – and a hope – he had not experienced in a long time.

Later, with the ship in order, Po and Arithon stood watching the waves as the sunlight failed and evening took hold.

"I did not kill. I let him go," Arithon said looking out at the rollers and thinking of the battle. "One on one is terrifying. I could not kill him like that."

Po listened as Arithon told his story.

"Do not be ashamed of mercy," said Po, after Arithon had finished. "Just take care of yourself. Not all men are as generous as you.

Chapter 9 Last Warning

Hermes, messenger of the gods, bequeathed unto mortals the
gift of running – but on land, if not in air– as he sped urgently to
tell Poseidon of the rage of Hephaestus.

"The *Dolphin* will be completed a few days after we float her," began
Alteron, a few weeks after Arithon's return. He was walking down a row of
pithoi deep in the basement of the food storage facility making mental
calculations in preparation for the evacuation. Arithon standing with his
own lamp resting on the nearest jar could see the flame of his father's
receding into the cavernous recess. He called louder so that Arithon could
hear, "Po took his team with him to Lesvos yesterday. You need to start
gathering your crew."

"I have," answered Arithon. He was holding a clay tablet nestled in a
wooden frame, scratching the symbol for the merchandise next to the
estimated weight his father called out as he roamed the magazine,
estimating the payload against the capabilities of the fleet, which he kept
stored in the hold of his mind. Since most of the established crews were
already away, Arithon recruited a crew of younger sailors; less
experienced, but trustful and intrepid. He soon had the forty men he
needed, including Sestos, Losius and Szaba whom he wanted in his First
Tier along with Hyssos.

"I count five hundred and forty-eight of the large pithoi – wine. Say
three talents apiece. That will require the *Raven*, the *Sunbeam* and the
Marlin."

Arithon scratched the symbol for wine, did the math in his head, and
marked <>//////....)))) the symbols for one thousand six hundred and forty-
four, next to it. He then made the symbol for the three ships to be assigned.
He marveled, not for the first time, at his father's knowledge and wondered
how the Therans could ever accomplish this evacuation without him.

"The Nile-born is doing well, yes?" asked Alteron, rejoining an earlier
thought.

"Szaba is quickly learning our language living with Po, but I am not sure he will ever love the sea as we do."

"I sense a hidden prowess there," his father said, trailing his lamp through the dimness back up to Arithon. "In time we will know."

Arithon shrugged in acknowledgement but paused to ponder his father's insight.

It was late afternoon under a thunderous sky when the two emerged with their tallies and started their trek toward the Council House, which had been set up as the staging area for the island exodus. On Paros Street, they stopped at the workshop of Pherthos to see what artwork he and his guild had created from the African ivory. Balanced on the center table in a sea of chips, was a magnificent tusk revealing a half-emerged dolphin of frothy white leaping in the exact curve of the horn. Muscular men stripped to the waist and coated in flour-fine dust gathered around the piece to soak up the praise of the respected visitors, smiling broadly at each compliment. Pherthos' mark was widely recognized and would command a high price from those who could afford it – and there were many city-state kings on the mainland who could.

"Beautiful work. Should help us," Arithon said as they re-entered the street.

"Yes. None too soon. We need ships – loaded ships – before the sailing season ends."

They pulled up under the sun awning canted out from the portico of the Council House, where tables were aswarm with ordered franticness. Half of Akrotiri must have been there, divided into groups organized to package the breakables, transfer the stores to the piers, provide meals for the workers, assign ships and destinations, set timetables for departures, and provision the ships for people and stock. Overseeing it all was an administrative organization led by Alteron.

Arithon hesitated on the edge of the crowd, holding his tablets as if he were afraid of entering the fray, daunted by the swirling eddies of humanity. Crowds worried him – in his dreams often.

"Hand me the tablets and go check the progress in the shipyards," his father suggested. "We launch the *Dolphin* tomorrow!"

***

Workmen were completing the launch way; greasing the timbers with buckets of tallow as Arithon meandered up to the port side cradle, which would make the slide with the hull. Over his head cheerful girls were draping a festoon of ribbon along the full length of the gunnel. He smiled up at a blue sky festooned with thunderheads. Tomorrow would be a maritime event of great joy – the birth of a ship, and the whole island was ready for the christening of their creation. For Arithon it was a perfect wind – the edges of the world were reachable.

"Beautiful, is she not?" asked a voice beside him.

"Oh! It is you, Kokini," bobbled Arithon, startled from his daydream. "Yes, she is."

"Come let me show you how I rigged her," he said. "This chock here and the other there are all that hold her. Knock these loose and she will start her first journey." They had moved around to the stern and he was pointing to two enormous wedges blocking the aft most timber of each cradle.

"Will she not lean over?" asked Arithon.

"Possibly, but we will have two teams at the bow – with the tackle to start her off nice and slow. If she tips, they can bit her down."

"I wish we could launch her now," Arithon said.

"No! No, that would not be proper! She must be blessed first."

"Come now, Kokini. She will always be blessed," Arithon said.

"Do not say that. The demons will hear you. It has to be done properly."

"As you wish, Kokini. Tomorrow – with a christening."

***

The next morning, Arithon was on the second ridge of his morning run, desiring to watch one more sunrise on his beloved Thera. It was to be a merry day; the 'Day of the *Dolphin*'; a day he had waited for with consuming anticipation and now it was here. He reached the top and bounded up onto EastPoint Rock to await the event, which always brought him a sense of continuity; a splendid power without malice. But something was different today, though he could not at first discern what it was. Thinking maybe it was his own state of mind, he stood uneasy, facing the east, slowly becoming aware of a weighty silence. The birds were always their noisiest in the softness of predawn, yet all was quiet. He felt a deep foreboding which overpowered his desire to await the sun. Something was wrong and it had nothing to do with him. He turned to look at the mountain, then back to the east and had just decided to leave when it struck.

114

He had not the time to turn, before the pressure wave knocked him forward off the rock, where he landed face first in a tangled maquis. The shock of the earth came next and it was so violent the entire hill heaved toward the sea, flipping him out of the shrubby growth and onto the ground. He rose on his elbows just as the sun rose over the horizon of the sea, and he looked down the hillside toward Akrotiri to witness an unbelievable site.

The water in the harbor disappeared – only rocks and stranded ships. A huge wave appeared; much larger than the first he had witnessed; at least thirty feet high, maybe more and he could see that it pushed out as a ring – like a ripple from a dropped rock. He had no time to think about it, for when he turned the blast was hurdling toward him like a diving bird. But fear brought him to his feet and urged him toward the harbor, moving at a downhill speed he had never attempted. But it would never be fast enough.

He pivoted to his left and ran under the ridge he had been standing on seconds before. There was a cliff about twelve feet high, overhung enough to form a slight indentation at the base. It was not much of a shelter, barely large enough to accommodate his frame as he dived to the ground and rolled face forward to the rock. He could hear it growing louder for a few seconds and then it was upon him: a boiling cloud of rock and broken wood hurdling the ridge and careering down the mountainside. The noise swallowed his head and the earth began to swallow his body, pressing him into the crumbled stone in live burial. He cupped his face to stave off the smothering, but breathing only gagging dust, he sucked a few frantic chokes and then lost consciousness.

He became aware of himself; his eyes pinched shut; his face jammed into the ground. He was breathing in short bursts, and as he came to full consciousness, he knew where he was and what had happened, but he had no grasp of time. As his senses awoke, he began to hear a continuous rumbling. The full realization of what was transpiring prompted him to push up to a sitting position wipe his face with powdered hands and looked out onto a smoke and dust filled world. The sun was an orange ball, which he could stare at, and from its position he knew he had been unconscious no more than an hour. The landscape was much different than when he had jogged up the ridge in the moments before dawn. The brush and trees, which greened the hillsides were gone; blasted away.

He struggled light-headed to his feet; dirt, stones, and splinters falling from his body. As he moved back toward the obliterated trail, he rounded

115

the cliff and looked up on a sight that buckled his already shaky legs. A red-orange flame glowed at the top of the mountain, belching fire and smoke, which rose to the roof of the heavens where it flattened to the south-southeast. But fire also poured down the sides of the great peak, the molten guts of the earth, flowing like a smoky black river on its way to the sea.

Arithon stood mesmerized by the sight, fear tingling the back of his neck, stirring a childhood fear he had yet to master. He wondered what it all meant and what the mountain would do next and then he was afraid – afraid for his family down in Akrotiri. He turned his back on the Creator and would-be Destroyer of his island and stepped his way down.

It was slow going. He wrapped his breechclout around his face and picked his way down through ankle-deep ash. His eyes burned from the soot in the air and his breathing was so labored he had to pause often to catch his breath. He wanted a drink to soothe his throat and wash his mouth and stop this awful gagging which convulsed him in fits of heaving wretchedness. What would have been a quick traverse any other morning, took him over an hour of anguish and torment. On the last ridge above Akrotiri, he saw to his relief that, though damaged, the town had missed the brunt of the pressure wave as it ricocheted off the surrounding ridge. But lava was moving toward the high boundaries of the city, as the flows which had already made it to the sea, grew with each new torrent pouring from the crater. If the eruption continued, the lava would soon enter the city.

As he trotted into the upper neighborhoods, he found that homes on every street had suffered damage; collapsed walls and roofs spilled into the roadway, forcing him to slow down and step over the unstable rubble. After his third fall, he attempted to swear, unaware of its impossibility in his choked throat. Frustrated and discouraged by the descent, he was lifted when he found his own home still standing. The door was shut, but no one greeted him inside, and the house felt empty. After listening to the upstairs, he shuffled to the kitchen to rinse his face and drink the sweetest water he had ever tasted. He put on a kilt, not taking time to wash his dust-caked body, before returning to the street calling for his family.

"I am taking too long," he croaked to himself, and then released the torrent of curses, which had been corked, but could now escape.

He hurried in the general direction of the harbor, though he had to alter his route three times to avoid the blockages on the lower levels. He found the citizens of Akrotiri assembled on the beach, and after a few inquiries, located his mother, Roa standing close to the pier. His little mother embraced him with tears lining her dust-covered face. As she gently admonished him for his absence, he thought for the first time in his life, how wonderful she was.

"You are a beautiful woman, Mother mine," he said into her ear.

"You have never told me that," she replied, releasing her hug, but continuing to hold his arms.

"I should have before today, and I will do so more in the future," he said.

"Oh, Arithon," she said. "Go help your father over on Cibo Knoll."

He kissed her dusty forehead and began to wind his way through the milling crowd when a young man, filthy and frightened, emerged from the throng.

"The lava has trapped those still alive in Kamari," he said, naming the hamlet on the east shore. "The only exit is by sea, but our few fishing boats are not enough – I was only able to bring four others in mine. We need help," he pleaded to those around him.

Arithon looked down on the port and remembered, on sight, that the fleet was gorged with payload: low and slow – all of them. He shook his head. A scan of the assembly told him that the leaders were all occupied with other rescues.

"Come with me," instructed Arithon. "What is your name?"

"Eskopi," he replied.

"Run ahead down to the dockyards, Eskopi. Wait for me by the fast hull."

Arithon hurried through the crowd, tapping those he knew, telling them to meet him in the yards as soon as they found two others in the crowd that could row. He kept his word to Eskopi and was soon under the scaffolding; searching; while confused sailors gathered round, watching him stooping and lifting as he wound his way through the grid of vertical supports. He found what he was looking for and stood erect when Kokini appeared with a look of terror.

"What are you doing?" he asked.

"I am going to launch the *Dolphin* and take her around to Kamari."

"You cannot! She must be blessed first. Take another." Kokini was dancing in anxiety. He had worked for two years on the magnificent ship and could not stand the thought of ruining her now.

117

"Wait?" he spat and pointed. "Look up there."

Arithon moved to the aft starboard cradle carrying an enormous wooden mallet and eyed the barrel-sized chock holding her in place. He glanced to the left to take note of the port chock.

"Arithon, I beg you. Do not do this. The ship will be cursed. You will be cursed."

Why was he doing this? Someone more senior – a leader – could accomplish this task: it need not be him. But … he was capable, and innocents were dying while he vacillated. If not him, than who?

"So be it," he said. "How many men are needed on the tackles?"

Kokini looked but said nothing. Arithon returned his gaze and repeated his question. Standing there caked in ash and dirt he looked more like a creature from beneath the earth.

"You need two hundred at least, and you have no more than fifty here," Kokini answered.

Arithon began to visualize all that could go wrong. Fifty men would only hurt themselves and someone would be killed if they attempted to restrain the ship once it started its slide. He thought better of his rashness and hesitated. Kokini saw him wavering and thought to cinch it.

"They are already dead," he reasoned.

Arithon looked up at the mountain, spewing fire and pouring waves of molten rock down her flanks, most of it headed for Kamari. He turned to look at Eskopi; thought of his own terror on Moonrise Ridge; and made up his mind.

"Stand back. I alone will be cursed." And not waiting for the crowd to give back, he raised the hammer and swung a mighty blow. The chock pivoted but did not part until the second hit shot it out onto the sand clear of the launch way. And as it escaped the mighty hull above him skewed to starboard and he could hear the tackle strain and complain. A handful of the verticals fell, crashing a wooden note and scattering the crowd further.

He then stepped to the port side and swung, once, twice, three times before the chock popped like a cork from a bottle and set the hull moving to crush him. But the tackle sang of stretching rope and whining sheaves as the hull rocked to a stop two feet closer to the water.

Arithon pivoted out from under the counter, snatched an axe from an onlooker and climbed the work ladder to the deck where the ropes were wound about her mast and angled out to the restraining posts set deep into the earth a hundred feet up the beach. He mulled whether he was doing the right thing and looked up into the city where a large work party was erecting the portable crane to save any they could, buried in a large collapse. His father was certainly there – as he always was – first to spend his strength in aid.

He swung the axe and the ropes parted with a whistling twang; recoiling off the deck like burned snakes. In that same instant the hull began her first and shortest journey, unbalancing the lone mariner standing on her deck as the scaffolding fell and she yawed to starboard. Arithon regained his footing as the rackety, jarring ride began in earnest; the ship waddling down the greased planks seeking the sea like a newborn turtle sprinting for the surf. The crowd followed alongside, keeping a safe distance, but anxious to witness the awesome event. The city, called to attention by the activity in the yards below, paused in their task and watched with fascination, as the hull seemed to free herself and run for the water. Only the lone figure standing on the deck gave any indication of human intervention. Alteron, standing from his stoop in the rubble, recognized the silhouette of his own son.

The stern met the sea first; splashing and pushing a rolling wave as she sought support for her fifty tons. Arithon almost fell again as the hull's headlong rush was slowed by the water, but held on as she continued in, floating free of the cradles and moving out into the harbor on a graceful glide. She was a live thing – a newborn lady of the sea.

"I name you *Dolphin*," called Arithon. "Men of the *Dolphin*, to me!"

"She is a cursed ship," moaned a dejected Kokini standing ankle deep in the surf. Many around him mumbled their agreement and shuffled nervously where they stood.

But not Hyssos.

He waded in and swam the few lengths to his new ship and clambered up the side.

"Welcome aboard," Arithon said. "We need to set the steering oar."

The two turned their backs to those on the beach and began fitting the oar onto its pintles. Twos and threes in the surf hesitated, conversed, and then prodded each other to help their friend, swimming out to join Arithon and that beautiful new ship.

With the steering oar set, Arithon began barking orders to pivot the ship and get her underway around the quay and out to sea. As they passed close to the dock end, Szaba, in full stride, joined them with a leap and a smile onto the moving deck. If they hurried, they could be in Kamari in time to help.

As the *Dolphin* cleared the harbor, their new viewpoint revealed the mountain's devastation. The initial explosion had rushed down the mountain on all sides, flattening everything that stood on its slopes. The protective ridge that guarded Akrotiri from the north winds also saved it from the mountain's blast, which skipped over, leaving the town relatively untouched. The eastern flank was a heat shimmering river of rock flowing down to the sea.

"We have stayed too long," Arithon said to Szaba.

"Perhaps this is the last ... what is the word for telling you danger?" Szaba replied.

"Warning?" Arithon offered.

"Yes, last warning." Szaba rejoined. "There may be time, my friend,"

"Perhaps," Arithon said. "Do you know that is the first time you have called me 'friend'– at least in Minoan?"

"You are my first friend in all my languages," Szaba said.

The *Dolphin* arrived at the cove below Kamari in record time; the crew pulling on each stroke, knowing they were in a race with the fire of Mount Thera. All their experience with the mountain heretofore did not prepare them for the scene they found.

Cliffs dominate the eastern side of Thera, and the homes of Kamari are perched on the zigzag path, which starts at the beach and climbs to the plateau above: once the upper orchards of the inhabitants, but now a field of lava dropping great ribbons of liquid rock over the precipice into the water below. One great rivulet had sliced through the center of the village, dividing it into two unscathed areas. Most of the survivors, perhaps forty-five Therans and a like number of domestic animals, were huddled on the beach on the north side; an island in the torrent, not yet obliterated by the flows.

But it was the water in the cove that frightened those manning the *Dolphin*. It boiled and steamed from the heat of the lava pushing in from the west. Most of the rowers were afraid to enter the mist, which smelled of burnt sulfur and seawater, fearful of what it might do to them or the ship. They hesitated on their oars and stared, wondering if Kokini was right.

"Row!" Arithon bellowed. To falter now was self-fulfillment of the curse.

He guided the ship toward the beach at a great clip, yelling, "Cease!" in time to ride up onto the sand. Those on the beach were panicked; clawing at the hull, while avoiding the surf; the water too hot to touch. The crew lowered the gangplank to help men, women, and children up onto the deck where they fell in coughing fits, gagging for air, and begging for water. Many brought animals with them: goats, sheep, the family dog, and one lone burrow, braying continuously in fear.

"Eskopi! Is there anyone else?"

"A woman believes her son may yet live on the south side, beyond that middle flow."

Arithon looked but could see nothing through the steam on their port side. The heat was becoming unbearable; enough to cause a handful of those on board to faint. They would all soon be overcome. On an impulse, Arithon decided to check the cove before they retreated.

"I will take the skiff around this flow to see if any are left on the south beach," he explained to Hyssos as he prepared the tender.

"Pull out as soon as all are aboard, and I will meet you at the entrance to the cove."

Arithon descended into the skiff and rowed out and around the growing mound of lava piling into the surf. As soon as he cleared, he pivoted shoreward through the steam, unable to see the water's edge or locate it by sound above the continuous hissing and popping of the liquid rock. A careless splash of water on his legs caused him to flinch. How could it be so hot? Cooked alive – what a horrible thought. He shook it off when he felt the bow touch the sand as his oars shallowed.

He stepped onto the beach, calling. He gagged on the stench and then straightened and ran a few paces up toward the cliff and called again. No one could be found in his first scans of the area and he was turning to leave when the steam cleared enough to see someone huddled under the cliff, alone and cowering. Sprinting to the spot as the mist closed again, he found a young boy, maybe five years old, clutching a toy wooden boat to his chest and trying to press himself into an indentation in the cliff much as Arithon had done earlier.

"I have a toy boat like that," he smiled at the frightened child. "Hold onto it and we will go find your mother."

Arithon scooped the boy up in his arms and pivoted toward the surf, just as the lava surged and swirled a great swath onto the beach in front of him. The heat shot up and a flame flickered in the steam ahead: the skiff had caught fire. Panicked, he backed away, his face winced back from the throbbing heat and the boy whimpered in pain. But he was up against the rocks now; trapped between the lava and the cliff.

Without thinking, he spun the boy onto his back and scaled the rock face in terrified haste. It was the only way out. Arithon had climbed sea cliffs all over the island hundreds of times and this one was no different; but he did not know what he might find at the top or even if he would make the top before lava spilled over the edge and wiped him from the precipice.

Halfway up his heart quieted, and he became aware of the boy on his back, gripping his neck and panting raggedly behind his ear. Arithon could feel the toy boat pressed up under his chin from the boy's death grip and laughed to himself at the thought of it.

"Just hold on, little mariner," he encouraged, "we are taking the scenic route."

Somehow the act of trying to assure the child assured Arithon the more. He felt better for making light of their plight and pressed on, finding footholds and handholds as he negotiated the ascent. Just as his confidence waxed, he heard a different sound than the popping and hissing of lava – a sound of cracking rocks. He looked up the cliff to see a boulder, pushed loose on the upper flanks, teeter off the edge, and hurtle past his right shoulder in misaimed malice. Sucking air through clenched teeth, he was startled to hear the same sound again, only magnified, as if the whole mountain were rolling and cracking its way down the slopes above. His confidence waned.

A quick look to his left revealed an overhang that might protect them, and he started toward it when the advance guard of the avalanche poured over the lip above. The stone legion charged to the edge in a tumultuous landslide as Arithon, with the boy clutching, sidled across the rock face in a precarious, unbalanced rush. With boulders smashing around him, he reached the overhang and ducked under, pulling the boy off his back, and pressing him into the cliff next to him. The main body of the slide showered down, splintering and cracking in a pounding roar.

It was over in seconds, and thinking he should hurry before it started again, he spun the boy onto his back and climbed toward the top, where he hauled himself up onto the plateau. He was about fifty feet above the water and to his left the plateau sloped down the southern headland, which formed the entrance to the cove. The flank of the volcano was surging with lava; moving toward him as fast as water flows down a river.

He darted to the south and then eastward down the slope just as the lava reached the edge and spilled over. Had he been on the cliff, he would have suffered a terrible death. But he was alive and moving ahead of the flows, which poured freely over the rim of the cove, covering Kamari forever.

Arithon reached the end of the headland and looked down. The cliff at this point canted outward, preventing any climb down and the water seethed and boiled. He could see, to his relief, that the *Dolphin* had pulled back and the crew was scanning the mist for a sign of his skiff. The south beach was covered in lava with more surging over the edge in great waves, beginning to stopper the cove with liquid rock. The steam grew ever thicker and the stench even more so.

Arithon looked back and saw he did not have much time. The lava, not content with its existing channels, was growing toward him in starts and stops. The peninsula would soon be engulfed.

"Szaba!" he bellowed in his loudest voice.

Why he called for Szaba, he did not know, but somehow, he believed Szaba would hear him. And his instincts were right. Szaba pointed him out to Hyssos, who set the ship in motion toward the low cliff where their friend paced like a caged cat.

Arithon's mind was boiling also, trying to formulate a means of escape. His first thought was to have a rope thrown up and he could see a crewman coiling a line in anticipation of the request. But it would be a mighty throw indeed that could reach them at this height. An idea billowed in his head and he called it down to Hyssos who responded, ordering those on board to execute the necessary preparations.

It was going to be close, Arithon thought. The lava was advancing, and so was the *Dolphin*, but he did not know which would reach him first. The boy on his back was silent, but he began to cling tighter as the lava approached and tried to pull himself higher onto Arithon's back.

"Do not stop," Arithon called to Hyssos, pointing back up the slope. "The lava will hit the *Dolphin*."

Hyssos understood, and ordered the men to maintain their cadence, while he steered as close to the cliff as he dared.

Arithon was staring at the *Dolphin*, trying to estimate its exact arrival. He could feel the heat on the back of his legs and hear the crackling of the lava as it approached. When it sounded like a bellows, he knew he had only seconds left to live, but the *Dolphin* was not quite in position.

The boy around his neck kept spinning his head. Arithon could feel the unbalance each time he did so, but he did not want to look back himself, concentrating on the approach of his blessed ship.

The boy squealed in his ear, and Arithon knew it was now or never. He leapt with all the strength of his young legs. The boy would have been jerked loose had he not had such a tight grip on Arithon, and they both flew away from the cliff like a startled pigeon exploding from its perch.

For Arithon, it seemed like the world had slowed down, just as it had in the battle with the bandits in Africa. He felt as if he were falling through water, with time to mull over his plight. To those on the ship, it looked as if he had taken flight, so far did he propel himself from the precipice.

His right foot caught the edge of the sail and he somersaulted in toward the middle, spilling the boy as he did so. Hyssos had two sailors to each sheet line pulling the sail back so it formed a steep slope, ending in a slight curl. The men had to climb onto the rear cabin to affect the desired shape, and both teams wrenched back on their lines at the moment of impact. The flying duo rolled down the sail to the cupped edge, where Arithon continued off, landing in the arms of Szaba, who was positioned to break the fall. They both toppled back onto the deck with an OOOFH that knocked the wind from them both. The boy caught in the curl.

Hyssos leaned hard on the tiller and pulled the *Dolphin* to port, just as a slug of lava poured over the edge and hit the water next to the ship, just missing the starboard oars, and soaking the rowers and Hyssos with hot water. The crew strained the *Dolphin* away from the cliff and into the safety of the open sea.

Just as Arithon rolled up onto his hands, an object fell from the sail above landing on Szaba's chest. The African looked down his nose at a tiny boat, upright on his torso sailing south with the *Dolphin*. The boy peeked over the foot of the sail looking for his toy and Arithon smiled and turned to acknowledge Szaba. They clasped hands and Arithon rotated onto his back, looking up through the rigging at the smoke boiling the sky.

CHAPTER 10 ACHAEANS

The Sword or the Oar,
Wisdom or War.
Though Cretan born
proud Athena was torn,
Henceforth who would carry her lore?

The funeral pyres burned for weeks consuming broken bodies pulled from the wreckage by screaming mothers and silent fathers. But the most devastating deaths were the trapped victims who died begging for water, while the rescuers worked with raw, bloodied hands in exhausted haste. The mountain continued to pour molten earth that flowed ceaselessly to the southeast corner of the island where it plunged into the surf creating a curtain of steam. On most days, the smoke from the volcano drifted southwest or southeast on the prevailing winds, but on bad days the wind would bear due south and Akrotiri would be enveloped in a cloud of ash that was sharp and caustic to the lungs and nose. The smoke and continuous earthquakes were threatening and difficult, but the destruction of the island's flora was catastrophic. The orchards had been wiped out on the entire southern end of the island; only a blasted, rocky landscape remained. From out at sea, Thera was only fire and smoke and mist – a hellish, rocky prison stripped of nurture and nourishment. Thera was no longer a nurturing home to its inhabitants, but a prison – a place to escape from. A gloomy foreboding enveloped them all; the mountain would not relent.

Only humans moved about in the choking cloud and they were busy with the frenzy of escape. Arithon worked and cried and grew hardened alongside his once joyous race; now grim and determined to survive a crippling blow. When there were no more dead and the ships had begun their shuttles, he was surprised by his father at breakfast the week his *Dolphin* was to join the fleet.

"You will need to sail on your mission to the Achaeans as soon as you can make ready."

"But won't the *Dolphin* be needed for the evacuation?" he asked.

"Of course, we need her, but we need a place to go to even more," Alteron replied. "As it is, we will have to divide the population into many groups and scatter ourselves amongst our friends and allies. We need a new site for a city, so we can amass there to begin anew.

"But none have returned with any alternatives. Our temporary refuges cannot last for long. No one will feed us, and our wealth will quickly deplete. We will be frighteningly vulnerable until we can unite at a new location."

"I understand," said Arithon.

"It cannot happen too soon, my son. Our family will be among the last to leave; we should be here when you return; but you should make utmost haste."

***

The *Dolphin* was the swiftest ship in the fleet; faster than the *Swallow* or the pirate wolf packs, as Po had anticipated. But to the superstitious she would never be anything but a cursed ship. The priests had labored hard after the inopportune launch, but there were those who refused to sail on her, thinking no number of blessings could free her of the demons haunting her timbers. Arithon was forced to recruit against the losses he sustained to religious misgivings, but in the end found a willing crew of the less pious.

On board for the expedition was a ship's complement of forty-two including Arithon's First Tier and his cousin, Glaxos, heir to their grandfather's seat on the Council. Theran leaders believed the Achaean mainland was a possible site for colonization and the mission needed a representative of title.

A cloudless sky domed a placid sea as they cleared the harbor and the rowers, eighteen to a side, began their cadence.

"Round Thera, and point Northwest," Arithon directed to Hyssos at the tiller. "Cut a straight wake. Let us see how fast we can push her.

"We racing?" asked Glaxos, as he ascended the small aft deck to stand beside Arithon.

"I want to be prepared for anything," Arithon answered.

"I know, I know. I was jesting," smiled Glaxos. "Grandfather thinks you are the finest captain we have."

"Po is better," Arithon said.

"Poius is the first generation."

"He has not returned, Cousin," said Arithon looking away to the north.

"Yes, he is overdue – troubling in this hour. We will need him before it is over."

"Perhaps a storm," offered Hyssos, creating an awkward silence.

Arithon doubted any storm could beat Po. Something else was keeping him.

The ship doubled Monkey Head and the mountain was wholly visible, belching its choking black smoke, which rose high into the heavens. All on board were silent, watching the spectacle and only the steady cry of the strokeman, Losius, was heard.

They proceeded without incident until the afternoon of the second day.

"She is Achaean," came the answer from the watchman on the mast.

"Achaean," repeated Arithon, as he stared off the starboard side of the *Dolphin*, at a vessel no more than a league away.

"Are you sure?" he called, looking up through the rigging at Jaros, standing on the yardarm.

"Yes, Captain. At least the ship is."

Arithon gazed out.

"Pointing to intercept," came the next report.

"Intercept," Arithon mumbled as his thoughts rolled back to his first trip to Knossos. There was no need to think that the Achaean was hostile, yet he had a long-nurtured distrust of the race.

Szaba and Sestos left the deck and went below, unnoticed by Arithon, who was watching the approaching ship and wasting precious moments in indecision. The *Dolphin* was heading northwest, and the Achaean was traveling south on a collision angle. Arithon fretted at their purposeful approach and became convinced it was hostile until the Achaean flattened the angle and started to draw up from the stern in a less threatening manner, clearly intent on coming alongside.

This comforted Arithon, and he could now make her out as a merchant ship, smaller, eight rowers to a side. Her captain would occasionally wave from his aft deck as if he were an old friend.

"Hello," cried Arithon in Achaean.

"Hello," came a friendly reply, "I will come alongside. Let us talk."

About what, thought Arithon to himself, this is hardly the place to have a conversation, and the sea was too high for them to lash up.

He moved to the aft-most corner of the deck a few paces behind his usual spot near the steersman, as the Achaean, still rowing, moved up within a ship-length.

A swell lifted the *Dolphin* above the Achaean, and then they switched positions, the Achaean high on the wave. The next swell was large and as they rose to its crest, Arithon could see over the rail onto the deck of the foreign vessel. At least twenty men crouched low behind the gunnels, armed, and waiting for a signal.

"Starboard, pull!" screamed Arithon, trying Po's trick. "Port, back water!"

The *Dolphin* had been slowing, but the Achaean continued to make way. The Theran rowers obeyed their captain, causing the ship to start the pivot. But she would take a few precious seconds to react to their efforts, and the Achaean was upon them.

The Achaean captain yelled his command and his archers stood and loosed their first volley. An arrow sliced across Arithon's shoulder, cutting him, but another better aimed pierced the back of his steersman and he fell forward over the tiller onto the deck. Arithon took his place at the rudder, hard over, as the *Dolphin* responded, and the stern started to swing toward the Achaean.

But they were not going to make it.

The sprit of the Achaean bow snapped its way into the last three oars of the *Dolphin* as the two ships surged toward their inevitable collision. On the next swell, Arithon's port side oars dug deep, as the ship climbed out of the trough, causing her to turn fast on the crest, and as the aft end swung around, the two ships collided. But the Achaean was at the bottom of the following trough as the *Dolphin* crushed into his port bow. It was not the hit the Achaean had intended.

Grappling ropes were flying in great arcs from the pirate and hooking up on the rails of the *Dolphin*. Two Achaeans made the jump to the Theran ship, bent on killing Arithon, who hesitated to abandon the tiller. Weaponless, he was considering a jump to the lower deck, when Sestos emerged.

"Arithon," he cried as he underhanded an axe, sending it grip-first toward his friend. Arithon caught the handle, and continued its trajectory, guiding it around to meet the oncoming Achaean, whom he cleaved in the shoulder, knocking him overboard. The young Theran would have been killed by the second boarder, who was about to catch him off balance in the act of finishing his swing, but an arrow struck the brigand in the face knocking him over into the sea.

Arithon regained his balance and swung his axe twice upon the rail, severing the grappling ropes nearest him before he again caught the tiller, wrenching it forward to continue the turn of the *Dolphin*.

"Port pull!" he screamed again, desperate to get the ship moving forward.

But the Achaean pirate had a dozen ropes attached like the arms of a giant octopus, engulfing its prey, and arresting its escape. He would not be shaken so easily.

A volley of arrows aimed at the *Dolphin*'s rowers, made three deadly hits, forcing Arithon to release the tiller and spin around to chop off the tentacles of his tormenter. Arithon flattened his frame to the deck, seeing the next volley was aimed at him, and then, without warning, a pair of black legs took stance next to his face and he looked up to see Szaba pulling the prize Nubian bow. With great purpose and composure, standing still as a statue, he waited for the ship to rise to the top of the swell, where he loosed his deadly messenger. The arrow found its mark in the chest of a pirate archer.

Arithon bounced up and continued to chop the restraining ropes even as the Achaean was trying to reel her in. The *Dolphin* was caught like a great fish. More ropes were finding a purchase on the Theran ship, but Arithon was soon joined by Sestos with another axe. The young captain turned his head to see Szaba, stock still, another arrow nocked and drawn to its fullest extent. The white feather was pressed flat against his black cheek, and his right eye, squinting slightly, was sighting down the length and beyond to a target known only to him. The *Dolphin* was at the top of another swell and Arithon looked over to the Achaean ship to witness the arrow's flight. But there was no twang, and Arithon glanced back to see Szaba, unmoved, and unshaken by the arrows, which now sought him as a mark.

Arithon chopped at two more ropes, but as the *Dolphin* climbed the next wave, he found himself drawn by sheer amazement to look over at the African and then back to the Achaean.

What is he waiting for, Arithon thought; there are plenty of targets. What does he aim for?

At the crest of the swell, he heard the bowstring sing and he looked to watch the arrow overshoot its mark, traveling over the heads of the nearest Achaeans. It was on a trajectory, which would cause it to pass over the full length of the pirate ship. And in that split second of flight, Arithon's eyes, just ahead of the flying arrow, saw him standing there, his sword raised above him: the captain of the Achaeans. The arrow pierced him in the neck and arrived with enough power that the point exited a finger's length out the back. The captain clutched at the feathered shaft protruding under his chin and dropped to his knees. It was an improbable shot – two ship-lengths away with both decks pitching in the heavy swells.

Confusion erupted on the Achaean vessel and Arithon and Sestos seized the opportunity to hack at the ropes binding them.

Szaba was shooting freely, his arrows never failing to find a target. Others in the crew had brought bows on deck and were giving to the Achaean in equal measure. Arithon raised his axe to strike the last rope when it snapped from the strain of the two ships and hurdled over the rail coiling at his feet. He leapt back to the steering oar and as the *Dolphin* pulled away the Achaean ship did not follow.

The *Dolphin* rowed away at a steady pace and when they were out of range, Arithon had Hyssos relieve him at the steering oar so he could help the wounded.

Regus and Lembre are dead," Sestos reported, as he tried to staunch the flow of a deep cut on the side of Inthos, one of the oarsmen. "Those were Achaeans – what did they attack us for?" he spat.

Arithon heard a cry of pain and looked across the deck and recognized his cousin lying on his side with Szaba holding an arrow he had obviously extracted from Glaxos's thigh.

"How are you, Cousin?" he asked coming to his side.

"Wounded and in pain, but it was shallow," Glaxos answered. "You?"

"Uninjured."

"There is blood on your tunic."

Arithon looked at his chest and saw the red. Remembering an arrow had almost skewered him, he pulled back the material at his shoulder. A cut across his flesh had bled freely but was now stopped. He felt the pain as soon as he looked at it, and marveled that he had not noticed it before.

"I have a slight wound, it seems," he spoke from the side of his mouth, as he poked at it.

How did we escape, Arithon?" asked Glaxos through clenched teeth. "I fell in the first volley."

"It was Szaba," said Arithon.

Szaba was applying pressure to Glaxos' wound and did not look up at the two men who were now staring at him.

"Szaba?"

"Yes, Szaba," continued Arithon. "He shot their captain. I have never seen a shot like it. In truth, I would not have believed it possible."

"I did not see it, but perhaps it was a lucky shot," ventured Glaxos, wincing in pain.

"It was not a lucky shot," answered Sestos, joining the three on the port deck, and dropping a piece of linen bandaging down to Szaba. "He hit his intended target. Did you not know that Szaba was an archer?"

"No, I did not," answered Arithon, "and how is it you know?"

"I saw him shooting once, quite by accident. I was on Black Rock Beach one full moon – late. I was with – well never mind that." The group turned in unison to look sidelong at Sestos. "We, uh, … I hid, not knowing who was coming. It turned out to be Szaba, carrying a bow. He set up a gourd 200 feet down the sand," continued Sestos, "and put five arrows into it."

"Is this true, Szaba?" asked Arithon looking down at Szaba who was wrapping the bandage around Glaxos' thigh. "Are you an archer?"

"Yes," he answered.

"Why have you never told me," began Arithon, annoyed – annoyed at himself for not knowing and annoyed at Szaba's enigmatic reticence.

"Is there anything else I don't know?"

Szaba paused and then answered, "I do not know."

Arithon opened his mouth, and then shut it. Sestos chuckled audibly.

Arithon gathered himself and asked, "Are you familiar with my bow?"

"Yes. The bow is from my homeland. It is Nubian. I am Nubian. Nubians are great archers and my father was one of the best."

"Keep it, it is yours," said Arithon.

"I will accept your gift, Arithon, and someday I will show you how to draw it. You have the strength, but not the skill."

Later that night, after the dead had been wrapped and the wounded were made comfortable, the young men sat on the aft deck. Sestos and Arithon talked about the battle, examining many aspects, while Szaba stared down at the deck. Sestos was talking about the shot – again, when Szaba, looking out to sea, began talking, interrupting Sestos in mid-sentence. He often paused to ask for the correct word or phrase in Minoan.

"We are Nubians – the archers of the Blue Nile. We were once mightier than they who now rule us. They were our allies and we fought for them.

But they became great in many things and then we were vassals, not equals.

"My father was the Lion of Nubia," he said, looking into their faces.

"He taught me. I wanted him to be proud of me." Szaba said. He paused and looked again over his knees at the deck boards.

"In my eighteenth year, the Nubians were called again to the side of the Egyptians to defend the delta. I went with my father. The Pharaoh's third son was head of all armies. We suffered a defeat in the deserts of Aqaba at the hands of the Mitanni army.

"The Egyptians fight with chariots. Do you know of chariots?" asked Szaba.

"I have never seen one, but I know of them," Sestos answered.

"An archer – sometimes two – man the chariot with the Egyptian who drives headlong into the enemy soldiers. We archers shoot them while moving at great speed. At times we must take aim at other chariots. My shot, which you praise, is one I have trained for – when both the target and I are in motion. But the ships go up and down also, and I am not used to that movement. Perhaps I was lucky today."

"Do not make light of your skill," said Arithon.

Szaba gave a slight dip.

"At the battle of Aqaba, I was in the Ptah Corps in a one-archer chariot, left flank, third rank. My father was the lone archer in a lead chariot in the general's vanguard: The Re Corps. It was a hot, windy day in high summer when we met their armies in Sinai. We outnumbered them and the son was sure of a victory and anxious to prove himself – as I was anxious to prove myself.

"I stood next to Iphis, holding his reins and telling him what a brave horse he was and how I would protect him during the battle as we lined up facing the enemy across the dry expanse: Waiting. Waiting for them to advance, but they did not, and the son became impatient as the horses withered. I remember thirst.

"At midday, the horns blew. I mounted the chariot and Iphis bolted to the lead of our Corp. The Mitanni turned and ran, and the Pharaoh's son pursued them.

"We were ahead of our infantry when the enemy turned to face us. They had archers behind the low hills who loosed a volley when we were in range. Iphis was hit in the eye but ran on until he tripped and fell. My feet left the straps as the chariot cartwheeled. The driver was killed, and the other chariots passed me by. I crawled over to Iphis, tangled in the wreckage, his front leg broken, blood pouring from his nose. I thanked him for his great heart and asked his forgiveness as I slit his throat. He was in such agony.

Szaba paused for a long while.

I lay back against him in my own pain and watched our chariots engage theirs. Re Corps was surrounded and destroyed – in a clash of armor and screaming horses. My father was with them. The other flanks turned back, for the Mitanni were inspired and pressed forward. Our army retreated and the fighting passed me by."

Szaba paused.

"What then – I mean how did it end?" asked Sestos.

"Shush," said Arithon, "let him be."

"No, I will finish," said Szaba, surprised at his own verbosity. "The Egyptians made it to higher ground and held the Mitanni off until nightfall. The enemy pulled back to their camp."

"I walked alone for two days, scavenging from the bloated dead, and joined our beaten army as it limped back to Memphis. "The Pharaoh was furious. I do not know the fate of others, but I was sold into slavery and there I remained until you bought me. That was three years ago. I have not handled a bow, until I borrowed one from Po and began to practice again. I am not up to my best and I will never equal my father."

A quiet followed, broken by Sestos, who hated quiet. "This Achaean rope," he said twisting it apart in his hands. "It is a farmer's rope; stiff and course – liable to absorb water and catch in the fairleads. They are not sailors. Not yet."

"They learn fast," observed Hyssos. "Those boarding maneuvers are tricky and he almost succeeded."

***

A gray surf of clouds was spilling off the continent and rolling out over the sea as Arithon stepped onto the deck. When he turned to look back, the rollers were already closing the slit framing the rising sun and in an instant the day was smothered before it could flame. An overpowering feeling of foreboding descended upon him as the sun disappeared and his mood darkened. Yesterday's encounter had left him brooding.

He had killed someone, and he wondered at it. Somehow it lacked the heraldry and portent he had expected – the warriors vaunted zenith; a rite of passage; a benediction. But no, it was empty and pointless. There was no glory. No one asked him about it later, or marveled at it, or even acknowledged it. He was attacked, he reacted without thinking, and the attacker was dead. It was a simple chain of events. Too simple he now thought.

The fact they were pirates helped his young conscience. As maritime traders, all Therans had a nurtured loathing for those who would prey on them. Theran stories were replete with the misadventures associated with cruel pirates. Children were taught at an early age to recognize foreign ships offshore, and even the smallest knew not to be caught unawares on a lonely beach where many a slave trader had plucked the hapless into a wretched life of servitude. Girls were rich targets, and therefore mothered compulsively. Families who had suffered from pirating – and there were dozens – harbored an intense hatred for the marauders. The pirates knew this, and were by and large a cautious lot, usually attacking the defenseless and only the strong when they felt bold; for if caught, they were tied, weighted, and dropped into the sea.

And this troubled Arithon the most. These pirates were bold and Achaean; a bad combination if it thrived, and a serious omen. If the Achaeans were embarked on a voyage from ally to enemy, the Minoans would soon be hard pressed. Arithon felt vulnerable with no home to take refuge in, and a troubling neighbor flexing his muscles.

When the distant land began to change from a dull blue stripe to valleys, cliffs, and beach, they began to encounter fishing skiffs and coasters. Two vessels altered course to traverse their wake, watching the Minoan cross the border into their waters. Arithon held straight, ignoring their maneuver, but glanced back like a lone man passing a gang of footpads. After a course correction, the *Dolphin* took the afternoon to row up the long gulf to the port which served Tiryns and Mycenae. The Achaeans had built the fortress of Mycenae in the hills a day's march from the coast, but Tiryns was only a short walk from the surf on a rocky promontory.

"Great Zeus, would you look at that," exclaimed Hyssos as they rounded into the bay.

Stretched along the beach, like a string of shorebirds on stilted legs, perched hull after hull of ships under construction. The three closest to the docks were almost complete with masts already stepped, and as Arithon's eye alighted on each in turn, he could see that the hulls became less

134

complete as they moved up the beach, so that the furthest one – the fourteenth by his count – was only a keel with the first row of planks.

"Look at all that wealth," said Sestos, ambling up to the gunnel where everyone stood gaping.

Sestos had voiced a similar thought taking shape in Arithon's mind. This was an organized effort – and state sponsored. Had private owners commissioned the ships, the line of hulls would not show the symmetry now displayed. And there was something odd about their loft.

"What was that you were saying about them not being sailors yet?" jibed Hyssos at Sestos. "They seem to think differently."

Hyssos' challenge was astute. But there was more than a desire to 'just be sailors' represented on that beach – much more.

Arithon, Szaba, Sestos, and Glaxos took the tender ashore, leaving the *Dolphin* manned and anchored far enough out to protect her if trouble arose. The ship's carpenter had fashioned a cane of ash for Glaxos, who could barely walk, though he insisted on not being carried.

The news of their arrival preceded them, of course, and many came to watch them pass on their way to the fortress. The locals were interested in the Minoans: they were especially interested in Szaba. While the Achaeans knew of Africans, the presence of one in their land was not a usual occurrence and many of the children along the path pointed and laughed excitedly at his passing. Szaba was by now used to such treatment, having experienced a similar reception in his first days on Thera. But unlike his arrival on Thera, he walked at Arithon's side, feeling an equal after his contribution in the pirate battle. The two men struck a commanding presence – Arithon tall and powerful, Szaba thinner of build but slightly taller than his friend, they towered over the average Achaean.

"This land is rocky and sparse, Arithon," observed Sestos, "why would we want to come here?"

"Shush," admonished Glaxos. "Do not assume that they do not understand. Many Achaeans know our language. Be careful what you say, or at least say it quietly."

"I hope the sea has more abundance," he now said quietly, "though I dare say they fish it hard themselves."

"I do not think we can be so picky," countered Arithon, "you may remember that our own beloved land is no longer hospitable and even poor land would be preferable to the Therans being scattered to the winds."

"Agreed, but surely we can do better than this," Sestos insisted.

135

"I suppose we could be allowed to colonize an unsettled part of the mainland. I doubt that it will be an area of choice, but either way, we will undoubtedly have to pay tribute to the Achaean king.

"Glaxos, what about our autonomy?" asked Arithon, as if he had just considered the matter.

"Of great concern," replied Glaxos. "Our best hope is to remain loyal to Crete, which still holds some sway here. But Minoan power is waning as the Achaeans become ever more powerful. They want to rule us someday, and for us Therans, that may be sooner than for the Cretans."

"We have a difficult task it would seem, Glaxos," stated Arithon, "I am glad you are here."

"And I you," replied Glaxos.

The band talked quietly, picking their way slowly up the heights upon which the citadel was constructed; Glaxos in considerable pain, but uncomplaining. The Achaeans were perfecting their fortifying techniques and could already boast walls, twenty feet wide at the bottom, even though they were rough and uncut. A history of tribal warfare and endless bickering had made the Achaeans formidable, but had also inspired a sense of independence. They lived in city-states, much as the Minoans, but there was much less cooperation between the cities and often intense rivalries. Mycenae, Athens, and Thebes traded heavily with the Minoans, but only begrudgingly with each other. On the accessible mainland, each city sought dominance over their neighbor, spawning the creation of fortresses unknown in the Minoan world. The walled cities were unnerving to the Therans, especially since they were considering moving there.

Arithon wondered at the terrible need that elevated such bastions. As they approached, he could feel the ponderous strain of each great block; the draglines snapping as an errant stone resisted the relentless energies of the mortals, and tumbled back down the slope; the men shouting to clear those below. And then the painstaking reset, and the triumphant cries when the determined finally won and dropped the shapened mountain chip into its pre-appointed pocket; sweating, triumphant, and victorious – but for only a short while; the colossal wall would remain long after its hope of eternal protection had vanished.

Arithon spied a sentry on the watchtower marking their progress up the hill, and he wondered if his new home would need walls.

"These Achaeans are numerous," offered Sestos, as they surveyed the populated areas, spread out on the surrounding hills. Beyond the buildings which lay like scattered stones, were tended groves of olive trees with barley sown beneath. Vines were woven cleverly along the slopes which rolled up from the wheat sown plains through which roads ran off north, west, and east. It was an important hub and it supported a large and thriving population.

"I do not see much room for us."

"Their numbers grow between each visit," said Glaxos quietly, "It is troubling and may explain the Achaean pirate. There have been other reports, throughout the islands, of Achaean raids and encroachment."

The final approach to the fortress was a winding path up an impressively steep hill, which became a stone paved ramp that wrapped itself smoothly around the great walls. Arithon reached out and trailed his hand along the massive blocks, wondering at their great weight. Glaxos stood straight at the gate and propped his cane against the stone and addressed the keeper in polite speech. The Therans were admitted inside the citadel but made to wait in a small alcove just inside the walls.

"Why do we wait so long?" asked Sestos, impatiently. "Are they trying to tell us something?"

"Quite possibly," Glaxos answered.

"What? That we are not important and must wait at the door like servants?" Sestos threw a pebble against the great wall; it pinged off its immovable bulk.

"Maybe. It is an old trick. Puts us at a disadvantage. But do not be hasty," Glaxos cautioned. "It could be that he is unavailable or otherwise engaged. After all, we are here uninvited."

"I have been sitting here for half the morning watching these people come and go," began Sestos, "and in many ways they seem like us. They are industrious and have some love of art and decoration, but not near what we enjoy. Achaeans are too serious. But more than anything else, I have decided that without a doubt, Minoan girls are prettier."

"Shh – I agree," said Arithon in a low voice, "They are watching us, also. We appear to be of interest to them."

He nodded toward an alley, where young Achaean boys were taking turns peeking at them from an alley wall. They hurried out of sight when they realized they had been discovered, laughing, and shoving each other trying not to be the last one to disappear.

Szaba laughed at their antics; his first reaction since they had entered the city. He was clearly uncomfortable and knew that much of the attention was focused on him, a standout in the group, both tall and black.

Presently, a slave came and escorted them to the palace. It was more fortress than palace, but the megaron, into which they were finally led, was impressive and comfortable, furnished admirably with things of beauty and craft.

"We are emissaries of King Selleres of Knossos," Glaxos introduced. "Please accept a small token of our friendship."

He then presented him with a beautiful ivory carving of a dolphin, leaping above the waves of its base. Arithon smiled inwardly, knowing that he had played a valuable role in its acquisition. Szaba, too, took note of the gift and Arithon could only wonder what thoughts he harbored about the wealth he contributed as a slave. It could easily have been the very horn he carried the breadth of the African desert.

"Very nice, and beautifully made," the Achaean king replied politely as he handled the gift with obvious pleasure, "but what favor could I give to so great a king as Selleres?"

"We are seeking land for a new colony," explained Glaxos. "The sites we have in mind may be within your influence?"

"My influence, hmmm," he answered carefully, mulling over the word influence. "And where would these sites be?"

"On the island of Paros, or possibly on the mainland in a harbor near Epidavros. Both are unoccupied."

"Unoccupied, yes, – for now, but we use both for our fishing fleets. Tell me why you want to colonize on my land? Have the Minoans run out of land to own?"

"Our land is deserting us. One island anyway. We are Therans and –"

"The volcano," interrupted the King.

"Yes," replied Glaxos.

An attendant whispered something to the Achaean, who hesitated before he began. "We have heard of the volcano, though I have not ventured to view it myself. Hephaestus is extremely angry with Thera it would appear. Have you not tried to appease him?"

"Yes, for many years, but it seems he will not be content until we have left," explained Glaxos.

"Then do you mean to move all Therans?"

"Yes," Glaxos answered briskly.

"How many?" asked the King, with a furrowed brow.

"Our population is industrious and –"

"How many?" the King interrupted.

"Twelve thousand," Glaxos answered.

"Twelve thousand," the King bellowed, "that is not colonization. That is invasion."

"We are not inclined to invasion or war," interjected Arithon.

"We know," said the King, looking straight at Arithon.

Arithon did not like the King's tone in this last statement and brooded while Glaxos continued to explain Thera's needs.

The discussion went on for almost an hour, but it was clear that the Achaean King was not interested in a Minoan colony and would settle for nothing less than all of Thera's wealth and subjugation of any colonizers.

Arithon became increasingly uncomfortable, especially when the Achaean began a series of questions about the wealth and strength of Crete.

Glaxos was a skilled politician and deftly avoided the probes while politely providing vague answers.

An impasse was finally reached. They respectfully abandoned any further discussion, made their farewell, and left for the *Dolphin*. As they were leaving, the King noticed Glaxos' limp, which he had tried to hide.

"Are you injured, Glaxos?" he asked.

"I was injured during the last eruptions," he lied, "and it still pains me some, but it is healing."

The Achaean nodded, but watched them as they left.

"I did not like his attitude," began Arithon once they were outside the gate, and I believe he was much more interested in taking advantage of us, than helping us."

"You are right, of course," agreed Glaxos. "We are feeling the pressure of the Achaeans more and more. They want our knowledge but would prefer to rule us rather than ally with us. Our mission was to test their sensitivity to our move. We own the trade of the Aegean, and we believe the Achaeans are jealous of this monopoly. It is the source of our wealth and they know it and desire it as well. We will have to seek elsewhere."

"Why did you lie about your injury," asked Sestos, "I wanted to complain about the Achaean pirate."

"Be careful what you reveal," he advised.

It was a somber company that made their way back to the harbor. Arithon did not want to return with this news and advocated a visit to Mycenae.

"We will fare less well there," Glaxos explained. "His brother is king in Mycenae. The Council expected this but thought Tiryns worth a chance."

"I had hoped it was more than just a chance," Arithon replied, frustrated by the lack of progress. "This feels like failure."

"No, we have learned a valuable thing. The Achaeans will not help, and we should be wary of them. They are no longer afraid of our navy, and this will be of great interest to all of Minoa. We should return with due haste."

***

"Do we run now or wait until morning?" asked Hyssos. It was late evening with a low mist already forming on the quiet waters of the bay.

If the night skies were clear, Minoans could sail by the heavens – a monumental feat of navigation accomplished generations ago. It was their edge in the maritimes, allowing them to sail over open water instead of hugging the coast, as the Achaeans were forced to do.

"Clouded night. Take bearings and we will anchor in deeper water, and wait for a clearing sky or early light," Arithon ordered.

He was hard asleep in the aft cabin when he was startled awake by the sound of scurrying feet. He sat up as Hyssos pulled the door open.

"Sestos asked me to raise you. There are pirates near!"

Arithon hurried to Sestos' side peering out into the night.

"The moon broke cover just now and Jaros saw three ships beached on an islet to the south. He insists one is the Achaean we encountered yesterday," reported Sestos.

Jaros was the youngest aboard. He had fallen from Suicide Cliff in the back harbor, leaving him with a stiff ankle and a noticeable limp, but he earned his living on the sea same as all in his family: his brother was lookout on the *Octopus*.

"Did they see us?"

"If they are watching, we must assume they did," Sestos answered.

"Any activity?" asked Arithon.

"He could not tell."

"I wonder," Arithon voiced aloud, but thinking to himself. He glanced up at the breaking cloud cover. "Rouse the crew. We are going to try and slip out. What time is it?"

"The moon was there," offered Hyssos.

When the crew was in position, Arithon had them up-anchor and row into the blackness.

"Starboard," he whispered to the steersman.

In his head he was recalling an image of the gulf and plotting a blind course out. They would row, even with a fair wind on their starboard quarter; unwilling to risk sailing onto a rocky shoal. His heartbeat was noticeable as they groped away from the anchorage, wondering if their escape could be heard. The men had quietened their oar looms with a leather sleeve, but the creak of *Dolphin*'s timbers groaned unsympathetically out across the still water. He knew the sound would carry, but were they listening so close? The answer was immediate – he could hear the unmistakable wooden thumps of ships getting under way, and he strained his ears on the port side to position the source.

What would they do? How did pirates think? With three ships they would probably send one to pursue and position the other two to cut him off to leeward – and they had the angle.

"Starboard. … Hold her there," Arithon whispered.

The *Dolphin* was slicing straight across the bay in an attempt to outflank. But she would not make it, Arithon decided as he continued to listen and work out in his mind the relative positions of things he could not see and only occasionally hear.

"Starboard. More. … More."

"I think we are going the opposite way now. Up the channel," Hyssos leaned in at his shoulder.

The lapping sound on the bow changed as she pointed into the wind.

"Hold her there," Arithon ordered. "And trust for no shoals.

"We will run up to windward and see if one of them will follow. I want to spread them out, before we dash back down."

Sestos came aft, working his way from the bow.

"Arithon, I believe I can hear ships up channel," he reported.

If true, they were trapped, and Arithon began a cold sweat. As the net closed around, he felt a fool, and worse – at least worse to him – he would lose his ship: the sleek and worthy *Dolphin*, on his first command. The curse would be fulfilled and that dog-faced Kokini would be proven right. This revelation goaded his mind to feverish activity, interrupted by a hail from Jaros atop the mast.

"Fire off the starboard beam," he called in a muffled shout – almost comic in its execution. Arithon turned and saw a fire on the hills – a signal – and bad news for the *Dolphin*.

A black shape loomed ahead; a ship under oar; and cries arose on both vessels. Arithon reached for the tiller, but Tropos had already put the tiller up affecting a quick turn to port. As if in answer to an unasked question, arrows began to whisk out of the darkness. The crew of the *Dolphin*, now armed, endeavored to respond, but the ships separated quickly in the darkness.

Arithon, wallowing in the despair of a squandered responsibility, was shaken from it by the appearance of Szaba at his side, standing stiff, bow in hand, an arrow loaded. They could hear the black ship turning to reacquire them and their rallying cries to the other ships to close the net. Arithon was struck by a memory of a boar hunt in his fifteenth year, when the hunters encircled a sounder of boars, slowly closing the ring. When the animals realized their escape was cut off, they squealed and charged the line, breaking through in a wild slash of tusks. If he did not do something soon, these hunters would skewer them all.

"Hyssos, bring the ship about. Tropos, raise the sail," he ordered in quick succession. Arithon had decided to slash his way out, and he needed speed and teeth.

"Into the bow, Szaba. The steersman first," he instructed, "and any who take his place."

Szaba giving only a slight nod started forward.

As soon as the sail was up the *Dolphin* began to surge through the darkness, running blind – a most unsettling predicament for sailors always wary in unfamiliar waters – and even more inadvisable: under sail.

"Watch the trim. Steer before the wind," Arithon ordered.

He looked up at the sky, wondering how much longer the enveloping darkness would hide them, when a rent in the clouds framed a silver bright moon. Blasphemies spilled from a dozen lips as their true peril was revealed. No less than seven ships could be seen within striking distance and worse, the hunters could see the *Dolphin* and estimate her speed and direction.

When the cloud cover closed again, Arithon nudged her to port to throw off their calculations and increased the cadence of the oars, no longer concerned with the squeaks and thunks they would produce. *Dolphin*, accelerating, was folding the wave on her bow when the encounter began.

Out of the blank darkness appeared the shape of a ship rowing upwind. The black ship spotted the *Dolphin* and on first instinct turned landward to avoid the oncoming collision. Arithon anticipated the move and ordered the counter turn, but, oh, Great Zeus, it was going to be close. The Achaean captain realized he would be caught broadside and yelled for his steersman to turn to port.

Szaba, waiting only for the distance to close, released his first arrow, leaving their helm unattended. The second was in the air before the steersman hit the deck and their captain fell beside him.

A second order from Arithon twisted the *Dolphin* as she came alongside.

"Ship port oars," yelled Arithon to his crew, who responded in a deftly executed maneuver.

The Achaean had started to ship his just as the bow of the *Dolphin* crushed into those on the forward quarter, snapping the outstretched looms as the *Dolphin* raked her length, tossing most of the near side rowers into the water. Slowed by the impact, the Minoans, nonetheless, darted off into the darkness, believing – no – hoping they had broken out.

With the clouds beginning to pale, Jaros, from his better view on the mast called, "They have set sail for a stern chase." And there they were, strung out behind them on different points of their port quarter, a fleet of Achaean ships, large and small, setting their sails and rounding to the chase. Arithon felt relief at the sight – ships behind, but none ahead.

As the day gathered light so the *Dolphin* gathered speed, and it was soon apparent that she was the much faster ship. The Achaeans broke off at the edge of the gulf like a dog pack at their border, and the Therans sailed unconquered into the open water of the Aegean.

CHAPTER 11 WATCHER'S ROCK

Hestia protected the hearth flame but for a while longer,
foreseeing that it would not survive the outburst of her cheated
nephew.

The ship spent an uneventful day and night at sea, relaxed, but watchful of the horizons. Arithon took the night tiller, and pointed her southeast, steering by the moon and the stars. He tracked the moon through the night; its late rise on the horizon and its march over his head. For a moment, he pegged it to the top of the mast, where it sat like a spherical lamp, lighting the deck and the sea around her. The wind was steady out of the northwest and even with the sail at quarter notch, she pulled the *Dolphin* at a smooth and unwavering pace.

Arithon remained there for the night, reflecting over the previous days. He was troubled by the posture of the Achaeans: they were building a formidable navy sponsored by the city-states. He was even more troubled by the overwhelming weight of responsibility that was crushing him like deep water. It had been a deep dive, this trip; with his first kill, first loss of crew, and a first encounter with a foe of immense resolve. These things had always existed on the periphery of his world, but a trader's life on the sea was the challenge he wanted to pursue. Why had this come in his time and where would it all end? As they sailed deeper into Minoa, the moonlight on the water, a fair wind, and the thrum of the tiller did much to soothe his soul.

His mood was more positive as the *Dolphin* neared her home waters and he napped until midday, when he heard the crew moving about more than usual. He emerged to see thick black smoke roiling up from an unseen source on the horizon. Arithon's mood again darkened.

The crew sailed the *Dolphin* around the north of the island to avoid the smoke plume and pulled into the harbor as the sun snuffed into the ocean: fiery orange behind the soot-soaked sky.

The dock and the beaches were piled with furniture, jars, baskets and rope-tied bundles: the personal possessions of a citizenry in full-scale evacuation and a distressing sight for those aboard the *Dolphin* as the full weight of what was going on pressed home. Sestos' family had coiled nautical rope of four different sizes from finger width to the width of a forearm in great skeins on the beach – their entire inventory. His father sat on a stool amid the piles, higher than his head, cutting or splicing lengths according to need.

"It has started," voiced Hyssos. "It has really started."

"Yes," Sestos said. "What did you expect?"

"I do not know," replied Hyssos. "It just hurts to see it."

"I am going to help my father," said Sestos to Hyssos. "Come and get me when your family is ready to move to the harbor."

Arithon made no comment; lost in his own personal melancholy he had nothing uplifting to offer so he released the crew and walked up the paved streets to his home. The walk was unpleasant and difficult as the streets were littered with debris and the air was filled with dust and acrid smoke, which burned the eyes and lungs. As he neared, he was heartened to hear his mother singing – she must be alone to sing so boldly intimate. It was a spinning song, an old round for many voices, which rose and fell to the rhythms of a rotating spindle. She sang with her circle or quietly to herself in a contented comportment, but it had been a while – a long while – since Arithon had heard her voice in melody: it warmed him like a hearth on a cold night.

"Arithon," his mother cried with an anguished smile, "I was hoping you would return today."

"Today," he chided as he hugged her, unable to keep from smiling "you were hoping only today?"

"You know I have wished it every day – do not tease your mother, especially now with all of this," she said with a flourished wave.

"Where is Father?"

"He is leading the first evacuation. He's been gone for three days and I do not expect him back for two or three more."

"We chose to send the neediest first, the oldest and the youngest and their families. Three of the Council went to manage temporary shelter. We are evacuating to Crete and Rhodos, you know."

"No, I did not know the final plan. Is it so desperate? Do we not have a permanent destination?"

"None will take so many, it seems. The reports from all our emissaries have come back with the same response. 'Too many and not here,'" she answered.

"I fear, I must report the same message," said Arithon.

"Where is Sis," Arithon said suddenly, as if he just noticed her absence, "has she gone?"

"No, not yet. She is helping the Scrius family prepare their move. You know Scrius – he went with Po, and the children are all so young. I was helping there myself all day and have just come home to prepare a meal. I expect she will be along soon. Are you hungry?"

"Some, but what of Po?" he asked suddenly. "Has he returned?"

"No," she said quietly, and returned to cutting a handful of carrots and onions for a lamb stew.

Arithon stared at her back for a moment, then glanced out the window at the vines on the terrace. The leaves were yellow and plagued. He turned a frown and then bounded the stairs, skipping the first two as he always did, and found his room tidy and clean. It was comforting to his mother to keep his room ready for his return: it somehow guaranteed that he would return. She suffered the worry common to all wives and mothers of mariners: that someday they would be late and late would become forever. His father routinely overstated his journey lengths so she would never think he was 'late' getting back to homeport. Arithon wondered at Po's 'late,' but pushed it aside and went to the wet-room to wash off. After oiling his skin, he returned and put on a fresh tunic before sitting on his bed next to his trove chest.

I will have to find a new home for this, he thought as he opened it. Inside were the ana of his Theran life: childish keepsakes and precious heirlooms.

"Hope no one ever sees what's inside."

He opened a woven lidded basket, grabbed a bronze comb that lay next to a matching bronze mirror, unbraided his hair, and combed it only enough to untangle. His mother had given him the set on his fourteenth birthday, thinking he might groom himself through to manhood. He always forgot to take it, leaving his hair braided, or in a horsetail for the length of a trip. Arithon smiled at his oversight, knowing it must exasperate her that the gift remained in his trunk, unjourneyed and unused. He would remember them in the future – for mother's sake.

In the corner sat his favorite toy as a child: a wooden boat, rigged with a square sail. It was a pull toy equipped with tiny wheels, enabling him to captain it across the storm-wracked courtyard, tethered by a length of string. After he was older, Roa used to place her doll aboard and mother it around the house. By then he had moved on to the real thing and lost track of the toy. Sometime back, the undoubted result of a cleaning mission, his mother had placed the memory in his chest and there it remained, anchored, and awaiting orders to shove off again.

A battered wooden box nestled in the other corner contained his collection of valuable 'keepers'. He opened it and smiled at the contents. There was a large white stork's feather he had found on a hike of Mount Thera, a dried seahorse – got that on Black Beach, a handful of unusual shells – who can remember where all these came from, a shark tooth of exceptional size – a gift from Po, five odd rocks, a cracked wooden spinning-top – originally Father's, and three bits of glass. He closed it and put it back, wondering why he kept such silly things, but unwilling to give them up just yet.

Toward the bottom was a box of cosmetics and perfumes, which he rarely used, though makeup was a mainstay of Minoan fashion for both genders. His mother, with a keen interest in fashion, had a box of makeup as large as his chest. He knew Sestos to have one just as large. He wondered how many ships would be required to transport the make-up boxes of Thera. Twenty he decided, with a smile.

In the center of the trove was a beautiful box of incised redwood. It had belonged to his father, but was passed on to him, when Raiha gave her husband a larger one made in Lycia. Arithon now used it for his real treasures. His jewelry, which he only wore to the festivals, was wrapped in little cloth swatches of green and yellow. He had an amber ring he was fond of, a tiny ant imprisoned inside the yellow crystal; and a bracelet of silver, with dolphins that swim round the wrist – an heirloom from his grandfather. A flash of gold at the bottom turned out to be the miniature double-sided axe his father had purchased for him in Knossos. He fingered it, remembering that day as he had remembered it a hundred times since.

The front door opened and closed; so he repositioned the lid and stepped down to the first floor. Roa was in the kitchen talking to their mother when he slipped up behind her. The girl's feet and hands were dirty from soot.

"Arithon," she squealed, throwing herself onto his neck.

He spun her so that her feet swung free before he checked her movement and held her in a warm hug. His mother turned to see them and pinched her lips between her teeth as if she were about to cry and then resumed feeding the fire blackening the copper pot on the kiln.

"You are a mess," Arithon said, "whatever have you been up to?"

"I have been helping," she replied, "haven't I, Mother?"

"I know," he said with a grin, "I know you have; and a wonderful thing for you to be doing. You are a good Theran."

After an offering prayer and a tip of wine to Hestia, they sat down for a meal of olives, barley bread, and the stew, which somehow tasted better than it ever had. Arithon had a feeling he might never again share a meal with his family in the house of his birth. He slept heavy that night and rose to a quiet mountain and fresh air. But Therans would never again trust the mountain.

The following day he was tapped to lead a second evacuation wave and spent the day managing the loading of goods piled all over the quay and along the beach. The *Dolphin* could take a hundred Therans, including their belongings, but it was problematic getting it all aboard in a manner that would satisfy everyone, and not everyone was willing to embark on the 'cursed ship' and had to be reassigned. The women, huddled at the rails, wiped tears on their best clothes knowing they would never return to their beautiful homes: empty, forlorn, and abandoned on the hills above. He followed his father's track to Crete but missed him in the dark the following evening at sea and did not encounter him for another week, until they were again in port at Akrotiri.

"I am worried about Po," said Arithon to his father on their first night at home, "I want to go and look for him."

"I share your feelings, Arithon," he agreed, "but we cannot spare the *Dolphin*, now, while the evacuation is underway. Afterwards we may get a chance if he does not return first."

Arithon would return many times over the next four months ferrying crying Therans to Crete and Rhodos, reminded by the diminishing piles, that his time would soon come.

An orderly, cooperative population accomplished the task with a great sense of solidarity, believing a long-term solution would eventually be found. Food was the greatest concern, as no other city could afford to feed so many mouths and the wealth to buy it would deplete rapidly. Foreseeing this, the Therans had prepared and had many stocks that would last a full year – if they were careful. As Alteron had calculated, it took over three hundred ship-runs to evacuate the population: transporting over twenty thousand tons in their bottoms. The last fifty trips carried perishable cargo: giant jars of oil, barley, fish, and wine; carried down on carts from the great food stores near the Hall. Arithon and the other men on Thera worked for weeks at this backbreaking work, treating each jar as if it contained their last meal.

The evening before final evacuation, a weary but toughened Arithon sat alone on Watcher's Rock, an enormous basalt column, eight feet across, thrusting out of the heights above the harbor's west end. Everyone in Akrotiri had perched on the rock at one time in their life, watching for a returning ship, or enjoying the strangely satisfying melancholy of solitude. The Theran fleet floated motionless in the gentle waters of the protected harbor, the finest in Minoa. Arithon had never seen all of Thera's ships in at one time, though he knew them all intimately: their capacities, peculiarities, assigned routes, and their captains. *Polus* and *Prados* were tied across from one another on the quay with the *Sea Monkey* at dock's end and the *Dolphin* tied to her.

"*Hoopoe Two, Loyalty, Sunbeam, Octopus, Gentle Seas, Marlin, Sweet Fussy,*" he smiled and continued naming aloud, "*Coriphenes, Ziphius, Thera, Stinella, Easy Sail, Sea Turtle, Grampus, … and Flying Fish,*" he finished, naming all thirty two at anchor.

"*Swallow,*" he added.

"She is not with us," a voice startled him, and he pivoted to see his grandfather climbing the step-like stones that wound up to his pinnacle.

"I did not hear you," said Arithon.

"I can move quietly when I want to," Tios smiled, as Arithon made a place for him on the rock. "Only I am slower."

Tios was like a length of well-made rope: lean and tough; pliable when handled, but unyielding under strain. He was the unmistakable grand sire of Arithon, though his thick hair was now foam white and he favored his left leg. Even now, no one would misjudge him as anything but formidable, though his fierce presence was now tempered with thoughtfulness and wisdom.

"I thought to have Watcher's Rock to myself this one last time, but I am glad to have found you here, Grandson. You soothe my heart," he said laying a hand on Arithon's shoulder.

"On the watchout for Po?"

149

"No, not really, but I miss him," Arithon answered.

A long quiet followed, as they continued to watch the harbor. A lone fishing skiff was rowing out to the *Sunbeam*.

"Regares has decided to join us after all," his grandfather pointed, as the old fisherman caught a line thrown to him from the tow ship.

"You know his skiff, even from this distance, Grandfather," Arithon said.

"I have watched from here many times in my life, and I take care to know all I can – even the look of old Regares' skiff," he answered.

"Yes, I am glad he will come. He taught me to fish," Arithon replied.

"The harbor has been as this only once in my life," Tios started. "The Cycladian fleet had assembled here, and you could step from ship to ship across the bay – as you can today. It was my twenty-third year: the year Selleres of Crete and Tios of Thera united and sailed against the Carians. ... What an armada!" he gleamed as if he could see it all again.

"Selleres told me you saved his life."

"Yes. I did," he said, pausing to recall. "We engaged the Carians off Kos. Selleres was on the flagship, which suffered a mortal blow – her hull was split, and she sank quickly. I commanded the *Swift* and we engaged the wolves as they were shooting the men in the water."

"The *Swift*?" wondered Arithon aloud. "I have never known a *Swift*."

"No," his grandfather chuckled, "I do not expect you would. ... She sank the same day in heavy fighting. Selleres was wounded and I kept him afloat until we were rescued. Another *Swift* was never built – in my honor I suppose.

"The swift is always on the wing," Tios mused, "looking for a home."

Tios looked over at Arithon, who acknowledged the thought with a nod but said nothing.

"Selleres has sent word that he wants you to come to Knossos," Tios rejoined.

"I would like that," said Arithon, remembering.

Again, they were quiet, each in his own thoughts until Arithon asked, "Is this the end of Thera's line?"

"For me, yes," Tios answered. "The tree is uprooted, but the seed will be planted on other shores."

Arithon released his harbor gaze and turned to face his grandfather.

"We have enjoyed a serene, happy, playful time," Tios continued. "There is no place like this … but it will now pass into legend. You will begin your own tale – tomorrow."

Arithon pursed a smile, and he and his grandfather talked quietly until stars foamed the black ocean of sky, and a soft waning moon rose in the east to light a path for them to descend.

***

On the following morning Raiha stepped out one last time onto the courtyard of her home and sat on the stone bench. Arithon had used the left seat edge to achieve his first stand after crawling out from the kitchen on a gray morning long ago. He smiled then as he does now when he triumphs. She could almost smell the jasmine of that day – there was a large vine over on the trellis: it was a landmark in the neighborhood. Down the hill, she could hear a religious ceremony underway on the dock involving a sacred flame carried in procession from the abandoned Temple of Poseidon. There would be no more fires in her home, or family meals with fighting children. The window up behind her was the room she shared with her husband – it looked forlorn and inviting in that instant. There they had revealed their hopes and fears to each other and yes, they had made love – often quietly, when he made her feel like a teenager again. The room was empty now. Oh, to have it all as it once was, but … It was time to go. Her companion and lover would be waiting for her by the *Sea Monkey*. She smiled to reflect on his strength and kindness and left her memories to seek the comfort of his presence.

The final sailing of the Theran fleet proceeded single file out of the harbor, thirty-one ships, packed with the dreams, history, and sorrows of a thousand generations. They stayed in formation, until well clear of the island. At a flag signal from the *Sea Monkey*, half of the fleet peeled away and struck south for Crete.

Arithon watched it all through tear blurred eyes from the Heights, having stayed behind to strike north in search of Po.

CHAPTER 12 ABANDONED

Hypnos, God of sleep, debated with his brother, Thanatos, god of death, while the mortal drifted between their realms.

No one waved from the watchtower or met ships at the quay. No dogs barked; no donkeys brayed; the wheels of the carts no longer squeaked on their trip up from the docks. Only the cry of gulls echoed off the walls of the city streets, where the wind blew dust into piles that no one swept. A lonely place thought Arithon on their last morning as he and his crew prepared to leave. Only the long-dead lived there now along with a few rats that ate what the Akrotirins had deemed unfit to transport.

The quiet would have been the most disturbing, except for something else now present. There were cracks in the ground where there had been none only weeks before. And the land was changing. In places it had risen several feet. An ominous feeling followed him as he wandered the upper city, inducing uneasy turns and the occasional look behind. It reminded Arithon of his moment on second ridge. Yet the mountain was not smoking or sloughing lava from its cone, though the tremors seemed to be more prevalent, warning that they were still not welcome. The crew felt it too and skylarked nervously on the quay after two days of loading the last of the stores.

Drawn to the heights of Akrotiri one last time, he was about to descend, when he noticed tracks in the ash that should not be. The city was blanketed with fresh fallout that should have lain undisturbed, but trampled paths wound through the alleys and into doorways. Realization washed over him with the attendant fear of one who stumbles into the lair of a waiting predator. He surveyed the city with a furtive pass but was drawn to an anomaly to the southeast. And there his folly was revealed. Two unfamiliar ships were positioned off Monkey Head and they were preparing to enter the harbor. How long had they been there? Long enough – and he had been negligent.

It would be no secret in the Aegean that the Therans were leaving. Vultures were picking Akrotiri's dead flesh and he realized they would do the same to him. He bolted for the harbor to give warning and escape the closing trap, feeling a fool for his complacency.

But his noisy flight gave notice to the invaders and a series of cries – foreign cries – repeated along the watch ways. It was a trap – and it was now in motion. The activity roused the crew, who moved toward the ship – except Szaba, who darted up-city.

Arithon caught glimpses of the intruders on his periphery moving down the streets to cut off his return. Altering his course, he ascended the back stairs of Omelkor's house and bounded onto the high roof above the surrounding homes.

"Hyssos!" he cried out, his voice echoing. "Take the *Dolphin* around to Black Cove. Ships off Leeward Point!" He believed he could go over land with the same speed and meet them – if he could get out of the city.

Hyssos was the only one he could see when he called, and he was relieved when Sestos also appeared, waved his understanding, and hurried the crew aboard. They had already pushed off the dock when Arithon began his descent to the alley, contemplating a safe route out.

"Arithon! Arithon!"

He could hear – it had to be – Szaba's voice, echoing up the empty streets, and moving fast. He should be on ship, was all he could think, and he continued to wonder about it right up until Szaba emerged on the far end of the lane.

"We are cut off behind," huffed Szaba when they met.

The two darted higher into the city avoiding capture until they found Kalliste's secluded patio, where they took up a watchful position. With the light fading, the lead ship and its follower rounded Monkey Head and proceeded into the harbor. It was the first full-on view of the intruders, as the hills had blocked their final approach. Arithon was so startled that he stood erect to gain a better look then dropped down behind the low wall, sitting with his back to the stones. He whispered to Szaba, "Sea Peoples! I expected Achaeans, but they are Sea Peoples."

"Who are Sea Peoples?" asked Szaba.

"The mystery of this age. Their ships roam the Aegean, though none can find their homeport. Some believe them to be a lost tribe of the Achaeans, others think they are a blue-eyed race of the north. The one certainty is they are dangerous. They tried to take the *Swallow* once – when I sailed to Crete. They must be pillaging all over the island and some have walked over the ridges from Kanakari and Finikia."

The Sea People's ships rowed to the pier and armed men stepped ashore, fanned out, and began hunting. Arithon ventured a last look.

"We haven't much time," he said to Szaba, but cut short his next utterance when he heard close voices – two. Szaba fitted an arrow and waited. The men were beating their way up the street, searching the houses. Arithon could hear others around them, but none as close.

After numerous smashing echoes that made Arithon wince, the approaching voices began to clear, and Arithon had time to wonder what a strange language it was; course and guttural, but not as barbaric as he had expected; no, it sounded intelligent and not unfamiliar.

"Let's go," he said.

They began their retreat, bending low as they hurried up the street toward the heights, hoping to elude the sentries in the twilight. But they were spotted by a watcher, who intended to kill them, but miscalculated their route and lost them in the maze of streets. As a last resort, he called aloud.

Arithon and Szaba knew they had been discovered by the sound of the cry, and worse, the voice was close above. They soon heard the clumph of hurried feet echoing off the walls. Arithon was getting that old sensation.

"They are closing the trap," he said.

As he spoke, an arrow whistled by his head. Over the wall before another could fall, Arithon took the lead, taking routes that did not lie along the roads. Like every child, he knew the back routes through the courtyards and gardens, but try as he might, he could not make the transition to a higher level. The invaders occupied the heights, with the intent of forcing him and Szaba down the hill.

Arithon turned onto Saffron Street and remembered something. "This way."

They hurried down his old jogging route; paused to look around; and then they slipped inside his father's house and closed the door.

"Over here," Arithon whispered.

In a corner of the main room, he dropped to the floor and ran his hands over the tiles looking for a crack with his fingertips. He located what he wanted and wedged the edge of his battle-axe between two rows and pried. A trap door appeared.

"Get your knife under it and help me lift."

They soon had it up, a dark hole beneath.

"You first," he said to Szaba, who gave Arithon a frown.

"Do not ask, just get in. It's a tunnel."

Szaba lowered himself into the hole and was handed the axe and bow. Arithon joined him and then positioned the heavy door into place with a satisfying thunk. It was black dark and they both stood frozen, disoriented, their eyes trying to find even the dimmest light.

"Hold on to my belt," said Arithon, "and duck your head. You will not be able to stand upright."

Szaba said nothing and did as instructed. Arithon stepped slowly at first, feeling his way along the wall with the other grazing the ceiling. The floor was smooth, but it soon began a steady decline and made sweeping turns. Szaba could hear Arithon counting his steps in the quiet of the utter blackness. When Arithon was nearing one thousand steps, he stopped as if listening, and then proceeded even slower.

"We should be close to the end," he said over his shoulder.

The tunnel did end after a dozen steps when the wall on the left disappeared into an opening. Arithon stopped Szaba in the tunnel and stepped into the chamber, pushing his toes ahead of him until he located a step he knew should be there. He sat on it for a while, and satisfied that nothing was amiss, joined the Nubian in the tunnel. He and Szaba slid to the floor, resting their backs against the wall.

"This tunnel is the reason my house was built where it stands," Arithon began in a low voice. "It existed before we came to Thera, except for the chamber behind us. Those living in the Hall wanted to have a secret escape, known only to the First Family. The best way to keep the exit a secret was to put a dwelling occupied by a relative over the outlet. This is just my third time here.

"I never thought it would be used to escape from my house. We can enter the Hall from here after it calms down above. I fear there will be many above us looting."

"Will they not find one of the entrances?" asked Szaba.

"The one in the Hall is well hidden," Arithon replied. "Doubt they could find the one in our house in the dark. You might remember it used to have a rug and tripod perched over it."

Arithon paused and then grew quite still.

"Did you feel that?" he asked Szaba.

"Do you mean the breathing of the earth?" Szaba replied.

"Yes."

"It rises and falls. I felt it when we first sat down."

Arithon quieted down in the blackness and perceived what Szaba said was true. The floor seemed to rise and fall in a rhythm reminiscent of slow breathing. The longer he focused, the more noticeable it became. Most of the movements were indefinite or subtle, but now and again the earth would heave upward; like riding a skiff on the swell.

"It is warm in here also," offered Szaba, "both the air and the ground."

Arithon, who had been sitting with his knees up and his arms folded around, put his palm on the floor. The rock was not cold as he would expect, but sunshine warm. The air, too, was stuffy.

"I do not remember how it was when I came here with my father."

And then, on one of the risings they felt a distinct vibration – not a single jolt as Arithon had grown to expect, but almost a humming in the rock. It increased until the air in the cave began to resonate with it. They were sitting inside the flute of a mountain giant and he was playing his lowest bass note. It soon became a throb which was uncomfortable, and they covered their ears to ward off the pressure.

Arithon became so agitated that he stood up, unwilling to remain in the tunnel any longer, when the last note played. He remained standing, restless, before again sitting down next to his friend.

After a while it was Szaba who stirred the silence. "The mountain is troubled. I sense mounting strength. A ... I do not know the word."

"Foreboding," suggested Arithon.

"Yes, that is your word. A powerful rage is building. The earth is troubled."

"I feel it too," said Arithon, "like I never have before."

The blackness was so complete that the eyes grew weary trying to function and ached for something to focus on. He closed his eyes and rested his head against the wall and waited. The earth continued to heave and sigh.

CHAPTER 13   LEGENDARY HERO

Pluto, counting his gems, missed the blue one, and wondered.
Had it stayed with the mortals or returned to the underearth?

Arithon was aware of someone shaking him, but he was asleep – deep sleep. The wakeful one was insistent, and he felt himself lifted to his feet. Whoever was handling him was unrelenting, but he could not hear a thing – only a muffled agitation. He opened his eyes, or thought he had, but his eyes would not work either: he could not see a thing. And what was this groggy headache? He began to awake, at least it seemed so, bit at a time, and then he could hear Szaba's voice.

"Arithon, Arithon, wake up. This place is … broken. I am standing, but asleep. Wake up! We must get out of here!"

Szaba's voice was tense – a panicked sound he had never heard from him.

"Over to the steps," he mumbled, "we can get out at the top."

Arithon was half dragged into the chamber and over to the steps; Szaba groping along like a blind man and pulling Arithon with the other. They reached the steps and began to climb on all fours as they felt their way up the stairs. At the top, the two bumped their heads on the stone roof.

"This one slides," said Arithon, beginning to come to his senses. His head hurt but not from the bump. He had drunk too much wine it seemed, like the time Sestos brought a huge krater to one of his clandestine beach parties. Funny that he could remember that, but his memory had yet to recall this present event.

Arithon then groped around to his left and found the latch and pushed it to the side, exposing a bar, which he swung down. He grabbed a handle forward of his position and pulled. A crack appeared and fresh air flooded their upturned faces. Arithon sprawled on the steps to recover his strength.

After a bout of dizziness, he slid the hatch enough to poke his head out into the open. It was dark outside the tunnel, but not as dark as inside, and one could make out the dim outlines of a large room. Satisfied that it was unoccupied, he pushed the hatch back enough to climb out and Szaba followed.

They were in a wondrous room, open and airy, with the night air washing in through columned openings on either side. There was a mural on the far wall, just discernable in the soft light. Ships of Theran design plied the waves with schools of dolphins, while monkeys and lions roamed the trees of an expansive landscape. Szaba turned to look at their entry point and realized they had emerged from under a pillar. Arithon closed the hatch behind them.

"We called this the Africa Room because of the murals. They were supposed to represent the savannahs of your continent. It was my aunt's favorite room. She and the other women used to weave and sew here – their spinning room."

They both walked over to a bench built into the wall.

"My mother spent her afternoons – the hot afternoons – in this cool and airy room. A perfect place to hide the hatch, don't you think – where the mothers worked," he said peering out. "Let's inspect the Hall and see if we are alone."

Arithon continued down the row of windows, avoiding full exposure to anyone watching from below, and exited the room through a doorway at the far end. Now in a long hall with rooms on both sides, they peered into each portal before stepping by.

"I am famished," said Arithon in a low voice. "Let us go down to the storeroom. I know we spilled much during the move that should still be there – if the rats haven't gotten it."

Arithon led down toward the lowest levels. He stopped at a storeroom halfway down and entered while Szaba stood guard at the door.

"We will have to chance a light," he said emerging with a chipped lamp. "This wick is moist. Discarded during the evacuation I would guess, but a treasure to you and me."

Szaba knelt on the floor beside Arithon, and produced from a leather bag, a piece of flint and a pinch of dried moss. After a few strikes, he handed the light to Arithon.

At the bottom of the stairs there were numerous storerooms with row upon row of pithoi too large to be transported. Three or four held their contents of spoiled wines and putrid oils, unfit for consumption. After a hurried search, Arithon was able to sweep up a cupful of grain left in the bottom of a large jar; a vessel so big he had to climb inside.

Arithon handed the cup of grain to Szaba.

"What happened in the tunnel earlier? Did I fall asleep? I only remember you waking me up."

"I think there was something, I do not know the word, but something not of our world," began Szaba. "I could hear you falling asleep, for your breathing came shallow. I too became sleepy, so I stood up to remain awake. Even while standing my head rolled dizzy and I felt myself slipping away. I slapped my face, but it did no good and this scared me. I thought the mountain was trying to swallow us whole but would smother us first – like the snake does the rat. I grew frightened; my bow was of no use against a mountain."

"I think it is the death fog," said Arithon. "People die from the air that flows from the rip vents. Two years ago, seven people died during the harvest in an olive grove on the north side – near Kankari. No wounds. They just collapsed, never to awake. We call it Thera's Breath.

"We need to check magazine number three. Grandfather told me of another tunnel when we were on Watcher's Rock.

Down the hall they entered a room filled with row upon row of Pithoi as tall as a man. Arithon stepped toward the back of the room counting the rows. At row seven he turned and walked between the jars until he came to the last in the line. The room was carved out of the foundation rock of the Hall, and the wall he leaned against was like the walls of the tunnel – rough cut, black and porous.

"The entrance is under this jar," he said, putting his hand on the lip.

"Under?" questioned Szaba. "It would take four men to lift it, even were it empty."

Indeed, the jar was pinned against the wall and surrounded by rows of equal weight and girth.

"Look inside."

Szaba peered over the edge holding the lamp and saw it was full of oil.

"Why do you grin?" he asked.

"Because I have a very clever Grandfather."

They heard the clattering of many hurried feet somewhere above them in the Hall.

Prompted to haste, Arithon took his battle-axe and plunged the handle inside the jar. It struck a thin membrane of pottery crafted to create a false bottom only a finger below the oil. It shattered to reveal an empty jar.

"Quick! Inside!" whispered Arithon as he pulled himself up to the rim, swung his leg over the lip and lowered in. His feet could not find a solid bottom but struck something that felt like a wooden handle.

"The lamp."

Arithon saw the jar had no bottom and was set over a hole, where the first rung of a ladder protruded out of the darkness. After finding the top rung with his feet, he climbed down into the jar and then disappeared into the hole. Szaba followed quickly, as the footsteps were accompanied by rowdy voices, which were fast getting nearer.

When they reached the foot of the ladder, they found themselves in a chamber like the one below the Africa Room; only it had no outlet. On the floor was a jar bottom, slightly out of round. Szaba, seeing it for what it was, carried it back up and placed it inside the hole, propped up on the ladder rails. Back down to Arithon, he lowered the ladder, allowing the piece to slip into position.

"They are in the storeroom," he whispered, "and I can hear a dog."

Still holding the ladder, Szaba leaned it against the far wall, where a ledge protruded six feet above their heads. Arithon wet his fingers and pinched off the flame as they both sank to the ground gazing up in the blackness, waiting to see if they would be discovered. They could hear the pirates' footsteps above them, and now and again, the excited yelp of a dog on the hunt, but after a while there was only silence.

"I do not hear them, anymore," ventured Arithon. "We must take a chance and try to escape."

Szaba lit the lamp once again, a bubble of light emanating from his hand and throwing flickering shadows on the cavern walls; a welcome solace in that anxious blackness. Arithon started up the ladder, when it slipped on the smooth floor causing the upper tines to hit the wall above the ledge. He would have fallen but he caught the edge to balance himself. Cursing the noise under his breath, he pulled onto the lip of the outcrop, while Szaba secured the ladder, and then followed bringing the lamp and its precious light.

"Do you hear someone?"

Szaba was turned away with his cheek to the wall as if listening.

"I hear nothing, but I feel a draft," said Szaba. "The ladder has knocked a hole in the wall and air is pouring in."

Arithon took his place by the stone and felt the cold leaking through the slit: the flame spluttered in the whispery air. Even in that uncertain light he could see it was manmade: skillful stonework with a plastering of earth.

After handing the lamp to Szaba, Arithon, on his knees, pushed hard on the wall shoving a stone inward until it plunked out on the far side.

"Where is this?"

"I do not know," said Szaba, crawling through after Arithon.

"Nor I," said Arithon. "Grandfather only mentioned it as a 'secret' of the palace. I do not believe even he ever came here."

They stood in what appeared to be the subterranean rooms of a long-forgotten Hall.

"It must have been part of the old Hall. The present Hall is three hundred years old or more."

They walked side by side along an ancient corridor, passing but one room on their left. At the end, they found that the hallway turned into another natural tunnel, which led off into the darkness.

"We must return to that room and see what it contains."

After retracing their steps, they paused at the portal, as a heavy presence washed them like a weighty wave at the shore. Arithon turned his head toward Szaba to judge its effect and beheld the Nubian, his skin shiny black in the lamplight with his enormous eyelashes blinking against the smoke. The African felt it too; Arithon could see it in his fixed gaze, and he wondered – not for the first time – what a man so displaced from his homeland must think of the obscure culture of another. Arithon's eyes focused past the African's profile to the lintel decorated with incised hieroglyphs and the jambs carved to look like elongated griffins. He traced his finger over the glyphs to brush out the dust, trying to read them as he did so.

"What do they say?" asked Szaba.

"This is the symbol for Thera, and this, Poseidon," Arithon explained, "but I do not recognize any of the others, except this one, which means 'forbidden.'"

"What is forbidden?" asked Szaba.

"To enter, I would guess," answered Arithon.

A cold air smelling of great age guarded the entrance – he could feel it standing watch before him. They continued to stand staring into the chamber until at last Arithon determined he was no coward, and stepped into the columned room, breaking the spell.

161

In the center was a large stone box: the tomb of a sovereign. Arithon ventured over and Szaba set the lamp on the marble lid, heavy with the dust of centuries.

"Let's look inside," said Szaba, noticing Arithon's hesitation, but sensing his desire.

"Together then," said Arithon.

The lid was not fastened in any way, but it was rock tight and stone heavy. After three attempts they wedged up one corner using Arithon's axe, shoving Szaba's sandal in the gap to hold it open. After raising another corner, they succeeded in pivoting the lid onto the short end after much straining. Arithon peered over the lip, the lamp raised high. He expected the shriveled corpse of an ancestor, or a smiting curse from Poseidon, but what he found relieved and puzzled him. Inside was a model ship of exotic wood, intact, but cracked with age. It was placed at a distinct angle to the box, sailing toward a stone tablet snug in the corner. Arithon lifted the tablet first.

"An old script," said Arithon. "I cannot read it."

He cradled the ship on its ends, but it split as he lifted it over, dropping the contents of its hold onto the mosaic floor: a pair of rings rolled in different directions. Arithon picked up the male, an enormous stone of deep-sea blue set in the yellow gold of an antique style. Szaba handed him the smaller female.

"The Stone of Poseidon, and his consort. But sailing where?"

The two looked at each other in the circle of the lamp's light and then peered again into the box. The earth rumbled and the flame flickered as if a door had opened.

Chapter 14 Watery Escape

Pan, the cave-dwelling trickster, thought why lure for fish when I can scare for a man.

With Szaba in the lead, they exited the tomb and proceeded down the tunnel. It was as black as the other, but now they had a lamp. The passage twisted and turned, sometimes rising, often descending; but maintaining a constant width, which allowed them to walk side by side. As they marched, Arithon tried to discern their general direction.

The storeroom was on a hall, which ran northeast, southeast. This tunnel was more or less perpendicular, so they must be bearing north-northwest across the peninsula toward the large bay of cliffs: it was the only logical direction, but there was no opening there.

After they had covered a considerable distance, the ceiling of the tunnel began to contract such that it became necessary for them to walk bent over for an uncomfortable period. But they kept a steady pace, anxious to find an end and especially anxious to know whether they would find a dead end. An almost constant quivering vibrated up through their sandals prompting Arithon to converse with Szaba about its looming power.

After a time, they were able to walk erect, but they could also sense, almost feel, a rhythmic throbbing in the air. It was different than before, more like a wave than a rumble. Arithon was about to mention this to Szaba, when the walls of the cave narrowed to a slit just wide enough for a man to slide through sideways. As they stood at the start of the crack, they could feel a wave of air moving back and forth through the opening.

"Odd, what is happening to the air here," said Arithon. "It moves back and forth through this break, as if something is breathing on the other side. Perhaps it is the lair of the Spirilon, and we will be walking into his mouth," he said.

"I do not know," said Szaba, "but we know what awaits behind. Perhaps it is only the wind through an opening from which we can escape."

"Agreed. Do you want me to get eaten first?"

Szaba smiled, rotated, and shuffled through, holding the lamp in his trailing hand to give as much light to Arithon as to himself. The narrow slit twisted and turned more than the preceding tunnel, blocking any glimpse of what lay ahead, but Arithon's nose was picking up a hint. He was about to speak when Szaba broke the silence.

"There is glow ahead of us – faint but there. I smell the sea in this air! We will get out."

But their optimism soon gave way to puzzlement. The slit ended and they entered a large dim-lit cavern. The light came from a large pool of water, which surged into and out of the cave, in the rhythm of the ocean.

"That explains the movement of the air," said Arithon, "but where is this soft light coming from?"

"I do not know, but if it were only a window, we would already be out."

Arithon stood at the water's edge staring into the pool as if it would tell him something. After mulling it over, he thought he had an explanation.

"The exit to this cave is under water, but it is not too far, and the light of day is what we see. I suspect we have crossed the peninsula. There are only cliffs on this side – no shore."

"Then we must return by the way we came," said Szaba.

"No. We can swim to the exit. It cannot be far if the light can penetrate to here."

"I am more afraid to do this than I am to risk an ambush. I do not swim as well as you, nor do I know if I can hold my breath so long."

"I will go first to make sure it is passable," offered Arithon. "Then I will return for you."

Arithon stripped naked, entered the cold water, and waded toward the far wall of the cavern until all but his head was submerged. He had deep dived countless times and was confident. He took five deep breaths to load his lungs and disappeared beneath the surface.

Following the light, he felt his way along the submerged roof, counting to himself as Mavro, the sponge diver, had taught him. He knew he could stay under for forty-five beats, but he was going steadily down: he could feel the pressure building in his ears. It was deep. As he reached his turn-back count, he crossed under a low lip and was bathed in light. Though still in the tunnel, he could see the exit ahead of him and after a moment of indecision he committed himself. If the surface was too far above his head when he cleared the sea entrance, he was not going to make it – in either direction.

Szaba waited in the cavern standing at the edge of the water, apprehension building with each heave of the pool. He lost sight of Arithon's kicking feet when he passed into the water tunnel and his mind fretted about the safety of his friend, forgetting his own predicament. Time passed. No one could hold his breath that long, and how could he help him now so far beyond his own ability to swim. If Arithon did not make it, what would he do next? They had not discussed it. But he could wait patiently, always patiently, and he could stand unflinching though the moments continued to pass – slavery taught you that if nothing else.

"I am sure he is safe," he repeated to himself breaking his usual self-possession. But time continued to pass, measured by the rise, and fall of the water in rhythm to the unseen waves.

I will suffer the fate of my friend rather than turn back, he thought after a frightening length of time had washed by. He stripped naked, and on his knees, laid the tablet and rings in his tunic. He stared at them and pondered how he could escape with them in tow. Lying on the sand next to him were his bow and Arithon's axe. How could he leave these things? Yet he knew he could not take them either – he was not a good swimmer. While agonizing over these decisions he was startled by a sound so faint that he was not sure he had heard it.

There it was again – a murmur of the cavern – an unwanted sound in the silence.

He arose and slipped over to the narrow entrance to the tunnel and stood still as the stone around him.

There were voices in the tunnel! His heart raced. He was trapped, and alone, but he knew his direction. He would follow Arithon, even if he were to share his death in drowning.

He stepped to the pool's edge and grabbed his bow and quiver – his only real treasures – and ignoring all else, waded into the water. When he was waist deep, thinking only of escaping his pursuers, a human head erupted in the pool in front of him. His adrenalin surged, even as he recognized Arithon, emerging from the ocean depths like a sea god.

"And where are you going?" asked Arithon.

"Quiet," whispered Szaba, composing himself, "they are in the tunnel."

"How close?" he asked as they both waded back to the water's edge.

"Not long."

Arithon knelt in the sand and threw his axe, and their knives on top of the treasures and gathered the tunic around them, cinching it with Szaba's belt.

A dog yelped back in the tunnel.

Arithon grabbed the bundle and threw it into the pool next to the far wall. He wrapped and weighted the bow and quiver in the other tunic, tossed them into the water, and then interlocked his fingers into Szaba's. They both waded in and were chest deep when the dog burst into the cavern. The mastiff, finding his quarry, elevated his pitch. Both Arithon and Szaba turned to see him standing with his two front feet in the water, his teeth barred. Trailing voices approached.

"Be calm, Szaba. Quiet your heart. It is a long swim, but well within your grasp. I will help you. Take four deep breaths and then we will dive."

Over they went, and had they known it, only just in time as an arrow skittered the surface near their upturned rumps.

Arithon pulled downward with the agility of one who has lived on the sea. Szaba was awkward, laboring with uncoordinated strokes and moving at half Arithon's speed. He dropped behind. The African would drown before he could even exit the cave. Get him to the light, Arithon realized, and maybe he could will himself to hold on. As they made the lip, he looked back and saw his friend was frightened. Arithon's own seasoned lungs were beginning to burn – Szaba was surely in pain. The tunnel opening was ahead and Arithon knew that it curved downward at the exit. Szaba would not know this and Arithon feared he would panic. He reached back and grabbed Szaba's wrist, pulled, and then pushed him through the portal, not giving him a chance. The surface was thirty feet above Szaba's head, but he could see it and began to use his arms and feet trying to reach the world of air. Arithon swam behind, guarding his flank, but halfway up bubbles began to issue from Szaba's nose, and he slowed. Arithon's own lungs were an agony – what torture must Szaba be enduring and could he last. Arithon knew Szaba would lapse unconscious and he would lose him here on the edge of escape – it sometimes happened: a sponge diver, too long on the bottom, would drown ten feet short of life. They were that close. He shot past and scooped the Nubian under the arm, pulling him up with determined might through the last of the water barrier. They popped through the surface like startled prey fish, gasping, almost crying for air; Szaba frantic and choking in his effort to inhale desperate relief.

"You made it – you held on, my bold friend," Arithon wheezed out between breaths.

They treaded water, squinting into the bright sun, and bobbing like cormorants fifty feet outside the surf, which dashed against the high rocky cliff.

"There is a place to land up to the left," Arithon pointed. "Can you swim there?"

"Yes," replied Szaba through labored breaths, "but are you not coming?"

"No, not yet. If I leave this spot, I will have trouble finding the entrance as I did the first time. I am going back for our possessions."

When it was apparent they had both recovered, Arithon sent Szaba on his way and dived. They had drifted from the entrance and it took him a few precious seconds to find it, forcing him again to surface. Swimming down was more work than rising and he expended most of his reserves getting to the entrance. While treading in the surf he realized with an acknowledgement to his own absurdity that he would not have sufficient air to enter the cavern and return without surfacing inside. What was he thinking? The pirates would be there this time. But their treasures were too precious to abandon and besides there would never be another chance.

The swells lifted him in a passing caress and nudged him toward shore. He gathered as much air as he could before diving for the portal. Inside he swam up the tunnel and past the lip, anxious that this could prove extremely foolish. The cavern was just ahead, and he slowed his ascent, wanting to break the surface unobserved as close to the wall as he could. He would need time to recover.

His hair, then eyes, then nose emerged into the dank air. A dozen men stood across the cavern on the narrow shore, arguing in the circle of a lamplight. One was staring straight at him and continued to stare for precious seconds before he realized his escaped prey had returned. He yelled in alarm. Bows were raised and drawn, forcing Arithon to submerge. He had not yet recovered – he would need another rest, or his escape would end short – like a hapless sponge diver.

Under water he swam to one side before surfacing again and took two breaths before an arrow cracked against the wall above his head. They could see his shadowy figure in the water backlit by the filtered glow beneath him. The hound was mad with the hunt, splashing at the water's edge with a heavy swinging tongue; his barks echoing off the surrounding stone in an earsplitting din. Arithon submerged again but rose in the same spot this time with his head tilted back so only his face broke the surface. He could see them out of the corner of his eye, shooting at the small target of his face as he gathered more air. One dart entered the pool on mark and grazed his chest – the full brunt of it muted by the water.

This forced a dive, but he found their weighted tunics in the sand, though it took too long to locate the bow and quiver, which had slipped into a fissure. He gathered them close to the exit and turned to chance one more surfacing.

As he turned to ascend, he was so startled that it took all he had to not expel the last of his air. Three men were in the water, one above – he could see his legs pumping – and two swimming down toward him. He reached into the tunic grabbed his knife and loaded his legs for a spring from the bottom. When they were within reach, he pushed off, propelling himself in the direction of the lone man treading water, intending to stab him in the torso.

But he too was waiting for Arithon and when he neared, brought down the powerful stroke of an axe. Arithon detected the blade piercing the surface and just avoided the blow. He sliced out with his knife, opening a deep cut on the man's forearm, causing him to release his weapon and recoil. At the end of his breath, Arithon emerged next to the wounded man, grabbed him by the hair, placed the knife against his throat and treaded back to the wall. As the other two surfaced Arithon used his captive as a shield against them and the archers on the shore. The man was bleeding into the water, using his free hand to hold his cut, and moaning in fear.

Arithon was trying to catch his breath, but the situation was demanding, and he would never be able to relax for his long swim. There was a momentary standoff with the men treading water only ten feet away; but others started to wade in: they would soon have him surrounded. As they advanced, he brought his knees up and placed them against the back of his captive and shoved, forcing the man forward into his shipmates and at the same time Arithon inhaled, pivoted, and dived. The two followed – he could sense their movements in the water behind.

At the bottom he grabbed the bow and jabbed it at the closest man, hitting him in the face and forcing him to back off. A few sinuous strokes brought him within reach of their prizes, and then he raced for the outlet, closely followed.

As he reached the lip, he turned as if to strike again and the pirate pulled up. Arithon ducked under and rushed through the last of the tunnel; moving fast as the frenzied exertions consumed what air remained in his lungs; they were already burning, and he had far to go. Out of the portal, he could see the surface as he kicked upward with his hands full, but his mind was devoid of any thought except the relief to be had from breathing.

Arithon broke the surface gasping as hard as Szaba had earlier and began to swim for the landing, fearing his pursuer would catch him, burdened with his possessions. But reef and rock! he did not want to drop his treasures after having brought them this far – those brigands could not have them; not without a fight.

He heard the pirate pop to the surface behind him, sputtering for his air, but in immediate pursuit. He must be just as winded and slower because of it, but he did not show it: the man was tenacious. To monitor his adversary, Arithon turned on his back, kicking hard, but he had no chance, swimming with only one arm against such a chase.

A splash erupted near the pirate followed by another. An audible thump told the third had struck home on the pirates back; a beach rock the size of a pomegranate. He halted and when another splashed in front of him, he backed off.

Arithon turned and swam toward the landing, espying Szaba hurling rocks, with serious intent. Arithon smiled despite himself: a strong-willed child pitching stones at an advancing mongrel might appear as Szaba did now.

Szaba helped him onto the landing, and allowed Arithon to sit in the surf, catching his strength. He removed the bow from Arithon's grip, fitted an arrow and said, "Come we must get higher."

Arithon stood and discerned four heads swimming in the surf heading their way.

After scrambling to higher ground Szaba struck his ubiquitous body-quiet pose and loosed an arrow. The lead swimmer was pierced, and the others pulled up and retreated.

After tying their tunic bundles around their necks, they pulled themselves hand-over-hand, up the cracks to the top of the cliff edge, throwing themselves over at last onto the withered grass. A survey of the open water prompted a crawl over to the precipice, trying to locate the pirates and deciding they were tucked under the cliff-face out of view of Szaba's bow.

"You had trouble in the cave?" asked Szaba as they caught their breath and searched the rocks below for movement. Arithon was too spent to do anything but hang his head. His eyes closed for a moment, then he stirred to answer.

"Yes, I had to surface for air, and they attacked me. I do not understand why they are so relentless. What do they think we have?"

"What we have," said Szaba.

"I suspect you are right – they guess what we have. The city is bare, and they will not find much.

"I should not underestimate their resolve again. Let us get to the *Dolphin*, before they find it too."

It was late afternoon by the time they reached the cove; their clothes now dry in the hot wind. Hyssos met them on the last ridge and hurried to greet them.

"Arithon! Szaba!" he started. "We were preparing to send a squad to look for you."

A sudden and violent tremor wracked the island causing Hyssos to lose his footing and fall; the ground appearing to undulate under them. When it ceased, they hurried the remainder of the way, relieved to be off the minacious island and on board the welcoming ship.

"It is time for us to leave Thera to Hephaestus' brooding and find Po," said Arithon to the crew.

As they rowed out of the cove, Hyssos called and pointed back up the ridge. Two men were visible against the sky, watching them row out to sea.

CHAPTER 15   THERA'S DEATH

Aphrodite's long-suffering husband, the deformed smith of the god's, his temper enraged at his adulterous spouse, rampaged in his forge until both erupted in a violence of fire and fury.

The *Dolphin* left Thera's shores and bowed into the north wind, rowing until midnight, when a watch was set while the crew slept, and the ship drifted. Szaba and Arithon relaxed, ate fish, drank wine, and fell into a dreamless sleep in the cabin.

In the soft light of morning they started into the wind's eye again. Thera was hidden on a misty horizon; no plume reaching for the heavens to mark her location. By midmorning, two ships could be seen trailing at edge of sight.

"So they pursue," said Arithon, watching from the aft deck.

"We might lose them in the archipelago," Hyssos said.

"Good idea. We will round Little Schinoso on the east and try to shake them."

The *Dolphin* remained conspicuous through the channel between an outlying islet, but after doubling the point, they increased their speed and began to circle the island. Arithon wanted to round the western end before the pirates could break around the east, like kids at chase around a tree.

"There is a chance they could round on the west and we will meet them head on," said Sestos. "What then?"

"We will run," said Arithon. "It is two against one. Do you think it a good bet?"

"No, it is not," said Sestos, "especially since it is my hide at stake. I have grown fond of it."

"No doubt," laughed Arithon. "Maybe you could relieve Klerata – he is not rowing well."

By midafternoon, they had turned the western end and found what they hoped they would not.

"I can see the two," Jaros called from atop the mast.

"Poseidon's rage!" cursed Arithon. "I am overmatched by these sea warriors."

"Turn about," he cried to the steersman. "We will have to outrun them."

After playing hide and chase for a half day, they reached the eastern side of the archipelago and broke for the open sea; reaching on a port tack. The *Dolphin* was a league out from the islands, while the pirates were still in its lee, when Jaros cried, "Ho! Hi!"

His exclamation was so uncharacteristic that the crew looked upward and saw he was pointing not astern, in the direction of the pirates, but southward toward Thera.

On the horizon was a scene so outside the ken of mortal mariners that none could speak; it was a wonder that Jaros had found a voice at all. A black cloud of proportions beyond comprehension was forming with such alarming speed that only a malevolent god could create it. A few of the crew quailed, believing Hades was rising from the sea to smite them. But something else consumed their attention. The sky to the south was distorted and wobbly, as if they were viewing the world through a heat shimmer. The distortion reached to the edges of the world and rushed toward them, closing the distance faster than thought; shearing the wave tops in an exploding spray. Before Arithon could speak, the ship was cracked with a monstrous unseen force, as if an invisible hand had slapped them. He felt a pressure on his chest like a crushing wave. The *Dolphin* heeled over on her beam, dipping the gunnel, and dumping the steersman and two rowers overboard. The mast snapped after pitching Jaros fifty feet through the air as if he had been fired out of a slingshot. It fell across the deck killing Kavos, the oarsman, and tangling the portside crew in the ropes and sail. Still on her beam ends, they were wracked by a sound, which vibrated the ship's upturned bottom, knocked three of the crew out cold, and rendered the others dazed and terrified. It was the sound of a volcano, but loud beyond human endurance. *Dolphin* righted herself and yawed to port, trailing her rigging as the shipped water cascaded off the deck.

Arithon, the wind knocked from him, lay on the deck under the sheet line with a pounding throb in his head. Up on all fours and then to his feet, he was the first to stand. His cursed ship – if she were one – was afloat: He could love her for that. But ropes knotted the deck and tangled wreckage trailed like a sea anchor twisting the ship northward. The crew, their heads

172

ringing to the point of deafness, began to rise from the ruins and follow their captain's example, unsheathing axes to part the stays.

Arithon chopped two ropes before he realized what had happened. Thera had destroyed itself. He paused for a moment, stood up straight and looked southward. The cloud was forming, boiling, rising, at enormous speed. He was transfixed by the sight, stupefied almost, but nagged by some other thought. And then all his memories of the volcanic events on Thera rushed upon him and the real world was blotted away: Roa moaning under the rubble while his mother sobbed; choking death; the heat of Kamari. His mind pitched in and out like a horizon out of focus and he could smell the stench of sulfur and the bloated bodies of trapped victims and his stomach began to betray him. A heavy roll of the deck unbalanced him, and he saw that Szaba was beside him, staring at him. A moment of gut-twisting fright washed over him and with it – realization.

CHAPTER 16 THE WAVE

Poseidon, disturbed and angered by the destruction of his gift, lashed out to announce his displeasure with a power to destroy even greater than his nephew's.

He spun around, his own master again, and saw the crew was trying to pull the mast and sail onto the deck.

"No!" he yelled, but they ignored him, their ears ringing and numb.

He crashed into their ranks and heaved the mast – the end now propped on the gunnel – with all his strained might, over the rail and into the sea. The crew stood dumb and uncertain, wondering at his intent. Had their captain been knocked senseless? He pointed at the remaining lines, which Szaba cut, not questioning Arithon's purpose or sanity.

He pointed the crew back to their stations, where they began to row. Arithon leapt to the steering oar and laid it over; willing the *Dolphin*, with agonizing slowness, to turn about. To the south. She must get her bow to the south. Jaros, forgotten in the turmoil, made it aboard climbing unaided onto the sprit as the dismasted ship began her pivot.

Before she had completed the turn, Sestos, standing on the aft deck, drained pale and steadied himself to the rail. The nearest crewmen seeing the fright in his eyes broke cadence and stood on their benches to follow his gaze.

An enormous wave was rolling toward them at an impossible speed, moving faster than even the fastest hawk. It was simply something that could not be. The crew, transfixed by the onrushing death, let their oars fall and bang in the wash as the *Dolphin* lost way. Inthos started shaking so hard he collapsed across his loom, wailing in prayer.

Arithon motioned to Hyssos to get them to their stations. The ship had not swung round, and she would need to be moving at her best speed when the wave struck if they had any hope of surviving. The crew, agitated by Hyssos back to the world of the still-living, realized what Arithon wanted and mastered themselves enough to again man their oars – and aid their ship. Hyssos jerked the crumpled Inthos off his oar and took his place.

Arithon himself could not believe the arrow-like speed of that rolling mountain of water stretching across the horizon. No wave of the sea could move that fast. Perhaps this *was* to be his death; Poseidon's Rage unleashed.

But Arithon stood his ground and held the tiller as the crew labored to bring her up to speed, Losius increasing the cadence on every other stroke. The wrath of gods could be overcome – at least that is what he had been taught. He could defy them with his will to live; he would not succumb: he would fight to the last, unwilling to surrender. This should not, could not, be his final fate.

But his stomach butterflied, and his knees wobbled in the fear which had mastered Inthos. As the wave neared the archipelago, a league distant, it mounted ever higher, until the wall of water stood to the height of the first ridge. It was a wave larger than legend; larger than anything any mariner had ever imagined in his worst nightmare. He steadied himself and muttered a short prayer in preparation for his imminent death when he noticed a curious thing. The section of the wave, which would strike the *Dolphin*, was not growing in height, but maintained its size. It would still kill them, but …

It began to crash over the first island and was indeed higher than the ridge. A few of the mariners pivoted their heads, while the others remained facing the stern praying as they rowed. Even at this distance, Arithon could see the froth, boiling with trees and dirt, as the vertical sea swept over the island, topping its highest ridge. The island would be stripped bare and all who lived upon her would die. Poseidon would be victorious, and Charon would have a full ferry in the underworld.

But he had not time to think about it or even wonder at it, for the wave was upon them. Arithon could see the crest high over his head, just before it shadowed out the sun. It had a shape he had never seen; a blue vertical cliff of water, standing straight with precious little approach. He wondered if the ship would even attempt the climb or just roll under like a toy boat in a beach surf.

"Lift your head, proud one. Lift your head."

And then the *Dolphin* did begin to climb, nose first, at an alarming rate. Arithon had angled her to the best possible position for an ascent, but even so, the *Dolphin* was almost stood on end, as the bow scaled the wall of water. Everything not tied in place fell careening down the deck or bounced about in the hold, crashing, and crushing crewmen and structure alike.

And still she climbed up and up and up, that impossibly tall wave, defying its power, even now, at the end of her short life on the seas. Arithon's cursed ship would die.

The bow encountered the rough of the wave top and then shot clear and hung there, still as a grasshopper on a wall. Arithon, his feet dangling for firm footing, sensed the ship was not sure of her next move.

More than likely she would fall backwards down the sea-blue cliff, killing them all, as she broke in half; crushed to splinters under the following water. But there was a chance, he thought, and a thrill of hope shot through his spine. She might just crest the wave and lay down upright: Po's noble creation could live; she could.

Still she hung there, unwilling to yield and unable to master her opponent; like arm wrestlers stalled at their maximum strength, both at once unsure of the outcome.

And then the grand ship moved, but not as expected. She began a slow, capsize turn, which accelerated as the wave passed, flipping the *Dolphin* over the frothing top. Arithon held onto the tiller as the deck deserted his feet but lost his grip as the ship rolled over his head with a monstrous groan.

Pushed under and caught in the chop, he was shaken and tumbled until his clothes ripped from his body. He rolled over and over losing all bearing of what was up or down, and began losing consciousness, when he found himself on the surface, sputtering and coughing, unable to get his breath. He expelled swallowed seawater in the calm ocean surrounding him, sick to his stomach, with a body that felt as if he had lost a dozen boxing matches. As his eyes cleared, he could see the wave receding on the horizon. Aegean swifts could not catch it.

What happened to the *Dolphin*, he wondered as he treaded water in a circle, bobbing on the swells?

There she sat to the west, a swim away; upright, but listing to starboard.

How did she get so far away, he thought? And then just as quickly: My cursed ship lives! Bless her!

No time to wonder how the ship had survived; his thoughts turned to the crew, as he started toward the *Dolphin*. Halfway, he encountered the body of Komba, an oarsman, floating sideways in the water, having taken a disfiguring blow to the head.

176

"I hope they are all not dead," he spluttered.

With the shortened distance, he was relieved to see three or four men moving on the deck. At least some of the crew were alive – but who and how many. As he continued swimming, something landed in the water ahead, startling him. It was a rock, or looked like a rock, but it floated on the surface. Despite all that had happened, he was curious enough to swim over and pick it up. It was warm, and appeared to be a pale gray rock, the size of his fist. He held onto it and swam for the *Dolphin*, when another rock landed near him, and then another. He released the one he held, now that it was not so rare an object, and looked up at the sky. He could see them in the air, floating down like large raindrops and beginning to patter on the placid sea.

After a calm but tiring swim, he reached the *Dolphin* and was helped aboard by Sestos – he was alive – and two crewmen. Szaba was not in sight. Sestos was clothed and must have stayed aboard somehow.

"Look," he said, pointing toward the south.

Turning, Arithon saw a dark cloud, like an intense thunderstorm, broiling from the sea's horizon to the limits of the sky, and headed their way. It was moving fast, but not as fast as the wave, so they had some time before it would reach them. Arithon coughed and grimaced.

"Take count, get the men out of the water, and assess the damage to the hull," he ordered. "Start a bailing crew. We need to right her and get underway. Thera is not through with us. I have been in that cloud before. It will choke the life out of us if it can catch us."

The men, weary from their ordeal with the wave, were spurred to action by the new approaching menace. Lightening raged: exploding through the dark cloud like white cracks in a black vase. None of the reverent aboard had any doubt the sky god and the volcano god were exchanging fire bolts. They were witness to an epic battle, which would change their world forever. Perhaps they could distance themselves from the battleground; maybe they were not the targets; only innocents about to be trampled.

Szaba was found floating with an oar under his arm, unhurt. Once aboard, he worked with those trying to get spare oars back in their locks. Others began bailing.

There was not enough time. It would take half a day to clear the water, and large sections of the oar-rails had sustained crippling damage.

177

"The hull is intact, but much of the rowing equipment is gone or broken," began Hyssos. "I think we can set a dozen oars. We have no sail or mast of course. You threw them overboard, you may remember."

"I do remember," said Arithon returning the smile, "and you are a good man to remind me."

Arithon turned to look south. The cloud consumed the horizon. Floating rocks were raining down and beginning to accumulate on the deck.

"Row slowly in two widening circles to find those still in the water and then we strike northwest to Naxos. There we can beach *Dolphin* and repair her," Arithon said, kicking a handful of the stones into the water.

Arithon joined the bailing crew, while Sestos and Szaba took up oars. The injured littered the deck onto which stones were falling in great swaths. The survivors were executing their final circle with Hyssos at the tiller when darkness replaced the evening dim; the cloud had advanced enough to extinguish the last rays of the sun. Their time was up, and the *Dolphin* was still too unwieldy with the water below; wallowing and reeling like a drunken sailor on the jetty. It took all their skill just to get her moving in the general direction of Naxos.

"Hyssos, have we left anyone in the water?" Arithon called from his cramped stoop below on the bailing crew as he felt the ship straighten out of her circular plot.

"None," came the reply.

"What is the count?"

"We lost eleven," Hyssos reported.

Arithon frowned and sniffed. The air began to smell of scorched metal and dust.

"Cover your mouth with a cloth," called Arithon, ascending to the deck. "The dust will choke."

As the crew complied, the vanguard of the cloud began to engulf them. The thickening smoke and dust burned their eyes and throat, but the shadow held no power of death, having unleashed its full fury on Thera. They rowed onward, but the deepening pall rolled and boiled past them until the islands of Schinoso, which had been on their port, disappeared in the gloom. The crew watched the light of the world extinguish with gathering apprehension. Stones continued to fall until the water was covered and the bow of the *Dolphin* was obliged to push them out of the way as they edged forward.

Hyssos, with nothing to gain a bearing, steered by the angle of the wind, hoping it had not changed. It was black dark – too dark to be on the water. The men were choking to the point of sickness and had to be relieved at the oars at short intervals. Close to midnight, weary to the point of blindness, they entered a cove on the east coast of Koufo, one island short of Naxos and dropped the stone anchor. The crew, too tired to make it to shore, fell asleep where they could with cloths wrapped around their faces.

CHAPTER 17 RHODOS

Poseidon's dolphins rode the wave of their master for a
thousand leagues, heralds to all lands of the loss of the pearl.

Roa was on the beach on the south coast of Rhodos when the pressure wave knocked her back onto the sand. She lay there stunned, and had just come to a sit, thinking about crying, when Fassa came to her side.

"What was that?" he asked the young girl, thinking the lifelong sea dweller may know more than him.

"I do not know," she replied, fear shaking her voice.

Her fear upset Fassa also, as he realized this was not a usual occurrence.

"Let's get back to the camp," he suggested, looking over his shoulder.

Fassa helped her up, and taking her hand in his, they began the steep climb to the sheltered valley which had been chosen for their temporary home. The leaders had decided their vulnerable encampment should remain hidden from the eyes of those who marauded the seas.

As they started up the new path, Fassa glanced out into the shallow harbor, where the *Palos* and the *Prados* lay at anchor, the only ships of the Theran fleet not on a mission of trade or negotiation. They were too unwieldy for anything other than massive transport, and the Therans on Rhodos were using them as a floating warehouse, their holds filled with heavy pithoi of oil and wine. The goats and sheep they had carried were grazing the fields above the ravine at the valley's head.

The Therans had accomplished a great deal. The camp had been laid out on the uneven and hilly terrain to accommodate the needs of the population, if not the individual. A communal kitchen was the first semi-permanent building constructed of sun-dried bricks with a thatched roof. A community well and a sanitary facility had been the second. Ugly and crude, they would serve for a few seasons – at least through the coming rains of winter. Those skilled in building quick, simple structures such as the shepherds were laboring to exhaustion, proud to be in the forefront for the first time in their lives.

The population apportioned the basic work of survival to all: cooking, building, hunting, and fishing were the primary pursuits. The fishing fleet was essential, though the new waters would have to be learned; the currents, shoals, and reefs – especially the local shellfish beds and fish gathering riptides. Regares, skilled in practical ways, was much sought after for advice and consultation: a salve to the widower's lonely displacement from his homeland.

Fassa and Roa gained the floor of the valley and met Alteron hurrying down to find them.

"Roa! Come I am going to the heights," he said, reaching for her hand. Fassa let go of her other and followed as they headed up the rough ground.

"The sound came from the west," he said to Roa, as if he were talking to himself.

It would take him a few moments to reach a spot where he could claim a view. He had a nagging suspicion that Thera was the origin of the noise and the thought of it made him shudder. Arithon was surely away by now.

He found the climbing to be more difficult than expected. With no trail laid down over thousands of years of occupation, he was forced to beat his way up, over and around obstacles of rock and maquis. He paused at the top of a clear rise, where he could see the valley of the encampment below and the harbor in the distance with the transports nudged stern first onto the beach.

Not much of a harbor, he thought for the hundredth time, but it will have to do for now.

Roa pulled herself up beside him, continuing to look to the southwest, while her father surveyed the south.

"What is that?" she asked.

Alteron turned to follow her point and gasped.

A rogue wave, stretching the full length of the horizon, was approaching the tip of the island at a magnificent speed; so fast, that Roa could not even recognize it as a wave, thinking it some kind of wind disturbance.

But Alteron knew it for what it was – a threat of enormous power.

"Great Poseidon!"

As the wave approached it reared up at an alarming rate, mounting and growing until Alteron believed it might never stop.

Raiha! he thought, and jerked to look down into the valley, where she was helping in the kitchen. But his eyes came back to the wave, seeing it strike the point and wash over it in its fury, boiling rocks, and trees into its froth. And it kept going, marching down the angled coast with undiminished speed.

But it performed strangely at this time. As it raked the southern coast it dragged the water away from the island, draining the beaches, and harbors of their water as it pulled it up into its flanks. Alteron watched in fascination as it progressed to their temporary harbor.

As it swept by, it drained their bay; grounding the *Palos* and the *Prados* and for brief seconds they lay like beached whales, one tilted to port the other to starboard, as if they were trying to comfort each other in their fright.

The wave that rebounded to fill the void was only a third of the height of the rogue, but it was still a thirty-foot wave. Alteron watched it return like the backwash in a slopped bucket, crashing its way across the harbor entrance.

"Oh!" he groaned as it smashed into their store-ships obscuring them in the foam of destruction.

But something unexpected happened. He saw the twins emerge from the froth, pop to the top of the boil like the marvelous ships they were and begin to surf inland on the crest of the wave.

The wave was high enough that it climbed into the valley cleft, surging inland toward their camp. But the camp was obscured from Alteron's sight by a slight rise.

"Raiha!" he expelled and started to pick his way down as fast as he could with the boy and girl in tow, silent and troubled.

CHAPTER 18 PURPLE STRANGER

Astarte Baalat bestowed to the Phoenicians a gift from the sea
so that all might know them wherever they may sail, and in this
way, she too might survive the Olympians.

A westerly wind had cleared the air enough to allow a small amount of light to penetrate the debris cloud when they awoke late the next day, still exhausted, their throats sore from the dust filled air.

"Is it morning or evening?" asked Sestos of no one in particular.

"Midday," came an answer from Arithon, his voice hoarse.

"This? Midday?" continued Sestos. "Will there ever be another sunrise?"

"Midday, and many more will follow like this, until the winds have cleared the Aegean of Thera's memory," said Arithon.

"Look in the water," voiced Jaros.

The crew kicked their way across the rock-covered deck to the starboard side, where the wave had ripped the railings off. There was no water – the surface was undulating mud, or so it appeared.

"It is the floating stones," said Arithon. "Stick an oar in and see how thick they lie."

A crewman complied and everyone gasped to see that the waves had piled the stones two feet thick in the cove.

"How can they float?" asked Leidas, one of the oarsmen. "And where do they come from? The underworld?"

"Maybe it is the flesh of Hephaestus," proposed another crewman, "and he lost the clash with Zeus."

"It is the flesh of Thera," said Arithon. "All that is left I would guess."

"Perhaps the stones will reform Thera – an island again – floating on the sea like a crewless ship," mused Sestos.

"When did you become a philosopher?" asked Arithon. "You sound like one of the poets. A crewless ship! Where did you come up with that?"

"You don't like it?" asked Sestos.

"No, I like it. It is a fitting testimonial. 'An island of knowledge and beauty, destroyed by jealous gods and doomed to float forever on the open sea.'"

"Maybe she will come to rest and be populated again," Sestos submitted.

"Or sink beneath the waves," said Arithon.

"A legend is born," said Sestos with a grin, "and a poet, too. Girls like poets, do they not?"

"Yes, girls like poets, but instead of practicing your poetry, why don't you form a work party to search the island for wood. From the look of things, the wave has swept all the trees out to sea."

"Do you think we will have another wave?" asked Sestos as if he had just thought of the possibility.

"There is a wave every time Thera shakes," started Arithon. "I doubt there is anything left to shake. Thank the gods our people had the sense to leave. We would all be in the underworld had we stayed.

"We are truly homeless now," Arithon whispered under his breath.

Six went ashore to scavenge, while repair crews salvaged what they could on the ship. With four feet of seawater in her hold and a shifted load, the *Dolphin* was hurt, and she showed it. The rollover had cracked a disturbing number of food and water jars, but the hull and most of their possessions were intact, including the ship's tender, lashed to her chocks behind the stump of the broken mast.

They had been enormously lucky – more so than they could imagine. The wave had traveled the breadth of the eastern Mediterranean, destroying ships at sea and at harbor. As the wave shallowed, approaching islands and coastlands, it had reared to heights of one hundred feet and more. Entire fleets were destroyed as far away as Egypt, and seaside towns vanished throughout the Minoan world. The blast was felt a hundred leagues away, and the rumble was heard in Mesopotamia, fully a thousand leagues distant. It would be many months before the true proportions of the cataclysm would be made clear to the survivors.

"We have collected enough wood to repair many things," began Kimilos, the ship's carpenter when they returned. "We have some sail material, but no mast and we will be short half our oars."

"There is a village – Alyko – on the southwest corner of Naxos," offered the oarsman Leidas. "My brother lives there."

"Tomorrow we will find our way there," Arithon said, "after we have the water out."

"The rocks," asked Hyssos, "can they lie this thick in open water?"

"Do not know," replied Arithon. "We will find out tomorrow."

***

The rocks were even thicker once they left the bay. At times, the oars only pushed rocks, never biting into the water.

"Why don't we just get out and push," said Sestos. "I could walk on this stuff."

"Give it a try," dared Hyssos, "but if you disappear beneath, we will never find you."

"What is that?" asked Szaba, suddenly looking ahead and to the right.

"I do not know," answered Arithon, "but I see it too."

Something white was peeking through the undulating mass. One of the oarsmen hooked it and when they got it to the side, they realized it was a sail: a white sail.

"It is the pirate's sail," realized Hyssos. "Their ship was near Ios when the wave came. For some reason, the wave was bigger there. They were broadside when it hit, and I saw their ships roll down the face of the wave."

"Bring it aboard," ordered Arithon. "We have need of it. We can sail as pirates for a while."

It was late afternoon, or so they reckoned in the dull darkness, when they turned into the harbor of Alyko. The bay, covered in rocks, was filled with other debris as well: wood shards, dead fish, birds, the occasional goat or dog, and a bloated corpse surrounded by quiet gulls pecking at its eyes.

"No, Hyssos, leave it. Proceed to the town," instructed Arithon in answer to Hyssos' question. A worried silence washed over the deck and only the creaking of the oars and the odd scrunching of the stones against the bow accompanied them the rest of the way in.

But they could not find the town. It was not where it was supposed to be. The wave had swept it out to sea and altered the beach so that Leidas could not recognize it. Going ashore, they found foundations, walls, and streets, but the dwellings had vanished. Poseidon had spent his wrath, and none had survived

"I wonder how many towns were hit this hard?" asked Hyssos, voicing everyone's thoughts.

185

"When I surfaced, after the roll, I could see the wave moving undiminished to the horizon," said Arithon. "I suspect hundreds."

"What of our families?" asked Abaki, one of the youngest oarsmen.

"Therans survived," Arithon assured, looking to the south.

Camping that night in a glen above the demolished town, Arithon was restless. It was late and everyone was long asleep, scattered about the dying fire. He lay on his blanket thinking about his home, now blown into the sea and sky, and his people marooned on other shores. An idea was beginning to form of what the destruction of Thera could really mean to the Aegean. Bad times were looming on the horizon of what he could imagine. If the fleets were damaged or destroyed, the thin thread of cooperation between cities would break as hardship cascaded through the Aegean. And many could take advantage by preying on the edges and gobbling up the weak. The Therans were weak now – no not weak, but vulnerable he decided, and he knew just who was poised on the borders. Prepared or unprepared, for the Therans, it would soon begin.

Wrapped in these thoughts, his body stiffened. He had heard, maybe just sensed, the presence of another nearby. A chill ran the length of his back, as he experienced that primal flush of being watched. He was unaccustomed to setting a guard; not on a Minoan island anyway; and he thought the southern end of the island must be empty of life. But he berated himself for such a slip. Pirates could easily be ashore. As he lay debating, nothing more could be heard and perhaps, after all, he was just edgy.

Feigning sleep, Arithon rolled over to face the beast, and perhaps catch sight of it, unlikely though it was, for the night was dark; the moon muted by the emissions of Thera. There was a glow from their night fire, but it only made the surrounding blackness more impenetrable. He lay quiet, breathing shallowly, straining to hear.

There it was again, a quiet rustle, moving away to the right above their camp. A deer perhaps. Arithon rolled over, grabbed his axe, and slipped into the darkness outside their firelight, leaving the crew to their dreaming. After a short wait, he felt he could see enough to proceed.

Working his way to the right, silent as any night animal, he stepped up the hill and into a sparse forest above the waterline of the wave. He was attempting to outflank the intruder, guessing at his direction, though he had not seen him yet. The young captain began to move faster, more sure of his stride as he became accustomed to the darkness and the terrain. Then he saw it, something large – much larger than a deer – a man possibly. But it was more a shadow than a someone, moving up and to the right. So faint was the outline that he was not even sure he had seen it. He stopped to listen, sweat beading up on his temples, his heart pounding. This was unnerving. No beast could be so difficult to see. Perhaps he was pursuing a demon, or some other unworldly danger. His sweat rolled down his cheeks and dripped onto his chest as he stood motionless in the stuffy air of the ravine, twisting the haft of his axe so hard that it burned his palm. He was beginning to quail, and fear of the unknown was conquering him. This was unwise, most unwise. Why was he doing it? He had nothing to prove.

He turned to rush back to the camp and as he did so that haunting, nagging thought was confirmed – you are a coward – and a clever one to rationalize so convincingly.

A-RE-SA-NA!! Enough! You are the son of a great man. He would not act so. He would face his fears and his foes.

He rounded and started up the slope.

When he was a dangerous distance from the camp, he glimpsed a fleeting shadow moving swift and quiet. It continued to move to the right, and if he hurried, he thought he could flank it. He doubled his stride, moving up an ever-steepening hill. As he approached the ridge top, he could detect the movement ahead. No outline, just moving blackness. And then his sandal slipped on some loose gravel and the sound exploded through the darkness. The shadow veered to one side and was gone.

Arithon remained motionless on his knees, peering into the darkness ahead. Where had it gone? It was now aware of the pursuit. Had it run away? He could not locate it again, and he was loath to move until he could.

Then the hair on his neck bristled. It was behind him; he could sense it. He stood, pivoted wildly, and swung his axe.

The shadow sprung aside and moved toward higher ground. Arithon swung again and this time his axe met with a reply. An odd sound occurred on the collision – a sound which Arithon had never heard. This was not a man, it was a demon, and he had picked a fight with it. Arithon waded in – committed. The shadow was adroit and moved with practiced grace, avoiding Arithon's best maneuvers. It was smaller, but he could sense the power that lay beneath; a worthy adversary; and Arithon knew the fight would not go his way. This Demon of Darkness was too good. As

Arithon spent his strength on their clashes, he felt as if he were being toyed with – like the cat does the mouse.

Then he caught a flash of its weapon, a broad sword of medium length. The demon used it as if it were an extension of himself, warding off or turning all Arithon's thrusts and swings. Then it moved in on the offensive; Arithon falling back and tiring. The shadow continued to maneuver for the high ground and Arithon was unable to counter, barely able to block the blows. And then as if to finish it, the demon reached skyward with its blade and two handed it down toward Arithon's weapon. Arithon held his axe aloft to thwart the blow, and the sword caught the haft just below the head and cleaved the wood, causing Arithon to topple backward and fall hard, lying with his head downhill, the head of the axe flying off into the darkness.

The demon was upon him, and Arithon felt the blade on his throat and a knee on his chest.

"Sit up," spoke the Shadow, and as Arithon complied, the Shadow pivoted behind him, the sword still on his neck.

"I am not trying to kill you," the Darkness said in perfect, but accented Minoan.

"Your actions do not back your words," huffed Arithon, out of breath.

"I do not murder in the dark," came the reply. "Besides, if I were to kill you, your tall black friend would skewer me. Even now he takes aim."

"Szaba," muttered Arithon.

"Do not loose your dart, Szaba," spoke the Darkness, "I mean your friend no harm."

Arithon could not see Szaba, but he did not doubt his presence.

Nothing was said for a moment – the tension remained and only their ragged breathing troubled the still night. Arithon could feel the weight of the demon's arm on his chest and the muscular torso at his back. He thought to turn and surprise his captor, but something told him he would not be successful. The demon was confident and assured, no trembling of exhaustion or fear in his limbs.

And then Arithon spoke, "Szaba, do not shoot. This Shadow does not seem intent on my death. He could have killed me already, had he wanted."

Addressing the stranger, Arithon said, "Shadow, lower your blade and Szaba will not shoot. You have my word. We do not murder in the dark."

The Shadow complied and removed his blade.

"Szaba, where are you," called Arithon into the night. "Come closer."

As soon as Szaba moved, Arithon could see him. The Shadow, not liking the approach, released his grip and stepped back into the darkness.

"How could you see Szaba?" Arithon asked the Darkness. "You must be a demon. You cannot be seen and yet you can see in the dark."

"I am a man, just as you, but I am cautious by nature and sometimes I do not wish to be seen," the voice replied.

Arithon stood up. "Like earlier, when you were spying on our camp?"

"Spying is an ugly word for what I was doing – investigating would be a better description," the Shadow replied.

"Are you alone?" asked Arithon.

"A dangerous question young man," replied the unseen. "But I will answer. Yes, I am alone.

"More than I would like these days," he added, almost as an afterthought.

"Accompany us back to our camp," offered Arithon. "Will you come and be seen then, Shadow?"

"You may call me Myros," he replied. "Lead the way."

They started down the hill, Szaba in front followed by Arithon with the stranger a few steps behind.

"How did you know Szaba was there?" asked Arithon, breaking the silence.

"Lesson number three," said the stranger, "always assume you are fighting more than one."

"Number three?" inquired Arithon. "And what are the first two? And are you now my teacher?"

"Yes, number three," came the reply from behind, "and as to the first two lessons – well that would depend on an answer to your last question."

"Are you a scholar? What do you teach?"

"A scholar? No, that is not my profession."

"What is your profession?" asked Arithon.

"Killing."

"Then you teach how to kill," said Arithon, surprised by the stranger's answer, and now a little uncomfortable to have him behind them.

"No, I teach how to stay alive – by killing. Something I deem you may need some scholaring on."

Upon reaching the edge of the clearing, Arithon and Szaba took a seat on the ground away from the sleeping men. The stranger sat opposite

189

them. The coals of the fire glowed a dying light; not enough for them to make out who or what he was. He was dressed in what appeared to be a long, black, hooded cloak, which hung low enough to cover his face. They offered him a skin of wine and block of cheese, which he accepted, pulling back his hood.

Arithon studied his opponent with renewed interest. He was a man approaching forty, with gray flecks that caught the light in a black head of hair which he wore in the style of the easterners; shoulder length with bangs now growing long. If he stood, he would be of average height, Arithon guessed, but he had developed upper body strength. His eyes were keen, bright, and black as pitch; they confirmed a mind of great intelligence and culture. He was not 'just another wanderer,' but indeed his face evinced the knowledge acquired in a long and varied history.

"Where are you from?" he asked before they could question him.

"We are homeless, though we once had a home," Arithon answered.

"Then we share a common plight," Myros replied, "but you do not appear long to the task."

"We are not. In fact, our homelessness was completed only the day before yesterday."

"Ah, … Therans? I thought as much. You too, have stories to tell. … What was that wave?" Myros asked, as if he had been pondering it. "I was inland atop this mountain when Thera exploded. I watched it all, including the wave, which must have been fifty cubits high or better when it hit Naxos. How did you ever survive it at sea?"

For the balance of the night, Arithon told all that had transpired with Thera and the *Dolphin*. The stranger told nothing of himself. The talk began to wane, as conversations do late at night, and the participants drifted off to sleep. Szaba remained awake long enough to set a sentry, and then he too closed his eyes, but not his ears, as he lay down to have a rest.

Arithon awoke to a day filled with smoke and ash, but the stranger was gone.

"Where is our guest?" he questioned.

"He departed earlier. Said he would return tomorrow," Ilias replied.

The crew set to work repairing the *Dolphin*, a daunting task, from the look of her, but a challenge they welcomed, using the ancient skills of their race to win back against the sea. Kimilos, in full glory, organized three teams carving oars from his patterns and hunted the island until he found a tree of marginal height – "it will have to suffice until we can purchase a seasoned piece."

The next day all hands were stationed on ropes, at the chocks, or holding mallets when Kimilos began the choreographed maneuvers that would take a horizontal timber into a vertical position, and drop it through the mast partners, down through the hold, and into the step in the keel. After wobbles, wavers, whacks, and near catastrophes it popped in with a satisfying thunk. Cheers erupted, Kimilos beamed, and Szaba nodded. It felt good. Therans would persevere.

"Impressive," came a new voice.

"You are a Phoenician!" said Arithon, turning to a robed figure carrying a pack and walking toward the beached *Dolphin*.

"Yes, my color gives me away in the daylight, but hides me at night," said Myros, lowering his hood in the last steps of his approach.

"It is a purple such as I have never seen!" said Sestos, offering a hand up. "Dark and rich. Those cost a few minas. You must be a man of wealth."

"Once I was, but no more," he replied, lowering his traveling bag to the deck. "I am a wanderer like yourselves. I would ask to accompany you, if I may." he said, turning to Arithon. "I am not without talents – some you may find useful."

"Why would you want to ship with us?" asked Hyssos, not yet comfortable with the stranger.

"My original destination was Thera," Myros explained. "I heard it was a place of great knowledge and beauty. I had made it as far as Naxos, but it seems Thera has come to me – or what is left of it. Since the island no longer exists, I request a place in your crew, for as long as it suits our mutual benefit."

There was an uncomfortable silence.

"What do you say, Arithon?" asked Myros.

"Join us," answered Arithon.

"I thank you," said Myros, with a slight bow. "I think we may make a good team."

"Perhaps you can enlighten me on your other lessons. I assume there are more than three, though I hope not quite as painful," Arithon said rubbing the back of his neck.

"They are all painful," said Myros.

Once on board the *Dolphin*, they rowed silently out of the dead harbor, only days before, the site of a thriving town.

"Make for Paros," ordered Arithon. "I believe it to be Minoan still, and not yet an outpost of the Achaeans. We may be able to secure supplies and tackle."

They rowed the great ship slowly but steadily to Paros Island, visible in the distance, and anchored in a sheltered cove that evening.

Overnight a southerly wind developed that brought a miserable amount of choking ash from the bowels of Thera, still being hurled into the sky in a massive mushroom tower which dominated the southern horizon. They struck north and hoisted the pirate sail. The wind brought the blessing of speed, but also the wretchedness of the dust and ash. The sea was still choked with the floating rocks which had_rafted_up in the tidal rips into enormous obstacles which they were obliged to circumnavigate. They tried to sail through one of the smaller ones but became mired and had to row clear. After that, the crew opted to chart a wandering course through the 'mud fields' as they now called them.

That evening they entered the large, protected harbor of Naousa, on the north side of Paros Island and were surprised to find that it had suffered the same fate as the southern facing towns. It had been washed away, and the harbor was now littered with debris and the occasional bloated body of one of the wave's victims. They anchored for the night, in one of the north hooks of land that formed the harbor entrance, and remained on board, too depressed to venture inland. That night a local survivor visited them on the *Dolphin*.

"*Dolphin*. Are you pirate or Minoan?" hailed a voice from the beach.

"Minoan," answered Hyssos, who could see a young man standing in the surf.

"Can I come aboard?" he asked.

"Certainly," called Arithon, thinking to lower their small boat. But before he could, the young man waded into the water and swam out to the *Dolphin*, and with help from Jaros, climbed aboard.

"I am Tinos," he introduced himself. "Your ship was Minoan, but your sail worried me. I have been watching you since you entered the harbor. You act Minoan and dress Minoan, but I wanted to be sure."

"We are Minoan – at least most of us," said Sestos. "What happened to Naousa?"

"Poseidon, I think," he replied, with reverence and awe. "I was on the hills above, tending to the olive groves of my father. I had stopped and was watching the harbor when an unbelievable thing occurred. First the blast

192

and noise hit me and knocked me down the slope. Then the water in the harbor disappeared. It just rushed out like an explosive tide. All the ships were grounded and lay on their sides in the mud. The whole fleet was at anchor, except for a few of the fishing boats. And then it all came back, except not like a tide, but a wall of water, higher than our tallest buildings. I fell to my knees and watched it crush our fleet, like toys in a Titan's hand – Poseidon's hand. The ships did not even have a chance to re-float, but were swept over, and their debris is all that came frothing to the surface. It hit the wharves and sloshed up to the third level in the city, crushing all that it encountered. And then it swept back out, and rocked to and fro, before it settled back to its normal height. But everything was gone."

Tears began to flow from the man's eyes, and he wiped the back of his hand across his nose. Szaba offered him a wineskin, which he accepted with gratitude and drank while he composed himself.

"Where is everybody?" questioned Arithon.

"Most of the town was killed, and the rest have fled to higher ground, afraid to sleep in what's left of Naousa," he replied. "I want to leave here, and I came to ask you to take me with you."

"What of your family?" asked Arithon.

"All were killed. We lived by the wharf. My family were traders. We owned our own ship." At this, he broke down again, and sat on the deck, where one of the crew brought him something to eat.

They spent a restless night at anchor and were away in the dark before dawn. Tinos was aboard, another homeless wanderer on a ship of wanderers.

CHAPTER 19 BALANCE OF POWER

Zeus asks who hath brought
knowledge of what can be wrought!
To mortals not west but east.
Prometheus, another beast?
Or to others shall it be taught?

A fine ash fell like dust from a beaten carpet, torturing their lungs and eyes, every league they sailed. But by midday the wind had swung around, bearing out of the north, relieving them of the ash and sail. The men were glad to row, exchanging the work for fresh air and they stayed at it until late afternoon, when they made anchorage in an uninhabited cove on Mikonos.

The First Tier was sitting on the deck after an evening meal, when Myros took his sword out from under his robe and stuck it into the deck. The hilt had a typical cross guard, with an ornate leather grip, capped by a bronze pommel; simple and functional, but the blade was unusual. It was straight, about two feet in length, and, in contrast to their bronze weaponry, it shone like silver.

"You have met Tektos before, Arithon," Myros began. "Do you know what it is?"

"I think it to be a sword," said Sestos.

"You are correct, my young friend," said Myros, with a raised eyebrow and a roll of the eyes that made them all laugh, "but do you notice anything special?"

"The blade," offered Hyssos. "I have not seen one like it."

"Hyssos, you are smarter than your young friend," Myros replied, drawing a chuckle even from Szaba.

"Lesson number nine;" said Myros, pulling it from the deck board and handing it to Arithon, "know your enemies' weapons."

Arithon felt a strange reluctance to pass it on. It was marvelous.

"Beautiful things can possess you," said Myros, reading his thoughts, "and always come with that price."

Arithon handed the weapon to Sestos.

After the sword had made it back to its owner, all were quiet, as if they, too, were overcome with desire for the object. Szaba, who had seen countless weapons of the bellicose, broke the silence first. "Of what is it made?" he asked.

"It is made of 'iron,'" said Myros.

"Our bronze is strong enough. What is special about iron?" asked Sestos.

"It does not require tin."

They all turned their gaze in unison to stare at Myros.

"Phoenician?" asked Hyssos.

"No, the Phoenicians do not have the ability to make such a metal," Myros said and then paused and lowered his voice for effect. "This is a secret of the Hittites, and them alone."

"Hittites," blurted Sestos. "Who are they?"

"No, I do not suspect you have," said Myros, "and for that you should be glad."

Myros stared into the deck. No one spoke. Waves lapped against the hull in a gentle rhythm with the night murmur of the men below deck. The realization began to form in each of their minds: a new weapon, and its making was a secret, known only to Hittites – the very name sounded ominous.

The moment was broken by Szaba who said, "The Egyptians know of the Hittites."

"Where is their land?" asked Sestos.

"To the east of Lydia and north of Phoenicia," Myros answered.

In their mental map they could place it, though they knew little of any place more than ten leagues inland. It seemed far away, and it put their minds at rest that they were in no immediate danger from people with such weapons – or so they each thought.

"Perhaps we could trade for iron," suggested Hyssos.

"Always the businessmen, you Minoans," laughed Myros, "but for this you cannot trade. A weapon that requires no tin gives the king of the Hittites an advantage. With these he can take riches – more riches than waves on the sea.

"No, iron is for taking treasure."

Silence again prevailed on the deck of a lone ship moored in a deserted bay. An orange twilight tinged the graying sea, but the evening was yet warm. A plopping splash near the ship caused Hyssos to pivot and wonder at the fish's size as he watched the ripples fade into smooth nothingness. Only a few eddy-built pockets of floating rocks still lingered here.

"How did you come by it?" asked Arithon.

"A long story. Some wine, and I will tell it."

The wind had swung round to the west and the air was clear enough for a half moon to offer a pale sleepy light for a stranger's tale. They all settled into their usual positions: Sestos sitting cross-legged as close to the center as possible; Hyssos leaning back against the gunnel with his legs straight; Szaba balancing on the new railing, as if keeping guard. Arithon leaned his back to the cabin facing Myros.

"We Phoenicians are traders, too," he began. "Not so great as you Minoans – not yet. But we have unique abilities and we are clever.

"Our one disadvantage is that we live in a vulnerable place, fought over by the empires which surround us. You Therans, until now, have had the advantage of island isolation. A conqueror would require a navy to fight you, and you have a formidable one of your own."

Hyssos nodded his approval.

"We are adept in diplomacy," Myros continued, "always trying to be neutral in a world of powerful kingdoms. We offer transport, trade, and ideas to our allies; it is our preferred relationship. We are, at times, asked to serve as the navy for a land power, but this requires us to take sides. And taking sides is dangerous.

"The Hittites came to Phoenicia two years ago and met with our king – King Daleth. They desired transport of one thousand men to Attaleia on the south coast of Anatolia. Their generals planned to march northward to quell an uprising in Ariassos.

"Their army required eleven of our greatest ships. This was a tricky negotiation, as we are under the yoke of Egypt. But because this action would transpire in an area not claimed by Egypt and appeared to be a Hittite internal problem, we agreed to it.

"Our king's youngest brother, General Mara of the Phoenician army, was asked to lead the fleet. I accompanied him on his ship.

"The Hittite army arrived and boarded our ships one night, secretive about their mission and weaponry. It took us three days to arrive at Attaleia, and by then I was knowledgeable of the virtues of these weapons and what they might portend."

"What do they portend?" asked Arithon.

196

"You can rightly guess, Captain," he said, addressing Arithon with the formality of service. "Bronze is expensive, for tin is scarce. If iron proves cheap and available, then vast armies can be lethally equipped. It means a shift in power. That is why the secret of iron is kept with blood."

Myros took a hard drink from the wineskin and passed it to Hyssos, beginning anew.

"On the morning of the day we were to arrive, our lookout spotted a distant ship, which he believed to be Egyptian, sailing south out of the bay of Attaleia.

"This was our first warning that things were not as we thought. The Hittite commander asked us to disembark half his troops out of sight of Attaleia and then had us sail into the harbor.

"This was our second warning.

"General Mara was suspicious at this point, but we proceeded, as agreed, into the bay. The Hittite commander on board our ship demanded a blockade of the harbor.

"Mara objected but the Hittites seized the ships and forced us to comply. The Hittite army, which had disembarked earlier, attacked the town. A ship on the wharf attempted to leave but was stopped by one of ours. Egyptians were on board and a few were taken hostage and the rest slaughtered. Our men, sickened by the carnage, wanted to abandon the blockade, and return home, but the Hittites would not allow it.

"General Mara was angry for having been duped into such an ugly affair. It would complicate our relationship with the Egyptians. Phoenicia was on the precipice of having to choose sides – a choice that would make the Levant a battleground.

"That night, while the Hittites were slaughtering the inhabitants of Attaleia, General Mara launched a recapture of his own ships. Eight of the eleven ships succeeded in regaining control. The Hittites were stripped of their weapons and thrown into the bay. The eight sailed for home.

"General Mara had all of the weapons transferred to his ship during the voyage back."

Arithon listened for the crew. None of the usual dice induced guffawing could be heard; only the gentle lapping against the hull. Arithon could picture them strewn about the hold, still and quiet, listening to the story on the aft deck. Secrets never remained so on a ship.

197

"The news was not welcome when the fleet returned to Byblos. The king knew a difficult diplomacy would ensue. We were all surprised at how rapidly it developed.

"Within two months both the Egyptians and the Hittites had sent emissaries to demand explanations, reparations, and," Myros cleared his throat, "someone's head on a stake."

Sestos shuddered, and the listeners shifted – except Szaba who remained impassive. He, no doubt, had witnessed it.

"The Hittites wanted General Mara – for a tortured death, along with compensation.

"The king decided to sacrifice Mara to the Hittites, and one of the officers would be given to the Egyptians – to pass him off as a rogue commander working with the Hittites.

"I was the officer to be executed by the Egyptians."

Myros paused.

"General Mara found out about the plot. He warned me. We were able to assemble a crew of shipmen loyal to Mara, and we appropriated the lead ship and the weapons."

"You escaped with the weapons?" asked Sestos.

"We did – and that is a story in itself," said Myros.

"The pursuit was immediate. They hounded us across the sea for months. Thrice they came within sight, but we managed to stay one port ahead, always moving west."

"Where is your ship? Where are the weapons? Where is General Mara?" asked Sestos.

"Patience, son," said Myros.

"We realized we would be pursued until we were caught, and the prudent thing would be to split up and lose the ship. Perhaps they would think we had gone down in a storm.

"Had I known Thera was going to erupt, I could have used it to my advantage," he said. "But I did not and so we devised another plan.

"General Mara also left with a considerable amount of his wealth, and so he was able to pay the crew and leave them in a city that will go unnamed. Mara and I retained the weapons and hid them here in the Aegean. The ship we sank.

"In all those wanderings I visited Thera once, and decided that was the place for me to disappear. But Thera deserted me before I could get back."

"I believe I saw your ship – the trader with the wide beam, yes?" Arithon said.

"The one. We stayed but a day. We may have met otherwise."

"Where is Mara, now?" asked Arithon.

"I cannot tell, nor would you want me to, if you knew him," Myros replied. "I understand you are on a mission – to seek a new homeland."

"Yes," nodded Arithon.

"These weapons," he said patting the sword sheathed at his side, "may prove useful, and I know where they are hidden."

"But do they not belong to Mara?" asked Arithon.

"And to me also," Myros replied, "and I can assure you he would trust me to make good use of them. And I can think of no better use then to bring their advantage to my adopted race."

"How much?" Arithon asked.

"In my exile I seek neither wealth nor comfort, but the acceptance and companionship of good men," said Myros.

"I am a lesser son of great men," said Arithon. "Po, the one we seek, and my father are greater Therans than I."

"Then I want to meet them," began Myros.

"You are welcome among us. May the gods protect you," Arithon said.

"Let us gather the weapons – they lie northeast of here," Myros said with a calm smile.

"Do you propose we go and get them?" Arithon asked.

"From your words, I am heartened you would have me, with or without them," said Myros.

Arithon gave a nodding bow.

"They are on the island the Phoenicians call Samos," answered Myros.

"We call it Imvrasia," acknowledged Arithon. "It is peopled by colonists from your land, I believe."

"Yes, it is," said Myros.

With the story over, the crew, including the First Tier, found their way to their sleeping areas, and a watch was set. Arithon remained at the rail peering over into the water, as everyone drifted off, including Myros, who had drunk a quantity of wine. Szaba slipped up beside him. His days as a slave had taught him much about non-verbal discourse. He was a gifted student in the protocol and expressiveness of the unspoken. They said nothing to each other, while watching the moon journey across the sky above them.

"What do you think?" asked Arithon, in a voice too low to be overheard.

Szaba acknowledged the question with a turn but only stared at him.

"What do you think of Myros?" he corrected.

"He does not tell all," offered Szaba.

"I sense the same," Arithon replied. "You are astute my friend."

"Do you trust him?" added Arithon.

"I think he is an honorable man, but he carries a burden – a secret perhaps," Szaba replied.

"Agreed," said Arithon. "What of the weapons?"

"I prefer the bow," Szaba said.

"I know that, son of Nubia," Arithon said with a smile, "but what of the swords – should we retrieve them?"

"It seems too good a gift to refuse," Szaba replied.

"That is what worries me," said Arithon. "But they are 'a secret that is kept with blood.'"

The two friends said no more and slept in relative comfort, for the air was clear and a breeze brushed the *Dolphin* throughout the night.

The next morning, the crew was up with the sun; the first seen since Thera's destruction. The *Dolphin* rowed northeast all day and spent a calm night at sea, rocking on the gentle rollers. A southwest wind aided their progress on the following afternoon but again brought the misery of Theran ash. A curious thing: the dust had changed color; it drizzled down in black and red instead of mud gray. The colors reminded Arithon of Thera's beaches: the secluded black beach had been his favorite. He spent many late nights there with his friends, drinking borrowed wine and enjoying the company of a rascal girl who had managed to sneak out of her father's house. It filled him with a hollow sadness that there was no longer a place for his memories to live save in his own mind: his contented childhood and indeed all of Thera's history had been blown to dust.

On the third day out, they entered the uninhabited island chain off the west coast of Samos and drifted into a hidden cove in preparation for a stealthy approach.

"On the northwest coast near the tall, wooded peak there is a crescent beach. Not far above the beach there is a canyon, which leads to a series of waterfalls," began Myros. "The approach is steep. We will have to do it in daylight, but we must be quick, because there are always prying eyes. We will need ten to fifteen men to carry it all in one trip."

"Ten to fifteen?" questioned Arithon. "How many swords do you have?"

"One hundred and fifty-three," said Myros with a wink.

"One hundred and fifty-three," exclaimed Arithon. "You pay much for your citizenship with a bunch of wanderers."

"I value it," Myros replied.

An adventurous crew guided their grand ship out of its anchorage before sunrise and by midmorning had located the beach. Half the crew went ashore with Arithon, Szaba, Sestos and Myros. A watchful Hyssos stayed on board.

"Through those trees," Myros responded to Arithon's question.

The hidden canyon was rugged and tight, stepping upwards through broken rock, and overgrown with tough, dwarfed trees and scrub. It became necessary for them to wade the stream and climb the waterfalls to secure a clear pathway; a vigorous but welcome respite after a week on the ship. After the third falls, Arithon wondered how any one person could have carried anything up so torturous a route. He was feeling uneasy about it when Sestos blurted out, "How did you get this plunder up here, Myros? Have you wings?"

"No wings," he replied, "but I did have help."

Help, Arithon wondered? He must mean General Mara. Perhaps he is on the island – maybe quite near.

They reached a waterfall with a pool beneath – big enough for them to swim in. It was an idyllic spot, shaded by tall trees nourished by the waters. As it was past midday, they halted and ate a meal of dried fish and unleavened bread – it had gotten wet and was spoiling. Sitting next to the pool, the four of them talked in the shade, while the others bathed in the cool waters or played near the waterfall. Crickets maintained a chorus of squeaks and tweaks in the thickets around them.

"Are we near?" asked Arithon.

"Very," Myros replied.

"Very?"

"A moment please," said Myros, who disrobed and plunged into the pool with practiced grace. He dived near the falls and was under but a few seconds before he arose, his head above the water, but not his arms. He grew taller with every step, though he waddled as if he were straddle-dragging something between his legs. Nearing the edge of the pool, he pulled a heavy pithos from the water; a large one with two handles. Sestos

201

jumped into the water and took hold of one side, helping him bring it to the bank. All crowded around, startled he had pulled such a thing from the water.

"A Phoenician trick," he explained, scraping the wax from the top plug. "We seal things of value in jars and submerge them in times of trouble.

"It was General Mara's idea to leave most of the swords at the bottom of a secluded bay after Attaleia. On our arrival in Phoenicia we possessed only about twenty. A trusted few knew we had many more. After our escape, we retrieved them and made our run."

He opened the jar and reaching inside extracted a sword similar in design to the one he carried, only it did not shine like silver, but was black-red and crusted.

"Are these iron?" asked Sestos.

"Yes. The red crust must be honed off with a stone for the shine to return. It happens to mine if I neglect it."

The other men had already started diving to retrieve the jars under the falls, and they soon had thirteen more on the shore.

"Only fourteen?" asked Myros, puzzled. "There is one more."

But they could not locate another. Myros dived numerous times until he was satisfied there were no more.

"Only one other man would have taken it," he said to Arithon pulling him aside from the group.

"It is only one jar," Arithon said, thinking the 'other man' must be Mara. "We have more than enough. Let us forget it and get back to the *Dolphin*."

"Yes, yes, let's get back to the *Dolphin*," agreed Myros, "but we cannot forget this. It concerns me."

"That Mara would take it?" asked Arithon.

Myros looked at Arithon and paused before saying, "I am concerned these weapons will find their way into the markets and they will leave a trail to me, and ultimately to you," he said.

"Do you really think they want you enough to follow you forever?"

"Iron is the new balance of power," he replied.

CHAPTER 20 THE MEAT HUNTER

Cruel Ares had delivered the metal of war, hiding the deed from
Zeus. He now delighted in the game he had wrought and
prepared to meddle anew.

"We must go into Vathi, the city on the northeast corner of the island. I
have to find my old partner," stated Myros, after they were on board. "I ask
this favor of you, though I am loath to put you or the *Dolphin* in danger."

Arithon felt an odd thrill. "What is the danger?"

"I do not know, yet," Myros replied, "and that is what I want to find
out. Lesson number two: 'know your enemy's plans.'"

"How do you know the city is still there?" asked Arithon. "None of the
others we have visited survived the wave. And there is damage to the
beach here."

"The city lies well above the sea and should not have been smashed,"
said Myros, thinking about something else. "Are there any supplies we
could buy? We need an excuse to be there."

"We could barter for a mast," offered Hyssos.

"Excellent," said Myros. "And Arithon, come help me. I need to look
like a Minoan."

"A Minoan?" repeated Arithon. "What do you mean?"

"I mean that you need to help me fix my hair, and I will need to borrow
a tunic and Minoan jewelry," he said.

"I will find you clothes, but get Sestos to help you with your hair,"
Arithon dodged. "He is always fussing with his."

"You are just jealous of my beauty," retorted Sestos.

"Sestos, of course that is true," said Myros. "Now help me. I need to be a
Minoan by tomorrow."

They spent the night at anchor and were away as the sun broke through
the tall pines on the hills above. Myros paced the deck for most of the trip.
The swords, sealed in their jars, were scattered in the hold disguised as
food cargo – the Therans had taken their first step as smugglers.

They rowed with an excited cadence, and reached the protected harbor, where they slowed their approach, and coasted in cautious and alert. The wave had called here too and not a ship was afloat. One great hull lay in two pieces: the bow pointing skyward out of the beach like a breaching whale with the matching stern section cast high above the waterline onto the rocks. Debris piled the shore, rolling in the sand of a lapping surf.

"Great Poseidon," murmured Hyssos, staring up the hill at the stranded stern.

The town, terraced upon the hill, was intact as Myros had predicted. But to Arithon, a mariner of many ports, it seemed naked and self-conscious without its fleet. The inhabitants watched them anchor from the heights as if they had never seen a ship before. There was no longer a wharf, so they pulled the tender up onto the beach, where men of the town and a press of children surrounded them. As Myros stepped about trying to be overlooked, Arithon noticed a slight bulge down the middle of his back. He also noticed, as Myros maneuvered into the background, that his hair was curled and pulled back on his head, and he had a flicker of green eye shadow in the style of a best-dressed Minoan.

Nice job with the hair, Arithon thought but did not voice; and only Sestos could have affected that makeup. Myros was also wearing a Minoan necklace, a Theran sailor's headband, and sandals borrowed from Hyssos.

The Vathians were mostly Phoenician extract, but the city was a mixture of many cultures, including Carians, Pelasgians, and a smattering of Minoans. Many on the beach were mariners of other lands, stranded when the wave pulverized their ships. Speaking Minoan with a trader he knew, Arithon explained he was there to purchase a new mast and food stores.

"No food!" came the combined and hurried response.

"The ash is killing our crops and our grapes – oh, our beautiful grapes are suffering," mourned a wizened man with the stained hands of a vintner. Arithon could appreciate this – Samos was famous for its superb wines, a mainstay of the island's wealth.

"And our fishing fleet is smashed," interjected another, not to be left out. "Just look at it."

Arithon followed his gaze past the empty harbor to the east beach. Fishermen and shipwrights alike were scurrying about the yard as if preparing for war. And they were. Like Akrotiri or any seaside town, the populace depended on the protein they could pull from the sea and the battle for survival was engaged.

The growing throng closed ever tighter, moaning, and complaining, but above all clamoring for news of the outside. The *Dolphin*, arriving unlooked for, was the first Minoan ship to call since the annihilation of Thera and the following wave. Surely, she would have information on everything they wanted to know of things abroad.

The Therans were invited to come up the hill to the town by an official-acting gentleman intent on getting them out of the pack and into a more private setting. He shooed the crowd aside and shepherded them off the beach.

The trail up the hill was broken and washed by the wave, but soon gave way to a stone-paved road of careful construction. The Vathians were a skilled and cautious people who built their town on the heights of the hill for protection against sea marauders. They were far from Phoenicia, and the Minoans did not trouble to protect them, though they traded with them.

They ducked inside a well-constructed building off the public square which belonged to the harbormaster. The participants were relaxed and polite as Arithon and Sestos took a comfortable seat and told them what little he knew of the other islands, and a long tale of the last days of Thera.

Myros slipped out the doorway, choked with a curious crowd, and walked unnoticed up the street. He was not sure where he would find his old shipmate, but he knew how. Wandering the town like a dog on the scent, he greeted everyone he met in Minoan, pretending to be a curious tourist or mariner. Nothing escaped his eyes: the layout of the streets, the through-streets, the dead ends, the open doors, the gardens, and the stairways. The warrior kept track of where people were working: the potter's shop, the carpenter, the rope maker's shop. Many women were cleaning last night's ash fall from the streets or gossiping at doorways: he greeted all openly. A cart, pulled by a hunched-over man, lumbered past when he spotted what he was looking for: a group of young boys playing in an alley. They were throwing pebbles at a stick man balanced on top of an upturned pot.

"Can I have a throw?" he asked in Phoenician.

The boys looked at each other, grinning sheepishly, until one found his voice.

"Sure," he said.

One of the smaller boys handed Myros a pebble but instead of throwing it he addressed the lead boy, "Show me how."

Flattered, the boy stared at the target and then lobbed an overhand. His pebble just missed, clattering onto the paving stones of the alley to lie in the pile of other missed shots against the back wall. He tried again with the same results.

"Something like that," he said.

Myros side armed his projectile and it found its mark, knocking the target off the pot and onto the stones. The boys gasped and giggled.

Myros, addressing the boy said, "You are a good teacher. I have never done that before."

A young boy ran and put the target back in its place and attempted to sidearm a throw just as Myros had done.

Keeping the lead boy's attention, he praised, "I bet you are the top boy in Vathi."

"I am," he replied. "At least I am the top boy of Murex Street and I am already nine."

"I bet you know everything that happens around here, too," said Myros.

"Most everything," the boy said, thinking he probably did not know everything, but it sounded important to say so.

"Good," continued Myros. "Perhaps you can help me. I am looking for someone. Someone who would be new here – say in the past six months. He would be Phoenician like me."

"Are you not Minoan?" interrupted one of the other boys.

Myros looked down at the boy and chastised himself for his lack of discipline – a deadly mistake in the wrong place.

"I meant he looks about like me, but he is a Phoenician," he corrected.

The boy looked puzzled and then his eyes brightened, "I know a new person who looks like you, but he is not Phoenician."

"What is he?" asked Myros.

"I do not know. He dresses different – maybe an Egyptian or another easterner," replied the boy, "but he looks like you and he came here a few months ago."

"Do you know where he lives?" asked Myros.

"He bought a big house on the third tier. My father says he is rich," said the boy.

"Where is this house?" asked Myros. "He is a friend of mine."

The boy walked out onto the main road and stepped into the sunshine, looking for a wider view, and said, "That one up there."

He pointed to a prominent house perched high on the hill. Beyond it were yellowing orchards and ash choked gardens, and beyond that pastures for the sheep and goats.

Fool, he thought. … Buys the biggest house in town.

"Thank you," he said to the young boy, and tossing another pebble at the target, stepped up the street.

The house stood a hundred feet from its nearest neighbor, most likely the former home of a wealthy landowner. It seemed to grow with every step as did Myros' uneasiness. There was no activity around the house and not a whisper could be heard within. A quick decision turned him into an alley, which ended on a trail leading up into the groves of grapes and olives. His sandals, damp from the surf, caked over with ash before he reached a stand of ancient olive trees. He wound his way through the shade to the left. After finding a large tree above the house, he sat down and leaned against its trunk, noting the ill-treatment he was giving to Hyssos' sandals. The hill was deserted; neither farmer nor herder walked the knee-high grass. Perhaps they were down in the town gawking at the mariners.

He picked a piece of grass and played with it in his teeth while he surveyed the estate. He became preoccupied with a pot leaning against a shadowed wall on the rear patio.

"Careless," he muttered through the grass stem.

Just about to rise, he caught an indistinct movement through a window on the top floor. His head drooped like a hunting cat deeper into the high grass. Someone was there in the shadows; heavy motion; a man. The shape crossed the floor again, moving away.

Myros bolted with unexpected speed off to the right, out of the view of the window, and down to a back wall of the patio. He slipped over the wall; a Demon Shadow once again. Crouching down next to the pithos, he recognized that it was indeed what he hoped it would not be; one of the sword jars.

An opening to the house was to his right. He stood and slipped in.

***

Arithon and Sestos were still answering questions, when Arithon's mind became more and more fixed on Myros – or rather the absence of Myros. Szaba had remained motionless through it all, standing against the wall, ever watchful of all that might threaten. Arithon made brief eye contact and cut his eyes to the door. Szaba remained still, unblinking, as if he had not seen the gesture. Sestos, who had captured the floor, made a joke about the pirate's ship being plundered asunder by the hand of Poseidon. The whole gathering laughed, including Arithon. When he looked up, Szaba was gone.

Szaba walked up the streets, wearing his bow across his chest like a decorative sash. It was so much a part of him that no one ever wondered to think that he carried a weapon. The African walked with purposeful strides as if he knew where he was going – but he did not – and was planning to either be found by Myros or discover some activity, which would lead him there. After negotiating a few levels, he stopped in the street to look and listen. Five boys were playing in an alley nearby.

"Are you looking for the easterner, too?" asked a boy at his side in Minoan, wide eyed at the sight of a towering black man standing on the paving stones in front of his home.

"Yes, I am," said Szaba.

"He is in that big house at the top," explained the boy.

"Thank you," said Szaba.

"Why are you black?" asked the boy, as Szaba started up the hill.

"The sun," said Szaba, pointing up.

***

Arithon and Sestos had finished their stories to the satisfaction of the crowd and were ready to discuss business. The press of those listening at the door and in the street, realizing the entertainment was over, began to disperse.

"We want to barter for a mast, if you have any available," began Arithon.

"A mast? You will have a hard time finding a mast here."

"The shipwrights and carpenters are felling every tree of girth on the island to build a new fleet, and besides there are foreigners in port who lost their ship and they are anxious to buy a new one."

"Foreigners?" asked Arithon trying to sound disinterested. "Where are they from?"

"The east. Most of the shipmen are Phoenicians, but the others are strange to me," he answered, glad to offer something of interest. His job as harbormaster was boring most of the time, and now with no ships at anchor, it was even more tiresome.

208

"Strange? How are they strange?" asked Sestos.

"A brutish bunch," he said, lowering his voice and cutting his eyes to the door. "The leader is a sinister type. Name is Zorkos. He has been pushing everyone around. We will be glad to see them leave. Maybe you could take them with you."

"No, I do not think so," said Arithon. "We are at capacity. Besides, I am sure we are not going the same way. Where are they now?"

"Do not know," he answered, "but they were all worked up two days ago, trying to get a ship to take them to the west side of the island. When they could not get one, a bunch of them went off on foot at a smart pace. Some are still here in town."

"They are?" said Arithon standing abruptly, and then tried to recover with a nonchalant: "Well, we must be off ourselves. Need to find a mast if we can."

Arithon and Sestos left the harbormaster and hurried down the switchback toward the ship. On the beach, six men, feet spread, were watching them descend.

"This doesn't look good," whispered Sestos.

"Be calm," said Arithon, but feeling a jab of fear himself.

The men cut them off before they could reach their tender. Arithon had never seen the race. They were not tall, but stocky. They had swarthy complexions with noses thick at the eyes that gave the appearance of having been broken. All had black, curly hair and beards with hairy arms and shoulders. Not a handsome race, they carried an air of cruel intelligence.

Hittites, he thought.

"Your ship?" one asked in poor Phoenician.

"Yes," answered Arithon in Phoenician also.

"We want," replied the stranger.

"No," said Arithon.

This was not the answer the brute wanted, for he and Sestos were seized and their arms pulled behind them. The squat nosed leader brandished a familiar looking sword in Arithon's face.

"Yes," he said with and evil grin, made even uglier by a missing tooth.

* * *

As Szaba approached the house he could hear a fight – a vicious fight. Before he could decide what to do, a figure dived out the top window, somersaulted across the first story roof, and then leapt to a courtyard wall, sword in hand. The man pivoted off the wall, erect and balanced. But four of his attackers were out the door and upon him.

It was Myros. A Myros unveiled. Now in his realm, he fought with a ferocity that astounded even Szaba.

The sword he held in his right hand, a dagger in his left. Clang! He met the first thrust sword on sword. A quick kick to the gut of another sent him back on his rump. Pivoting, he thrust the dagger into the neck of the one behind. Szaba, swift and sure, fell the fourth. The two alive retreated.

"Quick," he said to Szaba when they met, "they will try for the *Dolphin*."

The two ran down the inclined streets, Myros in the lead. At the top of the switchback leading to the harbor, he and Szaba ducked behind a low wall. Sestos and Arithon were next to the tender looking out to the ship, each pinned by a man behind. One of the Hittites was yelling at Hyssos to beach the *Dolphin* and threatening to kill Arithon if he did not comply. Hyssos, reluctant and unsure, was ordering the crew to their oars.

Szaba, sitting with his back to the wall, turned to Myros and said, "I can take the two."

"From here?" questioned Myros.

"Yes."

"Do it."

Szaba placed an arrow on top of the wall, then took a kneeling position to fit another. He stood erect, pulled, and released in one movement. He nocked the other, pulled, and released again.

Arithon heard the arrow in its last few feet of flight and felt the jerk of the man holding his arms. He wrenched free as the other arrow pierced Sestos' captor.

"Swim for it!"

The nearest tried to cut them off, but he, too, took an arrow, tripped, and fell face first into the water. The remaining two fell back, as Szaba and Myros charged onto the beach.

Unwilling to leave the tender, Myros pushed it into the water, while Szaba stood by.

"Come," said Myros when he had it afloat.

Myros manned the oars while Szaba took a braced position on the stern sheets and watched a confused crowd gather, including a squad of Hittites attending to their fallen. Moments after Sestos and Arithon had scaled onto the deck, the tender bumped up against the *Dolphin*'s side and first Szaba then Myros scrambled up and the crew secured the boat. Arithon, dripping-wet and shaken, gave the order to out-harbor, but before they could get her spun round, a dozen more warriors jogged onto the beach, hot and exhausted.

An armored man stepped out in front, brandishing an iron sword.

"Mara!" he bellowed in a deep and menacing voice. "You cannot hide. I will find you."

Myros stepped up to the rail as the *Dolphin* pulled away, and answered, "I will not forget Jalu."

Arithon steered her out into open water and turned east to fool the watching eyes, and when she disappeared over the horizon, he brought her back to north and they slept that night on the open sea.

CHAPTER 21 MYROS UNCLOAKED

Apollo blew the scent of laurel across the seas, seeking Daphne and truth.

"He called you, Mara," started Arithon.

The ship was creaking and groaning its way through a hazy morning of Thera-dusted skies and he and Myros were on the aft deck watching the terns following their wake.

"Yes," Myros replied.

"Yes?"

"Yes, I am Mara. Myros is my assumed name – I prefer Mara."

"You lied," said Arithon.

"Yes, I did," he said, then paused and waited for Arithon.

Arithon watched a tern wheel over and crash into the water. Others followed in formation, spearing headlong into the water in a tumultuous cascade of spray and feathers; corking back to the surface and flapping free of the soaking; an arching sardine trapped in their beaks.

"I know a bit about lying," Arithon said. "I did the same once – over a fig. 'Between the gale and a lee shore', my father had said. I thought about that for many years – my lie and father's words. I decided that a lie is a dangerous wrong – just as the gale on the lee shore. But we choose the one we are willing to face and endure the consequence. I chose a lie to save a boy a beating – and it cost me my word; but I made my choice."

"Your destiny, my fine Theran, is a leader of men," Mara said.

"A king once said that to me," said Arithon. "I do not know what it means."

"The tern does not know what it means to fly," said Mara gesturing, and his eyes flickered.

The strains of a deep baritone wandered up from the hold: Kimilos was singing an old carpenter's song and the two men listened.

"Who is Zorkos?" asked Arithon.

"You heard?" said Mara.

"Yes, the harbormaster of Vathi said he was the leader of the Hittites."

"He was the one who called to me from the beach," said Mara.

212

"You know him?"

"Oh yes, I know him well," said Mara. "He is half Hittite. His mother was Phoenician. He is a hunter."

"A hunter?" asked Arithon.

"Yes, he hunts humans," said Mara, "and he is good at it. He hunts me even now."

"Why does he hunt humans?" asked Arithon.

"Because he gets paid for it, and … and he enjoys it."

"How could anyone enjoy hunting humans?"

"People with hate can do most anything, Arithon."

"Does Zorkos hate you?" asked Arithon.

"Yes, mostly because I am so much trouble to him. I suspect he will get many talents of silver to bring me back to Hattusa. This was not the first time I escaped his pursuit."

"Then he will continue to pursue you – and us," said Arithon realizing what that might mean.

"Yes, he will," said Mara. "And you think rightly when you say 'us.' He is hampered without a ship, but he will soon remedy that, and the chase will continue. It worries me that he knows of the *Dolphin*. He will use it to his advantage – I know that much about him. I know a good deal more, but it is terrible and unworthy of discussion. I regret that you are involved in my plight."

"I might regret that too," said Arithon remembering the toothless Hittite gripping him on the beach, "but I learned in Africa to embrace an ally – especially one unlooked for. The foes will always be numerous – the friend scarce."

Mara nodded but said nothing.

"What happened to you at Vathi?" asked Arithon.

"My second in command was living there. He wanted to live in a Phoenician colony – I thought in obscurity, but in that I was wrong. It was he who helped me hide the swords and we had agreed to leave them hidden until I returned. My plan was to retrieve them, with your help, and then go to Vathi and convince him that he was not safe there. If he had waited for me, he might still be alive."

"Then he is dead?" asked Arithon.

"Yes, when I got to his home, I knew something was amiss. I slipped in on the lower floor and found him dead in the kitchen. They had tortured him to death – a bloody mess. Undoubtedly, he told them of our stash and the main press had marched off to retrieve it. I cannot believe our timing: after all these weeks we get to the swords only a day before Zorkos. They must have found our tracks at the pool and then ran back to Vathi."

"What happened in the house?"

"I was angry about Jalu and slipped up the stairs to deal with the guard," said Mara, glancing at Szaba. "I broke lesson number five: 'do not get angry – it clouds your thinking.' While I was up there, four more arrived and a fight ensued. The great African found me at an excellent time."

"One of his many skills." Arithon said and then turned to Hyssos: "Put down some distance before we rest."

***

Those not rowing worked on the repair of the ship: crafting oars and thole pins, replacing the stays, and modifying the pirate sail with sail material in the stores. The *Dolphin* had been the pride of the mighty Theran fleet, and many now wondered if it might not be the only ship in all of Minoa. The last two port calls had unnerved the crew, and many were despondent. Their world was in turmoil from the destruction left by the wave, and their survival of it had made them a valuable article – too valuable it seemed; enough to cost them their lives. Only days ago, ships had roamed the Aegean by the thousands, and now it appeared that they were the lone survivor; the others smashed to splinters. What is more, the ports had been a welcome destination heretofore; a looked-for comfort at the end of a journey. With no port to call home and no port to call on they were truly homeless wayfarers, and the Aegean was suddenly a much more dangerous place. A secure home never seemed more attractive than now.

But they were glad of their young captain, if not the new passenger, and gratified to be on a mission to find the *Swallow* and its captain.

Arithon had much on his mind, so he spent the day rowing, which he did from time to time. It relaxed him and helped him think. He had developed potent upper body strength for which he was proud, and he wanted to maintain it. Often he would swim for extended periods after they anchored or go ashore and jog like he used to on Thera, but for now he was content to relieve starboard station four and help the crew propel their floating home northward.

Worried about their ability to obtain food, the crew turned to the sea to supplement their stores. Sestos spent the day at the stern rail teaching Szaba how to fish in a variety of ways. Mostly they netted herring from which a wonderful soup could be made, but late in the day they were able to hook a huge tuna, requiring the help of Jalos and Pserimos to reel it in, spear it, and get it up over the gunnel. The whole ship, including Arithon, still rowing on bench four, cheered when they wrestled it aboard. Toward evening, a group of dolphins emerged to play around the ship, leaping in unison off the sides or darting and dodging under the bow of the ship as she plowed through the water. Mara, alone most of the day, walked over to Sestos at the rail.

"Do Therans eat dolphins?" he asked seriously.

"No," Sestos answered quickly. "They are like us; they make their home on the sea. Besides, it would be bad luck to kill our namesake, don't you think?"

Mara's eyebrows jumped, as if he just realized this.

"We certainly cannot afford any more bad luck," he said.

"What is that the rowers are singing?" he asked. The crew had broken into song as they often did; this time at the appearance of the dolphins.

"Oh, it is an old song," explained Sestos. "Do not doubt you can't understand it – sort of a sailor's jargon. Nonsense mostly, but it goes something like this:

> For the tired and hapless ro'er,
> A song to lift the languid oar
> From journey long
> The sailor's voice a hopeful song
> And the answer from the shore
> return again
> Row on by sun and moon
> The oars call the rhyme
> Our voices keep the tune
> The strokeman marks the time

Thunderstorms had been forming all afternoon and a wind was building out of the southwest. Hyssos and Pserimos had thought to spend the night at sea, but now advised that they sail north and east to find a cove on the mainland. Turning her to run on the wind, they began to row hard for the sheer thrill of making the grand ship cut through the water as fast as they could propel her. Rain began to splatter in large drops as a small storm cloud pursued and found them riding the waves. They were soon drenched, but continued to row at an unsustainable speed, switching rowers to maintain the pace, and laughing exuberantly at their own foolishness; a welcome release of all the tensions they felt.

The sail became dangerously heavy from the soaking, but still flapped madly causing the belaying pins to rattle and snap as the makeshift mast strained under the load, creaking and pitching, loose in the socket. The sea lashed and seethed off the hull, phosphorescent foam boiling in her wake; but they kept at it, until they sighted land. Exhausted from the exertion, they reefed the sail and coasted easily, while the black clouds rushed ahead, beating them to the shore.

Just before nightfall they found a protective cove and dropped anchor for the night. Sestos and Jaros prepared a feast of the large fish, roasting it on the large brazier, and after emptying a few wineskins and consuming the meal, the crew fell into a deep and satisfying sleep.

The next morning brought a cool, steady rain that washed the decks clear of the heavy ash accumulated since the eruption. The crew stayed below deck, playing games, and making small repairs to personal items. Arithon created a necklace from a skein of leather chord and attached the ring with the signet blue stone he had found in the hidden tomb. He was not comfortable enough to wear it on his finger, not knowing its history, but he was proud to wear it around his neck – a token of the past glory of Thera.

He lay back on his small bed, listening to the rain, when Mara asked to enter the small cabin.

"I see you have a new piece," he said sitting down on the opposite bench.

"It is from Thera, long ago," explained Arithon. "Szaba and I found it before we left Thera for the last time."

"Where did you find Szaba?" Mara asked as if he had meant to ask it before.

"Szaba? Szaba is from Africa. He is a Nubian," answered Arithon.

"I know perfectly well that he is a Nubian. I mean what were the circumstances that brought you together?"

"Circumstances?" questioned Arithon.

"Yes," said Mara. "Why is he so loyal to you? He protects you – always."

216

"I did him a favor once and … well, it's more than that," said Arithon. "He and I trust each other. He knows what I am thinking, and I know he will always be there when I need him."

"Yes, I see that," said Mara, looking down through his knees. After a pause he asked, "Do you trust me?"

"Yes," said Arithon with no hesitation.

Mara snapped his head up.

"Why?" he asked. "Do you have reason to trust me? I would wager Szaba has reasons to trust you."

"Szaba and I have a … bond," said Arithon. "With you it is an instinctive feeling. General Mara did the right thing at Attaleia. He was a leader who did the right thing, even though it cost him. For that I would give him a chance of trust."

Mara paused and met the gaze of the Theran and then said, "Then let us throw in together and test that trust."

Arithon sat up on the bench, eager and said, "You are knowledgeable in the arts of war, it would appear. Szaba told me of your fight at Vathi. He was impressed; and Szaba is not easily impressed. I feel the danger all around us now. Every port, every race, every country in the eastern sea is disrupted by Thera's destruction."

"Go west, then," said Mara.

"West? West to where?"

"There are many lands to the west, and many wonders. I went there once. I would go again and maybe stay this time. It would be far enough from the Hittites to begin anew."

"But, until then — the art of war."

"We Therans are adept at naval engagements," started Arithon, "and we are handy with an axe and spear, but we know little of land battle or sword work. We are now blessed, or maybe cursed, with those marvelous swords. Could you train us to use them – you know, lesson number seven or thirteen …"

"That I can do," said Mara smiling. "It is lesson number eight: 'know your own weapons and how they can best be used.'"

"You know, Po used to teach me lessons also," said Arithon.

"I will be glad to meet him here soon," said Mara.

The rain had stopped, and they had both gone out on the aft deck to stand next to Szaba. Hyssos was readying the ship to leave. The sun had emerged and was beginning to evaporate the moisture on the deck and in the sail.

Arithon moved to talk with Hyssos, leaving Szaba and Mara alone.

"Why do you protect Arithon?" asked Mara.

"Is he not worthy of protection?" questioned Szaba. "You seek to protect him, also."

"Yes, I do. He is a light in my darkness," replied Mara. "But why do you?"

"I was a slave. He bought me to save my life and then freed me the same day."

"Oh, I see," Mara replied. "You owe him a debt."

"Not debt – I do not have the words …" corrected Szaba, "I protect him because he is a noble spirit like my father."

"And his son," said Mara, patting the Nubian on the back.

CHAPTER 22 FIELD OF FLOWERS

Demeter felt the shortening of days as she stepped through the fields and watched guardedly for he who would come to snatch her daughter.

After raising the anchor and pivoting, they rowed out of the cove, which like many on that coast was surrounded by sheer cliffs; no way in or out except through a narrow entrance from the sea. Swallows which nest on the protected north face were diving down the precipice in a suicide drop, only to pull up at the last minute, skim the surface of the water, and rotate their bodies back and fro, so that their wingtips appeared to wave farewell to the inlet's overnight guests.

"There were thousands of swallows on Thera," said Arithon, "just like these.

"I used to watch them as a boy when we went egg hunting on the cliffs inside the inner bay. They would crisscross the water at great speed, avoiding each other with a slight tip of the wings as they passed. I used to wonder how they could so narrowly avoid the collisions. My mother loved them and used to say they brought good luck. Mother paid a Theran artist to decorate our bedrooms and the first floor living spaces with all kinds of things, but Mother loved the swallows most, and there was at least one on every wall in our house."

"Where is your mother now?" asked Mara.

"She is with my father on Rhodos with a large contingent of Akrotiri."

"Rhodos," repeated Mara, nodding his head.

"I liked the pictures of the ladies at your uncle's house," said Sestos, with a spreading smile.

"You would," said Arithon with fake disdain.

"You did too. Do not deny it. I saw you staring at them more than once."

"Perhaps you are right. We probably miss the women more than we want to admit."

"Oh, I will admit it," laughed Sestos, "I miss them, and I am sure they miss me also."

"You're sure?"

"No, not really, but I am sure they miss you.

"Arithon was the most desired man on all of Akrotiri," said Sestos now to Mara. "All of the young girls hoped they would be wedded to him."

"Do men take a wife at your age?" asked Mara.

"They could, and many do, but not all. Most bondings are arranged, but a few are not. And there are other women, also," explained Sestos. "Actually, it is quite complicated."

"It is always complicated – in every land and with every people," said Mara chuckling.

"Did you have a wife, Mara?" asked Sestos.

"I did," he answered, "but no longer."

Sestos did not pursue the discussion. Szaba had listened to the entire conversation and as usual, said nothing, but he had an odd look on his face throughout the interchange, occasionally looking south, presumably to his homeland.

"Was your mother Thera's Queen?" asked Mara.

"No. Therans are led by an oligarchy – the First Families. You might call them nobles."

"The King you spoke of?" asked Mara.

"King Selleres – of the Minoan League," answered Arithon.

"He means the Federation," inserted Sestos. "He always uses the old name."

Mara and Arithon turned to Sestos, who looked guilty for his interruption, but continued under their gaze. "Well you do. You sound like one of the codgers. The League was a joining of the Cyclades – when Thera held sway. It predates the Federation – The Minoan Federation if you want to be proper about it."

"And how is it that you are suddenly a history scholar?" asked Arithon.

"What do you mean 'suddenly'? I am a scholar of many things."

Arithon snorted and said, "History?"

"Well ... yes –."

"Where did you hear it?"

"From old Cardanos," Sestos answered a bit sheepish, before explaining to Mara, "He died in our last earthquake."

"What were you and old Cardanos up to?" asked Arithon, sensing one of Sestos' hidden schemes.

"Well it does not matter anymore. But if you must know, we were brewing. Experimenting with a wine and pitch combination that was going to be very popular – if we had finished it."

"So, I see! Was this a pursuit for wealth, or women?" Arithon laughed.

Sestos ignored him and jumped back on the other tack. "Cardanos knew much about olden times. We talked late many nights in his cellar. Crete needed us because Therans are the best mariners and shipwrights in the world. Old Selleres made a pact with Arithon's grandfather."

"I wish that Thera still lived," mused Mara. "I had thought to retire my warrior status."

***

They rowed persistently all day at a strong pace, but a north wind – a gale really – common to the Aegean and known to all who sail there, kicked up in the late afternoon. Forward progress soon became difficult, and at times they appeared to be making no headway at all, rowing head-in to a dangerously strong wind that continued to breeze up. They were hoping to make the south side of the Chios peninsula, but even this looked out of reach; the waves had been building with the wind, and two had topped the gunnels, soaking the portside rowers. After an hour of steady rowing and little progress, Arithon called the First Tier to a huddle on the aft deck.

"This meltemi could hold for days," stated Hyssos "and the men are frustrated."

"Let's pull up until it wanes," offered Arithon.

"There is a scattering of small islands or do you want to chance a harbor on the mainland?" asked Hyssos, agreeing with the decision to stop.

Arithon looked at Sestos and Mara, neither of which showed any preference.

"Mainland. We can hunt better there."

After numerous tries, they found a cove in the lee of the wind, with a gentle beach and so little surf that they slipped her stern gently up onto the sand after anchoring her bow. The wind showed no sign of letting up, and believing it might hold for days, they decided to take the opportunity to hunt for fresh meat. Therans were adept at hunting fowl, boar, and the occasional stag, using both spear and bow. One group led by Hyssos succeeded in killing a boar on the first day, which they roasted on the beach for a wonderful feast. The countryside was rough and hilly with

221

small streams running through tight, narrow valleys; some forming gorges along part of their length and winding off in unknowable directions. They saw no one and no sign of habitation.

For the next several days, the wind continued unabated. Mara organized sword lessons for the crew and remained on the beach, teaching whoever was not out hunting at the time. The crewmen were mariners first, but most had experience with the bow, spear, or axe, and were capable and earnest students; strong and coordinated. They were making progress and Mara was pleased, but they were far from a strategic fighting unit.

Arithon, as in all things, was first pupil; adeptly learning the basic movements, and even some of the nuance of the art. He and Mara were soon sparring in heated duels that exhausted them both. Mara was a stout and capable adversary, impressively clever at his craft. He was consistently able to best all sparring partners, including Arithon, but he knew the young man would soon be formidable and a worthy opponent.

Arithon and Mara were sitting on the beach after a particularly intense session, sweating and out of breath, when Sestos emerged from the brush, coming back with a hunting party. They were excited about taking a deer and were hollering at those on the ship to come and have a look. Sestos walked over to the two on the sand.

"Arithon. Mara. We found something on our hunt today."

"Yes, I can see," said Mara, looking over at the kill.

"No, not the deer – something else. It is about an hour from here. Come I want to show you."

While the crew was dressing the deer and preparing for another unique meal, the three set off into the brush. After a steep climb, the small stream they had followed from the bay, split, and Sestos took a right turn, finding his way to a cross ridge that allowed them to summit to the next parallel ridge without crossing the valley. They then began a descent into the far valley that ran at an odd angle to the prevailing lay of the land; a sort of hidden valley, which did not make its way directly down to the sea as the others managed to do. After a quarter hour of difficult walking down steep and unstable slopes, the valley flattened out into a small meadow. But the meadow was not a natural occurrence; the scrub had been cleared and it was being cultivated. There were flowers growing in abundance, and the land was managed to promote their growth via a crude, but effective, irrigation system taken off the small stream, which wandered through the valley bottom.

"Are these –," started Sestos, who was quickly interrupted by Mara.

"Yes, these are poppies, and they are producing opium," he said, turning over one of the flower pods to show the score marks.

"Who is doing this?" puzzled Sestos. "There is no dwelling that we can find."

They walked among the flowers, wandering apart from each other as they surveyed the area. Mara paused and then walked casually over to Arithon.

"We are being watched," he said quietly, his head still, but his eyes darting side to side.

"Are you sure?"

"I am certain of it."

"Are we in danger?"

"Lesson number five," he said with a small grin, "'assume you are.'

"Make your way over to Sestos and then both of you move slowly down to the right. I am going to feign returning the way we came. Listen for me. I will either call for you to run for the ship or come to me."

"I am anxious to have a rump of that deer," he said in his normal voice. "I am returning to the ship." He took off at a normal pace and soon disappeared into the brush.

Arithon walked over to Sestos who had stooped down to look at something.

"What did you find?"

"Someone has walked here. I can see where their feet have broken the grass."

"Yes, Mara says we are being watched. He intends to outflank them, I believe. We are to move down to our right – but not too fast. He will need time to get up and around."

"Where do you think he is – the person watching us?"

"I am not sure, but I sense the presence, also," said Arithon as they moved slowly through the field, pushing the flowers aside as they walked. "I do not know why I sense it, but I do."

***

Mara had entered the brush and when he was sure he could no longer be seen, he turned to his right and started up the hill at a heart-pounding clip. The warrior could move unexpectedly fast and undetectably quiet when he wanted to and was proud of his ability to do so. He kept his head up, always surveying the scene around him, taking note of the lay of the land and the best direction to take him where he wanted. He knew where that was – about half-way up the ridge and then back around to his right. He had good instincts on land, having spent much of his youth in similar terrain.

This was different than many Phoenicians, who spent most of their time in maritime pursuits. But he was the fourth son of the royal family, and his profession was chosen for him. The older brothers managed the population, politics, and the family's wealth – most of it tied up in the merchant trades. He was predestined to be the soldier; had complied; and was undeniably a good warrior, having mastered the art at a young age, and accomplished what many in his profession had not – staying alive.

He was high up the ridge, and out of breath, when he began his move toward the unseen watcher. Small scrubby trees lined the banks of the trickle which ran down to the meadow below. Crossing this in a quiet leap he continued before turning and starting down. He slowed his pace to aid his silence, and pulled Tektos from its scabbard, carrying it backwards in his hand, to avoid self-impalement in steep and unfamiliar terrain.

He was soon even with the meadow, which he could barely see through breaks in the brush as he slowed his walk. Satisfied with his progress, he sat down to watch, and trained his senses forward. He could catch the occasional murmur of Arithon and Sestos in the meadow below.

Continuing to remain motionless the sweat from his labors began to pour down his back, soaking into the loincloth. He was getting impatient – something he did not like to do. Patience was important for survival, especially now, but he was irritated that he could not find the watcher. No man should be able to elude him this long.

He duck-walked down the slope, unwilling to stand up, worried about a headshot from a bow. He wished under his breath that he had a bow, or better yet, Szaba.

There were a few taller trees on the edge of the stream; pine trees with dense foliage at their tops. Unable to locate anyone, he paused and found his eyes drawn to those trees: conical towers of green in a brown and tangled scrubland. His eyes were wandering the slope, when he half saw, half felt a movement in one of the middle trees.

Someone was in the tree.

He popped from his reverie and concentrated on the spot. The first objective was reached; he now knew the location of the watcher, but were there others?

He decided that they were in no immediate danger, so he stood and slipped quietly closer. Since he was the trespasser, and feeling cocky, he thought it only fair to announce himself.

"Are we in your field?" he called in Phoenician.

The watcher, suddenly aware that there were also strangers behind him, was out of the tree and on the ground, quick as a squirrel, and scurrying down along the stream in small leaps and bounds.

Mara gave chase, but his prey was quick, finding unseen paths through the underbrush, as he quickly outdistanced Mara.

Mara was about to give up the chase, when he heard a scuffle ahead of him, followed by the sound of Arithon's voice. After circumnavigating a half dozen more breaks of brush, through which the watcher had somehow found a direct path, Mara emerged into a small clearing, no more than ten feet in diameter, to find Sestos attempting to hold a young squirming boy in his arms. Arithon was offering greetings in different eastern languages, trying to calm him down.

"What have you got?" asked Mara as he approached out of breath.

The boy quit squirming.

"A young girl," Sestos answered while holding her in a bear hug.

"A girl?"

"Yes, I am sure, her tunic came up when I tackled her. I still remember the difference."

"Good! A good skill to retain," quipped Mara.

He noticed that she was undeniably a young girl, maybe eleven. Her hair was disheveled, but she wore a hair ribbon that Arithon recognized as Minoan.

"Do you know Minoan?" he asked her.

"Minoan," she repeated as if she understood the word, but not the language.

Arithon pointed at the hair ribbon, and said, 'Minoan,' then pointed at himself and said 'Minoan' again.

She looked puzzled for a minute, but then seemed to get his meaning.

"Let her go," said Mara, taking a seat on the ground and instructing Arithon, who now held her legs, to do the same.

This move comforted her, but she scooted backwards several feet, still facing them.

"Opium?" questioned Mara, pointing at the meadow.

"Opium," she repeated and then stood and motioned for them to follow her.

"Should we?" asked Arithon.

"Let us find her source," Mara proposed.

And so the young girl led them skillfully through the valley, but turned halfway down and walked over the ridge into the next ravine and down its gently sloping floor, until it began to open up into a wider gorge on its way to the sea.

On their way, the three talked.

"What do you know about opium?" asked Mara.

"It is valuable, and we trade it with everyone; the Achaeans, the Egyptians, the easterners such as yourself. It commands a high price."

"Where do you get it? Do you grow it?" continued Mara.

"No, we do not cultivate it," Arithon stated. "We leave that to others. I have been with Po when we traded for it in Ashkelon. Traded it to the Egyptians for wheat, which we traded on Crete for jewelry and pottery."

"I have heard it can be found south of here on the coast," offered Sestos. "Most of those supplies are taken to Crete. They are specialist with it."

"Do Therans use it?" asked Mara.

"The healers do, and sometimes the devotees."

"What about the others?"

"No, we avoid it, because it can enslave you, or so the stories tell."

"It can. I have seen it in the royal houses of the east. Those who use it often, must often use it. Soon, they can think of nothing else.

"But what of the Cretans? You said they use it."

"They have many ceremonies and festivals. They burn it almost like incense," said Sestos, echoing the commonly held belief on Thera.

"I have been told that they use it on the bulls – the ones the acrobats vault," Mara remarked.

"This may be true," added Arithon, again remembering his youth and his trip to Knossos.

"I attended once. I had guessed they used something to dull the bull's responses.

"There are other ingredients also – the king told me," Arithon said, but he was thinking of something else from that day.

226

"You will have to tell me about the bull celebration sometime," said Mara. "I never got to see it, but it was known as far away as Byblos. It is the theme of many art works. My family had a krater with scenes of the acrobats and the bulls."

"Perhaps we can go, when we return from Limnos after we find Po," offered Sestos. "I never saw it either."

"I would like that," concluded Mara.

She led them to a small hidden trail that wound its way cleverly through the valley. It appeared to be a game trail, no wider than one made by boar or deer. There was a small side rivulet off the main creek that formed a side canyon, which the girl entered, motioning them to follow. Inside behind a hiding break of trees and shrubs they came upon a single hut: a farmer or herder's abode of wattle and daub construction. A woman ran outside when she saw her daughter, followed by three armed strangers. She was clearly alarmed, and pulled the girl tight to her, an expression of anguished fear pinching her face. The mother's clothes were simple and functional, including a black stained apron, but her hair, tied in ribbons on top of her head, was a style recognized by Sestos and Arithon.

"They are Lydians," said Arithon, as they entered the cleared area.

"We are Minoan," he then said in a startlingly strange tongue.

Mara looked at him, much bemused by the sound of the language. "What was that? It sounds as if you have an olive stuck in your throat."

Arithon smiled, but had no time to respond, as the woman, looking a little less anxious, began talking rapidly.

Arithon held up his hands to stop her, unable to discern what she was saying.

"Tell her we want to trade for opium," said Mara.

"Minoans to trade for opium," translated Arithon.

She understood and motioned for them to sit down on a crude bench a few yards from the hut, but out of the sun. It was a workbench as evidenced by the chips of wood, bone, and stone littered on the ground around it. Arithon imagined the man of the house must have spent many hours sitting there, repairing or making the necessary tools for survival in a lone setting such as this. They must be entirely self-sufficient, he reasoned from all the shards lying about. Grabbing her daughter by the hand the mother disappeared down a trail which obviously found its way along the valley to the ocean. They could hear the waves in the distance.

While they waited, they talked.

227

"Why do we want opium?" asked Sestos. "Did you not just tell us to be wary of it?"

"As you said, it is valuable, and I can foresee a need for it.

"It is useful for the wounded," he added in a way that said, 'but we do not have to talk about it.'

The woman suddenly reappeared with a man weathered and doughty, though he carried himself with poor posture: his shoulders sagging forward and his head bobbing as he walked. The young girl was not with them, having been stashed in a secret and hopefully secure hiding spot. He was armed with an old, small dagger, and smelled of goats and sheep, but he was carrying eight sea bass, which the woman took into the hut, leaving the men to their business.

The farmer was visibly nervous, almost jumpy, but willing to talk with them, especially since he was so outnumbered – and by warriors, or so he judged them to be. He knew a smattering of Minoan words but was not fluent. Arithon guessed that he usually sold his opium to a middleman and was not used to dealing with the traders. This bode well, as he would be used to lower prices. Always the businessman, Arithon had a good idea of the market value of the opium.

After a short discussion, made awkward by language, they arrived at a deal. Sestos lost his dagger at the outset, and they eventually had to have the hunched rustic down to the ship to complete the transaction. They ended up with a goatskin bag of medium grade opium, as assessed by Tinos, the young man from Naxos, who was skilled in its gradations. Mara was pleased to have it aboard. What he had in mind for it he would not say, but he showed no desire to handle it and was content to have it stored safely away in the hold.

The carpenter and the crew had searched the hills near and far during their sojourn and had found and felled a tree of excellent proportions on the same day as the opium purchase. The wind tapered off the following day, but Kimilos asked to remain at harbor for two more days, while he prepared a new mast. Most of the crew took turns, working it to the right dimensions with their tools and all were on hand to step it into position. Jaros in the meantime had taken it upon himself to paint a giant bull's head on the white pirate sail, in the manner of the Minoans. He worked for days creating a pigment from tree bark and a red clay he stumbled on during one of the hunts which set the whole affair in motion. It was merely an outline, but meticulously executed and praised by the entire crew. It had been fifteen days since the wave had almost destroyed the *Dolphin* and she was again a mighty ship, crewed by hardened survivors. The complicated repairs were obviously not of shipyard quality, lacking the refinements made possible by better tools, but nonetheless she was again the most magnificent ship afloat on the eastern sea.

They started out the next day, waving to the little girl of the poppies, who had come to the beach every day since her discovery and was there to watch them leave. What she thought of such an odd array of men, she could not express, but she was genuinely sad to see them leave. Had they known it, she wished for them to take her also, and end her isolation from a world she could only dream might exist.

CHAPTER 23 SLAVE TRADER

Dionysus beheld the tragedy and drank to forget.

The wind, stiff and steady when they began to push north, moderated the same evening and was nonexistent the next morning, allowing considerable progress as gauged against the coast sliding by on their starboard. On a muggy afternoon they sliced through the narrow strait east of Chios, where the gentle breeze wafted an herbal fragrance not unlike the rosemary of their own remembered land. After another night on an islet, the travelers struck due north across open water, bound for Lesvos. Arithon was getting anxious to complete this journey. His instincts told him that all was not as he had left it in the southern Aegean, but he also felt a strange sense of purpose – fate perhaps – in this mission. They needed the *Swallow*, if she were still afloat, and they needed Po even more.

Unwilling to take the time to hug the coast they had to spend a night on the waves, a small row crew working to maintain their position. It was a calm and beautiful night, the first crew was preparing for the drift, when Mara found Arithon on the aft deck, preparing to retire for the night.

Arithon had rowed most of the day and was more than ready to sleep, but he always enjoyed talking with the Phoenician. Mara was wise in many ways that Arithon had yet to mature into, and Arithon eagerly absorbed all that he offered. He leaned back into the wall of the cabin, his hands behind his back.

"What is your plan, when we get to Lesvos?" asked Mara with interest.

"Plan?" said Arithon yawning. "I guess I do not really have one, other than to find Po."

"Do you not think that Po would have made his way back before now, if he had not found trouble?"

"Yes, I assume he encountered trouble."

"Might not we encounter the same trouble?"

"Yes, I see what you mean," Arithon said, sitting erect from his slouch.

"Do you have a plan?"

"No, but we could talk one through – with the First Tier – if you would like."

Not tired, as he was only minutes before, Arithon gathered Hyssos, Sestos and Szaba to continue the discussion seated on the aft deck.

"What do we know of these islands?" Mara began.

"That they both begin with 'Luh'," responded Sestos, feigning a word game.

The group ignored his attempt at humor.

"Lesvos is very large and close to the mainland. Limnos is four days to the northeast," explained Hyssos. "The main settlement on Lesvos is on the northeast corner.

"A mix, we believe, of Pelasgians, Lydians, others. But we also have rumor that the Achaeans are beginning to infiltrate these islands near the spont."

"We did not enjoy our last encounters with the Achaeans," Arithon understated. "There are indications that they have plans of dominating the Aegean – and us. The Achaean privateers appear to be state sponsored, and I believe they act as Achaean scouts, testing and probing our strength and resolve."

"Then Po may have found misfortune at the hands of the Achaeans, as you did, but he did not fare as well."

After a long discussion, it was decided that Sestos and Mara would go ashore to ascertain what kind of a welcome they could expect. Arithon lay awake thinking for a long time before he finally drifted off to sleep.

The company rowed the next day on a placid sun-drenched ocean, sheltering on the southern end of Lesvos that night. Arithon had never been to Lesvos and was surprised at its lush forests. The coast appeared uninhabited, so they sent out two hunting parties early. Szaba accompanied one and they returned with enough rabbits to feed the crew, and Hyssos' group took a large boar, though Pserimos sustained a ripping leg gore.

***

The following evening, they put Mara and Sestos ashore a short walk from the town and then moved south to a secluded anchorage. Mara had been with them twenty-one days. The plan was to stay out of sight and pick them up the same time next day. But they never returned to the *Dolphin*, though the ship waited at the rendezvous point.

"They are not coming," said Arithon to Szaba sometime after midnight.

"No, Mara would not be late."

"Tomorrow night, you and I go – quietly."

***

Sestos and Mara walked together down the main road toward the center of the town.

"Some wave damage – you can see the water mark. But there is something else wrong here," observed Mara. "These people are troubled."

"Are you sure?"

"Look at their faces. They are curious, but afraid to engage."

"This place is bigger than I thought," said Sestos as they began to wind their way through the maze of tight streets. "Where are we going?"

"Down by the water, to make our deals."

It was a rich port, which boasted a large quay and merchant homes above a seawall: the lower story served as an office with a storehouse in back. The trader and his family lived above. There was often a window which provided a view of the harbor from which the mistress could keep an eye for new arrivals.

But Sestos and Mara did not arrive by a visible ship, and so they were able to avoid the usual onslaught of proprietors pressing them to the dealing table in their office.

"What are we looking for?" asked Sestos.

"These traders specialize. We need to find one who deals in meat."

"Meat?"

"Yes. Human meat," said Mara.

"Oh, you mean slaves."

"Yes, the final destination of many a wayward mariner."

"What do you mean? We are free men."

"How do you think they get slaves?" asked Mara.

"War."

"Yes."

"And many are born to it."

"Yes."

"And I guess some are taken in raids – especially women," Sestos stated, as if completing the list.

"And many more are free men in the wrong place at the wrong time; waylaid and captured, to be sold into slavery. I think this is what happened to Po."

"You do?"

"Yes, and it could happen to us if we are not careful.

"Here, let's try this one," said Mara, standing in front of what looked like a prosperous trader. "Hello," he said through the open door.

An overweight man emerged from the cool shadows. "Hello," he replied. "Minoan?"

"Yes, we are Minoan."

The man yelled up the stairs in his native tongue, received a curt reply, and then turned to his new customers. "I told the wife she should keep a better look out for the ships, but her reply was obscene," he said with a smile.

"Oh, our ship is –" began Sestos before Mara interrupted him, "not going to be here for many days, yet."

"Oh, I thought you were here to trade," he said looking disappointed.

"We are comparing prices," explained Mara.

"Oh, then my name is Steno, and I have the best prices in Thermi. What is it you are looking to purchase?"

"Many things," said Mara, "wood, wine, spices, slaves."

"I trade in all but the slaves. Dagieri trades slaves," he motioned down the street. "Come in, I have not spoken to a Minoan in ages."

They went inside and spent a polite time discussing prices and drinking vinegary wine. Steno was attentive, wishing to hear news from the outside as much as make a sale. He was surprised at the destruction of Thera, and listened in awe, unable to even take a drink for fear that he would miss an important detail. The wave he knew about but did not attach it to the end of Thera.

"Yes, we heard the boom that afternoon and the wave arrived before sunset. We did not lose any vessels, but many other harbors did. How did Minoa's fleet fare through it all?"

"I do not know," said Mara. "Have you heard?"

"Not much, but one rumor has the southern fleets destroyed and all of Crete in disarray."

"You heard this so soon?" questioned Sestos.

"Yes. From the," he lowered his voice and glanced at the open door, "Achaeans."

"Achaeans?" questioned Mara. "You have news from the Achaeans? So fast?"

"Yes. Their fleets are mostly intact, and they are here now."

"What do you mean 'here now?'"

He lowered his voice another rung, "The Achaeans are here in ever increasing numbers. They bully us for cheap goods and slaves. The First Family is cooperating with them, but I think they are just trying to avoid an invasion."

"I saw no Achaeans here," Sestos said.

"Oh, they are here all right. There is an Achaean quarter in the city – hundreds live here. Their ships are always here."

"I saw no ships."

"They left three weeks ago, but they will be back – maybe today. They are never gone for long. You should trade with me today before they come back. I do not know how they will react with you in port. They want to control everything."

"Then we will return this evening. We will check with Dagieri for slaves."

"Very good, gentlemen, but come back to me for the wine and grain. I promise to beat his best price."

They walked down to the quay and looked out to the harbor as if expecting an enemy ship. "Achaeans," Sestos said, "they have been nothing but trouble. Do you think they have Po?"

"If he is alive, I think it is a good possibility. Let us go talk to Dagieri."

Dagieri was as wealthy as Steno, but he was a very different man. He was not a member of the aristocracy of Thermi, nor would they want him to be. The first families shunned him, and for this he hated them – he hated everybody in truth and would shackle and sell them all to a short, wretched life.

So he turned his attention to the accumulation of wealth convinced this would someday make him better than they. He sensed in the Achaeans a new power he could exploit to further his goals and he had been working with them for years. They were good customers, paying him both for the slaves and the information he could provide. What did he care if they had a desire to displace the first families – better for it – it would leave a void he could fill.

Mara and Sestos found him sitting on the front steps of his office dressed in clothes, though expensive when purchased, were dirty and too long worn. He was an ugly man: short, bald, fat, and hairy of limb, made even more ugly by his slovenly disposition.

"Dagieri?" voiced Mara.

"What," he replied, squinting up at them, the sun in his face.

"We were told we might purchase slaves from you."

"Yeah, who told ya?"

After a once-over he added, "And what might a Phoenician, posing as a Minoan, want with slaves. Didn't you know Minoans do not dabble in the slave trade? What are you really up to?"

"You are perceptive," Mara said. "Could we take this indoors, perhaps – away from unwanted ears?"

"Perhaps. But do not think you can rob me with that sword hidden under your cloak. I have a guard inside."

"Appreciate the warning," said Mara in a tone, which made Dagieri a little uneasy.

Nevertheless, he rose and led them into his office, yelling something to someone unseen.

"I told the guard to keep an eye on you – at least until I figure out your game."

"Game?" asked Sestos.

"Yes. What you two are really about. Now you boy, you are a Minoan," he said, pointing a fat finger in Sestos' face. "What are you doing in league with this Phoenician slaver?"

"Our partnership is newly formed," answered Mara.

"I hadn't heard that the Minoans and the Phoenicians were working together. This is awfully queer."

"Competitors will sometimes work together if it suits each. We hear that the northern islands are partnered with the Achaean mainlanders, for instance."

"Sometimes – if it suits us."

"So. Slaves," said Mara, trying to focus the discussion.

"What kind dya want?"

"What kind?" puzzled Sestos.

"You *are* new at this young Minoan. Yeah, what kind?" he repeated. "Dya want servants, cooks, spinners, field workers, shipmen, miners, or dya want what everybody wants: bedroom girls, young and pretty. Or boys depending on your taste."

"We would look at all," answered Mara.

Sestos for once in his life was struck dumb. The thought of a bedroom slave was causing his mind to reel.

"Look at him," laughed Dagieri, "he's drooling about having a girl to fuck.

235

"You fuck them whenever you want and any way you want," he said with a grotesque smile. "And they have to smile and like it, or you can beat them," he said leaning forward with a clenched fist. His breath smelled like cheap fish and rotting teeth.

Sestos was quickly becoming uncomfortable, as the filth of Dagieri's mind poured from his mouth, a dribble of spit rolling down the edge of his fat lip.

Mara interrupted the slob to bring the discussion back to business.

"Yes, we are interested in bedroom girls, of course. But we are in the business of acquiring wealth, just as you. We want slaves who are in demand – that will command a good price in the right markets. We need slaves for shipmen. It is our business after all, and we need experienced mariners."

"What dya got to trade?" asked Dagieri.

He did not like these two. They were up to something and they reminded him of the aristocrats of Thermi. They thought they were better than him. Well, he was ready to drive a hard trade and be done with it. Besides, he had a slave girl, recently purchased, lying upstairs and all this talk had made him want to go and rape her, and he planned to beat her – that excited him.

"We have many things to trade," responded Mara. "What slaves do you have to purchase?"

Dagieri had sold a large lot, almost twenty, a week ago to an Achaean. He had kept the young girl because she pleased him, and he was loath to sell her until his desires were spent. He was expecting a new shipment from a Carian raider any day, but he was not sure if he could stall these two, and he was not convinced they were really in the slave trade.

Maybe, he thought, they are just new at it. Perhaps he could get an outrageous deal. His business mind and his greed began to outweigh his distrust of these two traders without a ship.

"I can get you any slave you want. It might take a few days. I have a girl upstairs that I wanted to keep for myself, but I could part with her for a small sum. Would you like a young fuck?" he slathered at Sestos.

"Oh, I am sure he would," answered Mara. "I will tell you what we want. Do you need a scribe?"

This last statement made Dagieri rage inside, though he hid it. He did not need a haughty scribe to do his business. He could remember and calculate any deal in his head. Who needed a scribe? That was for the aristocrats like that pompous Steno.

"No, I can remember," he hissed.

"We are looking for shipmen, say ten oarsmen. And we need an experienced man, also, say one who could navigate and manage a ship. We also need metal workers – as many as you can find. And add say, six young girls. They would be pretty, would they not?"

"Does Lydian mean anything to you?" he asked with a prickish grin.

"Should it?" replied Mara.

"They are the prettiest girls you'd ever fuck. I can tell you that."

"Ok, Lydians it is. But what about the rest?"

"Uh, let me see? Those other skills are in high demand. The Achaeans are buying up the oarsmen. And well, metalworkers are specialized. So is an experienced mariner – a navigator and all. That's going to cost you."

"Have you had any like that recently," asked Mara, "or are these skills just too hard to come by?"

"No, I can get them. How long can you wait?"

"Not long on this trip, but we can come back soon. What can you give me today?"

"How about the girl upstairs – I will fetch her." And with that he huffed his girth up the stairs leaving them alone.

Sestos started to open his mouth but snapped it shut when Mara shook his head.

They heard talking upstairs and what sounded like someone falling on the floor. There were footsteps on the stair and then Dagieri emerged pulling a rope. Tethered to the other end was a young girl, naked, her hands tied together in front. There was also a boy, about fifteen, who appeared to work for Dagieri. He took a seat on a bench over by the wall.

Some bodyguard, Mara thought. This Dagieri is filth.

But Sestos first noticed the girl. She reminded him of his youngest sister – she was only a child. He shuddered to think of what she endured.

"You don't like. I can tell," he said. "Maybe too young for you."

In a way he was pleased he would not be making the sale, but it made him hate these two even more. Who were they to refuse something he valued? His hate was wrestling with his greed.

"No matter," he continued. "There will be something on tomorrow's shipment that you may find more to your taste."

"Good," said Mara, sensing the conflict in Dagieri. "What is coming tomorrow?"

"A trader from Limnos."

"Good," said Mara, wanting to move things along. "Now, what about a navigator? We have an immediate need for one of those. Do you know of any?"

"I had one offered to me months back. The Achaeans on Limnos have him. They want a good price for him, too. In fact, he's a –"

Dagieri stopped. His eyes darted up; his mind racing.

"He was expensive," he said as if to complete his sentence.

"No doubt," said Mara, noticing the change in Dagieri.

"What would you trade? A navigator will cost you a lot more than a pithos of wine or a basket of olives."

"We have something I am sure you would find of equal value," answered Mara.

"What? Tell me. I am getting tired of this."

Mara lowered his voice and said, "We have opium."

Dagieri's eyes opened.

"Opium," he repeated.

Dagieri then turned to the boy and spoke rapidly in a strange tongue. The boy left.

"I told him to fetch my scales," Dagieri said. "Now, how much opium do you have, and is it quality?"

"We have enough, and it is the finest. Syrian grown. I brought it myself from Phoenicia," he lied.

"Show me. I want to see it."

"It is here, under my cloak," said Mara, tapping a goat bag slung from his shoulder, "but I think I would rather weigh it tomorrow, when you have the slaves."

This angered Dagieri. He cursed them for wasting his time and accused them of having nothing to trade.

Mara noticed the boy had not returned with the scales. Uneasy, he stood and motioned Sestos toward the door, but the office erupted in a fracas.

Two men burst through the front door, the first wielding a club that he used to strike Sestos in the side of the head. Mara pulled his sword as he pushed past Sestos who had crumpled to the floor. Mara's aim, deadly and true, pierced the assailant through the heart; blood erupted in a fountain. He turned to deal a blow to Dagieri, but his cloak was pierced from behind.

The blade deflected off his left shoulder blade and traveled into the muscles causing Mara to roar in pain.

He pulled forward off the blade and wheeled to behead his attacker, when another club, held by Dagieri, struck his sword hand, crushing two fingers and causing him to drop his sword. The remaining assailant knocked him to his knees and then raised a sword.

"No," Dagieri laughed. "Don't kill him. I can sell him to the mines. Hand me the goatskin and that marvelous blade."

Mara remained kneeling on the floor, trying to hold his wound to staunch the flow of blood, while the guard cut the strap from his shoulder. He was getting lightheaded, and he was worried about Sestos, out cold on the floor, blood leaking from the side of his head. He heard Dagieri scream, "It's sand!"

He heard the whoosh of the blow and remembered no more.

CHAPTER 24 RAID ON THERMI

Satyrs played their lonely pipes throughout the night,
wandering the high hills above the plains, unused to sharing the
high darkness with those that pass on two legs.

The next afternoon Szaba and Arithon readied for an unexpected mission: find and save their friends from an unknown adversary. Mara's wariness of the previous days only accentuated Arithon's disquiet and underscored his own lack of experience. How could he possibly fare better?

Arithon slipped an axe into his belt and watched himself do it. He added one of the iron swords just in case. Szaba strapped one on to supplement his bow.

Like fading shadows, Arithon and Szaba hiked through the twilight avoiding anything which looked like a trail or a road. They passed through orchards and olive groves, arriving at the heights above town with the last of the light. There they sat huddled under a thick shrub, watching windows appear in the homes below as full dark descended. The two friends murmured past and future as the night progressed and a quarter moon cast a vaporous glow on the mists hugging the contours of the land.

"There are dozens of fishing boats on the shore, Szaba. The wave must have spared this port."

"No ships though."

"No there is not, but that might not be unusual."

Slowly the lamps began to extinguish: one here in the foreground, and then another on the far side, but as bedtime approached dozens all at once, as if the people in the city kept similar schedules.

"I never watched this before," said Arithon. "A town going to sleep. The stars echo in response; a bright one here or there, and then hundreds all at once."

"You see beauty in many places," said Szaba, "even here. But I am uneasy about this town. It swallowed Sestos and Mara."

The two rested until the town was asleep, and then started walking down the dusty path, which led to the first homes. It was quiet and so were they. There was lamp light in the odd home or two, but they avoided those and made their way to the harbor.

When they reached the street of the traders they walked openly, feigning a purposeful errand, but all the while looking for a slave trader, retracing the planned steps of Mara. As they walked, Arithon read the marks on the doorpost. There were symbols for wine, oil, wheat, linen – all the usual goods, and the dwellings looked like your typical trader's home. He paused outside the one with a slave icon. As he was standing there, Szaba tugged at his kilt and pulled him down to his knees. Moonlight reflected off the stone threshold.

"Blood," he muttered under his breath.

Bad move. He immediately heard movement in the house above.

Szaba pivoted him by the shoulders and they ran two paces and jumped over the sea wall and onto the beach, evaporating into the gloom. A gruff and angry man emerged from the doorway and looked up and down the street. He then huffed his girth to the wall and peered over.

Arithon and Szaba pressed tighter into the shadows, holding their breath. They could hear him cursing in a strange language, pacing to and fro. And then the call of a name, followed by light footsteps, and the voice of a young boy.

A few commands and the boy ran down the road at a quick pace.

Arithon and Szaba sidled down the wall toward the quay and soon slotted into the cavities of the large rocks of the breakwater. The place reeked of rotting seaweed and slimy marine life, and the water puddling at their feet soaked their sandals with sand and muck. No sooner were they hidden, than two armed men came trotting down the road with the boy. After a short discussion, the guards began searching around Dagieri's building, including beneath the wall where the Therans had been standing. They soon tired of looking and after another discussion with Dagieri, one of the men followed him back inside. The other started back.

Arithon and Szaba, without a word, began to parallel him on the beach side.

On the edge of town, he entered a plain and functional building: a storehouse. Arithon and Szaba knelt under the full shadow of the wall.

"If they are alive, they are in there," whispered Arithon. "We need to find a way in."

A quick circumference of the building showed no portals of any kind, save the vent slots high on the walls, too small for a man. They darted up an alley onto the street behind, hoping to gain access to the roof, but no easy way presented itself. Frustrated, Arithon stood looking out into the harbor.

Rounding into view was a ship. As a boy, he, and his friends, sitting on the roof in the early dark, watched countless ships returning late to the harbor of Akrotiri. The dark silhouette he now viewed was so familiar to him that it took a moment to realize it was out of place.

"The *Swallow*," he said aloud, frozen by rapid, disjointed thoughts. His heart raced and he could hear a pounding in his ears. He felt an impulse to cry out and would have if his eyes had not become distracted by another ship following in her wake, just clearing the headland. They were both headed for the dock.

Arithon continued to stand, mesmerized by the sight, but an Achaean hail from the *Swallow* set in motion several events. The door to the storehouse opened and the guard hurried to the quay to help them moor. Dagieri's house came alive with light and the young boy emerged.

"That is not Po," whispered Arithon, and they were off down the second-tier streets. They arrived at the back of Dagieri's when the ships were tying off.

"We need to get into the upper floor before that captain can enter the shop. I want to hear their conversation," Arithon breathed to Szaba.

But try as they might they could not scale the back wall to the lone window on the second floor. The stones were stuccoed too smooth for them to find any footholds, though a rope would have made the job easy, as there were wooden beams extending out from the roof.

"Wait here," said Szaba.

He disappeared into the dark alley. Arithon waited, listening to pick up what he could out front.

"What brings you in so late?" asked the proprietor in Achaean.

"Hello, Dagieri. An unexpected visit for us. Had a little trouble. I had to chase down the trader. As it is, we need to leave at sunrise."

"Come inside, I have some business for you."

Arithon heard the door shut. He could hear the voices, but they were too muffled. Frustrated he attempted the wall again but could find no means to climb even a few feet.

"I have a rope," said Szaba's voice, startling Arithon so that he spun around.

"Where did you get that?"

"A fisherman knows where to find a fisherman's rope."

He then threw the rope over the beam end, tied a slipknot, pulled it tight, and then walked up the wall and slipped into the window. Something diverted Szaba and he was away from the sill for a few seconds before returning to help Arithon.

As soon as Arithon was inside he saw what had distracted Szaba. A young girl in a filthy toga was sitting on the floor next to the bed. Her hands were tied in front of her and tethered to a ring anchored in the wall. Arithon understood her plight and the purpose of her bonds. He made a sign for her to be quiet, but she just stared at them, wide-eyed and silent. Szaba stayed by the window, while Arithon, ever so slowly, moved to the bedroom door, where he could eavesdrop on the conversation.

"The wool and the oil, we have decided on," said the captain's voice. "Now, what of the slaves?"

"I have two for you – well, really just one."

"Is it one or two?"

"One Minoan. The other is a Phoenician – injured – too much to travel. Otherwise, I would sell him to you today. I will have him ready when you return."

"And the other?"

"Oh, he is fine – a little sore-headed perhaps," Dagieri laughed snortingly, "but he will do nicely.

"A mariner for you. He can navigate and calculate – he is not your average rower."

"How much?"

"How about The Lady? Can we trade for her?"

"Do not anger me, Dagieri. She would break you. She is being returned to Limnos."

"Is she aboard? I want to see her."

"After we conclude. Now, how much for the navigator?"

"I am too tired to parley. For you – say two pieces."

"Done, put him aboard. Come, and you can see The Lady."

Arithon heard them moving out the door. He crossed the room to the window, where Szaba had already begun his descent. Arithon looked back at the girl. Still quiet, she looked at him with such an expression of pleading his stomach turned over. He thought to take her with them, but he knew he could not do it. For a moment he stared, like one does at a dying animal, and he knew it was hopeless. He walked back over to her and said in Lydian: "I will come back for you."

"Please do," she answered.

He walked back to the window, reached up and loosened the knot and slid out the window and out of her tortured world.

On the ground, he coiled the rope, talking to Szaba in the dark.

"I am going back to the storehouse to see if I can get Mara. You work your way close to the quay and see if they have Po; and keep a lookout for Sestos. I doubt you will have a chance to help him. If we cannot find each other, I will meet you at the orchard."

Szaba nodded, turned, and was gone.

Arithon finished coiling the rope, slung it over his head and ran down the second-tier street. He was not sure what he was going to do when he got there, but his adrenalin was pumping.

There were no beam-ends this time, but on the corners the last bricks were higher than the wall. If he could toss a loop over them, he could make it to the roof. Years of throwing ropes in the maritime trades had made him more skilled than he even knew. He had the rope secure after the second attempt and was on the roof on his first. He could find no skylight or entrance. Peculiar; the buildings of his world always had access to the roof: where else could you sleep on a hot sticky night?

He got on his knees and peered over the edge. He found that if he leaned as far as he dared, he could just see into the vent slots; but they were only rectangles of darkness. His nose was not impaired, though. The stench was human waste and misery. It was unmistakable and appalling. What went on in there? He had to chance something, so he tossed his voice down into the vent.

"Mara."

There was no answer.

He skittered along the roof edge until he could see the next slot and then tried again. There were a dozen slots on this side of the building, and he was running out of time. The activity at the dock was winding up – he could tell from the sounds. He continued, with no change to his luck, until he was at the front of the building.

He crossed the roof and started again. On the third slot, he called and waited. Nothing. He rose to move on when he thought he heard a faint sound. He sank again to his hands and knees.

"Mara?" he called.

"Arithon?"

"Yes, it is Arithon," he said. "Are you hurt?"

"Yes. Badly."

"I will come for you."

"No. Try for Sestos. They took him."

"Yes. I will. I want to help you too."

"I am chained to the wall, and I could not go even if you could free me."

"I do not want to desert you."

"Save Sestos – come back for me."

"But Mara –"

"Arithon, do you know what lesson number one is?" he interrupted.

"No."

"Lesson number one is 'live – always live. You can fight another day.' And on that day come back for me."

Arithon's brain was racing, but he did not have to wait long. His mind was made up for him. Several things began to happen at once.

He heard someone talking in Mara's cell and then the front door of the storehouse open. The guard ran out into the street and looked up at the roof.

Arithon crawled toward the opposite corner where his escape route lay. He had just grabbed on to the rope when a skirmish erupted on the quay. He paused to look back. Men were scurrying and shouting, and he could see bowmen on the *Swallow* shooting into the darkness of the beach.

Szaba!

He looked down and there was the guard; a large man looking up. Nothing was going right for him. His mentor was wounded and chained in a cell, his childhood friend had just been sold into slavery, and his trusted Szaba was in trouble. And here was an ugly jailer grinning at his new captive.

Arithon quit thinking.

He pulled the rope up, while moving to the middle of the roof and grabbed the end. He had done this many times off the cliffs of Thera.

Dashing to the edge of the roof, he hopped off, swinging down the side of the wall and around the corner to meet the jailer. He met him feet first in the face, snapping his neck back with an audible crack.

Arithon landed hard and it knocked the wind from him, jarring his senses. As he rolled over onto all fours, trying to get his breath, he looked back at the jailer; but the man would never move again. The skirmish echoed in the distance but sounded as if it were getting nearer.

It was definitely getting nearer.

Back on his feet, he moved to the street where he encountered another guard. This one carried a large club in his right hand and a dagger in the left.

Arithon went with his first weapon and pulled the axe from his belt. Two swings later he had shattered the club and with the other hand he pulled his sword. The guard was still for it and lunged with the dagger. Arithon executed a maneuver taught to him by the Phoenician lying in chains on the other side of the wall. As his assailant's arm extended, Arithon dodged to one side, and brought his sword down. The blow severed the guard's arm near the wrist, and his hand with the dagger still in it thumped to the ground, followed by the screaming man.

Where was Szaba in all this mess?

The answer soon arrived delivered by Szaba himself as he came sprinting out of the darkness, pursued by twenty men. His bow was stowed across his shoulder, a sign that his quiver was empty. Like a leaf rejoining the current, Arithon spun in beside him and they raced up the street.

The city was waking up. As the inhabitants emerged from their doors, lamps in hand, they assessed that the two running from the throng must be thieves or pirates. Arithon and Szaba found themselves darting through a maze of streets hostile with adversaries. After many pushes and near tackles, he pulled his sword and brandished it at any who might impede them. This worked after a fashion, but it only served to ignite the vengeance of a disturbed populace. By the time they reached the edges of the community, the pursuing mob jammed the street. Five of the younger men were beginning to gain on them, and their will did not wane when they passed into the orchards.

Both Szaba and Arithon had the advantage of conditioning and a long stride, but the activities of the night were beginning to take their toll. After an all-out chase through the orchards, they arrived in a pine forest, ascending a steep hill. The pursuers dropped off as the incline increased, until only a dozen hardened hunters remained. Arithon and Szaba had another problem though – they were going in the wrong direction: away from the *Dolphin*.

At the top of the hill, Arithon realized they were cutting across a peninsula, for he could glimpse a reflection through the trees. 'To the water' his sailor's blood told him and pulling Szaba by the tunic he veered to descend the slope. After a few falls and scrapes, and frantic scrambling they pulled up on a sizable sea-cliff – maybe eight fathoms. Eight fathoms would pause any man.

Arithon looked at Szaba, his face dripping sweat, staring at the water below.

"We will have to jump and trust for no rocks."

Szaba said nothing.

"We will need to jump out as far as possible and time it to hit the wave peak."

Again, Szaba said nothing.

"It's easy. We used to do it all the time when I was a child."

Szaba turned to Arithon, exhaustion and hesitation streaking his black face, "I grew up in the desert."

Arithon laughed despite himself. Szaba smiled but looked again to the crashing below.

"Take my hand. When I say jump, we go together."

Arithon watched the waves and tried to judge the height. He really had jumped this far before, but in daylight and into waters he knew. This was going to be tricky. If he could only watch a set of waves to get the rhythm, he could be sure, but there was not enough time: calling voices in the forest were getting closer.

He watched two more waves, crouched a bit, pushed his arms back and said, "Now."

They leapt in unison, almost as a practiced team and held hands all the way down. Arithon's timing or his luck held true and they pierced the water beyond the rocks. The cold water was a shock to their overheated bodies, and they emerged gasping.

He thought to swim across the entrance to the bay of Thermi and arrive on the southern headland, but even he would find it a long swim when he was fresh, and he was not fresh. Szaba would never make it; he had not the skill. Back through the town was the shortest route, but that was impossible. That left only one way – they would have to continue north until they could circumvent the town and start south. And then what?

It would take them at least three hours, maybe more, to manage the land leg and they might be in the water for some time yet. And what time was it? Night reigned, but dawn could not be far. If the Achaean captain were punctual, he would leave with Sestos long before he and Szaba could reach Hyssos.

Szaba grabbed his shoulder and directed his attention to the top of the cliff. There was movement on the rim, but it was hard to tell if they could see them in the water. The roar of crashing waves washed back any voices.

Arithon started to swim north, angling out farther, hoping they would not be spotted. They needed to be out of the water before first light or they would be visible; two heads floating just outside the surf.

They began a frustrating swim, burdened with their clothes and weapons. Arithon tied them into an awkward bundle which he shifted from hand to hand, and then back under his arm. Szaba was not an efficient swimmer and so slowed their progress even more. He was soon exhausted. Arithon had been watching the African, and it was clear that he would not be able to continue. Of course, he would never say anything – he would roll over and drown before he would complain. Arithon knew this and admired his devotion while he resented the responsibility it conferred. If Szaba would only yield first, it would free him of the decision. But this was a negative line of reasoning brought on by the frustration of Sestos slipping away. His father would not have thought so petty of another's noble efforts. He wondered where Father was, and if he had survived the wave. It was possible he had been smashed and drowned like so many others. He shook off these unhelpful thoughts, trusting Alteron could look after himself, and he could look after Szaba.

He started to swim shoreward and looked to see that Szaba followed. He was looking for a good landfall but concluded they would have to chance any. The whole coastline was rocky and treacherous. At least, it would prevent their pursuers from lying in wait; this was not a likely landing spot and they would not be expected here.

Arithon looked back over his shoulder and could just detect the black sky turning to a hazy gray on the horizon.

After a few attempts, Arithon found a rocky perch above the waves. He had skinned his shin, but it was a mild discomfort compared to the shaking cold; the swim had drained his last reserves.

He managed to get Szaba out of the water with no mishaps, and they started to ascend the cliff, both chattering; naked in the night wind. The rock face was not as high as the one they had jumped from, but it took a considerable amount of effort going up. By the time they reached the top, the eastern sky was a whispery blue and day was coming. Pushing into the pine forest they fell onto the soft needles and rested, almost dozing before they recovered.

They wrung out their clothes, while surveying the forest for the hunters, who seemed to have lost the trail. The two then began a tentative trek out, carrying their still wet garments and trying to get a bearing on the town. Arithon was surprised to learn, after climbing a short ridge, that they were a league north of Thermi. A crescent of the harbor was in sight, but they would have to pass around to the northwest to get a full view of the bay to see if the ships had left.

The hoped-for creek was not at the bottom of the ravine and by the time they ascended the next ridge their thirst was foremost in their thoughts – neither had had food or drink since the previous afternoon. Arithon started down the spine of the ridge, more in the direction of town than he had wanted, but he had decided that to increase their speed back to the *Dolphin* they would require water and if possible a bite of food.

On the knee of the ridge, they spotted an outlying farm of tilled fields ringed with olive groves. It was early, but farmers on Thera were up with the sun. There was no activity in the gardens or paddocks, as he and Szaba located the well and drank their fill. There was a vegetable and herb garden on the southwest side where they picked and ate handfuls of legumes, and two turnips apiece. They were not yet ripe but tasted a feast to a famished stomach. Thirsty from their thievery, they decided to risk one more take at the well.

Szaba was drinking when they heard the front door of the house bang shut. Arithon reached down to gather their bundles when a woman rounded the house on her way to the well with a jar balanced on her head. She came face to face with two, tall, naked men, one of them black and holding the bucket she used five times a day to draw water. The pot on her head slipped to the ground shattering on the stony soil and without a word she started to back up the way she came, but stopped in bewildered surprise as the two men showed their bare buttocks and sprinted away through her orchard and vanished into the trees beyond.

The water had been more refreshing than Arithon had expected, even if the root vegetables had been less than satisfying. But they were off at a steady trot working their way around the west side of the town. After a long run, they paused on a ridge west of Thermi and found an opening through which they could see the harbor.

249

Arithon's heart dropped. The two ships were gone. Chiding himself for not checking earlier, he cursed just as Szaba pointed higher on the horizon. "There."

The two ships were just passing out of sight around the north promontory.

Arithon glanced at the angle of the sun, and then unfolded his damp kilt and put it on. Szaba did the same. Arithon made a sighting on their direction, a few mental notes about the terrain and then took off at a withering pace, his tunic tucked under one arm.

"We need to be fast," he relayed to Szaba over his shoulder, "or we will lose Sestos."

Arithon did not have to see the slight nod of the head; he knew it had transpired. This allegiance – which earlier he had found wanting – now spurred him on as they covered the distance in a dedication to their friend. Arithon did not care if anyone saw them at this point. They would have to catch them, and he doubted anyone could. He ran as straight as the landscape would allow through the tilled areas until he found the goat paths where he pressed on even faster. A vague idea of how long it would take was hounding him, and he was determined to halve it if he could. On he raced, Szaba matching him stride for stride.

He reached the track that would take him to the beach where they had disembarked yesterday, but the *Dolphin* would not be there – she was in an unknown cove farther south. At the time this had not seemed an important detail, but now it was distressing not to know the shortest route to the anchorage. There was nothing for it, except to go to the coast at this point and begin to work their way down, looking into every inlet.

After an agonizing run that consumed at least an hour, they still had not located her hiding place and Arithon cursed the delay. Every moment of time he spent searching, Sestos moved farther away, and the chances of his rescue dimmed.

But he thought he knew where they were taking Sestos, and this gave him hope. 'I have to get her back to Limnos,' the Achaean captain had said. If the Achaeans sailed there directly and not by some side trip, there was hope.

But there were two ships. What if they split up?

He pulled up, heaving his words. "Szaba, did you see which ship they put Sestos on?"

"The other."

They started moving again. Arithon distracted himself from the pain by thinking about Szaba's activity last night. No telling what had transpired, or how he had incited the town. The quiver was empty. There was no doubt as to the final resting place of the arrows. He did wonder how it all started and … He pulled up again.

"Did you see Po?"

"No."

They took off again.

The responsibility of what loomed ahead could still not distract him from the torment he was inflicting on his body. The young Theran had led the race and his arms were bruised and scratched by the brush as he pushed it aside. After another half hour of dense scrub, he became too weary to hold his arms upright any longer. Szaba noticed his faltering steps and pushed ahead to break a path. It was disheartening to fight to the edge of the water and see only cliffs or broken coastline. Hyssos would not have anchored unprotected and may have rowed many leagues to find a safe harbor.

And so, they pressed on until Arithon tripped and fell to his knees. He rolled onto the ground and lay there panting in the morning heat, dry heaves conquering him. Szaba dropped to all fours, sweat pouring from his body. Arithon was no longer sweating, and Szaba knew this to be a bad sign.

But Arithon rose, and after his heaving stopped, began to walk, thinking he needed a change of fate – and soon. As if in answer, a stream emerged from the brush, making its way down to the sea, and Arithon lay in the water, and drank with measured pause. When he felt recovered enough to move on, he decided, on an impulse, to follow the stream down to the beach.

With Arithon leading again, they pushed their way through the brush made dense by the presence of water, often walking in the stream itself, until they came to a rock wall in the ravine. They could hear a gentle surf ahead, and when they rounded the rock face, there floated the *Dolphin*, riding on the undulating surface. Hyssos had found an anchorage so secluded that it had almost proved detrimental.

Szaba walked down to the water's edge and flopped down in the sand as if the strings which held him up had broken. The *Dolphin* was already lowering the tender. Arithon glanced around and noticed that the beach bore the signs of men encamped and the debris of a slaughtered mammal.

251

Hyssos stood at the rail. Pacing only moments ago, he was smiling in relief.

Before the tender had even touched the beach, Arithon called across the water. "Prepare to leave – all rowers."

The command created a stir on the ship as the men took their stations, either at the oars or the anchors. They were already slipping off the tension of the fore anchor rode to weigh the aft, when Arithon and Szaba climbed aboard.

"Quick as you can, Hyssos! We must catch two ships. They have taken Sestos as a slave."

Hyssos barked at the men and then turned to look at the two. From the look on his face they must have been an appalling sight; scratched and dirty, their hair in matted clumps, and shaking uncontrollably from their exertion. Hyssos called for food, water, and a wineskin and placed the two runners in the shade of the deck cabin.

"I was about to leave for Thermi," said Hyssos, handing a waterskin to each.

"Row north, and head for Limnos," began Arithon between drinks. "We are pursuing two ships which should be heading there. They left," – he paused and looked up at the sun, "three hours earlier."

Hyssos left them to captain the *Dolphin*, and when he returned, he found them both leaning against the cabin, their eyes closed. Arithon heard his approach and cracked an eyelid.

"I need to sleep for two hours – no more. Wake me if you see the ships."

He then slumped down on the deck and fell asleep.

CHAPTER 25 RESCUE

Akrotiri now played to Pluto's perfection,
But sent Poseidon a plea
Dispatch Polus and Prados protection
My grandson's son has need.

Someone was gently moving his shoulder. He tried to open his eyes, but the muscles would not respond. Then he heard Szaba's voice and sat up. He had been lying on the open deck, though someone had propped his head with a blanket. Squinting up into the bright light he could see Hyssos standing over him holding a cup. Arithon could not remember ever being so thirsty.

"You have slept the time you requested, Arithon," reported Hyssos. "We passed Thermi's harbor and are preparing to stand out. Who are we chasing?"

"Two ships – one is the *Swallow*, the other is half the size – a trader."

"Is Po aboard?"

"We do not know," Arithon replied, looking at Szaba for confirmation. "They are both manned by Achaeans."

"Then, we will fight them both?" asked Hyssos.

"Yes. Close the distance without exhausting the crew."

Hyssos stood still, paused, and then stated as if it were part of his job, "It is two or more days from here to Limnos."

Arithon went to clean up and gnaw on an overcooked strip of last night's boar. He had a lot on his mind. There were now three people to save from either violent death or a long life of misery; and each was a friend. He felt better after a bite and walked the deck from stern to bow several times. The carpenter did a wonderful job on the new mast, he thought as he passed it for the third time. The temporary mast they had used only a week ago lay on the deck. Hyssos had the ship in excellent working order. The cargo was strapped down, ropes and pins were stowed; and the weapons: axes, spears, bows, and shields were hanging within reach.

The *Dolphin*, after the wave, had a crew of thirty-seven, counting the First Tier, and all were expected to have at least two jobs. A few, like the ship's carpenter, carried special duties, but most could row and fight. It was a small force, but deft.

Arithon found Szaba shaving his head using an obsidian blade, which Arithon had awarded him after he swam across the bay of Akrotiri and back. He had changed clothes and eaten, and he looked much refreshed, as if their ordeal had happened far in the past.

"Expecting visitors?"

"No, my head burned hot on our run. All I could think about was shearing it smooth and cool."

"You were extraordinary on our misadventure," Arithon praised. "When I first met you on the deck of the *Swallow*, I sized you up and asked myself whether I could outrun you."

"And how did you answer?"

"I could not answer then, but I can now. You are my better in such play," Arithon said.

"I think not," Szaba answered, "but it honors me to hear you say it."

Arithon smiled and looked off the port side.

"Mara is injured and captive in the storehouse," he started. "I talked to him through the vent, but I could not see him."

"How is he injured?" asked Szaba.

"I do not know, but he said he is too hurt to travel. I did not have time to save him. The whole town erupted. What happened?"

Szaba looked uncomfortable. "I hid behind a fishing boat on the beach near the quay. Dagieri had gone aboard the trader.

"While I watched, three figures approached from the storehouse. The middle figure was clearly Sestos. He was unsteady on his feet and holding the side of his head. One of his guards was a man, the other a boy.

"As they stepped onto the quay, Sestos fell to his hands and knees. The boy moved to help him up, but the man," – and here Szaba's voice changed – "kicked Sestos in the side, knocking him onto the ground."

Szaba hesitated before he continued, "The man threw back his head and laughed so that the crews on the quay looked over to see what was happening. I have been Sestos.

"Before I could even think not to, I had put an arrow through his upstretched neck.

"And then it erupted as you say. I found myself the target of many archers, and I responded. I tried to get to him, but they pulled him down the quay and onto the ship."

He led Arithon up the deck where they sat down on the temporary mast. Arithon was the man he admired above all others, but he was an impulsive, unplanned warrior. Nubians had spent generations at war.

"We will need to board the trader to get Sestos, yes? On the open sea," Szaba said.

"Yes," Arithon replied, "But they will attempt to prevent this."

"And there are two ships," said Szaba. "Perhaps we could do something unexpected?"

"Perhaps," agreed Arithon.

Szaba patted their wooden seat and began, "We had a device on our chariots ..."

***

Arithon rose and called to the carpenter in the hold.

Kimilos was the eldest in the crew, a methodical and patient man, who had spent his life repairing the blunders of sailors. He took great delight in fashioning clever solutions to knotty problems in adverse conditions. His formal speech, almost an ancient dialect, made him seem a Minoan of the past and had always amused Sestos – he often mimicked him in his entertainment routines.

"Can you place a fitting here," he said pointing to a spot, left and forward of the mast, "which would serve as a brace?"

"I do not understand. What do you want it for?"

Arithon took the time to explain Szaba's idea and listen to the carefully formulated objections of the woodworker. As the problems found answers, Kimilos became, what was for him, excited. The carpenter looked at Arithon, and then down at the spare mast, smiled and said, "It might work. I will start on it."

Arithon joined Szaba and talked through several plans. Szaba had many ideas for a landsman and a surprising strategic view of battles unfought. At sundown, Arithon called a break and they shipped oars.

"I had thought we would spot them before nightfall, but this has not proved true. They are Achaeans, so they will go ashore tonight and try the crossing tomorrow. We will have to position ourselves this side of Limnos and wait."

They set drift crews through the night, while Jaros and Kimilos worked on the mast, and Hyssos maintained their bearings by the night sky. At first light Arithon scanned the horizon and seeing nothing from the rails, climbed the mast with the same disappointing results. The morning passed, marked by nothing but steady rowing and sailors' songs. Near noon, Jaros called from atop that Limnos was in sight.

"Ship oars," Arithon called, "Eat and rest – sleep if you can."

Arithon returned to his cabin. There he braided his hair to one side on the back of his head and tied his colors – the blue dolphins arching his temples. He cinched his loincloth before he put on a Minoan kilt skirt; cloud white, embroidered in gold by his mother.

He reached under his sleeping bench and pulled out his trunk. He had placed it there when they left Thera, thinking this would be its new home until he again had a homeport. He pulled out the cosmetics case and painted on his chest a blue dolphin, leaping over his left nipple. The *Dolphin* had proven lucky so far, despite the misgivings of those who thought her cursed. And besides, the Achaeans should know it was a Minoan they had picked a fight with. He thought to remove the signet ring, but instead removed it from its cord and jammed it to the bottom of his finger: the stone might afford ancestral protection. He slid the trunk back, belted his sword, and carrying his axe in his left hand walked out onto the deck; ready and resolute.

The *Dolphin* drifted, waiting. But the sailors could sense a shift: the wind was backing, and horsetail clouds were visible in the northeast sky.

"A meltemi is coming," said Hyssos, pointing. "I would say –"

"A ship!" The crew cast their eyes aloft, watching Jaros. Finally, he called down again.

"It is the *Swallow*. I would know her anywhere. And there is another with her."

Arithon clapped his hands together in relief; excitement; fear. "Turn to the south."

Addressing the main deck, he called, "To the oars, prepare for battle!"

The ship stirred into crisscrossing activity. The weapons: shield, axe, sword, and spear were passed out to each station. A peg on the bottom of each shield was fit into a socket on the oar rail, erecting a short wall along the cockpit. The spears were scattered about the deck in locations devoid of interfering rigging. Every third oarsman placed a grappling hook with a stout coil of rope close to his shoulder and each laid an axe on their bench.

Six of the crew were bowmen and would forfeit their oars. Their shields were like the rowers', but taller, and fit upright into slots on the deck.

Szaba took his station at the bowsprit, where he was exposed, but unimpeded.

Arithon began a discussion with Hyssos next to the steering oar.

"The meltemi will aid us," he began, "if it does not lay us over."

"Can you judge the switch?"

"I … I can," said Hyssos.

Arithon paused and changed his mind. "I will make the call," he said to Hyssos. "Watch for my signal."

"Very good," agreed Hyssos.

Arithon stepped along the deck over the array of weapons to Szaba at the bow. He looked back to see the coming meltemi foaming the wave tops in the near distance. He was needed at the sail and as he worked with the three sheet men, the initial blast of the meltemi flattened his tunic and whipped his braid into his face.

"Bring her up as high as she can take," he ordered. "And you will have to drop her as we turn."

They nodded their understanding, and hoisted the sail, two feet at a time, to allow the mast and her stays to adjust to the pressure: The painted bull's head billowed full; staring ahead; midcharge. The *Dolphin* began to pick up speed so that the rowers were obliged to quicken their cadence. When the sail reached the eighth notch the mast was bending against the load.

"One more notch and lash her down," he ordered.

The *Dolphin*, running before the wind, was racing through the water at an exhilarating speed; slicing through the breaking waves; a soaking spray drenching the first five of the fifteen row stations. The crew, encouraged by this gift of Boreas, saw it as a propitious omen and the speed pumped them with madness.

"Angle her toward the other. I want to see how they respond."

Hyssos complied, and after a few strokes they could see the *Swallow* angling to intercept. The Achaean had recognized their hostile posture and was screening the trader, forcing the *Dolphin* to take on the vessel with the most fighting power. The Achaean ships were trying to close the space between them, but the worsening weather was making it difficult.

Arithon, walking the deck with nervous energy, encountered Inthos, whose lip was trembling, and eyes were unseeing. He felt a flush of this contagious fear, but said, "Inthos, look for Po – he will need us."

Arithon nodded at Szaba, who returned the gesture, and then hurried back to Hyssos at the tiller. The speed of Arithon's ship was twice that of the Achaeans, giving him a significant advantage on the first pass. But they were two and he was one.

"Hyssos, aim at the *Swallow*.

"Slowly," said Arithon, "Not too fast. I do not want him to commit too early. When I give you the first signal, make him think we will pass on his port. Then watch for the switch."

Hyssos nodded, eyes fixed forward on his target.

"I will have to get to the mast," he said to Hyssos. "Watch for my commands!"

Arithon bounded forward. Two of the youngest crewmen, looked up at him, but his return stare bent them back to their oars. He took a position, where he could watch the approaching ships and Hyssos could see him.

The Achaean was holding steady. Arithon could see their rowers were in full cadence, trying to maintain their speed for maximum maneuverability. Their archers stood ready with helmeted men holding swords positioned behind them. He could see the captain standing on the very deck, where he had stood as a boy with Po.

"It's not your ship," Arithon muttered.

"Come on," Arithon continued under his breath. "Come on. Hold it, … hold it, … hold it."

The *Dolphin* was surging through the water faster than Arithon had ever experienced. He felt the exhilaration of speed and the impending battle take him. The boy who had thrown a javelin at the Sea Peoples was now that other Theran. A Theran of old. A warrior at charge. It was time.

Arithon raised one hand in the air, and Hyssos began the slight turn to starboard. Arithon waited, his breath held, eyes staring at the approaching *Swallow*, now only six ship-lengths away.

The Achaean captain took the bait. The *Swallow* began to turn, trying to angle off the Minoan and keep the *Dolphin* off his port side oars.

"Good, good," said Arithon, staring at the approaching ship.

"Get ready, … get ready, … get ready," he said under his breath.

"Now!" he cried, crossing both arms over his head.

Hyssos cut the steering oar so hard that those standing lost their balance from the surge. The *Dolphin* veered hard to port and leaned heavily but maintained the bulk of her speed.

The Achaean saw the maneuver, hesitated, and then tried to correct back to cut the *Dolphin* off on the other side. But it was too late; he was not going to make it, and he was in great danger of having his starboard oars sheared instead. Knowing this, he pulled back to port, hoping to miss the oncoming enemy. His archers and spearmen had prepared an onslaught to punish the *Dolphin* as she raked his side. The Achaean did not know it, but she was not going to.

"Ship oars," screamed Arithon, "shields and bows."

The rowers on both sides shipped their oars and protected themselves with their shields.

Hyssos kept turning the *Dolphin* to miss the *Swallow* altogether. The merchant ship, which bore the insignia of a stag, was not going to fare as well.

But the Achaean captain on the *Swallow* loosed his arrows at his attacker as she sped by, so close the Achaean could feel the weight of her presence. The bowmen on the *Stag* launched their first volley, so that arrows rained on the *Dolphin* from both sides. It would have been a punishing barrage, but only Szaba and Arithon were exposed.

The *Dolphin* was crashing through the water, when Arithon started to drop the rake. Arrows swarmed across and through. He heard a cry from a bowman behind him, but ignored it, intent on deploying his new weapon. Hyssos was steering toward the *Stag*, on a collision course with her port side oars. They shipped them as soon as they saw their danger, but to their dismay a spar as large as the mast was being lowered from the vertical: they could see it behind the *Dolphin*'s sail as it bounced down in fits and starts. And then the stinger was horizontal, like a giant knife positioned to slice them in two.

Arithon judged his rake was too low and with seconds to go, raised it and bent over to pound a wedge in with the side of his axe. An arrow twanged into the mast, missing his stooped back.

The rowers on the *Stag*, about to be beheaded by the beam, abandoned their stations, making themselves easy targets for the *Dolphin*'s bows and spears. Szaba, unscathed through the first volley, shot their captain and the steersman only seconds before the rake started to splinter their oar rail. The momentum of the *Dolphin* was unaffected as she drove past the ship, her stinger cracking through the timbers in a rolling cascade of splintered debris. A noisy panic erupted on the *Stag*.

Arithon began to drop the sail of the *Dolphin*, as something stung him on his left shoulder. The rake was still decimating the *Stag*'s upper railing, when Hyssos lay over to pivot around her stern, but the meltemi, catching the exposed side of the *Dolphin*, caused her to skate. The bowsprit crashed into the aft quarter of the *Stag*, and a shudder rumbled through the *Dolphin*. Arithon was thrown to the deck by the collision.

"Grappling," Arithon screamed, as he jumped to his feet.

He spun his head to ascertain the present position of the *Swallow*: she was completing a turn to port to re-engage. The *Dolphin* had only moments before she too would risk being crushed and boarded. He seized a grapple and swung it onto the *Stag* as the *Dolphin* continued her pivot, her nose stuck fast in the *Stag*'s hull.

Szaba tossed his bow and empty quiver onto the deck and climbed the sprit. Arithon was trying to secure his own line when the *Dolphin*, still spinning, broke free. Grappling lines snapped, unable to withstand the force of the *Dolphin* rotating through her pivot.

Arithon looked up to the bowsprit as it pulled out from under Szaba, leaving him hanging on the *Stag*'s gunnels. An Achaean above him, brandishing a spear, was preparing to strike.

Without thinking, Arithon bolted and reached down to secure a spear in stride. Three steps later, he released his throw. The spear sailed over the half-length of the *Dolphin*, passing over the heads of her crew. It struck Szaba's foe full on in the chest as he raised his own.

Continuing past his own crewmen and the weapon-littered deck, Arithon bounded up the bowsprit and jumped in one smooth motion across the widening gap to catch onto the rear rail of the *Stag*.

The *Dolphin* spun away, leaving Arithon and Szaba clinging onto the enemy ship.

Arithon turned to locate Hyssos, and hanging by one hand, motioned to him to come around. But the *Dolphin* was head in to the meltemi and slipping out of reach. What had been an advantage was now a disadvantage. She would have to reset her oars; stop her backward momentum; and fight the wind to again reach the *Stag*, which was floundering, unhelmed, in a choppy sea.

Arithon realized he and Szaba were the only two who made it aboard, and the *Swallow* was bearing down fast. This was Sestos' last chance.

Climbing the rail, he leapt onto the deck square footed. Though he did not know it, he was an overwhelming sight to those still alive on the *Stag*. His black braid whipped behind him in the fierce wind like a slashing tail, and his face was hard. Blood from his shoulder wound had reddened his left side, so that the dolphin on his chest was leaping into a red waterfall. He pulled the sword from his side and charged. He was a man possessed.

He struck the first with a force that knocked him into the water. The next two he met one at a time with the same result. His sword demolished shield and blade alike. But time was short – the *Swallow* was on the periphery of his vision and bearing in. Wild with fighting madness, he was determined to free his friend before he would stop his onslaught.

Others came at him in groups, and it would have gone badly for him, but Szaba was on the boards, working his way down the port side, fighting just as mad, and protecting Arithon's flank. Both whirled, and feinted, thrust and chopped their way through the ranks of adversaries. Arithon picked up a discarded shield and fought with abandon; deflecting spear thrusts and axe blows, he dealt hacking, painful death to all he encountered.

The sight of a wrathful warrior god accompanied by his black ally convinced three crewmen to jump headlong into the water. Those who remained swarmed toward the bow, save one, and he knelt behind a body lying on the deck. Arithon leapt over a fallen enemy and lifted his sword to strike when he held his blow. Horror struck him as the Achaean turned over the body of Sestos and held a dagger to his throat – the position of sacrifice.

"Stay back!" barked the Achaean.

Arithon halted and realized Sestos was not dead, but very much alive, staring up at him, expressionless. His hands and feet were tied, and he had a blood-matted bruise on his temple. Arithon glanced over at Szaba standing on his left, and past him to the *Swallow*, a few ship-lengths away, archers taking aim from her decks.

I guess we will die together, he thought. Fitting perhaps, but not the outcome he wanted. His fury raged, but he stood unmoving, his sword held over his head.

And then the Achaean cried out in pain, as a sword slipped up through the deck boards and sliced into the back of his thigh. He released his dagger to grab at his leg.

Arithon's sword came down with a force that split the Achaean's head like a melon, blood and brains splattering his kilt. He jumped down to cut Sestos loose as Szaba sprang before them to ward off what was left of the crew.

Arrows started to whiz by their heads as he helped Sestos to his feet and half carried him to the gunnel. "Jump!" he cried, "Swim for the *Dolphin*!"

Arithon turned to wave Szaba over the rail, and as he ran by the hatch, a figure jumped out in pursuit.

Szaba bounded past Arithon in one continuous movement over the gunnel. Arithon raised his sword to strike at the diminutive pursuer but was astonished when in perfect Minoan the warrior said, "Do not strike, I am Minoan, and I am coming with you."

Arithon realized two things in that instant: it was a girl, and she was not Minoan.

But he had no time to consider these things and his astonishment overcame his impulse to strike her down. She stood on the rail, said, "Better hurry," and dove into the sea. An arrow pierced the shield he was holding. He dropped it and taking one last look at the *Swallow* he raised his sword in defiance and followed the girl.

* * *

Hyssos had mastered the *Dolphin* and she was working her way back to the battle, but still ten ship-lengths away. He saw the four dive into the water, and he was encouraged, for he recognized three of them. But he was too far away to help them, and he would not arrive before they came within range of the archers on the *Swallow*, which was coming around the wrecked *Stag* to pursue them.

Arithon was the last of the swimmers, and after he had reached a safe distance he paused and turned in the water to assess the situation. The *Swallow*, her sail up and charging downwind, turned to pivot around her companion and bring the swimmers in range of their bows again. Arithon looked back – the *Dolphin* was too far away. He needed time.

"No, this way," he yelled at the three swimming ahead of him.

They looked, and he was pointing to the north, away from the *Dolphin*. Arithon thought to circle the *Stag*; to use it as a screen – they could be quicker – maybe. Szaba and Sestos complied, and the girl followed. The swells were packed and foaming, folding over the swimmers on every roll and spraying their faces as they surfaced to suck a breath and make a few strokes before the next dunking. Arithon pulled to catch them, craning to look over at the *Swallow*, hoping the Achaean would turn too fast into the wind with her sailed deployed. Arithon was disheartened as the Achaean dropped the sail. But as the *Swallow* came broadside, she heeled over and shipped water.

The *Dolphin* meanwhile was making headway in the breaking seas, her crew intact and rowing strong. Hyssos was desperate to re-engage, feeling he had failed to keep the *Dolphin* in a position to help Arithon. He now saw a slim chance after the *Swallow* lost ground to leeward.

Arithon reached the other three and realized Sestos was laboring, too weak to speak. He pulled him to his chest as he was slipping below the water.

"Relax, I will hold you," he said. "Get your breath."

They were near the bow of the *Stag*, which was rolling and yawing as the wind and waves pushed her to and fro.

"Hold here until he commits," Arithon said.

The *Swallow* was turning onto the starboard side of the *Stag*. If they timed it right, they could pass her on the away side. They bobbed a few waves and then started down the stricken ship. Arithon pulled Sestos to him and began to swim with one hand, but it was just too slow: the *Swallow* would clear before he and Sestos had created a safe distance.

Szaba and the girl made it just as the sprit of the *Swallow* came around. The Achaeans tried a few shots at them, but the angle was bad, and the seas were pitching.

The *Swallow* then concentrated its volleys on Arithon and Sestos: exposed and within range. Arrows peppered the water around them. Maybe Szaba had killed their trained archers, or maybe the seas were too heavy, but the arrows were not finding their mark until Arithon was halfway down the trader. A powerfully shot arrow pierced the water and gouged a path along two ribs, eliciting a cry of pain from Arithon as he released Sestos. He pulled the arrow with another scream, and then recaptured Sestos before he could slip beneath.

Gritting his teeth, Arithon continued, swimming so close to the *Stag* he was bumping Sestos' head along her hull. Odd that the ship Arithon had tried so hard to destroy was now protecting him. He could see the *Swallow* turning again as he popped out from under the stern.

Quickly losing his strength, Arithon looked southward to see the *Dolphin* had closed half the distance. This encouraged him to start swimming again, though his progress was slow. When he thought he was truly spent, he turned to see the *Swallow*, grappling the trader, and abandoning the pursuit. Continuing to chase Arithon would bring them within range of the *Dolphin*.

Arithon saw the *Dolphin* tossing ropes to the girl and Szaba, but she did not stop and continued to bear down, while his wound bled into the water and Sestos head rolled into unconsciousness.

When the *Dolphin* pulled up beside him, he was too weak to seize the ropes. Four crewmen jumped into the heaving waters and hauled them up onto the windy deck.

After a fit of coughing, prone on the deck, Arithon turned over to see a circle of faces staring down. He located Hyssos and made eye contact. Hyssos leaned close: "What next?"

Arithon lay too exhausted to think. Someone pressed a cup of water to his lips and tilted his head. He swallowed and then said, "Find a safe harbor."

He lay back and closed his eyes and then heard a strange voice, a girl's voice perhaps, and it said, "Get me some linen. This bleeding must be stopped."

He felt himself lifted and laid in a warm soft sheepskin and then lost consciousness.

CHAPTER 26 THE GIRL

The Graces of Splendor, Mirth, and Cheer, – Aglaia,
Euphrosyne, and Thalia; Zeus' daughters all three; must be
invited to feasts of plenty for the triad cannot be broken – first
guests to arrive and last to leave.

Arithon could hear the wind through the rigging. He was lying under a
sheepskin and he was hot. He tried to move his arms to push it off, but a
dull pain throbbed in his chest, and he opened his eyes, remembering.

He was in his cabin, it was daylight, and the ship was riding anchor; he
could feel the gentle fall and rise, and then the tug.

"Water?" asked a warm voice.

Arithon turned his head to see a girl, about his age, on the opposite
bench, a cup in her hand. Soft light filtered through cracks in the boards
and one slit-ray crossed her chest like a sash. A black braid fell across her
shoulder reaching to the waist. She was wearing a girl's tunic but a
crewman's kilt. Her eyes were fiery, clear, and bold like a cat suddenly alert
to something unseen. She was beautiful to the point of desire, but instinct
warned great caution.

"What?"

"Would you like a drink of water?"

He nodded.

She stood up and bent over him, raising his head to help him drink. Her
braid caressed the side of his face as she reached behind his neck. He was
staring straight at her covered breast and he watched them rise and fall
with her breathing. And he felt, well he could not put words to it, but he
felt a presence about her which bathed him in a warm glow, like sunshine
on a cold day. She stepped back and the link was broken.

"Sestos?" he exhaled.

"He is fine. He is sleeping," she replied.

Arithon lay back and considered the feat. Sestos alive and sleeping.

"Szaba?"

"I will get him, Arithon," she said, and slipped out the door.

Szaba appeared, followed by Hyssos, and they sat on the open bench. Hyssos wore an irrepressible smile; Szaba was satisfied.

"I hear that Sestos is sleeping. How is the rest of the crew?" Arithon asked in a throaty voice.

"Eight wounded, but we lost no one," reported Hyssos.

"No one?"

"No one, although Pegaia took an arrow to the gut, and is in pain. Vori is attending to him and expects that he will live. He is using a pinch of opium to calm him. But yes, Arithon – we lost no one."

"That is …" sighed Arithon, unable to find words to express his relief. "Where are we?" he asked instead.

"We are on an island five leagues south of Limnos."

"Szaba, will you take this skin off me? I cannot move my arms."

Szaba complied and Arithon saw that he was bandaged around the chest and left shoulder. Blood stained the chest wrap and his hands were tied to his waist. Arithon noticed, bemusedly, that he was without a loincloth.

Szaba untied his wrists and sat down again.

"So, tell me. What happened after you pulled us out of the water?"

"You passed out. You were bleeding from your chest wound. We brought you here and Lucina bandaged and cared for you."

"Lucina? Who is Lucina?"

"The girl," said Hyssos. "Did you not know her name?"

"Uh … I did not. I forgot to ask."

Hyssos and Szaba smiled, but Arithon missed it as he examined his bandages.

"Anyway," Hyssos began anew, "Sestos was unconscious, but alive. He was weak, as his head was cracked open on Lesvos and he had eaten little. He has regained himself, but he sleeps now."

Arithon took a deep but painful breath and exhaled. Hyssos continued:

"The wind was roaring, and the seas were high by the time we reached you. We were lucky to get you out of the water. The Achaeans had no more fight in them and pulled the remainder of the *Stag*'s crew onto the *Swallow*. They tried to put the trader in tow, but the gale was too fierce. It snapped their lines twice while we were still in sight and I suspect they may have abandoned her.

"I obeyed your order and sailed south to find a safe anchorage."

"I gave you that order?"

266

"Yes, you said 'find a safe harbor.' So, I headed for this island. The following sea lashed us all the way, but the mast held, and we made it here before dark. A fine ship."

Arithon nodded agreement and it struck him that she might have been lost – he was, after all, not at the helm. "You did well, Hyssos; like your father. I am proud of you."

Hyssos looked away, pinching his lips between his teeth.

Arithon then laughed and said, "Szaba, when I saw you hanging off the back of that ship – a one-man assault! What were you thinking?"

Szaba arrested a spreading smile and said, "Thank you for coming to help, Arithon."

"Szaba said you were a grand warrior," praised Hyssos, his voice thick.

Arithon stared at the ceiling, "I slaughtered them. I have never felt such madness. Or hate. Mara warned me – the warrior's bane. The savagery … it is numbing."

There was silence in the cabin. You could hear the wind in the stays and the water lapping against the hull.

"You did it to save Sestos." Hyssos said.

"Thank you, Hyssos. I just wanted … Did anyone see Po?"

"No one. Though we have not asked Sestos yet."

"Was the battle yesterday?" Arithon asked.

"You slept through yesterday. It is midmorning of the second day after."

"Two days," Arithon exhaled. "What was the *Swallow*'s heading?"

"When we last saw her, she was northbound toward Limnos."

"I need to get up," he said straining against the pain to rise. "I am already too stiff."

He grimaced but made it to a sitting position, his back to the wall.

"You better not let Lucina catch you. She labored hard to clean and dress your wounds."

"Who is she?"

"We do not know," answered Hyssos. "We thought you brought her along. She acts as if you did."

"She jumped with us, she … wait … she must be 'The Lady' Dagieri spoke of."

"Lady?" questioned Hyssos.

"That is what Dagieri called her, though I believe he was being sarcastic. I suspect she was a captive … or maybe a slave," he said.

"Why don't you ask her?" said Hyssos.

"That is not appropriate," Arithon said. "But I do need to find out about her."

"Where does she sleep?" Arithon asked, as if he was beginning to think about it.

"She has not slept," said Szaba. "She has remained here on this bench for two days."

Arithon was silent and stared through his knees at the floor.

"The meltemi still rages, unless my ears deceive me," he said.

"Yes, it is a strong one," agreed Hyssos. "I would guess two or three more days. Do you want to attempt Limnos?"

"No, I suspect the *Swallow* will hold up there for as long as it blows. When we do go, I want it to be at night."

"You look weak, Arithon, you should rest. We can talk with Sestos this evening."

"Agreed. I will rest but bring me something to eat. I am famished."

They both got up to leave.

"Oh, and send the girl to me," he added.

She appeared outside the door; he could see her bare feet through the crack at the bottom.

"Come in."

She slipped in and took a seat on the bench. Arithon was sitting up, but he had draped the sheepskin across his lap.

"I am Arithon," he said, thinking to correct his impoliteness.

"I am Lucina," she replied under his gaze. She dipped her head ever so little.

"Szaba and Hyssos tell me that you have nursed my wounds. I thank you."

"You are welcome," she replied in the politest Minoan.

He saw again how beautiful she was, but he also noticed her fatigue.

"I want you to lie down and go to sleep."

"Here?" she asked, and her head bobbled as if in agreement to the suggestion.

"Yes."

"Is that not inappropriate, even on Crete?"

"Yes," he smiled, "but I am not from Crete. I am a Cycladian, from Thera, and it would be considered inappropriate on Thera also. But this is unusual – at least for me – and I do not think it would be good – or appropriate – for you to sleep on the deck or in the hold with the men."

"I am tired," she agreed with a great yawn she tried to stifle. "I appreciate your – well, I might could …"

She teetered over, her eyes closing on the way down, and she was fast asleep when her face touched. Szaba appeared at the door with a fist-size block of cheese and a strip of dried meat. He also carried a skin of water, one of wine, and two cups. He looked at the girl and then at Arithon.

"Stretch her out and cover her up, if you would," said Arithon. "And sit down with me here and eat." Szaba emptied his hands and covered the sleeping girl, before joining Arithon.

They sat in silence eating, Arithon slowly, for he was full as soon as he started, but he ate what he could and drank at Szaba's insistence.

Moments after Arithon had taken a great gulp of wine, Szaba looked over and saw he was asleep sitting up. He laid him down, covered him and took one last look at both berths and left without a sound.

***

Light filtered in from a new sky when Arithon awoke again. He listened to the sounds of the ship and water and somehow knew it was early morning and not late evening. I have slept through, he decided.

The throbbing of his chest-wound had lessened, and he thought this a good sign, plus he felt stronger. He rolled over onto his side and saw her sleeping under a linen blanket on the bench across. He had forgotten about her; it all seemed so foggy. But there she was.

Her hair spilled across the arm she had tucked under her ear. She must have loosed the braid in the night. Long eyelashes formed two lacy crescents on her bronzed cheeks and her mouth was relaxed and slightly parted in the center.

He stared at her for quite some time. She was so still. Was she even breathing? She inhaled and her chest rose and fell in a tranquil sigh.

He felt light footsteps on the aft deck which interrupted his trance. That would be Szaba.

Arithon rose with a sore, but quiet push. He did not want to disturb the warm serenity. After completing a woozy stand, he made it out the door as best he could, proud that he had not awakened her. But he had. She watched him under parted eyelids.

It was, as he had guessed, morning, though the sun had not yet risen. He waddled to the gunnel in a needful hurry. Szaba met him when he finished and asked, "Would you like some clothes?"

Well, yes, he did seem to be naked. Szaba returned with a robe and a breakfast of barley porridge and a skin of diluted wine. Arithon walked back and forth, trying to limber up, chewing great mouthfuls.

"How is Sestos?" he asked.

"He was up late yesterday," answered Szaba. "He is talking again."

"That's a sure sign of recovery," laughed Arithon, wincing in stiff pain from the effort.

"Szaba, could you help me ashore? I would like to go for a walk."

It was more work than either of them would have believed, but Arithon made it ashore. The wind was blowing, and it tired him after a short walk inland. He sat in the shade of a rock shelf with Szaba beside him.

"You have found your bow I see," said Arithon. "I wondered if you lost it in the battle."

"No, I threw it onto the deck before I jumped. Jaros stowed it."

Arithon made other small talk, until he asked, "What are we to do with the girl?"

"She is unexpected."

"Good word, Szaba. For someone new to our language, you can be very precise sometimes."

"Yes, she is unexpected," Arithon began again. "This island looks uninhabited, and I do not have time to take her anywhere. We must make Limnos when the meltemi wanes, and I doubt Limnos is where she wants to go."

"Ask her," said Szaba.

Arithon thought to laugh but flinched against the pain. "Szaba, you are elegant and exact. I am starting to understand you are more gifted than I know. It is a bad trait of mine – underestimating friend and foe. Something I need to work on."

"Now if you could help me back to the *Dolphin*, I have exercised enough this morning."

When they got back to the ship, Hyssos was waiting for them.

"Good to see you up, Arithon. Are you healing?"

"My shoulder is sore, but it was not a deep cut."

"And the chest?"

"The wound is closed, but it is painful."

"Thank Lucina. She asked for many things, which we did not have, and ended up searching through our herbs and oils. I do not know what she finally concocted. She kept us away."

"Really?"

"Uh, yes." Hyssos shifted from foot to foot. "I worried about leaving you with a stranger, but she was so insistent, and I thought – well, she ..."

"Do not fret about it, Hyssos.

"Is she awake yet?"

"She went ashore. I thought you saw her."

"No. Szaba and I were walking. ... Leave her be."

Arithon worked until midday cleaning himself up. It was exhausting, but he knew he would feel better after shaving and donning a clean tunic – or so he told himself.

Sestos joined him for a joyous reunion at midday and they talked most of the afternoon. He told them about their meeting with Dagieri and waking up in the storehouse with a busted head. It was a blurred nightmare until he was dragged up onto the deck and saw Arithon standing over him.

"I almost didn't recognize you," Sestos remembered. "You looked like you had stepped out of one of those murals back home or a legend of old. You were a demigod!"

"Do not say that. I was just ... mad."

"I am glad you were mad at them and not me. And have I said thank you?"

"Countless times," said Arithon.

They decided to have a celebratory feast on shore that evening: those injured were on the mend, and they had retrieved their shipmate. The wind howled, but Pserimos had discovered a sheltered area behind a rock wall, where a fire could be made.

When all were ashore preparing, Arithon grew concerned for the girl, for she had not returned.

"Has anyone seen her?" he asked Hyssos.

"No, but she said she would be gone a while. She asked if we would be leaving today, and I told her no. She asked for a few odds and ends, and then I put her ashore and she walked off up the hill."

"What odds and ends? What did she ask for?"

"Oh, nothing strange really: a knife, a basket, a waterskin. She borrowed a needle and two swaths of material from Felos' stores. Said she was going to repair her clothes and hunt for medicinal herbs."

Arithon fidgeted for a while, watching the men build a fire. The crew was drinking wine and preparing to spit roast the shellfish they had foraged.

As sundown approached, he paced; his chest was throbbing again. Perhaps he was trying to do too much too soon.

Restless and uncomfortable, he drifted up the hill wanting a distraction from the pain. He passed those on firewood patrol and arrived at a rivulet where the water crew was dipping cups into larger pithoi. "Do not be gone long," they said, "we are going to make Theran snail soup."

He continued to walk up the watercourse, interested as all wanderers are, in where such things begin and how they trace their path through the wilderness.

He had gone far enough to be out of sight when he noticed the footprint of a girl: light with a high arch. She had paused at a tiny basin, where the water collected for a moment before it spilled over a rock lip and continued its path to the sea.

So, she made it this far, he thought. I wonder where she is.

He continued up, telling himself that he would only go a little farther and all the while thinking of her.

But he should be thinking about Po. He stopped and turned back to the feast.

"How are your wounds?" came her voice behind.

He pivoted, startled.

She was carrying a basket filled with the cuttings of different plants, plus a half dozen tubers.

But the most startling thing was her appearance. She had altered the male Minoan kilt to a more female version; but too short: it only covered to her knees. She had sewn two colors of material to imitate the flounce skirts that were popular with the women. The tunic covered her breasts.

He thought to tell her the breasts should be exposed if she was going to dress as a Minoan but thought better of it. He once teased a Theran girl about her attire and his mother overheard him. She informed him that inflicted embarrassment, whether intentional, or unintentional, was unworthy behavior. She had a way of making you feel terrible when you disappointed her, and this had been one of those times.

Her hair was washed and wavy: the curling-ribbons had left telltale marks. It was a Minoan style with a bun and two braids in back. A decorative ribbon interlaced the arrangement and wound through the braids, hanging from the tips like a tassel. Little curls bobbed before her ears. She knew the Minoan style, but she was not Minoan. He was sure of that.

But more than her dress and her hair, he felt her presence. And it centered in her eyes and pushed ahead of her like the glow of a lamp. She barely reached his shoulder, but he sensed power – power and intelligence – and he was drawn to it.

"They are healing – you did well."

She dipped her eyes.

"We are having a feast. Will you join us?"

"Of course," she answered, "my fate is entangled with yours.

For a time," she added, as she stepped in beside him with the basket in the crook of her arm.

"What is your fate?" he asked.

"To determine it – or so I hope," she answered.

"Because you are now free?" Arithon probed.

She hesitated and looked at him.

"Were you a captive … or a …" he trailed off.

They walked a few steps while she pondered her answer.

"A captive," she said and cut her eyes to see his reaction. She was relieved to see he was staring ahead.

"We are going to Limnos," he said, "and I expect your captors are there."

"They are," she agreed.

"I have to rescue a friend," he said, as if he were apologizing.

"Someone from the crew of the *Swallow*?"

"Yes, how did you … well of course you would know of the *Swallow*."

"Whom do you seek?" she asked. "I may know of him."

"His name is Poius – "

"Oh, I have heard your men speak of Po. Are they one and the same?"

"Yes."

"Describe him," she insisted.

Arithon understood what Hyssos meant about her persistence.

"He is about this tall, forty, and bald across here," – he made a sweep of his hand over his upper forehead. "Wears a horsetail like …"

"I know him," she interrupted. "They call him Cretan. He is on the *Swallow*."

"How –"

"I was on the *Swallow* … for a while."

"For a while?" he questioned.

"Yes. But my presence was … disruptive to the crew. The *Swallow* captain transferred me to the *Stag*."

She continued as they walked, "Do you know why the Achaean dropped his knife? The one who was going to kill Sestos."

"No," he answered, "I have not thought about it until you brought it up just now."

"Because I slit the back of his leg with a dagger through the boards," she said. "He was an ugly man.

"Twice, men of the crew tried to rape me," she said with no expression. "The first one, I broke his nose so it will forever be crooked. He was punished – they whipped him cruelly – and he threatened me from then on.

"Another tried later, and I escaped by jumping overboard. The Achaean captain on the *Swallow* was so angry he placed me on the *Stag*. I was tied from then on and guarded by one he thought could be trusted.

"But the one who later brought Sestos on deck was bribing my guard. They would talk in front of me, thinking I could not understand. Their plan was to rape me together – either in Lesvos or on the way to Limnos. Your arrival upset their plans."

"How did you get away then?" asked Arithon.

"I was napping when a flurry of activity told me something dangerous was coming. That was something new for me – a naval battle.

"I was desperate, knowing I would drown if the ship sank – like a chained slave."

Arithon's eyebrows went up when she said 'slave,' and she saw it.

"I implored the guard to untie me, but he refused and stood to peer out through a spot in the hull. My heart was pounding when the battle commenced, and I was feeling trapped and frantic when I heard the splintering of wood and the cries of wounded men. As soon as the raking stopped, the whole ship shuddered, and your sprit crashed through the hull. The ship heeled and my guard fell against me, dropping his sword. I wrapped my legs around his neck, intending to squeeze the life out of him.

"I have strong legs."

"I have noticed," he said. Which was true, but he regretted the statement as he uttered it. She stared up at him, slightly askance before she continued.

"I had enough play in my bonds to reach the sword and hold it between my tied hands. I brought it down into his heart – an awful thing – and then freed myself. I was peering through the boards trying to figure out what was going on, and how I could get away, when you landed out of the sky.

"He is a Minoan, I said to myself."

"How could you tell?"

"I think it was the dolphin," she smiled.

"I watched you make your onslaught across the deck. I was fascinated by your intensity. It was overpowering, Arithon. It really was."

Arithon pursed his lips.

"And then I thought, perhaps I can escape with him. I was trying to decide how I could help you – and so help myself – when I saw you stop above me.

"I heard that hated voice say, 'Stay back.'

"I crept underneath him and jabbed the sword up. I had hoped to hit him somewhere else," she laughed, "but it accomplished the task."

Arithon squirmed, and said, "Yes, you saved Sestos' life, and mine too."

She nodded and stopped talking as if she had said too much. And maybe she had. Arithon began to wonder at the violence which defined her life and her ability to talk about it as if she was talking about someone else. Arithon knew the world was dangerous and deadly, but to him it had always been an impersonal peril with plunder at its core and he just an obstacle. Her dangers appeared to be directed or centered on her. What kind of 'captive' was she?

She perceived his mind and directed him away. "Is Po your friend?"

"I have known him all my life; my father's greatest friend. He helped me to grow. Taught me to be a man."

"He did well," she said under her breath and he missed the reply as she intended.

"What is Po doing on the *Swallow*?" asked Arithon.

"It is a Minoan ship. He shows them how to sail and navigate. He is a captive."

Arithon chewed on his lower lip. She noticed.

"Who has the *Swallow* now? What is her homeport?"

"The Achaeans. Poliochni, on the island of Limnos."

"How did they get her? Do you know?"

"A little, but what is your interest in the *Swallow*?" she asked.

"It is my father's ship."

"Do you intend to rescue Po or take back the *Swallow*?" she asked.

"Both," he said as they approached the feast and he hurried to his final statement.

"I must go to Limnos, and I have no time to take you elsewhere. I do not think it is good to leave you here, but it will be dangerous at Limnos, and –"

"Arithon, I will go to Limnos," she interrupted. "I can help. I have lived on Limnos. Just do not leave me there."

"I will not leave you there," he promised.

***

The evening was a whir of eating, drinking, and laughing. Sestos was himself again, telling jokes and making light of his ordeal. Only his closest friends noticed the subtle change.

The girl was popular. So much so that Arithon dropped his intentions of spending the night planning and instead let the crew relax and forget.

They slept on shore that night, the girl a little apart, but close enough to the First Tier to feel safe. Neither she nor Arithon knew it, but Szaba kept a watchful eye over her.

Szaba was up before dawn, followed by Lucina, who found her way up the stream and disappeared. Arithon slept until the sun climbed over the protective rock wall and began to warm his skin. He lay with his eyes closed, testing his sore body, when he realized the wind was not droning through the brush. This brought him fully awake. It would be today.

CHAPTER 27 THE SWIFT

The Fates of Atropos, Clotho, Lachesis, set a man's birth, life thread, and death. A melody of pipes, lyre and voice floated to earth for the second time, though mortals would not yet remember the first.

Now was their chance and they might not get another. The wind had dropped in the hour before dawn, and the sea, though heavy with rollers, had fallen enough for them to attempt Limnos; and if they left by early afternoon they would arrive under cover of night. Worried he had not recovered, Arithon spent the morning stretching his body with Szaba's help. His shoulder was no longer painful, and he had full use of his left side, but his right chest was piercingly sore. Though the drainage was clear he feared fever; he had experienced none so far; probably a testament to Lucina's skill; but its onset would cripple him for weeks – if he lived through it.

Hyssos took charge of the rested crew and had the *Dolphin* ready by midday. The girl returned in the late morning, her basket brimming with sprigs and late summer blooms, which she stored after a consultation with Vori.

Hyssos, judging it time, steered the *Dolphin* into open water, and the crew began a hard row for Limnos. The seas were jarring but by early evening the swells had diminished enough for the First Tier to convene on a dry deck.

"Rescuing Po is our first objective," Arithon began, "but I want to retake the *Swallow*. Therans will need any ship still afloat in the Aegean, and the *Swallow* is one of our best."

"She," and he nodded at Lucina, "was on the *Swallow*."

The gathering turned to look at her. She hesitated under the stares and then began.

"There is a city, Poliochni, on the east side of Limnos where the Achaeans have set up an 'arrangement' with the local First Family. They want access to the spont – do you call it that?"

"Yes, we call it that," Hyssos confirmed.

"The Achaeans are setting up long trade routes into the Black Sea and they want a base here at the entrance. It has proven profitable. They trade in grain, oils, pottery, metals, gold, amber, and of course slaves. What they lack are good ships. They have not your skill, yet," she looked around the circle, "in the maritimes. They are supported by and serve the mainland city-states, but they act sometimes as traders, sometimes as privateers, whichever suits their needs."

"How do you know all of this?" asked Sestos.

"Because I have been a pawn in more than one of these agreements," she answered, "and I have learned to pay attention to the power shifts."

This was the same talk Arithon had heard from Mara. The tides were changing, and the Minoan high-water mark was passing. Arithon, dismayed by the crumbling of his orderly world, was beginning little by little to accept the bitterness of its passing. The choices he once thought he had were narrowing quickly.

"Please continue," he said, realizing she was waiting for his mental cogitations to conclude.

"The *Swallow* arrived months back, and the Achaeans took her the first night. There was a horrible fight – a score were killed. Po sustained a head wound, but he has recovered and is now a slave aboard his own ship.

"What of the crew," asked Arithon.

"Those not killed, were sold," she said.

Hyssos and Sestos cursed. Po's crew were their friends and hailed from the best families of Thera. Arithon immediately thought of Scrius, the family Roa had assisted. This news would go hard, as he was the head of the family. The rest of Minoa might hesitate, but for Arithon and his companions, a war with the Achaeans was underway.

They talked into the fading light, asking her a string of details: the numbers of Achaeans permanently stationed there; how and where they anchored the *Swallow*; and the geography of the port and the surrounding land.

"There is a large gulf on the south side which we can enter," she said. "If we anchor in a cove on the east side of it, your men can cross the peninsula and be back before morning."

Very late in the evening, Jaros called down that he could discern the peaks of Limnos in the distance.

"Your timing is as good as ever, Hyssos," complimented Arithon. "They will never see our approach tonight."

It took them almost three hours to find a suitable location and hide the *Dolphin* as best they could from unfriendly eyes. Szaba and Sestos prepared to depart, as the night was already old, and Arithon was anxious for them.

The girl came to the rail as they were lowering the tender.

"I will go with them," she said.

"No," said Arithon, "they need to move fast."

But she was resolute and retorted, "They will be faster with me to guide them and I can keep up."

The three looked at her in the darkness; none doubted that she could keep up, and her knowledge would, in truth, help guide them rapidly over unfamiliar terrain in the darkness.

Arithon hesitated, and then said, "Agreed, but I will go also."

Sestos and Szaba looked at each other and Sestos said, "Arithon, rest. We can do this without you."

Arithon started to protest but Szaba caught his eye and Arithon knew Szaba agreed. He also knew it was the right decision.

"Go with haste," he said, "keep each other safe and return by morning. We may have to leave if we are discovered."

The three nodded and deftly climbed into the tender so Jaros could row them ashore.

***

Arithon surprised himself and fell asleep around midnight, but awoke an hour before first light, worried about the three scouts. He was feeling strong again – almost battle ready – and the chest wound, though sore, appeared to have closed. He stretched on the deck, and then took the tender over to the beach and began to jog up and down, exercising his legs and lungs again. It felt better than he even thought it would, so he continued, until he had worked up a sweat. The girl had referred to herself as a 'pawn in more than one of these agreements.' He had let it pass but now he wondered what it meant. He was deciding she was more than the accidental captive – but what or who he did not know.

The three appeared on the far end of the beach. He met them standing by the tender. They all looked tired, but otherwise unharmed.

"They were preparing for us," growled Sestos, "and they know we are here."

"Who knows we are here?" asked Arithon.

"Let's get aboard and we can discuss it," Sestos suggested with a slight edge.

"One moment, please," said the girl as she disappeared back into the brush.

Szaba and Sestos looked at each other. Sestos waited until she was out of sight and then said in a low voice, "There is more to her than we know."

"What," replied Arithon, "what do you mean?"

"She slipped away from us for 'a moment', and was gone for almost an hour, and shortly after she returned, we were found."

"Are we in danger now?" asked Arithon.

"I do not think so but let us get back aboard."

They began to push the tender off, when she reappeared, "Taking me along, I hope," she called, trotting up to the water.

"Yes, get in," motioned Arithon. They paddled silently to the *Dolphin* and assembled on the rear deck, after gathering cheese, raisins, and water for the breakfast.

"Who knows we are here," asked Arithon, "the Achaeans or the locals?"

"Both, but the Achaeans are actively preparing for us – or watching for us. The locals assist them," answered Sestos.

Arithon expelled a breath and waited.

"The *Swallow* is tied to the quay and guarded," Sestos began again. "And an even bigger surprise is the *Stag* is there."

"Are you sure?" said Arithon.

"It is the one," said Szaba. "They are rebuilding the oar rail."

"So, they are better mariners than we at first gave them credit," mused Arithon.

Hyssos looked a little uncomfortable. Arithon noticed.

"Not just you, Hyssos, I made the same mistake. I make it often – underestimating my foe," said Arithon. "We learn together."

Hyssos nodded.

"So, they managed to tow her back – and in those winds – no small feat," said Arithon. "They will not be so easily caught off guard next time."

"No, they will not," said Szaba. "They are expecting us."

"And they have dead shipmates to avenge," Arithon added in a whisper.

"But we have scores of Therans to avenge," said Sestos, "and at least one to rescue."

280

"Did you see Po?" asked Arithon.

"No."

"Then he may not be aboard."

"He is not," interjected the girl.

They all looked at her, but no one said anything, and the silence became uncomfortable.

"I left to make contact with … with a compatriot. I knew you would not send me into danger, so I went on my own counsel," she then said.

Szaba and Sestos were staring at her.

"Did you know you were being followed?" asked Sestos.

"No, I realized it same as you when Szaba figured it out."

Arithon looked at Szaba, who nodded and blinked his eyes, so he knew the matter had been taken care of.

"Are we in danger now?" Arithon asked. "Should we move the *Dolphin*?"

"We may want to move the *Dolphin*," said Sestos looking up into the hills. "At least we should not stay in one place too long."

"But how do you know Po is not aboard?" asked Arithon.

"He was brought ashore and is being held in secret. They suspect he is valuable to you, and could be a bargaining piece," she added.

"Dagieri?" said Arithon looking at Sestos.

Sestos was thoughtful and then said, "Possibly. Our inquiries obviously would make him suspicious. He would have told the Achaeans."

He was quiet in thought again before adding, "And it would not have escaped their notice that the only thing you took from the last encounter was me."

Arithon's brow furrowed. Many things were going through his mind, but the fact his adversaries would know his true goal complicated everything. He had hoped for a quick raid, like he had executed on the open sea, but now this was unavailable.

All in the circle were silent, watching him. He became aware of their stares.

"I need to know where they are holding him," he said looking straight at the girl, "and," he paused, "and how long they will be in port."

Without waiting for an answer, he turned to Hyssos, "Move the *Dolphin* to the south. Find another hideout."

While Hyssos prepared the crew, Arithon thought to continue the discussion, but the three remaining looked out-all-night tired. Arithon sent them off to sleep the morning away, leaving him to think.

In the late afternoon, he knocked softly on the small door of his cabin, "I would like to talk," he said.

"Come in," she replied. "It is, after all, your cabin."

He entered slowly, saying, "Yes, I know, but I did not want to, well I did not want to …"

"You were being polite," she interrupted. "I thank you."

He sat down on his usual sleeping bench, she across, under a blanket, sitting with her knees up under her chin. Her tunic lay across the foot of the bed. He saw it and it caught his attention, distracting him. She noticed and smiled slightly.

He shook it off and began, "I have been thinking while you slept, and I have much to ask you."

She looked at him waiting.

"First," he began utterly businesslike, "I want to know if you can help us, and what you want in return."

"And second?" she said, tilting her head ever so slightly and raising an eyebrow.

"Uh … second," he stammered, "well …"

"I was playing with you," she interrupted.

Arithon smiled looking down and said, "I am sorry to act so direct but …"

"But your friend's life is in the balance," she again interrupted, "and you do not know if you can trust me. You are right to act so."

Arithon chuckled quietly.

"Why do you laugh?" she asked.

"I was wondering if you would always complete my sentences for me."

Now she was off guard.

"I am sorry. I am not shy, and I often speak my own mind, and –"

"Keep your own counsel," now interrupted Arithon.

She bowed her head and smiled, "Match."

"Match?" he puzzled.

"You know," she said, "we are evenly matched – like in a game. Do you play games?"

282

"Dangerous ones, these days," he said, "but as a child I played all the games. I understand your meaning now. I have just never heard it used like that."

"I can help you," she asserted. "And you are correct – I want something."

"But what I want is *your* help, and I had hoped it would be something we would not have to bargain for – each other's help.

"But I also understand we have only been together a short while and trust needs to develop.

"I believe, though, that the Fates have brought us together, and in this I am much encouraged," she added.

"Fates?" he questioned.

"Oh, I am mixing beliefs. The Achaeans believe in three goddesses that determine Man's destiny, weaving the thread of their lives."

"Do you believe in these Fates?" he asked.

"I am not Achaean, but I do believe in a kind of destiny for us all."

"I am glad you are not Achaean … but what are you?" he asked.

"I am someone in need of help. Is that enough?" she asked.

He paused and then answered, "It is enough for Arithon, but it is not enough for the captain of the *Dolphin*."

She wavered, then said, "I do not wish to mislead you, though I already have."

As he stared over at her, he felt, for the first time, an inner turmoil.

"You guessed I was a captive, and I agreed because it is true … in a way."

"In a way?"

"Yes, but it is complicated. I want to tell you. I will tell you. But I am looking for the right time and this is not it, I judge."

"But you expect my help, when I know so little about you," he stated.

"Yes," she said with no hesitation.

"Why?"

"Because you would," she whispered, holding him with her eyes before looking down.

Arithon was dumbstruck. He had no argument. She was right – he would. He was not sure why he would, or even how she knew, but somehow, she was right. He sat there, staring into nothing, then looked up and saw she was staring at him. He felt her presence – it enveloped him. Again, he was powerfully attracted to her.

"I will," he said, "What help do you need?"

"I need the freedom of another, and transport to the eastern shore – near Troy."

"Can the other's freedom be bought?" he asked.

"No," she said with a shake of the head, "she is a hostage – a royal hostage."

Arithon was quiet again, then said, "Who's enmity will we earn?"

"That which you have already begun," she replied.

"The Achaeans," he voiced.

She said nothing.

"I have plans," he added. "Let us get the others and discuss them."

He stood as if waiting for her to rise, but she looked up at him and said, "I need to dress."

Arithon looked awkward and said, "Oh, yes, forgive me," and started out the door.

"I do," she said, mocking his seriousness.

CHAPTER 28 LUTEA

The Dryad slept at the top of the great oak, its home and life, pondering its own Fates.

The First Tier discussed for hours their options and stratagems, weighing the consequences of each. It was proposed they might try to buy Po, and take the *Swallow* later, but they now had the added complexity of the hostage. Round they went until nearly dark when they finally arrived at a workable but dangerous plan. Each agreed to it, knowing the risks, and for that Arithon was grateful.

When darkness covered the water like a thick blanket, the *Dolphin* slipped out of the shallows and moved quietly north. Only the creaking of the oars, and the soft cry of 'ho' from the lead oar could be heard over the wash on the shore. Even the gulls, floating in the surf, or perched on the sands, were not disturbed by their passing. When they reached the anchorage of the night before, the tender was lowered and two unlikely figures were paddled ashore, slipped across the beach, and disappeared into the brush.

"Follow me," she challenged, "and see if you can keep up."

Arithon started to retort, but knowing she would best him verbally, kept his tongue.

Though shorter, her legs propelled her along at a clip that surprised Arithon. Pushing over the low hills, she did not hesitate, nor stop for any reason, always finding the path she wanted. Arithon found himself watching her in the darkness, her silhouette floating ahead of him. He had never watched a girl run before. Her stride was smoother than his, but more things were moving – in graceful arcs. He would have enjoyed it any other time, but now he had a head full of troubling thoughts to occupy his mind, and his wound was throbbing.

After an hour, she came to a stop and they rested and drank from their waterskins. "Slower from here on." she spoke quietly, "We are approaching the outlying farms."

For the second hour they moved more stealthily, often stopping and watching the trails ahead for movement.

"Where did Szaba detect the follower last time?" he asked on one of their stops.

"We are taking a different path," she answered, "a more wandering route, but safer I hope."

Arithon nodded approval and they continued. They reached the outlying neighborhoods with no encounters and sat down in a small, sheltered scoop in the hill which looked down onto a city, Arithon reckoned of five or six thousand. Lucina reached down and grabbed a few pebbles, which she tucked into a fold under her belt.

"That is the Temple of Artemis," she said pointing at one of the larger buildings.

"Can we get to it without being seen?" he asked.

"I can," she quipped, "but I don't know about you."

Arithon raised his eyebrows but said nothing.

"I made it there last night," she said more seriously, "but I picked up the follower – on the way out."

"None tonight," he said.

She looked at him and pulled up one corner of her mouth in an odd sneer. This was something new for Arithon and he was not sure how to react. It was funny and ominous all at the same time, so he smiled slightly. She relaxed and smiled also, and then rose and started into the town with him behind.

The streets and paths were familiar to her and she knew the exact route she wanted to take; one she deemed the most hidden from peering eyes. Earlier, while running, she had maintained a consistent, efficient rhythm, but now she was more catlike in her movements. Slicing in and out of the shadows and hurrying across the open areas, she constantly adjusted to the obstacles. She would jump to the top of walls, light as air, and pivot over in a coordinated kip, landing softly on the other side. He worked hard to keep up, but more than that, he was astounded by her athletic ability. He had always prided himself on his own agility, but her nimbleness was a level or more above his own.

The Temple of Artemis was an imposing structure set on a hill in the city; the entire compound surrounded by a six-foot wall with one main gate at the south end. Inside the walls, the land was terraced with wide stone steps which the devotees would ascend to the two heavy, wooden front doors: the only entrance to the building.

The doors stood open that night and a soft light glowed from within, spilling out of the opening and down onto the stairs in a fan shaped column which only made the edges of the temple complex even darker. It was into this darkness they landed, after scaling the north wall.

The second floor of the temple was ringed with windows, those in the front lit by the same flame as the doorway: the front chamber being two stories high. But the three windows in the back were dark and it was under these she crouched. Arithon stood twenty paces away under a well-pruned olive tree.

She took two pebbles from her belt and jumping away from the wall, threw them one after another through the center window, before sliding back against the building.

After a brief pause, the face of a teenage girl appeared, peering out into the night.

"Lutea," said Lucina in a hushed voice, "it is Lucina. The rope."

The face disappeared and a knotted rope was tossed out the opening, the end hitting the wall next to Lucina.

She grabbed it with one hand, turned to face the wall, shinnied up the rope as if she had done it a hundred times, and vanished into the black opening. The rope slithered up the wall and disappeared behind her.

Arithon waited in the darkness.

What was taking so long? She had plenty of time to execute their plan – unless she had been captured. His scalp began to prickle with sweat imagining all that could go wrong, but he remained still, an unwanted intruder in an unknown land.

And then the rope appeared and Lucina's hand motioned. Relieved, he bolted to the rope and tied a bag to the end, jerked twice and darted back to the safety of the shadows.

Time passed, and to Arithon it felt a longer, more anxious wait than the first. His eyes were fixed on the black rectangle on the high wall, when he picked up a familiar movement. Odd that he could already discern her signature motions after so little time. There was comfort in that.

The rope sailed out the window and he saw Lucina perch for a second like a bird on a cliff. She then slid to the ground and flew to him.

Arithon could not help but feel proud of her.

Swift, he thought; and graceful.

Arithon noticed she carried a well-made leather bag, strapped like a sash. She started back on their entry route, when Arithon grabbed her shoulder and pulled her ear close to his face.

"Did you find out where Po is?" he whispered.

She nodded, still looking ahead.

"I want to see," he whispered again.

She shook her head no.

Arithon squared her around and realized she was crying. He assumed the worst – at least the worst for him.

"Is Po dead?" he asked.

"No!" she said.

"Then why are you crying?"

"Aaaauuu," she uttered a little too loud. "Forget it. It will pass."

He looked at her puzzled, but also knew he had missed the chance.

She mastered her feelings, changed her mind and said, "I will show you where they are keeping Po. Come."

She led him through the city until they were within sight of the quay. The *Swallow* was anchored on the south side of the dock and the damaged *Stag* was moored opposite. Four armed men were stationed between the two vessels. Arithon could hear their muffled voices floating up the hill to where he and Lucina were hiding in the lee of a stone wall.

"The buildings below are the Achaean Quarter. That one there is where Po is kept.

"Do they guard that building?" he asked.

"Two," she said.

"Will your friend be able to bribe them?"

"I told you she would," she blurted and then softened, "Yes, she will do what she has to do."

Arithon was puzzled by her anger but busied himself scanning the harbor and the buildings below. When he had memorized as much as needed, he turned to see that she was staring ahead, but not seeing – her mind somewhere else.

"Time," he said.

Roused from her trance, she looked at him with a sad smile and said, "Yes. This way."

She took off with her usual grace and speed, on an intricate route through the streets, alleys, and courtyards. She seemed to know every twist and turn and anticipate all the obstacles. After a handful of scrambling climbs, at times balancing across the length of a solitary wall, they were on the edge of the city and moving at a rhythmic pace across the rolling hills. Arithon kept turning to look for pursuers, and when he was satisfied they were not being followed, he began to think of a host of other things: Po, Mara, the Achaeans, and his plans to retake the *Swallow*. But his mind kept coming back to her tears after her visit to the temple.

A short run from the *Dolphin*, they came upon a hidden recess in an overhanging bank.

"Can we stop here?" he asked, causing her to pull up. They were both sweating, and winded; neither of them aware of how hard they had been running; lost in their own thoughts.

"Yes," she replied. "Do you need a rest?"

He laughed at her competitiveness and said, "We both do."

After their drink, Arithon had them nestle into the alcove away from searching eyes, but in a good position to view the trail they had come down. It was a space so small they had to sit shoulder-to-shoulder with their backs to the rocks.

"What happened at the temple?" he asked.

She was quiet, thoughtful for a moment. She knew what he wanted to know, but she was upset and not sure she was ready to have the conversation.

"We discussed the plan," she answered.

Arithon shifted and pulled on his bandage. She saw his discomfort with a start, "Arithon, I am sorry. I had forgotten your wound. I have run you hard tonight. I have much on my mind."

"Judging by your performance, I would have thought you did that every night," he said.

"I do – or I did," she said with a small smile.

He knitted his eyebrows so amusingly she laughed aloud.

"I lived for a time in the Temple of Artemis," she began, her tone softening as if she were admitting something personal. "In that very window. That was my rope you saw.

"I used to slip out almost every night and romp through the countryside like a wild goat," she laughed.

"Like a night swift," he said.

She paused and repeated, "Like a swift. ... I like that better than a goat."

"I needed to breathe the outside air," she continued. "I needed to feel as if I were free, if only for a night. It is so stifling in that temple, and we are never supposed to leave. But I did."

"I would expect that," he said.

"I was never caught, although I came close a few times. I learned every possible pathway through the neighborhoods, and every trail in the countryside within a night's run."

"A night's run?"

"Well, yes. I had to be back before sunrise. As I learned more and more of the terrain, I kept going farther until my only limitation was my ability to run all night – and there were times when I did."

"But it is an island, and you cannot really escape without a ship," said Arithon.

"Yes," she said, "and that is why you are my best chance – the best chance for the hostage and I."

"Is she in agreement?" he asked.

"Yes, but ..." she hesitated. He turned and she turned away, talking to the darkness, "Lutea cannot execute our plan exactly as you and I discussed it."

He waited for her to continue.

"The guards will not be bribed by the opium as we had hoped – not that alone."

"How does she know –" Arithon started.

"She knows one of them – he comes to the temple every day. Lutea says he will not take a bribe."

"Then how will she do it?"

"He may agree, if she offers ... offers to meet him," she stuttered.

Arithon looked at her puzzled as ever.

"Don't you understand?" she said, tears starting in her eyes. "He wants her!"

Arithon did not know what to say. He blurted out clumsily, "But she is in the Temple. A hostage or priestess, or whatever you call it. Is this not forbidden?"

She laughed, staring up at the sky, tears flowing down her cheeks. "Of course it is. Are you that inexperienced? What do you think really goes on?"

Arithon was taken aback. This was not the conversation he thought he would be having, and he was unprepared for it. He had no first-hand knowledge of the world of hostages, slaves, and priestesses and their subtle degrees of difference. She, in contrast, seemed to have a complete understanding. And she had total disdain of his innocence – as if he were somehow at wrong. He knew nothing to say, and so said the only thing that was true.

"I do not know."

"It is all mixed up," she continued. "Some of the hostages live as part of a family, or as a teacher, or a confidant. A handful end up as priestesses attending to some god's temple and, of course, the luckless end up as slaves – bedroom slaves if they are unfortunate enough to be desirable."

"And some," she said, "are all of those put together, depending on the circumstances."

"And what are the captives of that temple?" Arithon asked.

He stared into the night, waiting for her to answer.

She knew where he was aiming, and she answered carefully.

"Priestesses are not harlots – as a mariner would think of the word. But condemned to the confines of a single building, they will often resort to physical favors, to get some – any – chance at life. Can you understand that? You have always been free, so do not judge the devices of those who have never been."

"I do not judge. But have we asked Lutea to do something she has never done, and if so, why are my desires to free Po, worth that which some prize even greater?"

Lucina went rigid, not expecting such a reply. She softened, turned to Arithon, tears flowing freely and said, "I am sorry for my harsh words, Arithon. You think beyond your own needs to the needs of others – even those you do not know. I ..." she checked herself before she let her defense down – a defense she had adopted to survive a perilous world which Arithon was only now beginning to enter. She wiped her tears with both hands and then continued, "As to Lutea, it is I who have counseled her in this plan, and it is I who will bear that burden. You hold no blame in it."

"But I do," he protested. "I doubt she would do this for me, if she did not think her freedom was to be bought by it. I would attain her freedom if you but asked."

"I know," she said taking his fist and cupping it between her two hands. "But do not worry so much – it may not come to pass as you think.

"There are ..." she looked embarrassed and stammered for words, "... there are other ways – well I cannot talk about them so freely with you.

291

Besides, her main goal is to distract him and the other guard with the opium. She is resourceful. Trust she will do what we need without too great a cost to herself."

Still holding his fist, she rose and pulled him up. "It is late Arithon, let us get back to the ship. But first I will have a look at your wound."

And so they ran the last half hour in silence. She seemed much relieved and ran light on her feet back to the beach where Jaros ferried them back to the ship.

While Hyssos roused the crew to move the *Dolphin* to another location, Arithon and Lucina stood on the aft deck eating olives and drinking diluted wine. Lucina yawned.

"Lucina, take the cabin. Get some sleep. Dawn is not far."

"That is the first time you have called me Lucina."

Arithon looked at her and raised his eyebrows.

"But you will need to sleep also," she added, "and it is your cabin."

"That leaves the hold with the men, or the deck – which would you choose," he said laughing.

"Wherever the captain deems," she replied.

"Off to the cabin," he commanded.

She turned to go but Arithon stopped her. "Forgive me, but I am curious to know why you advised Lutea so?"

"Because she is in more danger than she knows."

Arithon paused and then nodded. "Rest," he said.

CHAPTER 29 PREPARATIONS

Hera, protector of women, played with the swifts in her garden, eating an apple. She touched them with her scepter as they rounded on the wing, turning each a different color of the rainbow.

A lone crow perched on top of the mast as if laying claim to a piece of harbor debris. The sun was well up and he was stretching his wings and looking at the left one, where a lost feather had created an unseemly notch. Szaba was watching the bird of omens and wondered if he might ought to send it flapping before the superstitious in the crew arose. But Arithon emerged from his cabin before he could act, and the bird took flight and distracted Arithon for a long moment as he watched it make a broad circle and settle in a teetering dance onto the shore.

"Ai," he expelled, before he noticed Szaba watching him. "Not exactly the bird I wanted to see this morning," he offered in response to the look.

"What bird would you have?" Szaba asked.

"Well …" he wavered, "a swift, maybe." Arithon pursed his lips and looked at his friend. "Szaba, you have sent many to the ferry," he began, looking away toward the bird. "How … What do you think of it?"

Szaba paused so long that Arithon wondered if he had understood the question, but when he looked, he saw the African was deep in deliberation. A flock of seagulls left the beach in a rowdy caucus.

"I think it is wrong," he said.

"But …" Arithon started and realized what he was about to say. A gull wheeled over in a dive near the port side, then thought better of it, pulled up, and flapped toward open water on bended wing.

Szaba nodded a short agreement to the futility of further words.

In the evening, while the crew was preparing for a long and dangerous night, Lucina helped Arithon wrap his sore chest. He was sitting in the cabin as she stood in front of him.

"I am going to wrap it tightly because it will loosen through the night. This should help prevent the wound tearing open," she said as she pulled a piece of linen around his chest.

"Not too tight," he petitioned, "I need to breathe."

"You will be fine – just a few more wraps. Only you will have no room to paint your dolphin."

Arithon smiled, having already forgotten his dolphin. "Then I will paint it under my wrap – wait." He started to unwind the wrapping.

"Sorry I mentioned it," she said feigning irritation. "What did you use the first time?"

Arithon was already pulling his trunk and rummaging through to extract a box.

"I have a collection of shadows and pigments," he said, sitting back down on the bench. "Minoans – men and women – use them to … well … to change the way they look. Have you ever –"

"Of course," she interrupted. "I am just without my things. You may remember that I came aboard with nothing but my tunic."

"Yes, I remember you ran past me and jumped into the sea."

"I wanted to ask you," she said, "Why did you not strike me as I ran to the gunnel. You thought to but did not."

"I do not know," he answered, fumbling with his jars, "You called to me in Minoan, and I realized you were a woman, but it was more than that. There was something about the way you move – it caused me to hesitate and then you were beside me on the rail."

"Is it nice, the way I move?" she asked.

"Yes, uh, yes, of course – but – well, I do not know how to describe it. Have you ever experienced something, and you feel like you have done it before – in your past or in a dream?"

"Yes, of course. I know what you mean. You Minoans are not the only ones with dreams.

"Give me the pigments and sit down. We want a big and beautiful dolphin this time."

Arithon thought to protest her critique of his previous artistry, but before he could say anything, she dropped to her knees in front of him, dipped her finger into the jar of blue pigment and began to trace it across his chest.

Chills ran down his back so strong that he shuddered.

"Are you all right?" she asked.

"Yes, it tickles," he lied.

He felt again the aura that glowed from her body and the tip of her finger focused it upon his body, causing bumps to rise on his arms and neck. He had never been so moved by the touch of another human and it threw him into a stupor. Tingling waves would start on the back of his neck and travel down to his knees. It was the sensation of being cold, only it made him strangely warm.

She changed colors to something earth-colored and smeared it with her four fingers inside the body of the outlined dolphin. This new pleasure coursed through him and he found himself staring past her face at her breast as they shook under the tunic and swayed from the movement of her arms.

And then she was done and stood up. "How do you judge it?"

Arithon looked down and concluded she had indeed created a better dolphin. "It is wonderful," he murmured, as if he had been given a precious gift. "I am sure it will protect me through the night."

Warmed by his praise, and encouraged by her success, she was excited to continue the game.

"Turn around and let me braid your hair," she said.

He complied.

She first groomed him with the ornate comb she found in his trunk, and then began a skillful braiding of his long black hair. At times, her own hair would fall across his back adding yet another new sensation to his young body. Again, Arithon found the stimulation to be intoxicating and he wanted the waves of pleasure to continue forever. But then, oh too soon, she was done.

"There, and I braided it on the side, according to your preference," she said. "Now for the wrap."

She rewrapped his chest with the linen and fastened it on his back with a large pin she had borrowed from Vori.

Turning him around, she admired her work, and then settled onto the opposite bench.

"And now it is your turn," he said, picking up the jar of blue paste.

Surprise filled her face and she flushed but recovered quickly. "Are you going to paint a dolphin on my chest?" she asked.

"No," said Arithon, "not a dolphin – but a swift."

She looked at him with a mixture of emotions, and he enjoyed knocking her off guard. He let the moment age and then added, "And on your face."

She exhaled.

"Besides, there is no room for it on your chest."

She pursed her lips and squinted but said nothing.

"Kneel down and close your eyes," he motioned.

She looked at him sideways; suspiciously; but knelt before him.

"Close your eyes," he entreated. "I cannot do it with you looking at me."

She looked askance again, but recognized that he was genuine in his intentions, and closed her eyes.

He looked at those crescents of lace across her cheeks and remembered watching her sleep. Her face was a dark flush when he made his first tentative touch on her forehead. She flinched and wrinkled her brow.

"Smooth your forehead," he admonished.

She opened her eyes and started to retort but hesitated when she saw him leaning close to her, his blue-tipped finger paused in midair. She closed her eyes again and smoothed her brow.

"I hope you are not going to make me look ridiculous," she said, as if suddenly thinking about it.

"If you do not like it, you can wash it off," he invited. "Now be quiet, I cannot do it, while you are moving your face. Here, put your elbows on my thighs to steady you."

Arithon began again, and the effect was the same for her as it had been for him. As soon as she relaxed, she found that she enjoyed his touch: bumps appeared on her skin, sending waves of pleasure down her body. With her eyes closed, she found herself thinking about his hands. She held a memory of holding his fist the night before and she found it soothing to revisit it in her mind. She sought no words to describe his hands but soaked in the feelings they evoked: surprising strength guided by grace and passion. She could feel all these things now in his gentle touches.

Arithon, meanwhile, was concentrating on his artistry. He drew the outline first with the head of the swift on her left cheek. One of the wings cut down across her mouth and the other cut across the brow of her nose and onto her forehead.

He used three different colors to outline and accentuate details as the bird began to take flight across her face. He noticed that she was tranquil, swaying, as if she were performing an erotic dance or rocking to sleep. Whatever she was doing, it was becoming difficult for him to focus.

He was almost done but wanted to add a few strokes to the bird's head and leaned in close. He could feel her warm breath on his hand, and it distracted him. He moved closer to finish and found himself staring not at the bird, but at her mouth. Without thinking, he leaned in and touched her lips to his. Neither moved for that eternity of time, and she did not open her eyes, but her chest rose as she pulled a breath.

Arithon, awoke from his trance, touched her lips again, and then backed off.

"It is done," he said.

She opened her eyes and gazed at him. He inhaled. He had never been pressed by such a stare, and he could no longer see her face or her lips, or the swift. He could only see her liquid brown eyes and he fell into them and they held him. And he could feel her radiance as it fell across his body, penetrating to the depths of his being. It lasted forever and, in an instant, it was gone – like a ripple on the water.

She stood and floated back onto the bench, faltering, but recovering her composure.

"Do you have a mirror?" she asked, finding her voice.

"Yes." he answered. "A gift from my mother." He rummaged through the trunk to find the basket containing the buffed bronze mirror.

She stared at her own face and the design upon it.

"It is better than I could have hoped," she said.

"It suits you – a swift."

Quiet and afraid to look him in the face, she put the mirror on her lap and braided her hair with lithe hands. They sat in awkward silence until Arithon rose and said, "I need to continue preparations."

"Of course," she agreed, but a bit disappointed, nonetheless.

Later, Arithon was talking with Szaba and Hyssos when Lucina called from the door of the cabin. "Arithon, could you help me when you are available?"

He continued to talk with Szaba, to finish his thought and not appear too anxious to respond, but he eventually went back to the cabin and knocked. She was seated on the bench, and had a blanket wrapped around her shoulders, holding it together in front of her chest.

"This is embarrassing, Arithon, but I need you to help me with something. There is usually another girl around to do this for me, but I have no one else to ask."

Arithon was apprehensive and showed it. She laughed and said, "I do not know what you are thinking, but do not be afraid. I am the one who should be uncomfortable."

"Uh, what do you need?" he asked.

"I need you to tighten and pin this for me," she said dropping the blanket. She had wound a piece of linen around her chest and was holding the final coil.

"I want to pin it in the back, but I cannot do it tight, and now I am frustrated."

"Turn around," he said, a puzzled grin on his face.

She stood with her back to him, holding the end of the linen in one hand and the pin in another.

"I want you to pull it a little tighter, and then pin it in the back like I did yours."

"Are you wounded?"

"No, I just need to … hmmm, I want to hold myself … uhhhh, flatter – do not ask, just do it. Please."

He started to laugh, but she cut him short, "Do not laugh at me."

He moved up to do as she asked and was performing as required when he found himself looking down at her bare shoulder. It distracted him. Her hair was different than he had seen it – more of an Achaean appearance, with the braids wrapped around the back of her head. And she had scented her hair with something light that he had never smelled before.

"You smell … nice," he said.

"I brought back a purse with some of my things last night," she explained.

"Done," he said, opening both of his arms with a flourish.

"Thank you," she said.

She turned to face him and reached up to clasp her hands around his neck. Rising on her toes and pulling him to her, she kissed him, and then hugged him, her head on his shoulder. "Thank you," she murmured, "and be careful tonight."

"I will," he said, continuing to hold her, "and you do not have to come – you can stay here, as we have discussed."

They broke their embrace and she said, "No, this is my best chance and I learned long ago I must be the one to change my fate. I just need a little help."

"We all do," he said. "You too must be careful tonight."

"I understand," she replied. "You will be needed many places."

He nodded and then left the cabin and joined his First Tier.

The weather had been threatening all afternoon, and by nightfall, it was apparent thunderstorms would be rolling through.

"Do you want to postpone our attack?" questioned Hyssos, looking at the sky.

"No, it has to be tonight," Arithon answered. "There are other plans in work, which cannot be recalled."

Lucina emerged from the cabin and walked over to the standing group.

Sestos was taken aback, "A swift!" he exclaimed, "It is marvelous! How could you do it so well?"

Arithon did a sharp shake of his head. She deflected it saying, "All of you need a protector – let me get the pigments."

She was back with the box before she was gone and preceded to give the three of them a small but spirited symbol.

On Hyssos' cheek she painted the bull's head of Crete. For Sestos, at his request, she painted a pair of crossed axes, also on his cheek. Szaba approved a crescent moon on his forehead above his left eye.

***

Lightning was flashing in the distance when they dropped Arithon and Lucina on a different beach, 'to throw off anyone who may be watching,'" Arithon had said.

"When the moon is there," he pointed for Sestos who paddled them to shore.

"We know the plan," he responded. "You two be careful – we will meet you in the harbor."

Lucina took the lead, repeating her speed and stamina of the previous night, but traversing a different path through winding valleys folded between low wooded hills. She really could run every night, as she had asserted, and Arithon paused to recognize what a singular life – certainly one outside his own experience – had brought it about. And here she was united with them in an unlikely alliance on a perilous quest. She pivoted her head to look back at him and smiled as if she had read his thoughts. Arithon, self-conscious, checked again that he was carrying his sword, dagger, and axe, waterskin, and leather purse of dried peas. Lucina, he noticed, carried a dagger strapped into the small of her back: the one he saw Kimilos present to her from his locker.

The pair ran without stopping until they found a suitable hiding place sheltered under a venerable olive tree on the heights above the town. They settled in for their wait. Lightening had tracked them the entire run and now flashed from every point, illuminating dark heavy clouds fraught with power. Arithon could smell a warm rain in the charged air. He did not know if this was a good or a bad sign, but the threatening weather might at least hide some of the noise which was soon to come. Perhaps it was a good sign.

They sat sweating and gathering their breath, munching the peas, and sharing the water. He could feel the disquiet beside him and ventured a discussion.

"How long do you think?" he asked pointing down to the building where Po was held.

"Not long," she said. "I hope Lutea's ordeal is over."

He put his hand on her knee, but she pushed it off – she wanted no comfort. She wanted to be mad. She wanted to be mad at everybody. She would cry for Lutea, but that would be later. For now, she wanted to believe she was doing the right thing and his sympathy made her feel like it was the wrong thing.

"Curse the men," she said under her breath.

Arithon assumed it was directed at him and he started aback.

She saw it and said, "Oh, I am sorry. I did not mean you. I meant the men who would make my life miserable. Men who would use Lutea. Men who would use me."

"You?" he asked.

"Yes, Arithon. I have been a pawn."

"How long have you been a pawn?"

She hesitated as if debating a cautious answer, but then committed to the truth, "All my life," she said.

Arithon turned with a puzzled but sympathetic expression lacking any accusation. "Who are you?" he asked.

"More than I have told you," she answered. "I think you know that."

"I do," he replied. "You speak our language with only the slightest accent, you talk of your time in the temple, and power shifts in the Aegean. You have killed. You can heal. You are quick and bold. And as I re-examine my perceptions, I do not think I ever took you for a hapless captive."

"You are a gifted navigator," she smiled.

"If we fail tonight, my story is of little consequence," she continued. "I am risking more than you know and I deem the best course is for me to carry that alone tonight. But I would still ask you to trust me. Can you?"

"I am committed," he replied.

She reached over and cupped his fist. "Thank you."

He looked up trying to locate where the moon should be in that turbulent sky and then down onto the town. "We will not wait much longer."

CHAPTER 30 STRIKE

Zeus, the cloud gatherer, spoiling for a fight, polished his thunderbolts and scanned the Aegean for a worthy foe.

While Lucina and Arithon were traversing the peninsula, the *Dolphin* rowed around it, and stopped in a cove south of town. Szaba and Sestos disembarked with twenty men. This would leave the ship shorthanded and slow on the water, but they were outnumbered and decided to attack on many fronts.

Hyssos would stay with the ship. His role required bringing her around to the harbor and his great challenge was going to be timing. He needed to arrive after the diversions had begun, but in time to acquire his objective – the *Swallow*.

The land party split into two groups. Szaba, with ten men, angled off toward the south side of town to engage the Achaeans near the quay. Sestos, with more ground to cover, hurried off with the other ten around to the west to protect Szaba's flank and push toward the harbor. Neither knew it, but they would not reach their goal in time.

***

Arithon was growing restless and was deciding it was time to act, when tense movements on the street below startled him to his feet, followed by Lucina.

"Lutea," Lucina moaned.

Two figures emerged from the building they had been watching, one dragging the other by their wrist. Even at that distance, they could see the first was male and he was pulling a girl, dressed in a long tunic.

"Something has gone wrong," said Arithon. "We must get to Po before Szaba arrives or they will kill him."

"But Lutea," she pleaded, "What is he doing with her? She has to come with us."

"Po first. They will not kill her," he said.

"You do not know that."

Arithon knew she was right. Anything could and would happen before it was over. He made a decision, hoping not to regret it later.

"Follow them. I will go for Po and then come for you and Lutea. If we miss, I will try for the temple. Do you understand?"

"Yes," she nodded.

She started off, but he grabbed her arm and spun her. Pinching her chin, his thumb caressed the wing tip of the swift. He started to speak but could find nothing to say. She blinked, turned a smile, and ran off into the darkness.

Arithon barreled down into the town, unmindful of anything except saving Po. But immediately loud voices off in Lucina's direction caused him to pull up and listen. Only silence now, but the pause goaded him to think. He was being too rash. Discovery would mean the death of many. He forced himself into a cautious trot and proceeded to the rear of Po's jail.

It was a building of three stories with no openings on the ground floor except the heavy front door. There were windows on the third floor, but none on the second. He had not foreseen any requirement for a rope: the original plan was for Lutea to signal and then sneak them in; but now with her captured he wished he had a coil.

In the darkness, he edged along the building and after checking both directions, pivoted around to face the door, and pushed it open. Waves of apprehension flooded his chest so he could not take a breath. This was the moment he had been striving months to attain and now that it was upon him, he had a paralyzing fear that Po could already be dead and the ignorance of not knowing was falsely more comforting than what the truth might prove. But he knew that self-deception was a fool's path and Po's need transcended all his selfish placations. He stepped in.

The first two rooms on either side of the hall were dark, but he could see a room on the far end lit by a flickering lamp. There was a sweet pungent smell in the air, like the incense burned in the temples, but all was quiet – too quiet. He walked on his toes, checking into the other dark rooms along the corridor until he was a step away from the shaft of light; and there he froze, listening. I am taking too long, he would think, and then just as quickly think, no, I must not be rash – a mistake here could end it all. And so he waited, until there came a muffled thump upstairs, which unnerved him enough to chance a look into the room.

A naked man lay on old bedding, asleep or unconscious – Arithon could not be sure –with his lower body hanging off onto the floor. Arithon bit his lower lip and crinkled his face at the unsavory sight. Strewn around him, as if there had been a struggle, was a clutter of plates and cups – a few broken, some still with food or drink. Wine from an overturned jar had puddled under a table, where a single lamp burned next to a sword and belt.

Arithon stepped into the room and over to the guard. He raised his axe to kill him. He looked down on the prone man and could see that he was unconscious, his mouth hanging open and his eyelids half closed. Lutea had managed her part.

He grabbed the sword and lamp, backtracked to the stairs, and started up. At the top, he was startled to hear the sounds of men sleeping – dozens from the sound of it. Fear gripped his throat so that he almost gagged, his breath coming in labored pants. The thought of Po trapped here for months stiffened him. He tiptoed down to the first room, peered in, and then snapped back. Five or six men were sleeping on mattresses lining the walls, a pile of clothes and shoes next to each. From their smell he guessed these to be mariners more than warriors. He flitted across the opening and checked the next two rooms in their turn, finding the same results. That would be fifteen to twenty men, bivouacked in a temporary scatter.

He returned down the hall, past the stairs to the next two rooms. Before reaching the opening, he paused. It smelled different, of men yes, but not mariners. He wondered at it and wondered even more that he could tell the difference.

He chanced a quick look. There were men asleep here too, but as he had guessed, they were more permanent to the place. Their armor and weapons were hung on pegs, and there was a table in the center with die and other game pieces strewn across. Along the four walls there were sleeping benches – six or eight, it was hard to be sure. He did not bother to check the last room, guessing that it contained similar numbers. At least thirty men, then – a few too many for him alone.

But I am alone, and Po is my responsibility, he continued with himself, standing companionless in a dark corridor. He had come this far and there was nothing else for it – up to the top.

He started to ascend the stairs to the third floor, when someone inside the adjoining room awoke enough to either hear him or see the light.

"Pervelos?" a sleepy voice questioned.

Arithon froze, and without thinking replied gruffly in his best Achaean, "Go back to sleep." Hearing no response, he started up the stairs.

The third story occupied the back half of the floor plan – the forward half was an open-roof terrace. He sidled down the wall to find the first room empty. A quick glance into the last room revealed a form lying in the far corner, his back to the door. Arithon remained motionless in the hallway when he heard the softest whisper, "Ari."

Arithon hurried across the floor, dropped to his knees, and pulled the man up to a hug.

"How did you know it was I?" he whispered into Po's ear.

"I would know your footsteps anywhere, young son," he replied, tears streaming down his face.

"We have to go," Arithon said.

"I cannot," Po replied.

Arithon wiped the tears streaming down his face, though he was not aware of them.

"Why?" he uttered.

"I am chained."

It was true. They had hammered a chain about his ankle and fixed it to the wall. Arithon stared, his anger swelling.

"You must go. Save yourself."

"No! You will go with me," he said, examining a link.

Po reached over and fingered Arithon's linen wrap.

"I saw you take Sestos off the trader," Po whispered. "It reminded me of a young boy who threw a spear at the Sea Peoples on the way to Knossos. You were magnificent. But you were wounded it seems."

Arithon glanced at the bandage; disinterested.

"I can cut this chain with my sword," he said in a hushed voice.

Po looked at him askance and said, "Even if you can, it will take numerous blows and you will wake everyone."

Arithon frowned. Po was right. He could free him, but they would both be trapped. He stood and treaded down the hall and out onto the terrace. The soldiers were in the rooms below him and at least one of the mariners was sleeping lightly. He looked over the edge and judged it to be three fathoms: a jump to break an ankle and they would need healthy legs if they made it that far. Arithon found a protruding beam on the roof edge, and again berated himself. He would never do this again without rope he vowed – if he got another time.

Standing at the edge he adjusted his bandage and then looked at it.

'You will be fine – just a few more wraps,' repeated in his mind.

He fumbled with the pin in the back and pulled it free, unwinding the bandage and laying it in circles on the roof. The last few winds were stained with the dolphin. He smiled thinking of that memory and then pulled the linen, chin to fingertip five times.

More than enough. The sailor braced and leaned over the roof edge, mimicking a position he had used countless times over the gunnel, and tied one end to the protruding beam using more than he wanted for the knot, but it came within a short jump of the ground. He pulled the end back up so that none might discover it.

Quiet, but hurried, he tiptoed back to Po.

"Out on the roof," he said, "on the left I have tied the bandage for us to make the ground."

Po nodded, looking at Arithon's chest. Thunder rolled in the distance.

"Take this sword," he said, handing the guard's sword to Po, "and when I free you, get to the ground. If I do not follow, get to the harbor. The *Dolphin* will be there soon.

"I will," Po replied.

Arithon looked down at the lamp. "Wait here."

He then gathered up Po's straw mattress, and took it out into the hall, laying it on the landing. Searching the other room, he found another, which he piled on top. Not much of a fire, but it should afford them a few seconds.

Kneeling next to Po, he arranged the chain like he wanted and told Po to remain still. He then walked back to the stairs and stood motionless trying to recall his plans and weigh his options: Lucina had to be found. Should I wait for Szaba? Sestos? No, the other guard would return soon. And the others might never show up.

He then took the lamp and set it under the dry straw, which blazed and crackled.

It had begun.

Arithon went back to the room, pulling his sword as he walked, abandoning any effort to be quiet. He raised the sharpened weapon over his head and brought it down with all his might. Wham! The whole floor shook. The blow cut into the chain and drove it into the packed earth of the floor but did not sever it. Po's rescuer raised his sword twice more and brought it down with a force that finally cut through the chain and the floor too, raining the occupants below with plaster. Had they looked up they

306

would have seen his blade slicing through their ceiling, but they were already scurrying for their sandals and weapons.

Arithon pulled Po to his feet and out the door. The whole building was astir with well-armed Achaeans crowding the stairs in a race for the third floor, where the intruder had somehow entered. As Arithon passed the stairs, he kicked the burning mattresses down into their faces and pushed Po in the direction of the terrace. The mattresses disintegrated into a spray of flames and smoke that only caused a moment's hesitation.

But Arithon awaited them at the top, intent on giving Po time to escape. His axe in one hand and sword in the other, he struck the first two, before they could reach the landing, sending them backwards into the men below. The next two were better prepared, advancing with rectangular shields that protected them from his blows.

Arithon glanced up and sank his axe and then his sword into the beam above his head. Holding onto the hilts of both, he raised himself and kicked forward against the shields. The men were catapulted backwards, causing the press to topple one against another until their bodies jammed the stairs.

Seeing his chance, Arithon pulled his weapons free of the wall, sheathed his sword, put his axe in his belt, and ran onto the terrace. He jumped over the wall in one smooth movement, caught the cloth in midair and pendulumed across before sliding to the ground next to Po hiding in the shadows.

"You have learned much," Po said.

A dagger landed at Arithon's feet, encouraging him to press flat against the wall as others pronged into the ground. Without a word, he and Po edged along the wall, turned the back corner of the building, and began their escape up the streets.

Men – angry men – poured out the front door in a noisy pursuit. Arithon could have outrun them, but the months of captivity had taken a toll on Po. Though spirited, he was thin and exhausted with an ugly scar above his left temple. Arithon, acting as rearguard, eyed the diminished silhouette of his lifelong friend, and realized he was not going to make it.

"Sestos will soon be pushing through the city from the west," he said to Po as he moved up beside him. "We must try and meet up with him."

Po nodded, too out of breath to speak.

"Keep moving that way," Arithon said. "I will try and slow them down."

Arithon could see a few men behind, chasing them up the slopes. They rounded a building, and there, one hundred paces ahead was a barricade of men with torches. The men trailing behind stopped and blocked their retreat in similar fashion.

Trapped! A feeling Arithon loathed. Like a caged animal he surveyed the restraints, seeking an escape. There was a high wall on his right next to Po, and on the left were the walls of a home with a door flanked on both sides by large, lidded pithoi. Arithon kicked at the door in a desperate rage, but it yielded not – barred from within.

A triumphant laugh echoed down the street and a man stepped in front of the shields. He stood under a magnificent, gnarled oak, which grew to a great height with spreading branches that hung over the street. It had been planted generations ago, no doubt, and they had constructed an alcove in the wall to make room for its mighty trunk. Arithon took a second to admire it and wondered at his own foolishness.

"You are trapped, my young Minoan. Not to your liking I would guess," he said in a loud, proud voice.

Arithon said nothing, panting in unspent rage.

"Why are you so quiet?" he asked. "I understand you speak Achaean very well."

"I do," said Arithon.

"You have caused us much trouble," he said.

Arithon recognized him as the Achaean captain he had seen on the deck of the *Swallow*. He was not as tall as Arithon, but strong muscled on a sturdy frame. He wore a cuirass of leather and a helm of boar's tusks, and he carried a large sword in his left hand, a round shield in his right. Dressed for battle, he wore his panoply as one used to such attire.

The men behind started moving in measured steps, but Arithon sensed them and began moving forward. They would rush him soon. Arithon stood staring at the Achaean, contemplating his own death. He thought it odd that it should end here in this place at this time, but then anyplace and anytime would appear unwarranted. His stomach grew cold, but his resolve hardened. He inhaled and fingered the haft of his axe.

The captain saw his intent and raised his hand to stop his men.

"Why do you parley?" said Arithon. "I am ready."

"Patience. You have something I want; and for this I might bargain – in exchange for your lives."

"Name it," said Arithon.

"I want Lucina," he replied.

Good – she was not yet captured. "If I turn her over, then we are to go free?"

"You are getting greedy, young trader. I offer you life. It may be life as a slave, but it is life.

"Bargain now and perhaps your father can buy your freedom later."

Arithon reset his stance.

"A lesser man am I than my father, but I make my own bargains," he said.

"Then what is your bargain?" the Achaean asked.

"I want what I came for: the ship of my father, and my father's friend – my friend," he turned to look at Po, "to return to Minoa – to be free of you Achaeans."

"It is our time, young man. Minoa will be Achaea. We are the new masters."

Arithon realized now he had only been putting off the inevitable. If he were to produce Lucina, his life would be forfeit. He looked over at Po and saw the same truth in his eyes. He nodded at Po who returned it. Someone watching in the darkness saw his intentions and cried out.

"Vorkoros!" Lucina was standing on a wall on the level up.

The captain looked up and ordered men from both ends of the trap to 'catch her.' Arithon reached over and pulled the lid off the pithos as half the assembly broke off in pursuit. The captain, refocused from his distraction, waved his hand and stepped to the side. A gap opened in the shields and two bowmen, arrow and aim at the ready, loosed their darts. Arithon saw them in flight and placed the lid in front of Po, where the arrow meant for his friend, pinged against the clay shield, and fell to the ground. The other sliced through his kilt as he leaned over, cutting him across his hip.

Before Po's arrow had hit the ground, Arithon released the lid and prepared his throw. He pulled the axe back and loaded the muscles of his body with all the strained energy he could muster and with a mighty pitch forward launched his own projectile with that power awarded to him by the Immortals.

The axe spun end over end, flying straight and true with a sound like wind in the branches: on target to cleave the Achaean's head. But he saw it coming and was able to move only enough to miss the full assault.

It cracked through the side of his helmet, cutting a slice across the side of his head, and lopping off the top of his ear. Continuing its flight another twenty feet it struck the trunk of the tree so hard that the old oak shuddered from the blow – the sound of the impact resounding down the streets.

The captain dropped to his knees as his men watched. And then it was eerily quiet as if something powerful had been unleashed. The combatants froze, staring across the space between.

The hair on Arithon's neck stood on end, and the air crackled like seashells under a mallet. A bolt of lightning struck the tree and it exploded with such a concussive force that all those on the periphery were knocked to the ground, while deadly splinters cut through the ranks of those arrayed under its mighty boughs. The accompanying crack deafened them, and the flash was so bright that none could see for a brief time afterward. Then the tree, burning like a torch, started a slow, cracking, snapping fall into the street to lie on all that had fallen there – living and dead.

CHAPTER 31   FIRE AND *SWALLOW*

Hephaestus carried his fire from Thera in search of a new forge
but lent it to his mortal children while he slept.

Arithon was on his back, unable to hear or see, though he believed his eyes were open. Perhaps he was dead; maybe lying unnoticed in a lost spot in the underworld. He lay there for how long he could not tell, in a mental state where time came in and out of focus. As if from far away, he could hear someone calling his name. The god of the underworld finally noticed his appearance and was summoning him to account for himself. He listened, trying to concentrate. No, it sounded like Po. He turned his head in the most likely direction and as his eyes cleared, he could see a reposed figure, up on one arm facing him. He stared, and in a flickering light, he decided it was Po. And then he could hear him calling his name.

Arithon sat up and studied the burning tree, and then over at Po, who was attempting to rise. He remembered all that had transpired and saw his danger and his chance. An acorn was trapped under his hand, and he picked it up and tucked it into his pouch. Rising to his feet, he helped Po stand, and they walked down the street away from the crackling oak and past the unconscious men of the rearguard.

It started to rain; a burst of giant, warm drops began splattering the paving stones. Arithon, his self-possession mounting with every step, tried to hurry Po along, but saw he was not going to snap back as fast. He bent down, pulled Po onto his back, and clasps his arms around him. The rain was refreshing and Arithon felt alive, having escaped certain death by fated luck or the will of gods. He ran toward the harbor remembering his mission there.

The two Therans stopped in a side alley and Arithon put Po down just as the cloudburst ended. He picked up the chain and examined it closer, seeing that it was wrapped numerous times around Po's ankle with the end link hammered shut. It was too close to his leg to take a swing.

"Lay your leg flat," he instructed.

Arithon turned the chain until he had exposed the link he wanted and then jammed the point of his sword into the gap, trying to break it, but the link held.

"Wait here," he said as he walked back to the street. He looked one way and then the other before he uprooted one of the paving stones and returned to Po. He then pounded the sword until it spread and then sheared through the softer metal of the chain. After some pulling and unwinding, he had Po free.

"Thank you, Arithon. I am pleased to be free of that leash."

"It is good to see you, Po."

"It is good of you to come for me," Po said, laying his hand on Arithon's shoulder. "You have grown since I last saw you. I wonder at the change."

"Much has happened, but I have not the time to discuss it. I have work at the wharf before the *Dolphin* arrives.

"And Po, I need to move fast. Can you make your way down to the harbor, and wait for your chance?"

"Yes."

"Are you sure? I do not want to lose you now that I have found you."

"I am sure. I know my way around this town, and I can stay hidden. Do not worry about me. Go get my ship."

Arithon stood up, anxious to be on his way.

"You have a wound on your leg, Arithon."

Arithon looked down and parted the torn kilt.

"I do not believe it is deep. It can wait."

"And Arithon," Po said, pointing, "I like the dolphin."

"I had help," he called back, bolting down the alley. Po watched him proceed to the main street, where Thera's son turned and vanished.

The thoughts darted with every footfall. Was Lucina safe or captured? She was resourceful and could move fast through the obstacles: she had a fair chance. To think otherwise would incapacitate him.

I have broken rule number two: 'Know your enemies plans,' he reprimanded. The one who had taught him that lay in a filthy cell back on Lesvos – a worthy man at the end of his fate – perhaps.

Now rule number three – that was my first lesson, he continued with himself. Number three is: 'always assume you have more than one adversary.' This thought alarmed him into clear headedness as he pulled up where the street teed into the harbor. The Achaeans would be arrayed in more than one spot and must be found out before the Therans arrived.

He surveyed the harbor from a concealed position, noting that the sentinels on the docks were wary, holding shields and spears – a half dozen or so. But where was everyone else?

He looked up into the town and saw a few lamp-lit homes; probably due to the lightning strike. The tree, high on the hill, was still burning, but the populace had not emerged from their homes. This struck him as odd, for if such a thing had happened in Akrotiri, the whole town would have assembled. And if pirates were to attack Akrotiri, he thought further, the whole town would rise in defense. He guessed it was only a matter of time before the general alarm was given.

Worried, but determined, he pivoted and sprinted up to the second street and turned right, moving so fast that he almost outran his ability to stay upright. Arriving at the building barracks where Po had been held, he crashed through the front door like a wave upon the cliffs. Lamplight filled the rooms, but most of the building had emptied, seeking the escaped slave and his lone rescuer. At the noise, a guard bolted into the hall, not expecting anything more than an agitated comrade, but found instead an ascendant warrior provoked. Arithon swung to behead him, but the startled man ducked, and the blade demolished the wall instead. Before either could recover, Arithon brought his knee up, catching the guard under the chin and knocking him upward to the pommel of his sword.

Arithon stepped over the body into the room and took the lamp off the table. As he reached the doorway, a spear point thrust out of the darkness of the hall, aimed at his gut. His sword came down in a sweeping movement that deflected the point and broke the haft. He sliced out into the darkness at the unseen adversary, felt the sickening hack of sword on flesh, and then struck again on the side of a neck he could now see. Arithon kicked him backwards, where he fell across the other body lying in the hall. He listened up the stairs and heard men on the landing above. His own experience there earlier sent him out the door and around to the side of the building.

The linen bandage was hanging there, but his hands were full. Sheathing his sword, he first jumped and caught the linen with one hand and then placed the handle of the lamp in his teeth. The flame flickered into his face, but he climbed to the beam, wrapped his arm around it and lifted the lamp up to the edge.

On the roof, he pulled his sword and charged into the hall, catching the men looking down the stairwell, waiting for him. He smashed into them like a drunk in a crowd, knocking them headlong down the stairs, where they began to untangle and regroup on the lowest floor. After retrieving the lamp, he hurried down the hall.

In that hated cell, he raised the lamp to the straw roof above his head, lighting it in numerous places, before he ran to the next room to do the same. Checking the stairs, he bounded down to the second floor. They could hear him, but it took them a while to figure out his pyric behavior, lighting the straw packed ceilings and mattresses in every room. Smoke filled the building by the time he was finished, and he could hear the men below, scrambling to get out.

Down to the first floor he searched the soldiers' abandoned room. He could hear the fire crackling as smoke filtered down the stairwell and crept along the ceiling. After some fumbling, he found two large rectangular shields and what he most wanted: torches.

With unwarranted patience, he slipped his left arm through the hoops of the first shield and found that he could grip three lit torches in his left hand. He did the same with his right arm but instead gripped his sword under the shield. A quick look into the hall revealed that the front door was ajar; smoke rolling out under the lintel like boiling surf. He endured a spout of coughing and when it ceased the rising heat goaded him to mind his own danger in this self-set trap.

Now! was all he could think.

Arithon exploded through the great cloud of smoke billowing out the front door, roaring like a bull of Crete, startling those awaiting him. Three released their arrows, which he could feel as they struck home in the shields, but most were too terrified by the appearance of this raging vision of smoke and fire to do anything but give way. The two who did not, he hewed and slashed, opening the way before him. And then he was gone – a flame retreating into the night.

Arithon pulled up and dropped to his knees to catch his breath and cough the smoke out of his lungs. To the north he could see flames starting to lick up through the roof of the barracks. The Achaeans were already at work cutting away swaths of the roof to save the structure. The population was awake, judging from the homes lit from within, but few citizens had entered the streets. Arithon had two more targets in mind; and the next would distract the town.

He found an alcove where he discarded one of the shields and jabbed two of the torches into the ground. Now where was it? He did not know precisely, but he knew how to find it.

Keeping the remaining torch and shield, he headed up the main road from the harbor. Twice he bent to look at the road surface; finding and then following the ruts of the market carts, which led up into the city center toward a large building of odd proportions perched on a slight rise. It looked as if it had sprouted from the hilltop, like a cluster of mushrooms on a fallen trunk; the older, taller rooms crowded into the center with the newer and shorter additions sprinkled about the periphery. This would be it: the food storage building.

"I will pull them from their kitchens and give them something more to worry about than the *Swallow*," he said aloud.

He ran around the building complex analyzing its arrangement, deciding there was one short wing, almost an out-building, which he could set aflame without engulfing the entire structure. He did not want to starve them; just occupy them for a short while.

Pulling his arm back, he heaved the torch up to the roof.

Waiting only long enough for it to take hold, he started sprinting back down toward the harbor and cried out in his loudest voice, "Alarm! Fire in the food storage! Everyone up! Fire in the food storage."

His powerful voice rolled down the streets like the thunder of night rain, reverberating off the plastered walls and echoing back; warning of the torrent to come.

And it was effective too. People poured from their homes armed with jars of water, blankets, and rakes. The populace moved toward the center of town, and most important, away from the harbor.

Arithon arrived back at his torches without incidence, as he had rolled past the homes faster than the occupants could exit. He paused to catch his breath. A cloudburst headed for downpour, the mighty Theran picked up the two remaining torches, unsheathed his sword and started for the ships with no plan, except to provoke the Achaeans lying in wait before Szaba or Sestos stumbled upon them. Only speed and confusion would save him in this next venture. He hoped his luck would hold.

* * *

Szaba and his ten men had been beating their way through the brush and broken rock south of town. Unable to find a suitable trail, they had been beset with numerous delays. Unexpected gullies and tangled maqui's had caused them to backtrack and circumvent the obstacles, much to the consternation of the unflappable Szaba.

Nevertheless, he pressed them on with ever more urgency, knowing that his inability to arrive could result in disaster. He had a good sense of time and when they hit upon a trail that appeared to be heading into town, he knew they should already have been there. As soon as they stepped onto the footpath, he turned to Kuteros.

"I am going to run ahead. Bring the men as quickly as possible."

Kuteros nodded, and Szaba disappeared down the trail like a deer through the forest; his two quivers bouncing on his back; the arrows clicking together in a rhythm that matched his footfalls. Szaba, uncomfortable at sea, was at home in the brush. Only the most wary would know he had passed. He turned his head from side to side as he ran, using all his senses.

And so, it was that he smelled them long before they knew he was come. He pulled up, sniffing the air, and listened, but they were silent and yet well hidden. Seeking the higher ground, he left the trail and scrambled up the hill, his ears and eyes straining to find what his nose had already confirmed – Achaeans were waiting ahead.

The African hunter hurried along, afraid his men would arrive before he could locate those in ambush, and that would never do. There was an enormous flash to the north, followed by a crackling boom, which echoed through the surrounding hills. The event startled the Achaeans and they let out gasps of exclamation and talked amongst themselves for seconds afterwards. It was to be their undoing. Szaba pinpointed them long before they stopped talking and crept above them.

A bend in the trail cut close under a rock embankment almost ten feet high, where they were well positioned behind a lump of ground. Szaba counted six; four armed with bows, crouching low behind tufts of grass. The Nubian discerned the sound of his own men tramping up the trail seconds before the Achaeans heard them and rose onto their knees to load their bows.

While they were distracted, Szaba moved in closer above them, pulled his bow over his head in a smooth maneuver, and stuck three arrows into the ground, nocking a fourth. With his own men coming into range of the

Achaeans, Szaba loosed two arrows so fast they struck home before the others even realized their danger. The third had time to turn, still on his knees, before he was pierced, and the fourth had stood before he was toppled backwards down the rock wall onto the trail. The other two ran into the bushes before he could load again, but no matter; Szaba was moving down toward the path at crashing speed, knowing they would do the same as soon as they could break free of the brush. He leapt the wall and landed on the trail without breaking stride.

Over his shoulder he called, "Kuteros!"

He saw the two Achaeans enter the path up ahead and charged across the gap, his sword slashing through the darkness quicker than they could respond. Kuteros arrived seconds later.

"They were waiting in ambush," explained Szaba. "Let us go even quicker. I fear for Arithon."

And with that he was off again, outpacing the men, who followed as fast as they could. The trail led him around an impressive promontory of rock that framed the south side of the harbor and deposited him on the heights above the edge of town. He could see the burning tree and wondered if it was the result of something done by Sestos or Arithon. He needed to be there already. Arithon would need him. His men arrived as he was surveying the town.

"We will head for that area over there," he said, pointing out a stretch of beach south of the dock.

As he was pointing, he saw a building catch fire on the far side of the harbor. Three bunched torches moved through the darkness at magnificent speed away from the burning structure.

Only Arithon could run that fast; Szaba was sure of that.

Szaba did not know what Arithon was up to, but judging from experiences of late, he knew that the Theran would soon be in more trouble than he had the ability to master. He broke into a full sprint and waved on the men behind him.

He was in sight of the harbor, but out of range when he saw Arithon, clearly Arithon, careening down onto the wharf, a bull at charge, fire streaming from his nostrils, his braid flying behind him and booming at the top of his lungs like the elephant of Africa.

317

As Arithon approached, the men on the dock launched two spears. The first glanced off his shield, the other stuck fast, but neither slowed him down. He met the guards at full bore, slicing first one then the other, pivoting to kick up at another before pulling the spear from his shield and sweeping it in a great arc to keep others at bay.

Szaba had seen him like this, days before, and he thought then, as he did now, that there was something majestic in his ferocity, like a lion in the midst of hyenas. He is magnificent, he thought, and he shall not die tonight.

Szaba was within range.

Arithon could hear the men in both ships scrambling to get out of the holds. The four left on the wharf had called the alarm as soon as he struck down the first two. He had only seconds to live, he knew, but he would do what he came to do.

He tossed the first torch down into the hold of the trader, as a man thrust at him with a sword that broke the spear he wielded. Arithon jumped onto the oar rail of the *Stag* and set the torch against the sail piled under the spar. He dodged another spear, while gripping the torch … waiting … waiting for the fire to take. Counts passed, though they seemed like hours, before it began to crackle. By then four men had emerged onto the deck.

Arithon seized an oar and swung it into two of them, knocking them into the far gunnel. One he kicked back into the entrance of the hold, blocking the exit of those below. He caught the movement on his right and raised his shield to thwart the blow, but it was a heavy axe and it destroyed his shield sending him flying backward onto the boards. The man raised his axe again, this time to kill, when an arrow pierced his head, tipping him so that his stroke went wide.

"Szaba!" cried Arithon, and it gave him hope where there was none.

He looked behind and saw men streaming out of the *Swallow*. Two with bows were nocking their arrows but fell with Szaba's arrows in their backs before they could take aim.

The sail on the *Stag* was burning; flames licking up and moving down the length of the yardarm.

Arithon jumped to the dock, shieldless, but undaunted, and cut down two that opposed him, before jumping onto the *Swallow*.

He had one more thing to do before he would attempt an escape. And where was Sestos?

He leapt up onto the rear deck and brought his sword down on the mooring rope. Arrows, a hail of arrows, began to rain down on the *Swallow* – Kuteros, thank the gods, had arrived. Arithon in danger of the darts himself, started to work his way forward, hoping his own men could discern his shape in the chaos. He fought two more men before he made it to the bow, where he cut the final mooring line. When he looked up, Achaean reinforcements were pouring down the streets trying to make it to the ships, but Szaba could pin them back.

Men on the trader were trying to put the fire out and those on the *Swallow* were targeted as soon as they emerged from the hold. The focus on him no longer, Arithon grabbed an oar, and pushed against the wharf, hoping the wind would catch the ship's side and help him get her away. Slowly, ever so slowly, she began to move until Arithon was prone, pushing and straining every fiber of his body.

And then the zephyr got between her and the dock to assist. He was at the end of his stretch when he could feel her starting to pivot. And then she was free of the pier and drifting. In the confusion, no one seemed to be paying attention until it was too late. Those on the wharf tried to reach her, but with no results. Others launched spears at him, or threw axes – all of which he dodged, moving too fast to present a target. He paused and looked down, thinking of what lurked below, and an idea struck him.

"See who is left in the hold," Arithon cried in Achaean, "and kill them all!"

To his utter amazement, the simple trick worked. Three men emerged. The first jumped overboard without even a look, but the other two put up a fight. Grabbing a spear stuck in the planks, he skewered one with a javelin throw and met the other with his sword. He swung against him, once, twice – both times deflected by the Achaean's shield or sword. This one was undaunted; a seasoned warrior of countless fights, not willing to surrender the ship to just one Theran, despite his size and ferocity.

They dueled back and forth across the deck, neither able to gain an advantage. Arithon, fighting without a shield, was finding it difficult to protect himself from the skilled strokes of his opponent, and unable to press forward on the offensive. He was backing up, when he fell over one of the dead bowmen, and the Achaean moved in to deal his final blow. As he swung down toward Arithon's gut, Arithon felt a bow under his arm,

319

which he raised, poking the warrior in the face, causing his stroke to miss, and cut into the planks next to Arithon's side.

Arithon rolled over and swung at the man's outstretched arm, but his opponent deflected the blow with his shield. On the next swing, Arithon's sword met his opponent's. The superior metal of Arithon's sword broke the bronze sword in half. Amazement rattled the man's face. He paused, and Arithon swept upwards, catching him across the middle. The stroke sent him backwards, but he wore a toughened cuirass and it did not slice his flesh. He kicked out at Arithon's face but missed as Arithon rolled back to his right.

As Arithon gained his feet, the Achaean grabbed a loose spear and thrust it at his opponent's torso, but the Theran broke the haft with his sword and raised it for a final blow. The Achaean sprung aside, turned and ran to the gunnel and jumped.

He knows rule number one, Arithon thought.

"Rope," said Arithon aloud, "I need a coil of rope."

He jumped into the hold of his father's ship and found it exactly where it should be.

"Good for you, Po."

When the *Swallow* had drifted three ship-lengths away from the quay, he heaved the aft and forward anchor overboard, hoping they would set. In case they did not, he tied one end of the coil to the anchor line, and clutching the other end, jumped into the water and started swimming ashore, where he could see Szaba and his men taking up a defensive position near the seawall.

Achaeans were beginning to reach the quay, trying to make sense of the confusion, but no one seemed to have figured out a course of action.

Arithon walked up through the gentle surf and handed the line to one of his men.

"Szaba," he yelled over, "Thank you!"

Szaba touched the bow tip to his forehead and saluted back.

"Get your men aboard and hold this ship!"

Two at a time the Therans pulled themselves along the line out to the liberated *Swallow*, while Szaba and the others protected them from shore. Men filtering down from the town and those from the trader were assembling on the dock for a counterstrike. A dozen Achaeans had formed a rank of archers that were shooting at Szaba's men in the water and on the shore.

"They will rush us soon," said Arithon, standing next to Szaba. "You do not have enough men to move the *Swallow* or hold her for long. I need to find Sestos."

Arithon looked over and saw there were only two of his men left on shore; the others were aboard or in the water. Andamos lay dead, an arrow through his eye.

"Send everyone on, and then you follow. I need to slip off before I am noticed."

Szaba nodded.

Arithon faded into the darkness, jumped up the seawall and spun over it to hide in a crouch. He watched as Szaba entered the water, pulling Andamos' body with him on his way to the ship. Men on the wharf ran down the beach, intent on shooting Szaba in the water, but Kuteros provided a covering barrage from the *Swallow*. Szaba would make it, he was sure, so he slipped up the side street steering for the Temple of Artemis but looking for Sestos.

CHAPTER 32 BACKWARDS THEN FORWARDS

Clotho spun her yarn, humming quietly to herself, for this night was hers.

A large crowd had gathered at the food storage in a controlled riot. A line of men and women were moving foodstuff out of the rooms adjacent to the fire, while others were cutting away the burning roof. Children were weaving through the throng, jumping, talking, and pointing at the fire. Pickets of men were assembling – not all were armed but those who were had a grim look.

Arithon skirted the edges of the mob and scrambled toward the temple on higher ground to the right. On the way, he came into view of the burning oak. It only smoldered now, a few whiffs of smoke curling off a charred trunk. There were no bodies in the wreckage, and he wondered what that might mean. He was not anxious to meet with a group that large again, for he was feeling the weariness of a long ordeal. He also wondered for the hundredth time where Lucina and Sestos were.

And Po – where was he? He was the reason for all this. But Po was wary and would not be trapped again; somehow Arithon knew this. Po will make it – if any of us do, he decided, and pressed on.

High on the slopes near the temple he looked to the eastern sky, where he could detect the faintest change in the darkness. As he leaned back against a wall, he heard Lucina's soft voice above him.

"Arithon."

Startled he looked up and saw her head peering over, her fingers wrapped over the edge. Swinging a leg over to straddle the top, she reached down, offering her hand to assist, and with surprising strength pulled him to the top where he pivoted over and jumped to the ground. With both hands he grabbed her waist to assist. They both slid to a sit, their backs to the stucco.

"Here," she said, handing him a jar of water, and a piece of jerky. "You have been occupied."

"Thank you," he said, drinking half the jar, and stuffing the food in his mouth.

"Where did you get this?" he mumbled.

"I borrowed it," she said.

He drained the rest of the jar and leaned over to put it on the ground next to him.

"You are wounded," she said, pulling open the tear in his kilt. "But it can wait. It is not deep."

Checking the rest of his body, she looked at his chest and frowned.

"You have lost your bandage, I see, and you have torn this old wound."

Arithon looked down and noticed fresh blood on the underside of the cut. His dolphin was so smeared he could not recognize it.

"And my dolphin is wounded also."

Scanning her face, he saw that sweat had caused her swift to run, but it was largely intact.

"But your swift is still good. Let me fix it."

He traced his fingers across the parts that had broken, rubbing excess pigment from the lines that remained.

"There – a swift once more!"

"Where is Lutea?" he asked.

"In the temple – guarded."

He rose to his feet and pulled her up.

"Wait." She traced her finger around the smudged dolphin, creating its outline again. "You will need the protection."

"What is your plan?" she whispered after the short trip to the back of the temple.

"I do not have one," he replied. "I was thinking of barging in the front door and taking it from there."

She bit her lower lip and looked at the window.

"She is probably tied in her room. I can enter from the window and see if I can free her."

No rope again, he thought. "How will you get in?"

She squared his shoulders round to face her. "Interlock your fingers like this.

"Bend over and I will run to you and place my foot here where they web together. At the same time, you will straighten up and throw me. I will catch the sill."

He looked at her askance, "You can do that?"

"Yes, I have done it many times," she said. "Hurry!"

He doubted but obeyed and ran to place himself under the window. She followed him, turned, and counted her paces back as if she really did know what she was doing. Looking up at the window to gauge its height, she raised her hand to get his attention and then commenced her run. He did as she said: leaned over, fingers interlocked, and watched her rush, pacing her strides, and staring at his hands. She took one quick look up at the window, and then pushed off the ground in her leap. He felt her right foot in his hands and threw her skyward with all his strength.

His head snapped back as he released and he watched her float through the air to alight on the wall, soft as a butterfly, catching her fingers on the sill. The sight of her soaring, skirt fluttering with her speed, and unbound to the mortal's earth, moved him in a powerful way. That vision fixed itself in his mind and he forgot for an instant where he was or what he was doing. She pulled herself up until she could get an arm over, then the other; finally, she threw her leg up and climbed in.

His mind snapped backwards then forwards – he shook it off. She did not need a rope.

She peered out the window and waved at him. He motioned for the rope, but she held the palms of her hands up and shrugged her shoulders.

Shield and a rope, he thought, – next time a shield and a rope.

He ran to the corner of the building, while drawing his sword and peeked around, but saw no one. He did the same on the other side. Back, standing under the window, he wondered what was taking so long, when he heard a scuffle above. Anguished, he moved farther back to see into the room, unwilling to call out and bring enemies upon them. A powerful thud as if someone had been thrown to the floor brought him back to the temple wall, trying to scale it. But he fell back in frustration with no handholds available.

Arithon backed up again – just in time – for a man's body flew backwards out the window, as if he had been kicked with great force. He landed on his head, with an audible crack. Arithon turned him over and saw Kimilos' dagger buried deep in his chest. He pulled it out and stuck it in his belt.

"Arithon," she called. He looked up and Lucina was leaning out the window, with Lutea by her side.

"Help me with Lutea!"

Lutea was already beginning to straddle the sill; timid, but game. Soon she was hanging over the edge. Lucina, wedging herself behind the sill, took hold of both Lutea's wrists and lowered her as much as she could. Arithon raised his arms but could not reach her feet. He was about to call for Lucina to drop her when Lucina cried out.

Lutea slipped free of Lucina's grip, and fell onto Arithon before he could brace for it, causing them both to tumble to the ground; she on top of him. He looked up and saw the edge of Lucina in the dark room wrestling with an unseen foe. She was struggling to get out the window, and her assailant was trying to pull her back in. Before Arithon could stand, she fell, her attacker clawing at her clothes, tearing her skirt off as she rolled out the window.

Falling sideways, she almost corrected her fall, but landed off balance on one foot, oomphing to the ground next to them. Arithon looked up and saw a man looking down from the window. He turned into the room and Arithon heard him calling out as his voice faded into the recesses of the temple. Arithon bolted up. Warriors would be here soon. Lutea was already on her feet when Arithon reached down to help Lucina. She tried her leg and collapsed with a wince.

"I have hurt my ankle," she said fighting back tears.

Arithon scooped her up and ran to the back wall of the compound. Dropping to his knees, cradling Lucina in his arms, he looked down at her right thigh, now exposed, and saw an ugly scar, long healed. Something snapped in his head and he spiraled inward like never before. Waves of memories crashed in the surf of his mind: her fall from the window – a lithe form, in violent motion, rolling out of control; her vault from his hands at the temple; the way she crossed the deck of the *Stag*. His mind rolled like a ship in heavy seas: the smell of the incense; the drums; memories of how she moved – how she looked. Something he had dreamt of all his life – the exotic young girl – the bull leaper at Knossos!

All he could whisper was, "It is you."

CHAPTER 33   CHANGING HANDS

Ares, god of war, took up Zeus' challenge and prepared for the contest.

"Go, I cannot walk. Save Lutea."

Try as he might, he could not think. Guards were closing in; he could hear their noisy approach.

"Go," she pleaded, "Go! Get her to Troy"

He was mentally helpless – a wounded man unable to rise to the demands upon him. "Hide here in the shadows. I will lure them away and then return for you."

He kissed the swift on her forehead, lay her down behind a tree, threw Lutea up onto the wall and he bounded over. They dashed off in a noisy clatter of sandals on stone, drawing four plodding soldiers into a chase. Guided only by unthinking instinct, he charged off in the direction which would intercept Sestos. Dawn was coming and the eastern horizon was tinting blue, when he heard, and then saw Sestos and his men breaking their way through the city, almost halfway to the harbor. A quick look back revealed men on the wall where he had left Lucina.

Arithon hailed Sestos, requesting covering fire. The four chasers pulled up and retreated in the direction of the temple, as Sestos' squad launched a barrage. Arithon relayed their peril and need to Sestos as they covered the remaining ground down to the water.

The Achaeans in the harbor had organized and were beginning to strike back. Archers kept Szaba and his men pinned down on the *Swallow*, while a troop of Achaean swordsmen boarded the *Stag*. They were paddling away from the dock to board the anchored *Swallow*, when Arithon and Sestos arrived within bowshot. Arithon knew what to do with the archers on the dock, but the trader was beyond his reach.

His mind was reeling from the delay to retrieve Lucina, and the night had been so long he almost despaired from exhaustion. He looked out to the east and its promise of a new day, wishing for an end to this madness, when he saw the *Dolphin* moving into the harbor on a collision course with the trader.

"Look," Arithon pointed for Sestos. The sight of the *Dolphin* had started his brain again. "Let Hyssos deal with the *Stag*. You rush the archers on the pier."

"Is Po aboard the *Swallow*?" asked Sestos.

"I hope so," Arithon replied.

Sestos stared, for Arithon had an odd look and his voice seemed to come from far away.

"Wait until they launch another volley and then charge them."

"What about my sister?" asked Lutea in broken Achaean, pulling on Arithon's arm.

"Sister – Lucina is your sister?" he asked.

"She did not want you to know," she replied, wide-eyed and fearful.

He turned and looked back up the hill and then stared out onto the harbor.

"Arithon!" snapped Sestos. "Arithon! We need to go. The city is converging here. Soon it will be too late."

He had left Lucina – the thing he had promised not to do.

"Get her aboard one of our ships. I am going back for Lucina."

"It is too late, Ari," said Sestos. "We cannot remain in the harbor. We will be too vulnerable in the daylight.

"Take the ships out of the harbor. If I am not aboard by quarter day – leave."

"How will you get aboard?" asked Sestos.

"I do not know – swim if I have to."

Sestos looked at his bedraggled friend, anguish all over his face and said only, "Yes."

"Give me a shield and an axe," Arithon said. "Do you have any rope?"

Sestos looked puzzled and answered, "No rope, but take my axe and shield."

"I will make it," he said, turned, and bolted up the hill.

Arithon was through with thinking – he could not do it anymore. He was hallucinating from exhaustion and imagined himself a bull charging ranks of predators. All those he met, whether they gave way or stood against him, the result was the same – none could withstand him. He swung his axe as he ran; a madman in the streets, protected by his own madness, or maybe the will of gods. He did not even see his opponents anymore; they were just a haze on his periphery, as he whipped past, like a sirocco out of Africa, blasting the landscape in its fury. Somehow, he

327

sensed their spears and arrows in flight; seeking him, intent on his destruction; but protected by some force of will, none found their mark. The world around him had slowed down.

And then he was there, standing halfway up the terraced steps of the temple, looking up at the open doorway, the flame within.

The newly forged Theran warrior walked up the stairs, stood at the entrance, spread his arms, shield in his left, axe in his right and roared out. "Lucina!"

There was a clambering of weapons and heavy sandals on stone; two men emerged from behind the altar, both bearing long pikes rushing to skewer him. He stood immobile until they were upon him, and then released his axe, with a quick backward load and throw.

This time the intended target had no time to duck, and it split his head, hurtling him backwards like a straw doll. The other continued bearing in, but Arithon angled the thrust with his shield, deflecting it into the open door. Arithon pivoted on his left foot and bringing his right up, he kicked the hardened shaft with a blow that cracked it free at the head. His opponent, holding only the shaft, reached for his dagger, but Arithon drew his sword as his foot came down and he swung it into the head of the pikeman, sending him sliding across the floor.

Arithon entered the temple.

"You are very persistent," came a strong voice behind the flame.

The warrior captain emerged from the shadows, dragging Lucina with him. The right side of his head, now without helm, was caked with blood from the wound dealt by Arithon's axe. Otherwise he appeared unchanged – armored and weaponed, he stood motionless, Lucina in his grasp.

"Have you all you came for?" he asked.

"No. One more," Arithon answered.

"But she is not yours," he said.

"Nor yours."

"If she belongs to neither of us, then why are you here?" he asked.

"To fulfill a promise," Arithon answered.

Lucina raised her eyes, tears welling, and turned a melancholy smile.

"A promise I cannot allow," he said dropping Lucina to the ground and advancing to within a few paces of Arithon, who reset.

"You are exhausted, my young Minoan and you are not my equal in sword play I would wager. But if we must, then let me repay you for this token you gave me earlier."

328

He lunged forward with a powerful stroke that Arithon only partially deflected; the blade clipping his shoulder, drawing blood. The Achaean jumped back.

"A good start, but not full payment," he sneered, and attacked again. But this time Arithon met him blade on blade and the sound of the blow startled the Achaean, giving Arithon an opportunity to strike him on his wounded head with his shield, forcing him back reeling, but not daunted.

"You are a worthy foe, my young Minoan," he said, wincing from the pain in his head.

He thrust for the gut this time and Arithon sprang backwards and swept his sword across, knocking the Achaean's blade out of the way and exposing his opponent's middle, which he kicked with his left foot sending the Achaean onto his rump. But he was on his feet before Arithon could take advantage and they thrust and parried in a coordinated dance of supremacy – the young bull against the seasoned lion; they each gave as good as they took.

Clenched in a brutal exchange, Arithon heard the doors behind him creaking closed and the sound of the locking bar dropping into the cradles. He could not look to see what was happening for the Achaean was wearing him down and his strength was past spent. His opponent could sense it and moved to finish him, but Arithon had trained well under Po and Mara, and had a few moves left. He drew the Achaean in, on a three-maneuver feint and caught his right side undefended, slicing deeply into his forearm and causing him to drop his sword. The Theran warrior pressed home and with two overhead swings shattered the Achaean's shield knocking him to his knees. The Achaean looked up, no fear in his eyes, staring at the face that would deliver his death. But Arithon hesitated, gasping for air. He hated this Achaean who had twice tried to kill him; had killed Po's crew and enslaved him. The Achaean stared him in the eyes, fearless, waiting: a worthy foe.

Arithon raised his sword for a quick but vicious kill.

"No!" screamed Lucina.

The shaft of the broken spear whistled out of the darkness and cracked against the side of the Achaean's head, knocking him to the floor. Arithon took a step forward and raised his sword again, but Lucina moved between them.

"Arithon … Arithon …" she was pulling his arm down. "Do not kill him. Please." She looked over at the senseless man with a strange expression of sympathy and respect.

She leaned onto Arithon as he sheathed his sword.

"Help me over there," she pointed behind the main altar.

He half carried her to a room in the back and set her down on a bench.

"Here, move this block," she said, holding onto a stone, which formed part of the bench. He got on his knees and found that he could slide the stone away from the wall, where a dark hole appeared.

"It is the escape tunnel," she explained. "You will have to crawl."

She slipped into the blackness of the underworld and disappeared. Arithon followed her and pulled the stone back into place, obscuring what little light had been available. He started to crawl, feeling his way along the wall with his right shoulder. He could hear her breath reverberating in the tight confines so that it seemed she was next to his head. After some uncomfortable crawling, her shuffling ceased, and he bumped into her rump with his head.

"Watch it. We are at the end."

"I found your end," he jested, giddy with fatigue, "but where does this tunnel end?"

"It comes out inside a storage shed outside the temple grounds. But before we go up, tell me – did Lutea make it?"

"She did. I left her with Sestos."

"Good, then if I … we do not make it, at least I will know she did."

He heard her groping the surface above, looking for some handle or lever and then he heard a dull pop, and a sliver of light appeared in the tunnel. She was kneeling in front of him with her hands over her head, and, as she opened the hatch, light illuminated the tempest of dust swirling about her. She pulled herself up on one leg and then pressed herself out with her arms. He crawled forward and looked up through a square hole of light framing her face looking down.

"Come up, there is no one here," she said.

Limbs quivering with exhaustion, he followed her out into a mud brick room with a thatched roof. The daylight before dawn filtered soft light in through the cracks. Lamps, pots, tools, and baskets cluttered the floor. A broken door leaned against the entrance, having waited a long time to be fixed. Arithon stood, stepped across the floor, peered out the door and then turned and said, "Let us go. Daylight will not aid us."

"Where are we going?" she asked. She was sitting on the dirt, rotated onto her left hip. He could see the tip of the scar under her right arm.

"To the water. If the *Swallow* and *Dolphin* escape, they will be outside the harbor."

"I cannot walk," she said as if informing him of something he had forgotten.

"I remember. I will carry you."

"You will not be able to move very fast with me aboard," she said with a quirky smile.

"My hope is that the population will be down on the quay, and only a few will be looking for us. We will try to slip into the water on the north side of the harbor. That will leave us a half league or less to swim."

"Arithon, you are spent," she said. "You will not be able to carry me and then swim that distance. Why don't you go and save yourself? I release you from your promise – the one which brought you back."

"I would have come back for you without the promise," he said, looking at her scarred thigh.

"And why is that?"

"Because you are she," he said staring down at her.

She returned his stare and repeated the words, "'Because you are she.'" She then knitted her brow as if remembering something.

"Earlier you said, 'it is you.' What did you mean?"

"You are right - our destinies are intertwined, Lucina. I dream of you. I just did not know where you were. I would have searched all the seas for you – in another time – and here you appear to me leagues from where I expected to find you."

"How could you dream of me? Did Morpheus place me there – in your dream?"

"No, you appeared to me in Knossos, where you received that scar," he said nodding his eyes at her leg. "The gifted bull leaper."

She tried to pull her tunic to cover it and said, "Yes, I was a bull leaper – long ago it seems." She stared down into the hard-packed earth of the shed. "So, you remember me for my accident."

"No, I remember you for the way you move. Your strength, your grace, your courage; I fell in love with that image and I have carried it with me."

She looked up, her eyes brightened, but her face showed challenge. "You are in love with an image?"

He smiled, knowing he would not better her in this play. "Yes. And I am in love with you," he said, reaching down. She came to her knees and he scooped her up into his arms; she put her hands around his neck and buried her head into his chest. "You came back for me," she said.

Arithon said nothing but feeling refreshed, he moved to the entrance and she with her hands free, pushed the door aside. Dawn was coming and the rain clouds of last night were swept away; replaced by a fresh blue sky promising warmth and light winds.

"That way," she pointed down a long alley, which wound its way north and eastward in the general direction they desired. He took off at a quick pace but was soon winded by the effort.

She felt guilty causing him to labor under the added weight of her helplessness, and exposing them to such risk; for he had to stay on the paths and roads, unable to scale obstacles that would have afforded him some measure of cover. They came to a rise, where they were able to get their first glimpse of the harbor. Lucina slid out of his aching arms onto her good leg.

Arithon bent over trying to catch his breath. He was weary beyond any weariness he had ever experienced, or even thought possible. His night with Szaba on Lesvos was but a practice run compared to the loss of strength he felt. Lucina studied his face with grave concern.

"Arithon, you are going to pass out," she cautioned, feeling the heat on his forehead with the back of her hand. "Let me try and walk some. If you can help me on my left side here, I may can hobble along."

"Look," he said, ignoring her, his eyes focused on the harbor. Hundreds of people were gathered around the dock or on the road leading to it. Many more were in the surf where a large crowd had gathered around the *Stag*, which was beached on the south side of town. Dozens of fishing boats were in the water, hovering around the grounded vessel in the process of trying to get lines attached to re-float her. The *Swallow* and *Dolphin* were nowhere to be seen. He hoped this meant they were both in the hands of his crew, but he could not be sure – perhaps one was chasing the other. Further to the right a diminishing column of smoke emanated from the food storage building, where the town's populace had managed to arrest the fire with only a partial loss of the roof. Arithon was thankful none of the damage had been catastrophic. He had regained his breath, if not his strength, and was ready to attempt Lucina's suggestion, when they were spotted from below.

A cry rang out and many hands in the crowd pointed up in their direction. They had stayed too long exposed. In his weariness, Arithon had gotten careless, and here at the last of a long night, he was to be caught and torn to shreds by an angry mob: he could hear it in the din. A large contingent of the crowd began to move in their direction, first slowly as they were packed together, but their speed increased as they spread out – like the start of a footrace.

Arithon swept her up and started running in one movement, adrenalin driving him now, as he had no reserves left to call on. But fear is a powerful motivator and he surprised even himself with the pace. If he could hold it, he may make the water ahead of the mob trying to cut him off. Unseen by Arithon or Lucina, one of the fishing boats noticed the clamor and moved to intercept – if they should reach the water.

He ran with all he had, Lucina bouncing in his arms, holding on as best she could. The thought of a mob, pulling his dream apart, her body broken and scattered on the streets, spurred him on. He forgot the pain in his legs, and the searing of his lungs as he pushed his mortal frame beyond the limits of what he ever thought he could endure.

They were converging on an intersection near the seawall of the harbor which at his present speed, Arithon would reach before the pack. But four in the main press, realizing his rapid descent, broke away to ensure they would be there to stop him. Arithon saw the fleet-foots and realized he would have to deal with them. Lucina saw them too and decided she could aid their escape.

"Keep moving," she instructed, "But I am going to get on your back."

He slowed to allow her to pivot around his neck and land piggyback in a deft maneuver. After she was balanced aboard, he was grateful for the change in position and once again accelerated. He felt her reaching down to pull his dagger out of the sheath. His arms were so cramped and weak that he doubted he could even raise his sword to the men who were coming upon them. The chasers reached the intersection ahead and turned to meet them, charging up the slight incline. As they approached swords drawn, Lucina spoke into his ear.

"Keep running, but I am going to raise up. Do not fall," she warned.

The men were only twenty paces ahead, when he felt her push up on his back and pivot hard, almost twisting him into a fall. He saw the dagger as it crossed over his head and came into view on its flight to land point first in the chest of the lead man, who fell back, tripping the man behind him.

Another violent twist announced the flight of yet another dagger, which found a similar target, creating the same tangling of followers. Arithon leapt onto the chest of one of them and bounded over the jumble of arms and legs to see a clear street ahead.

And then he was on the seawall, where he hesitated only an instant – the mob paces away – before jumping to the beach with her on his back. They fell forward and she tumbled off his back to land upright on her knees with Arithon behind her face down in the sand. A spear struck upright beside him and then another. He jumped to his feet and scooping her under the arms, they splashed into the surf.

As the water impeded his forward momentum, he threw her forward, where she landed on her belly and began to swim. He took two more high-step strides and then dived into the water, swimming up to her side.

But then he saw the fishing boat that had been shadowing them across the city and he could see many more following from the main harbor. His heart sank, for he was spent and doubted he could even swim another hundred feet, much less outpace a fleet of pursuing boats.

The skiff was only a short throw away, the rower pulling hard. Arithon pulled up and put Lucina behind him to protect her from the spear he could see propped up in the boat.

"Dive, when he strikes and try to get around to the other side," he told her. And then the boat was beside him and he looked up to dodge the thrust, the risen sun in his eyes.

"Dive," he called as the spear was launched.

Lucina complied and swam under the attacking boat. But for Arithon, the spear did not pierce, but hovered in the air in front of his face.

"Hurry, Arithon," said Po.

Arithon squinted and could see the silhouette of Po, holding the haft of the spear for him to grab. He did so, and as Po pulled him to the side, Lucina surfaced on the other and grabbed the gunnel, trying to upset the skiff. Po would have fallen overboard had Arithon not steadied him and called out, "No, Lucina, it is Po. Get in."

Po pulled Arithon in, as Lucina balanced the boat, and then she too slipped aboard. Lucina jumped onto the cross seat next to Po and grabbed the oars.

"I am rested," she said. "I can row."

Arithon, lying on his back, looking up at the sky, was so relieved that he passed out on the bottom of the boat and remembered no more.

CHAPTER 34 GREEN HILLS

Anteros, god of Love Returned, left Eros sleeping, and
fulfilled his quest in the dark of night.

It was black dark when he awoke with a start. His heart was racing, and in his dream, he had been running, but not fast enough, and he was going to be caught and killed. He lay there in the dark; his heart pounding against his chest, short rapid breaths, eyes wide open seeing nothing. He could hear the gentle lap of the water against the hull and the wind in the rigging; all else was middle-of-the-night quiet. He knew where he was: on board the *Dolphin* and in his bed under a light linen blanket. He lay rigid, trying to shake the fear of the dream which gripped him.

And then she came, and he felt her beside him sitting on the edge of the bench. Her warm fingers slipped behind the nape of his neck, and cradled his head forward where a cup touched his lips and the water inside was cool and delicious and he drank, slaking a thirst he had just become aware of. He drained the vessel and as she was lowering him, her hair fell onto his face and he could just discern the wisp of an exotic perfume as the tresses caressed. She pulled back to rise but he slipped his arm around her waist and pulled her body back to a firm placement on the edge. He rolled and put his hand on her upper back and started to guide her gently but insistently down toward him. Rigid at first, she yielded, and her upper body undulated down. She sighed into his ear and he embraced her in a determined grip soothing to them both. He felt again her powerful presence and it bathed him in its glow and nurtured him, filling his body with life's energy.

He would not let go, so powerful was the feeling. She kissed him on his ear, and it sent shivers down his body, so that he held her ever more tightly. But she pulled back enough to free her trapped arms and put her hands on either side of his face, guiding her own face down to meet his lips.

They kissed.

She felt his chest rise as their lips brushed, and she sensed he was losing himself in the intoxication of the moment. And she was too, and soon there would be no turning back. His hands slid down lower on her back and she could feel him pulling on her tunic, bunching the material at her waist as he tried to pull it free from the trap of her legs against the bench. She lifted her hip and the material yielded. Her breath was coming short and shallow as he slipped his hand up under the tunic and rubbed her back along her spine and side-to-side. She loved the feeling and when he slipped both hands under and massaged her skin from her neck to the small of her back, she got waves of goosebumps that flowed over her shoulders and down her arms, almost to her hands. She put her forehead against his and let her hair fall on either side of them, creating a tent that only their faces could occupy and the warmth of their breath inside was stifling and made her feel drunk. His desire for her enveloped them both and she could sense its insistence and that stimulated her – he wanted her, and she wanted him to want her.

And then she felt flushed and passion took her body, and she became more insistent, matching his desire for her. She sat up and crossing her arms behind her head, grabbed a corner of the material on each shoulder and pulled the tunic over her head, tossing it to the other bench. He reached up and pulled her down to him and she followed his pull until their flesh matched. He held her head and brought her face once more to his, kissing her closed eyes – one and then the other as delicate as you would kiss a puff of air; but the tenderness only inflamed her passion more, so that as he brought his lips to each cheek she pushed back the remaining cover from his lower body, as he pulled her down, her breast mashing against his chest. She turned from her sit and brought her knees onto the edge of the bench and he slipped his hands under her arms and wrapped them around her shoulders to pull her tight. He then eased off his grip to skitter his hands down the length of her back, to her buttocks and then up again. She wanted him to run his hands all the way down, but he stopped each time at her waist and tingled his way up to her shoulder, teasing her. She was squeezing her thighs together rhythmically, wanting something to crush between them and the desire became so strong that she swung her left knee over his body, and lowered her whole body onto his, causing him to arch up his torso, seeking to touch all possible areas of skin to hers.

Her cheek was on his chest and she could hear his heart beating and feel the rise and fall of his breathing, and the quivers of his body – anticipating her offer. She could smell him, and he smelled like Arithon and his scent filled her head. She wanted to give herself to him – right now at this time

336

she would, because she wanted to. She rose a little to accommodate him and he drew his breath in sharply through clenched teeth. He belonged to her for that moment and she knew it, and the sense of power it bestowed inflamed her with lust – the act was primal – it aroused her. She slid down upon him slowly, enveloping him in her flesh and he moaned for the first time. She placed her fingers over his lips to quiet him, not wanting to be heard by the crew – and his struggle to be quiet only added to her excitement. She rose to sit astride him, gripping him with her powerful thighs as she rocked back and forth. She interlocked their fingers and threw back her head, wanting to scream at the pleasure of his body trapped under her. She could feel his insistence and she wanted to hold him, so she undulated onto his torso, pulling him to her as he did the same to her and she squeezed him with all of her body as he arched into her.

He felt as if his body was melting into hers, like hot wax into cloth, and they became one entity for that moment – no longer separate – one body, one life. And his mind went clear of all things present, and he could think of nothing, for he had no control of this joined entity. He was almost unconscious, but an image was there – only an image – no thought. He was on a rocky hill, covered with green grass, as if it were just newly spring and the rains had nourished the fresh growth under a soft sun. And he could see to the horizon, hill upon hill, all the same sort marching up into the heights, obscured by rain clouds low on the mountains. And he knew he had never been there.

And then he was back with Lucina, and they were both panting from their effort. He was holding her so tight that she could not breathe and the scent of her body as he nuzzled into her shoulder bound him to her like an exotic opiate – an addiction to her feel and smell – to her life. And with his passion spent, he could again feel her radiance, and it washed over him like a wave on the shore, enveloping his every fiber. And it gave him life and relaxed him to the depth of his being. He held her tight but allowed her to slip to his side where he cuddled her under his arm and fell asleep.

He awoke once, later, as he felt her slip from under his grasp, but as he grabbed onto her arm, she squeezed it reassuringly and he fell back to sleep.

CHAPTER 35   RETRIBUTION OF ARTEMIS

Artemis, goddess of young girls, troubled and displeased,
prepared her bow for the shot.

She was not in the cabin – he could sense it before opening his eyes. The early morning light filtering into the cabin gave an unnecessary confirmation. Every muscle in his body resisted the roll to his side and he lay there exhausted from even that effort. Her leather bag was missing. He listened but heard only the wind, the waves, a seagull crying in the distance. To the mariner's ear, all harbors are distinctive; an ambiance of sounds and smells unique to its geography – and this anchorage was familiar – he had been here before. Keen to rejoin the living, he rose in a painful unfolding, and left the cabin having remembered to grab a loincloth. As he stepped onto the deck, he squinted at their anchorage and glanced to port where the *Swallow* was anchored two ship-lengths away. Po was standing on her deck and he waved. Arithon returned the gesture, and shuffled around, like a baby learning to walk. After a time at the rail, he ambled up and down the full length of the deck, weak to the point of giddiness. It seemed that every muscle from face to foot was sore, and he was famished. He had just decided to descend for anything that resembled food when Sestos popped his head out of the hold.

"Arithon! How are you?" he asked.

"I am hungry, Sestos, and I was wondering –"

"Speak, no more, I will have you a feast in moments."

Sestos' head disappeared and Arithon continued to pace the deck, his flexibility returning. Sestos reappeared with baskets under each arm, jars hanging from his fingers and two skins slung over his shoulders.

"You look like a peddler."

"Sit here. I have more yet to bring."

So it was that Sestos soon scrounged a feast from hoarded supplies and arranged it on the deck around them as the sun rose and warmed their backs. Arithon said little at first, content to eat all his friend had brought. Sestos had found olives and nuts, three kinds of cheese, dried fish, and a jar of raisins, which Arithon found particularly scrumptious; sweet and full,

338

their texture and taste a delight. He must have eaten two cups before he felt sated.

"Where is Lucina?" he asked.

Sestos, his mouth full, held up a hand to signal that he needed time to swallow.

"If she is not attending you, then she must be aboard the *Swallow* with Szaba."

"Szaba?"

"I thought you knew. He was wounded when we took the *Swallow*."

"I did not know this," he said fighting his tortured body to stand. "What is his condition? Who else is injured?"

"Slow down, Arithon. You have just risen yourself. We were as worried about you as anyone. Lucina thought you might die of exhaustion. You passed out and we could not revive you, so we made you comfortable and let you sleep. Lucina got a few cups of water in you and kept you bathed most of the day, as you were overheated. She has also been working with Szaba. He took an arrow to the thigh and has a sword cut across his neck. Our friend lost a lot of blood, though he kept fighting until we were clear, and now he is weak and feverish. Lucina has used a Cretan concoction on his thigh wound. She is afraid it might go poison.

"You should see her hopping about. She cannot walk a step, but she orders Lutea or anyone else in range to get her this or that. Po treats her like a daughter. He and she have nursed the wounded together."

"How many of the crew did we lose?"

"Three were killed outright – Dirantos, Andamos, Tiron – and we have four others who are too wounded to perform any duties."

"Tiron? So, his faith in me was unwarranted."

"What?" puzzled Sestos.

"Oh. Nothing," deflected Arithon, but his heart sank. Tiron had chosen to ship with the *Dolphin*, though his mother had railed against the cursed ship and its captain.

"Seven," Arithon said. "The world is whittling we few Therans down."

"That is a certainty," Sestos acknowledged. "We had a wearisome time rowing two ships to here."

"We have Po back," Arithon responded.

"Yes, and his ship, too," replied Sestos.

"I am going over to the *Swallow*. Want to row me there?"

"Of course," he said with an animated bow, "and is there anything else I can do for you?"

"Yes. Help me stretch."

The sailors had a practiced regimen of stretching to prevent cramping of the back and leg muscles: a constant annoyance on the rowing benches. Arithon lay on his back, as Sestos attempted to push one then the other of his extended legs toward his chest.

"What of the burnings – for the three?" asked Arithon, grunting from the pressure Sestos was applying.

"Po prepared the pyres yesterday. He thought today if you are up to it."

"Yes. After I have met with Szaba."

As soon as Arithon was limber, they rowed across to the *Swallow* for an emotional reunion. Po met him at the rail and helped them aboard, where he hugged Arithon long.

"Thank you, Arithon," Po began with tears in his eyes and so choked up he could barely talk. "You risked much for the life of one old man."

"You would come for me, Po," said Arithon. "You cannot be a slave. It could not be allowed by me or my father. ... Szaba?"

"In the cabin," said Po, gesturing behind him.

Lucina was sitting on the edge of one bench with Lutea asleep behind her. Arithon extended his hand, which she squeezed; communicating all that bound and separated. Szaba lay stiff but cut his eyes; bright though weary. Arithon dropped to his knees beside him, while Lucina watched.

"Szaba, you look ... slightly worn."

"I am not my best," he smiled. "I will be up tomorrow."

"Of course," responded Arithon, "but you can rest. You were courageous and you saved my life – as you do each time. You have repaid me back many times," he added, "and I will take you back to Africa myself."

"I desire to remain with you, Arithon, if that is not too much to ask," he replied.

"Why would you want to ship with a wanderer?" Arithon said gently.

"Because he is my friend," Szaba replied, "and though I have never been allowed to have friends, I find I value it."

"As do I, my friend, as do I," Arithon said, grabbing Szaba's arm with both hands.

Lucina, sitting at the foot of Szaba's bed, had tears in her eyes, but mastered herself and pushed Arithon aside to offer a drink to Szaba.

Arithon stood and said, "One more night here, and then we head for Lesvos to retrieve Mara. Get your sleep."

"I will take care of him," she said as he exited, and he knew she would and that Szaba would be the man he was before.

Ashore he followed Po up a short slope and around to a headland which poked into the sea: a stony rise with a flat top. The ships floated at anchor in the clear water below; silent and unmanned; for the crews stood with grim faces, staring at the bodies of their shipmates lying on three pyres. This remote island had not changed, but they had.

Arithon had attended many funerals on Akrotiri; the sailor's life was after all fraught with mortal danger; but he had never presided over one and felt quite unprepared to address a war death. The Achaeans were to blame. Or maybe he was. Po sensed his hesitancy and caught his eye with an offer, but Arithon shook him off. He looked now at his men and saw their grief.

"Dirantos, Andamos, Tiron," he said, looking out, "sailed with us on the sea of our fathers. They were our shipmates – and remain so. May they know the honor in the underworld they earned here with us."

The crew murmured – prayers, goodbyes, and sailor's incantations.

"To Hades' realm you sail."

Pserimos handed Arithon a torch and he stepped up to the pyres and set them each ablaze: the black smoke rolled into the wind and the crew stepped back from the heat, solemn and unsure. As the fire roared and consumed they walked single file back down to the beach; only Pserimos, brother of Andamos, remained behind, unmoving in his grief.

***

Arithon called on the wounded, while the crew repaired damage to both ships. He emerged from the hold in late afternoon, troubled and regretful, and watched a hunting party rowing the skiff back into the bay, two harbor seals in tow. When another group returned with seven sea ducks, buckets of snails and a string of rock perch, the crew suggested another celebration feast – to honor their shipmates and the repatriation of Po. Arithon consented and those who could went ashore to the rock alcove now christened Celebration Hollow.

Lucina refused to leave Szaba's side, which endeared her to Arithon, but disappointed him the same. He missed her more than he thought he could and often his mind wandered to some experience he had had with her:

341

when he first saw her on the ship, their time in Poliochni, his interlude with her last night, but always he thought about the first time at Knossos and he wondered where she had been since. And who she was? Why did the Achaeans call her 'The Lady'?

"I never heard what happened while I was up in the temple?" he asked Sestos and Po as they handed him a generous portion of roasted fish and snails on a broad leaf.

Hyssos joined them, bearing four skewers of seal meat, a wineskin, and a water jar.

"I watched you run like a madman up the street," began Sestos, "and I thought I would never see you again, but I hoped I was wrong and as it turns out, I was.

"I turned my attention to Szaba who was in trouble by then. He was scavenging arrows from the deck or waiting to be shot at from any and all directions. I saw him take the arrow in his leg, and while he was down, trying to extract it, four Achaeans climbed the backside of the *Swallow*. One of them slit the side of his neck in the ensuing fight. I rushed the archers on the wharf – they were focused on the *Swallow*, and we were upon them before they knew it. Their swords were sheathed, and we made short work of them, though we lost Tiron there.

"The trader was another story and I should let Hyssos tell you that."

"No, you tell it Sestos," Hyssos conceded. "You are a much better storyteller than I."

"Of course, I am a better storyteller than you, Hyssos. I am a better storyteller than anybody here. And a great many other things besides."

Hyssos shook his head and Sestos continued.

"The trader was going to be the end of Szaba and our bid for the *Swallow*, for they had thirty men aboard. I was standing on the quay, wondering how I could help when Hyssos rows by and hits the stern of the *Stag*, making a mess out of our sprit as he drove the trader past the *Swallow* onto the beach. Hyssos the Ram."

Hyssos laughed at the attention.

"My team jumped in the water and swam over to the *Swallow*. We scrambled aboard and got her off anchor in record time."

"I'll say it was a record time," interrupted Hyssos, "– he cut the rodes."

"Only one line, my dear Hyssos. We pulled up the aft as we rowed past."

"Then you only attempted half of the job for your record time."

"Yes, yes, so maybe it wasn't a record time – but it was fast. People throwing spears and shooting arrows at you prompts one to 'tighten your line,' as Po would say."

Arithon laughed heartily. He was enjoying listening to Sestos, talking like he used to do.

"We were soon out of range and headed out. Hyssos turned *Dolphin* in mid-harbor and followed us."

Arithon nodded and then asked, "Is that all, or do you have more to say?"

"You know perfectly well I have more to say, but I will only say this one thing more," he said, his voice constricting. "You give me hope, Arithon of Thera."

Sestos and Arithon exchanged a nod and ate in silence until Arithon mastered himself enough to ask Po, "How did you end up on that fishing boat and not on the *Swallow* or the *Dolphin*?"

Po grinned and looked down at the sand for a few seconds and then said, "After you left me, I worked my way down to the beach, thinking I should get out into the harbor. An old mariner like me feels safer on a boat.

"I found one to my liking and watched you raise more mayhem than you did as a teenager on Thera."

Everyone laughed; Hyssos loudly.

"I was not in much condition to help anyone, but I wanted to, and I thought, just maybe, Arithon would need me before the night was over. I spotted you again when the mob did, and I assumed you would head for the water. The rest you know."

"I do not know what happened after you got me in the boat."

"You passed out. You should have been killed a dozen times, son of Alteron, and it is a wonder you did not die of weariness."

"The gods protect him," Hyssos interjected between chews.

"Lucina rowed the boat. She got us within range of our archers before they could overtake us. She is a yare ship, Arithon. And there is more hidden in the hold."

Arithon nodded, staring with unseeing eyes. He was consumed with an overwhelming desire to go to her, sit next to her, and hold her tight to him without a thought in his head or a word spoken. He thought to rise but could not think how to accomplish this simplest of tasks. When he refocused, he realized that Po was studying him. They looked at each other as if a secret had passed between them and Po nodded so gently that only Arithon received it.

"Tell me news of your father," Po said.

Arithon responded but wondered if this was Po's deft hand on the rudder. One discussion steered to another and the course led them back to memories of Thera, home, and family. It was late when they all fell asleep on the beach, tented by a milky swath of stars in a cloudless night.

The next morning Arithon was restless. A providential northwesterly had kicked up pointing toward Lesvos; a gift of Boreas and Zephyr that would do the work half-crews could not. Szaba and the other wounded were the question and concern.

"The fever has broken," Lucina explained, as Arithon stood over the reclining Szaba in the dim cabin of the *Swallow*. "And the wounds are clearing, but ..."

"Do not wait, Arithon," Szaba interrupted. "I will live, Mara may not."

There could be no better argument and Arithon did not wait for one. He pivoted, left the cabin, and found Po.

"Po, if you will agree, we can leave for Lesvos."

"You do not need my agreement, Arithon."

What was that – an odd inflection in Po's response startled Arithon – he had never heard it in all his days with Po on sea and land. He looked at his friend's face and detected an emotional pain he had not been aware of.

"I am no captain," he said so that none could hear. "I lost my ship and my crew. An unworthy thing."

"Po ..." Arithon's voice trailed off lacking anything to say. What could he say? It was true and no words would change a wisp of it. Arithon could imagine how he would feel were he to lose the *Dolphin* and her crew – it was in fact his greatest fear, heretofore. But at this very moment his greatest fear was that Po would not recover from so deep a wound – deeper than any arrow might bite.

"Po, take the *Swallow*," he said loud enough for the crew to hear, "and lead out as quick as you can." Arithon turned without awaiting a reply and climbed down into the tender. There was an uncomfortable silence as Arithon set to the oars, but then a welcome, "Prepare to heave anchors," issued from the deck, and the voice was Po's.

The *Swallow* was aweigh in a skilled time. It was natural she should pace them to Lesvos as she was a trifle slower than the longer *Dolphin*. As she slipped by, with Po standing near the steering oar, Arithon was reminded of seeing him and the *Swallow* hundreds of times sailing out from Akrotiri. Po, as he had always done, interlaced his fingers, palms together, raised them to his forehead and then pushed them forward in salute. Great Zeus! that was a marvelous sight. Arithon had a lump in his throat, as he cheered for Po along with the others on board the *Dolphin*. They were mariners, from a race of mariners, and it felt good to be underway: the old masters of the Aegean.

Arithon hurried his own crew along with a rapid series of commands. They were in danger of being left behind; already the *Swallow* was out of the island's lee and filling her sail. The *Dolphin* rounded out, set her own sheet, and gave chase to her sister now settled on the run. Perhaps Po had something to prove, or maybe his natural ability could not be suppressed, or perhaps his pride in the *Swallow* would not allow him to disappoint her, but whatever the reason, the *Swallow* was being sailed so smart the *Dolphin* could not close the gap. The competition brought a smile to Arithon and he trimmed the sail and took the rudder himself: let us see if we can catch her. Great Poseidon! it really did feel good to be underway.

Arithon was reminded of his father's wish that Po and his son might sail the two ships together, although he had envisioned a trade mission, not a trial of survival.

"Po knows his ship," offered Hyssos, watching the distance.

"He is the last of Thera's great captains," answered Arithon, with unexpected melancholy – at least unexpected to Hyssos, who could not know Arithon's internal deliberations.

"Last?" he questioned.

"It will soon be over for us, at least in the Aegean, dear Hyssos. There will never again be a great Theran captain. The future captains of the Aegean will be Achaean."

"Those are bitter words, Arithon," petitioned Hyssos, whose great heart told him to follow his father's course; to captain his own ship was surely a possibility.

"Bitter, yes, but true, nonetheless. There is after all no Thera."

"True, but could we not continue on other shores?" Hyssos was clearly in pain from these words and Arithon realized, too late, that he was torturing him.

"Perhaps. We are already embarked on that quest. Our homelessness may be a gift. We have been prodded out of our complacency and maybe we will fare better in the end than the others of Minoa."

Hyssos looked at him still puzzled and Arithon realized that his thoughtful musings were no comfort to Hyssos' deliberate thinking mind.

"You will be a captain, Hyssos – when we settle again. Look to that day."

Arithon juggled these thoughts as they plowed forward through the blue water, chasing the *Swallow*. Only one task remained for him before returning south – Mara. Then others could make the decisions and lead the Therans.

The wind held all day and into the night. The *Swallow* and *Dolphin* lit night-lamps to maintain visual contact and sailed through the darkness, Po pacing the *Swallow* so as not to sail the *Dolphin* under. By the next morning, the two ships were on the southern coast of Lesvos and by that afternoon they had found a secluded anchorage on the southeast corner within striking distance of Thermi, port of the slave trader, Dagieri.

Arithon was struck once again by the beauty of Lesvos, one of the lushest islands in the Aegean, with dense, green foliage and running water. The men were glad to be back, and hunting parties were soon ashore, while others sought out water and firewood to replenish that which they used in great quantities.

Lucina ventured ashore with her sister to gather herbs; never satisfied with what the Minoans kept on board for medicines.

Arithon had not spoken to Lucina since their conversation in the temple tool shed, and he had much on his mind regarding her, not least their lovemaking in the cabin. He was a young man, and these things preyed on his mind, but he was distracted by his duties as leader and the oppressive responsibility which sailed along. In a way it was a blessing, for given free rein, he would have pursued her unabated, but separated he was forced to reflect on Mara, his family on Rhodos, and, yes, Lucina's ultimate goal.

The herb party had not returned from their foraging when Arithon decided to act on his final rescue. He left Po with the *Swallow* and took the *Dolphin* with all the healthy seamen for a sea-based approach on Thermi. After midnight they pulled up at the entrance to the harbor, pulled Po's stolen skiff alongside and two men got in. Both had a dolphin painted on their chest and were armed for war with dagger, sword, and shield. The larger one also had a coil of rope draped around his shoulder like a sash. They rowed into the harbor and the *Dolphin* slipped back south out of sight.

"What is the rope for?" Sestos asked.

"I do not know – but I always need it when I do not have it."

346

They landed among all the other fishing boats on the beach a short walk south of the quay, where only ten days before, Szaba had started the melee with an arrow pinned to Sestos' jailer.

"This place makes me uneasy," whispered Sestos.

"We will not be here long – all we want is Mara."

"Do we go to the storehouse first or to Dagieri's?"

Arithon thought, his chin in his hand, before saying, "Dagieri's."

"I was hoping you would say that."

"He is no use to us dead, Sestos. We need to know where Mara is."

"Agreed. I will follow your lead."

Arithon stole toward Dagieri's place with Sestos on his heels. When they reached the building, Arithon thought to go around to the back window as before, but instead hesitated at the front. He then drew his sword and tried the door – it was barred. He backed away and started to remove the rope and head for the back when he lost patience with the whole affair. He was mad and he wanted to get Mara back and be done with it.

He kicked the door splintering the bar cradles; it pivoted around on its far edge and crashed to the floor. Arithon entered the shop.

"So much for being quiet," Sestos said under his breath.

Seeing no one on the first floor, Arithon headed for the stairs, but was met by a large bodyguard emerging from one of the downstairs rooms, sword in hand. But the guard was unprepared for the strength and will of the intruder. Arithon broke his bronze sword with the first blow and his head with the second. Out of the corner of his eye he saw the teenage boy break for a window.

"Sestos!"

"On him," replied Sestos who caught the boy with one foot over the sill.

Not waiting for Sestos, Arithon bounded the stairs and kicked open the door to Dagieri's room with alarming power. But Dagieri had armed himself and was hiding off to the side waiting to behead the impudent intruder. Arithon saw the poor, wretched girl tied naked to the foot of his bed. She recognized him from before and squealed, pointing out Dagieri as Arithon crossed the threshold. Dagieri struck, but Arithon had advanced his shield, and he weathered the blow. He leapt into the room, standing near the girl. Dagieri was not done, and struck out again, this time sword on sword and Arithon heard the clang which told him Dagieri was armed with Tektos, Mara's iron sword.

347

Arithon had a problem: he could slay the man – Dagieri was not his match – but he did not know how to subdue him otherwise. Sestos remedied this, coming up the stairs with the boy in his grasp, he stabbed Dagieri in the rump, causing him to cry out in pain and turn, whereupon Arithon caught him across the face with the hilt of his sword, knocking him to the ground; Tektos clanging its way to a corner of the room.

Arithon put his foot on Dagieri's neck. "Be still or I will slice your eyes out."

"Arithon. Your rope, please," said Sestos. "I want to tie this one up."

When the boy was trussed and gagged, they both turned their attention to Dagieri, who was wide eyed with anger, and in pain from their treatment.

"Sit up," Arithon ordered, the point of his sword on his chest, "and no noise, or I will skewer you here and now."

"More filthy Minoans," Dagieri spat. "It is you who will die tonight."

"No, not tonight," answered Arithon.

Sestos stepped into Dagieri's sight. "So it is you." Dagieri snorted, "How is your head?"

Sestos started to move but stopped and waited.

"Good boy," sneered Dagieri. "Your new master does not want me hurt."

Sestos remained quiet.

"Mara," said Arithon.

"Oh, so you want the Phoenician. How much will you pay?" he sniggered.

"I have no patience for this, Dagieri. Tell me or I will make you into a eunuch. You will lose your desire to rape children."

"You are not so cruel, Minoan, and if I tell you, I have nothing to bargain with," he answered.

"I have become more cruel than any may believe," Arithon responded. "I will not kill you tonight, but I will sell you into slavery."

Dagieri sneered to himself: he had won. He doubted not he could buy his own freedom after they sold him. He had tin thrice his worth, hidden for this contingency, and he knew he could bargain with any slave trader in the Aegean – in truth he believed he knew them all.

"Tie him up and gag him," ordered Arithon.

"Yes," replied Sestos, "and … Arithon … the girl –"

"Yes, of course," interrupted Arithon. "And grab Mara's sword."

Sestos cut the girl loose, noticing she had been beaten; her lip was swollen, and she had old bruises and whelps over much of her thin body. He gestured for her to get dressed. She said nothing, but her eyes were wide with hope.

He then worked on Dagieri and tied his hands tight behind his back with a loop, which wrapped around his neck.

"Get up," he ordered Dagieri, but he did not comply.

Arithon reached down taking hold of one of his fat ankles and hauled him across the floor. When Dagieri realized he meant to drag him down the stairs and out onto the street, he squealed into his gag and tried to get up.

Arithon pulled him up by the loop on his neck. Sestos followed holding the girl's hand. She appeared to know what was going on and welcomed any change to her present suffering. Anybody who would treat Dagieri in such a manner was an ally of hers, she felt sure.

At the bottom of the stairs, they stepped over the body of the guard and walked straight out the door and down to the beach. Once there, Sestos bound his feet and tossed him into the bottom of the skiff where he trussed him up so he could not move, but only look up at them with hate in his eyes.

"What now?" asked Sestos.

"Let us go to the storehouse and see if he is there. If not, one of the guards may talk."

"What about Dagieri?"

"You have tied him up. We can leave him. Can you tell the girl to wait here?"

"I can try."

Sestos spent a fair amount of time gesturing for the girl to wait there beside the boat. After trying a few different hand movements and tossing out a few words in Achaean, Lydian, and Minoan, she seemed to get the gist.

"I am uneasy leaving her here, though I think she understands," said Sestos, chewing his lower lip. He paused for a moment more and then said, "Our only option, I think. Let us go."

Sestos started off, but first leaned into the boat and said in Achaean to Dagieri. "Don't cause any more trouble, or I will come back and smash in your head like you did mine."

He then joined Arithon and looked back at the girl to make sure she understood. She was sitting obediently next to the skiff as he and Arithon stole up the beach.

When her new friends disappeared, the comfort they provided disappeared also. Apprehensive, she thought to follow, stood, and looked into the boat at Dagieri, who mumbled through the gag for her to untie him. She continued to look at him and he became more abusive, making it clear she should comply, or she would suffer. Cowered by long months of subjugation, his threats frightened her, and she understood what he wanted.

She walked over to the breakwater and found a large rock, not yet smoothed by the waves, rough and broken with jagged cutting edges – sharp enough to cut the ropes of her master. She could barely pick it up but did so and carried it back to the skiff, and rested it on the gunnel, winded by her effort. Dagieri smiled inside. He was already planning how, once free, he would have his sadistic overseer burn the flesh off those two Minoans while he watched and listened to their cries for mercy.

"Hurry, you little scum," he screamed at her through the gag, "or I will beat you tonight."

Dagieri watched her intently as she raised the chopping stone high over her head, and he squealed as loud as he could into the gag as she brought it down with all her teetering force into his upturned face. She repeated the motions over and over, until she was too weak to lift the blood splattered rock and so dropped it onto the beach beside the skiff and sat down in the sand to wait for her new friends.

Arithon and Sestos reached the storehouse without incident and found the door unlocked. What luck! Noisy entrances, they had learned, were not advantageous, so they slipped in and located the guardroom. They could not see into the darkness of the windowless room, but they could hear breathing: it sounded like two.

Sestos disappeared into the front room and emerged with a lamp and he had managed to light it. With Sestos holding the lamp, they stepped into the room; and as the men awoke, they each found their face at the end of a sword, held by a man with a dolphin painted on his chest.

Arithon asked in Achaean, "Where is Mara?"

They did not appear to understand Achaean, but one of them caught the name Mara and repeated, "Mara," with a shake of his head.

Arithon gestured, 'well, where is he?' and the guard understood.

"Troy. Polos Troy."

"Sold to Troy," Sestos interpreted, disappointment in his voice.

"Tie them up."

They left the building and headed for the skiff. The little girl jumped up when they approached and ran to them, smiling but quiet. She had spent a fearful time on the beach.

When they arrived at the skiff, Sestos and Arithon looked in at a ghastly site. Repeated blows had split and crushed Dagieri's face, and his brains were oozing out; a puddle of blood pooled in the bottom of the hull. They both looked at the girl, who repeated over and over in a sort of broken Achaean, "Smash head in. Smash head in."

"I guess she heard me tell Dagieri I would smash his head in," shrugged Sestos. "I am sorry."

"Do not be sorry. A fitting end I would say," replied Arithon. "Let's get this mess out of the skiff and be on our way."

Arithon was despondent on the trip back, having missed Mara. He had to re-plan his rescue and this disappointment was debilitating, but by the time their skiff pulled into the hidden anchorage, he had a working scheme. They pulled up alongside the *Swallow* and the *Dolphin* and slept the few hours before dawn, the young slave girl alone in Arithon's cabin.

CHAPTER 36 PATARA

With Artemis' silver arrow and capricious fury spent, she slept peacefully and awaited the new day.

Po rowed over to the *Dolphin* as soon as he saw movement and Lucina accompanied him. As she climbed the gunnel, Arithon caught her eyes and held her so that she hesitated at the rail, unsure of what he wanted. As she finished her steps onto the deck, Arithon's heart skipped, and he wondered if it did the same to her. But he shook it off as Po approached, asking for news of the previous night. As they discussed the latest turn of events, Lucina listened with interest, but her face was troubled. Toward the end of their discussions, the young slave girl emerged from the cabin. When Lucina saw her bruises and swollen lip, she motioned her over and hugged her. The girl allowed the embrace but showed little emotion.

"Sestos," Lucina said, "did you feed her?"

"Yes, Luci, I gave her all she wanted."

"Hyssos," Lucina said, "have one of the crew take us over to the *Swallow*. This child needs care." She glared so hard they all became immediately uncomfortable.

Hyssos looked at Arithon, who nodded and Hyssos did as she asked.

Before she left, she turned and said, "Arithon, can you meet me ashore?"

"I can," he said.

She held his eyes and then pivoted, clutching the girl tight around the shoulders. But Sestos called to her, met her at the rail and pulled her aside. Arithon could see her eyes narrow into angry slits as she cradled the girl tighter. When Sestos returned to the group, Arithon nodded his thanks – it was not something he had wanted to broach.

Arithon finished his discussion with the First Tier and left the crew to prepare. He wanted to leave midmorning, hoping to reach Troy before Mara could be transferred. He was worried his captors would figure out who he was, and then no price could free him. If the Hittite, Zorkos, caught up with Mara, they would lose their friend.

Impatient as he was to get started, he was apprehensive about this conversation with Lucina. He knew what the discussion was going to center around, and he was distraught about its inevitable conclusion. But it could not be avoided, so he put ashore, and not finding her on the beach, began to follow her tracks up the stream which wound its way down through the low hills. He heard them – sounds of bathing – before he saw them and called out. Lucina came and shuffled him back down the path. They stopped and sat on a comfortable set of rocks near the stream; within calling distance of Lutea and the slave girl.

"That poor child," Lucina began.

"Yes, she had a hard time," Arithon agreed.

"She is scarred, and I am afraid she will not find much happiness. I have seen it before, but perhaps I am wrong. She is so young. She may find a decent life somewhere."

"I could not leave her there," said Arithon, "but I have no clear idea what to do with her either."

"Lutea and I will take care of her. We can take her with us," she offered, and looked over to gauge his reaction.

"Where are you going?" asked Arithon.

"Arithon, when we first met, I asked to be put ashore near Troy. Do you remember?"

"I remember all you have said to me."

She smiled then sadly replied, "The destination and the need have not changed."

"Can I change it?" he asked.

"Why would you do that?" she asked.

"Your strings of fate … Must we break them?"

"You do not know me – by my design – for if you did, you might feel differently," she said.

The two girls approached, and Lucina hurried. "Arithon, take me and Lutea with you to Troy – and Patara."

"Patara?"

"Yes, you men did not bother to get her name – it's Patara."

"Sorry," he said.

"Arithon – I criticize but it is easy to dismiss a girl as nameless property. I have longed, many times in my life, for the simple act of someone just asking me my name – acknowledging I had one."

Arithon dipped his head, remembering, with the level of guilt his mother could bestow, that he had failed to ask Lucina her name when they first met.

"Be aware of her feelings. Now let us be off. We have two days to – "

The girls had arrived and cut her off. She nodded at Arithon to acknowledge they would continue when they could be alone.

Arithon agreed the three would accompany them. As it happened, there was only a minimal crew left behind on the *Swallow*, with the trusted Hyssos in command. Po transferred provisions and the balance of the crew to the *Dolphin* to aid their speed and asked to accompany them. Po, healed by his beloved *Swallow*, sensed an impending storm that Arithon did not, and wanted to be there to help him weather it. Szaba insisted he was strong enough to go and would not be left.

With twenty-eight rowers on the benches, the *Dolphin* pulled out of south Lesvos before midday and started her race to Troy, hopes high She might beat the trader if it should tarry along the coast. The Therans made good time around the east side of the isle of Lesvos and gave a wide berth to the harbor at Thermi, not wanting to become entangled in the aftermath of Dagieri's demise. Patara, recognizing the terrain, ran and hid in the cabin until they had passed, fearful she was being returned. Lutea and Lucina spent most of the day trying to communicate with her as they fed her an endless array of foodstuff. The child ate everything they offered, and neither could imagine where she was putting it. They also busied themselves making her another tunic and altering a pair of sandals to fit her feet. By the end of the day, she was newly outfitted with her hair clean and braided, and a full stomach – something she had not experienced since her capture. She felt so at-ease she climbed up on the bowsprit and found a perch for her small frame; and remained there with the wind in her face, squinting into the late afternoon light reflecting off the waves, as the *Dolphin* moved one swell at a time northward.

"She looks content up there," remarked Sestos to Lucina who was sitting mid-deck with Lutea.

"Yes, she is quiet, though, so it is hard to know what she is thinking," Lucina answered.

"Her time with Dagieri –," Sestos started.

"Do not talk about it," Lucina said, her brow compressing. "It disgusts me."

"Do you know who she is?"

"Only bits and pieces – she talks to Lutea, but we do not understand all she says. Apparently, she is from a village in Lycia, close to a river, and she lived there with her parents and two brothers and one or two sisters – I cannot get that part straight. She was sent to the well early one morning and men grabbed her. She will not talk about what happened after that. It is as if her history resumes yesterday when you two rescued her – she talks about that often. Has Arithon spoken to you about what I told him?"

"No, Arithon isn't talking much."

"He isn't?" she said, but let it pass. "The poor thing is fixated on you and Arithon, so I want you to show some interest in her."

"Interest?" inflected Sestos. "What do you mean interest?"

"Just be kind – talk to her – show her something, teach her something. Give her a bit of your time. It will help her immensely and besides, she will only be with you for another day."

"Another day?"

"Never mind," she responded. "Why don't you and Lutea go play with her for a while."

Lucina watched Lutea and Sestos talk Patara off the sprit and engage her in a game of 'what is the word for this' in the three languages represented. Satisfied they were absorbed, she slipped unnoticed into the cabin, which had been given over for the three girls to occupy. She gathered the few items she had managed to collect or borrow from the crew and pulled Arithon's personal chest out as well. She spent the remainder of the afternoon alone, changing her hair to the Lydian style and applying makeup to match.

If someone had looked in on her from time to time, they would have seen her crying as she worked – something she rarely did in front of anyone, but sometimes engaged in alone. This time it made her feel better. It also improved her mood to be making herself attractive. This not only appealed to her femininity, but it also gave her a sense of power – and power was a stimulant for her in many of its forms. She detested the ugly side of power she often experienced with men and their petty desires that brought ruin and death, but she was drawn to power's other side – the power of intellect, art and music, the power of a strong, supple and skilled body and the power of life. She possessed all these things – in abundance – and she saw them in Arithon also, and she desired him. But it was more than a desire to possess him – there was some of that – but she wanted more to be with him, accomplish with him, grow with him and make him better, and in her dreams of a future she knew could never be, he would do the same for her. And he was drawn to her for the same reasons: he had told her so. He applauded her for her 'grace and courage.' She liked that.

He was attracted to her for all the right reasons – for the things she liked about herself, and this endeared him to her like no one she had ever met in her fractured life.

But their next meeting was going to be difficult and she wanted to look her best. She wanted that edge and she wanted to please him too: it was such a mixed-up emotion, but it made sense to her and she embraced it.

Lutea came in later with Patara, and helped Lucina fix her hair and scent it, as she loved to do.

"You look like a royal Lydian," Lutea said.

"I am," Lucina laughed, "and so are you."

"I never feel like one," Lutea replied. "I feel like a harlot."

"Do not say that," Lucina responded. "It is I who carry that guilt – not you. You did what I asked."

"But no one will ever want me," she replied, tears beginning to well up in her eyes.

"Nonsense. You are young and beautiful and only you and I will ever know."

"Promise?" Lutea entreated.

"Promise," Lucina replied and hugged her.

"We will soon be home," Lutea said.

Lucina frowned at this, but Lutea missed it, still in the embrace.

By late evening they had rounded the southern spit of the peninsula which contained Troy on its north end, and reckoning they were about halfway, decided to anchor for the remainder of the night so the crew could eat and rest. The jagged coastline, jumbled with stony cliffs, offered little protection to the intrepid mariners. They found an inlet with enough room to accommodate the *Dolphin*, and with Po at the steering oar barking orders, they were able to slide her in past the rocks guarding the entrance.

"Well done, Po," complimented Arithon. "I do not think anyone, but you could have accomplished that."

"You could have, Arithon," Po replied, "but you help my journey back. And Arithon ..."

"We need you, Po," Arithon interrupted. "The Therans need you, the *Swallow* needs you. It is enough." Po met his eyes and then turned back to his work and his thoughts.

The First Tier gathered on the aft deck and began to heat a meal on one of the portable braziers, when Lucina and the other two girls emerged from their hideout in the cabin. The men were astounded at their appearance, especially Lucina, who had been dressing and wearing her hair like a Minoan.

They were unaccustomed to the Lydian style and it struck them as exotic; foreign; an eastern look. Arithon had seen it before – once – in Knossos, and it struck a chord. His stomach butterflied and a chill ran down his back. This was the girl he had seen as a bull leaper: the image he had carried with him through all his journeys, and the image he would carry for the rest of his life. He would never forget. It moved him far more than even Lucina could gauge, though she instinctively knew some of its power.

"You three look – well, you look like princesses," said Sestos.

"We thank you for your compliment, Sestos," she answered, with a tiny bow. "You at least are a gentleman and notice."

Sestos had captured the moment and Arithon was left in an awkward position by Lucina's reply. He kept quiet but looked uncomfortable.

During the boisterous supper that followed, Lucina spent much of her time interpreting for Lutea, and she in turn tried to translate for Patara. And there was a lot to translate. Sestos was relentless, making puns or just clowning around, embarrassing someone in the group.

As the other center of attention, Lucina shone. Her smile and laughter were infectious and attractive to everyone present. Arithon could not take his eyes off her and was caught looking more than once. Lucina was nervous but determined to enjoy this night with the Minoans and her time in the center. She hoped it would somehow go on forever, but as the night deepened, those who had spent the day moving the ship grew tired and drifted off to sleep one by one until only Po, Arithon and Lucina were awake.

Po, sensing something lay between the two, thought to push it along.

"Arithon, you and Lucina go ashore for a while? I will stand watch."

Arithon felt a wave of apprehension and saw it mirrored on her. Po grabbed food and drink and threw them into the tender along with a few blankets. Arithon and Lucina climbed in.

"You might get cold," he said; handed them a lamp and added. "See you in the morning."

CHAPTER 37 THE HOSTAGE

All feared Eros, god of love, his arrows deadly to the mortal
and immortal alike.

The beach was small, but they found a place out of the wind, and sat down shoulder to shoulder, their backs to a tuft of earth and the lamp at their feet. They had so much to say to each other that neither wanted to start the conversation. Neither knew how to start it. They stared at the flame, or out across the water to the ship and to the stars on the horizon beyond. The full moon had risen behind them but had not cleared the cliff to shine on the two lonely figures, unsure of how to spend their last night together.

"Sestos was very funny tonight," she opened. "Is he like that often?"

"Yes, he was quite himself," Arithon said.

"Even Lutea enjoyed herself."

"How is Lutea? I mean after Poliochni," Arithon asked.

"She will be alright, Arithon," Lucina replied.

Silence followed, and then: "You are beautiful, Lucina. Like the first time I saw you."

Lucina was elated he found her so, but said, "You were a boy the first time you saw me. How could you think I was beautiful?"

"Something about the way you move. It was beautiful to me."

Arithon was stripping a piece of grass in his hands and looking out into the night, a bit embarrassed to be talking about something so intimate – even with her – the subject of his intimacy.

"How do I move?" she asked, enjoying his discomfort.

"You move with confidence, without fear, but … slightly self-conscious. You are aware of all that is around you and your place in it."

"And you like that?"

"I am attracted to it."

"Why?" she now teased ever so gently, wanting to hear him say it.

"I sense your intellect, your grace, your aura."

"And you knew this then?" she asked.

"Yes, but not consciously. Somehow it struck my core and over the years I have had time to put words to it. A sailor has time to revisit his memories. And for me that memory was you."

"But how could you make such a judgment on my intellect or my personality?"

"It is all there. What you are – what you will be – it is all in the way you move."

"What I will be," she repeated under her breath and then asked, "Then I would not have turned out to be someone mean or horrible who just moves nice – you knew I would be this person you like?"

"Yes."

"But Arithon, how could you know me? I have hidden that from you."

"I can discern some of it," he began as if she had really asked a question. "I knew in Knossos you were not Minoan. You were exotic to me; eastern; mysterious. It made a big impression: a girl my age; not Minoan; present in a sacred Minoan festival. How did that come to be?"

"That is my story, is it not?"

Arithon said nothing but pulled another blade of grass and waited.

"I am Lydian," she began. "At least I was born so. I am from a city in the interior, where my father is king."

"Then you were a hostage, yes?"

"I was. I still am."

"Still am?" he repeated.

"Yes, Arithon. It is complicated … and dangerous. I am sorry I let you believe I was just a captive, but only my full story would explain who I am and … and what I have done,"

Arithon sensed as he had before that her past may tarnish or even shatter the image he had built, and she, knowing this, was reluctant to do so.

"You said to me only a few days ago that you deemed it not the time to tell me who you were," he began. "You were wise in that. But I am ready."

"I hope so," she said.

"What is your city," he asked?

"Thyateira."

"I have heard of Thyateira," Arithon said. "We trade on the coast with those who sell linen."

"Yes, we are quite well known for it."

Arithon smiled; glad to have at least a passing knowledge of her land.

"What is your father's name?" he asked.

"Alikees," she said, as if referring to a stranger.

"Did you know him?" Arithon asked.

"Some," she responded. "My mother is the second of his three wives, and besides two sisters, I have a full brother."

"And the first wife?" asked Arithon.

"Three daughters – no sons. The wives are locked in a bitter struggle to assure one of their children can ascend. My mother is Lydian, but the first wife is Trojan."

She waited for this to sink in. Arithon turned and made eye contact. "Trojan?"

"Yes, it is a long story – do you want to hear it?"

"Yes. I want to know all there is to know about you."

"Maybe not all," she said.

"It starts with our land," she began. "We produce wonderful olives and linen as you know, but we are also rich in minerals. We trade these to every point on the wind, the Hittites to our east, Cyprus and Egypt to our south, north to the inland sea, and west via the Aegean to the Achaeans. All of these nations are more powerful than Lydia, and so we enter into agreements and alliances."

"Mara says the same of the Phoenicians," added Arithon.

"Yes, there are many who survive as we do, some waiting for their chance at the front, others content to hide in the pack for generations. But the winds are shifting again, and Lydia feels the weight of all who surround her.

"The Trojans are our closest neighbors and they pressed first."

"Who are they – the Trojans?"

"Newcomers to the Aegean," she said. "Their language is different. We can, at any time, bypass their control of the spont – overland to the north or west, and they did not like this, but it was not worth their trouble for linen, olive oil and a few talents of gold. But we made a mistake with tin."

"You have tin?"

"We have a secret source. Even I do not know its origin. Some believe we mine it and others think we get it from the Scythians and the Cyzicusians. The Trojans found out and threatened our northern border."

"When was this?"

"Thirty years ago – I think.

"My father worked out an agreement with them and took his first wife as part of the contract – a Trojan of the first house.

"But he was really in love with my mother – or so my mother has told me – and he took her as his second wife after years of consorting with her. She was from one of the first families of Lydia. As you can imagine, the two women are in a constant battle to control my father."

"We have heard of these practices. We consider them 'Eastern,'" Arithon said.

"It is commonplace in my world. As the eldest of my mother's children, I was involved early.

"We had another dispute with the Trojans, and I was dealt off as part of the agreement – at the influence of the first wife, Araxa. My mother fought hard but capitulated to gather leverage for her true goal – the ascendancy of my brother."

"How old were you?" Arithon asked.

"Eight," she said. "One day I was a common Lydian girl, and the next I was on my way to Troy."

"Somehow, I do not picture you as a 'common' Lydian girl."

"Umm, maybe not 'common.' I was a little untraditional."

"Now that I believe," he said.

"Why would you believe that?" she asked.

"You are strong willed."

"I thought you liked that about me," she challenged.

"I do."

"Yes, I guess I am," she softened. "But not everybody likes that – I am pleased you do. My mother liked it about me. She encouraged me in everything. I think she knew my time with her would be limited, and she tried to temper me to survive without her."

"What did you do in Troy?" he asked.

"I was in the First House – a kind of maid to the lady, she said looking down; remembering. "They were good to me, but I was nothing but trouble to them. I wanted to go home and tried more than once."

"How far is that journey?"

"Six or eight days," she laughed.

"And still you tried?"

"Yes, I was fiendishly resourceful – even then. I made friends with the boys of the house and learned all their secret ways in and out of the city walls."

361

"Then how did you escape from Troy?" he asked.

"The first time was quite simple. I lied to the gatekeeper. Told him I was on an errand to the fish market outside the walls and when I was out of eyesight I ran.

"They found me asleep the next morning five leagues away."

"What happened to you?" he asked.

"I was punished of course – the upstart Lydian. They started calling me 'Lady' to mock me. I hated it, but it stuck, and followed me from then on."

"Yes, I have heard you referred to as 'The Lady,'" Arithon admitted.

"Who?"

"The Achaean you whacked with the spear shaft."

"Vorkoros," she sighed, and then regretted she had said his name. Arithon started to ask about him, but Lucina raised her hand and shook her head. Arithon acknowledged her wish. She began again.

"The Trojans told me I was never going back – to make me cry, I think. But it only made me wonder why, and so I started asking questions – innocently at first, but as the days went by, I learned more and more of the internal workings, agreements, plots and subplots, which permeate a First Family and their allies. I gathered pieces of information, until I felt like I understood the 'arrangement.'

"I was a guarantee of good faith on the part of the Lydians – a royal hostage. If the Lydians broke the agreement I would be forfeited.

"At first it scared me, and then I believed it had nothing to do with me. I reasoned if I were not there, someone else would just have to take my place. Never thought it would be someone I cared about – someone more fragile than me. I assumed it would be a stranger. So, I bided my time.

"Then one day I met one of the princes – a boy name Lysis just a few years older than me. I was sent to the kitchen to get a basket of grapes for the lady and he was there pilfering sweets. We became friends, keeping secrets and participating in mischief. We used to spy on members of the household and slip into their rooms when they were out and look through their things – childish antics."

Arithon was watching her face, bemused by her story, and she was looking ahead into the night, reliving her life.

"Once we were snooping around in one of the royal chambers – off limits to us – and we heard someone coming. Afraid of being caught, he opened a secret tunnel entrance and we slipped in. That was my first experience with tunnels, but not my last," she said looking over at Arithon, who was watching her.

"We hid behind the stone, but left it open a crack. It was one of the young maids. She was meeting one of the men of the house for a tryst. We watched the whole thing. That was something else new for me – the sexual liaisons of the royal households."

Arithon was looking down at his hands, with a small grin on his face, imagining a young Lucina peeking out from behind a stone block, watching the affairs of adults.

"When they left, he wanted to exit back into the room, but I asked him where the tunnel led. He was nervous about me knowing, so it was sometime later before I ventured alone to discover its end. It led out of the palace and under the wall, exiting into a ravine behind the city. Once I knew its purpose, I decided I too could use it to escape, so I made my plans and waited.

"Months later I chanced on a piece of luck.

"Land traders from Lydia were in Troy but leaving for Thyateira the next day. I watched them leave on the main road south. Sometime after midnight I made my way to the chamber. That same maid appeared and caught me – demanding to know what I was doing. I told her I knew what *she* was doing there – a mistake – and she shuffled me off. I had to wait until the next night.

"This time I waited until I was sure the maid was asleep, slipped into the tunnel and crawled to the end where a stone blocks the exit. It took everything I had to move it enough to slip out. It was so dark that night. I can remember trying to find my way to the road. By the time I caught up with the caravan, I was a mess.

"I made it home, thinking mother would be ecstatic, but I was confused by her reaction. She cried and hugged me, but I could tell she was nervous. After I told her how I managed it, she showed a mixture of pride and fear, complimenting me on the one hand and admonishing me on the other – talk about my duty to my father and Lydia and how I needed to stay in Troy for a while – all of those things.

"My father was more understanding than my mother expected and proud of my pluck, but I had to return; he blamed the Trojans for their lack of diligence and put them on the defensive. None of it worked out the way I had envisioned. Once back in Troy, I was treated differently – as someone not to be trusted.

"It would have been unbearable if it had lasted, but I was there only a short while.

"More and more the Trojans collide with the Achaeans. As in all these matters, sometimes they negotiate, and sometimes they compete. The confrontations were escalating regarding the Spont – the Achaeans wanting to trade farther into the Black Sea for exotic goods such as amber, gold, and tin.

"So, they made an agreement with Athens – do you know of Athens?" she asked.

"Yes – we trade with them," he answered.

"This 'agreement,' surprisingly, included me," she said.

"Not long after I was back in Troy, I found myself on a Trojan ship bound for Athens."

"You lived in Athens?"

"Yes, it must have been eighteen months or so. When I first arrived, I was placed in the keeping of the temple maidens, where I learned about their world, as we have discussed before. Some are harlots and others are devout priestesses, and others are a combination of the two. It is a sad life in my estimation, for they are ever at the whims of the temple patrons, and never make any decisions about their own life. But that was not to be my destiny.

"Athens has a long-standing relationship with Crete; dependent on them for many forms of trade and transport.

"Because of a time-honored agreement, Athens has supplied bull leapers to Knossos. Boys are easy to find and train, but girls are a rare commodity – sort of like tin," she laughed.

Arithon laughed with her and added, "Yes, you are a rare commodity."

"Why thank you, Arithon. You always make me feel good about myself."

"I would have thought you always felt good about yourself."

"Oh, no. I have self-doubt like anyone else – so your compliments are a 'filling wind,' as you sailors would say."

"You do pay attention," he said.

"Another compliment?" she asked.

"As many as you like, and I can make them all sailor talk," he added as a mischievous threat.

"Oh, no," she said. "I have heard the banter below deck.

"Where was I?" she asked.

"Rare commodity."

"Oh, yes. My antics in Troy did not escape notice and I was deemed a perfect candidate for the acrobatic ranks."

"But why would Troy send you to Athens to be an acrobat?" he asked.

"Because Athens has trouble finding girls who are capable *and* expendable."

"Expendable," Arithon repeated.

"Yes," she said, and for the first time, Arithon detected a bitter resignation in this strong woman he so admired.

"Again Arithon, I did mislead you, but my path is complicated as I have said. To the Trojans I am a royal hostage, but to the Achaeans I was, *initially*, a valuable exchange commodity – like an expensive slave."

"Yes … complicated … and 'slave' is alarming," he agreed. "But what do you mean by 'initially?'"

She hesitated. "I have watched you captain the *Dolphin* many times. You adjust her point on the wind, you reef the sail, you watch the waves and the sky. You make quick decisions – sometimes they work, and sometimes the conditions change faster than you can respond."

"Is your life a ship at sea?" he smiled.

She smiled back. "In many ways. And like you, sometimes my adjustments are a mistake."

He nodded.

"I will get to the 'initially,' soon," she added.

"I was living in the Temple of Athena, in Athens, training with the acrobats, for a role in Knossos.

"Remember, I was a child at the time," she added.

"I loved it. The acrobats adopted me as one of their own. I soon learned that they valued the things others despised in me – my athleticism, my coordination, my – "

"Courage," Arithon interjected.

"My 'filling wind'," she said, and laughed.

"Yes," she began again, "they liked my fearlessness – how I got up after every fall to try again. But I have a secret. I am not fearless. I am afraid of failure because failure scares me more. Remember I am expendable."

"Your secret is everyone's secret," Arithon said.

"As they nourished my sense of worth, I began to excel," she started again. "Without a family, I adopted them as a surrogate and tried very hard to please. The head of the school was a married couple, whom I grew to love in many ways. They taught me the very things of life: the value of intellect, a developed physique; and respect for my own abilities and skills.

"The Achaeans have many worthy attributes," she added.

"I hate them," Arithon said.

"No, you fear them, Arithon. And you should. But do not hate. It is not how I want to think of you."

She turned to look at him, but his gaze could not see her, and she began again: "I learned much in Athens and I was soon the young favorite of my troupe. I learned to juggle, throw knives, perform leaps, tumbles, and feats of balance."

"Knives," Arithon said, as if acknowledging something.

"Knives?" she asked.

"When you threw the daggers."

"Oh, yes," she said, "That was one of our routines. I would ride on the shoulders of one of the men and throw knives at targets as he jumped and spun and ran around a courtyard – it was quite exciting."

"Yes, it was exciting for me, also," Arithon remembered with a resigned smile.

"Thank you," she said accepting a cup of wine he offered. "We performed in numerous festivities in Athens and the other Achaean cities: Tiryns, Mycenae, Thebes, even Sparta. Some unknown bureaucrat declared me ready and I was sent with eleven others to Knossos to train with the bulls."

"So soon," Arithon commented.

"Yes. As I said, they were keen to have girls and it takes a while to learn the skills of bull leaping. I spent the better part of a year training near Knossos with others from many cultures. I was considered part of the Athenian contingent even though I was Lydian. No one cared about all the other arrangements – I was a representative of the Achaeans.

"We trained every day on a 'horn vault' – a kind of fake bull. It has real horns and a place to land on the back. We sprang off this giant drum and rotated over the horns. The trainers would try and catch me, but that did not always work. I have a few scars you have not seen."

Arithon raised his eyebrows. She pinched her eyes at him.

"They have a more complicated vault where the horns are tensioned like a bow, which they release when you grab on. It is awkward at first, and you wonder how they ever figured it out, but somehow it was important to them and so they did.

"A few months to master and then they brought in live bulls for us to work. They were older bulls which did not have the strength to throw us very far. It is a wild ride, though; especially the first time you do it. The first bull I attempted threw me over his back to the ground behind."

"It is hard to believe you could do it, at so young an age," Arithon said, tipping the cup.

"Many did not make it through the training – either through injuries or fear of the bulls. It is deadly, do not doubt it. Heat and power. Face to face you grip their weapons, their eyes flame, their hot breath snorts onto your chest. It is like catching death.

"I was young, and maybe fearless in a way, because I knew by then I was on my own – and that knowledge hardened me. Whether I lived or died was largely up to me, and so I vowed then to seize the rudder whenever it was in my grasp. I was supposedly the youngest girl to ever vault the Minos."

"The Minos?" Arithon questioned.

"It is what they call the huge black bulls – the 'Minos Tor.' As I excelled, I grew to enjoy it. The, attention, the challenge of controlling something perilous."

"You were excellent."

"Do you remember my performance?" she asked.

"Every moment," Arithon answered.

"It is sweet, Arithon. I moved you so much, so long ago," she said, touching his hand for the first time that night.

The contact stirred them both, so she pulled back, afraid she would not get her story out before the sun rose – and it was important for him to know before tomorrow. It might help him.

"After perfecting the routine, I performed in festivals all over the island and became the crowd's favorite."

"You certainly were at the one I attended. Was that your first performance at Knossos?"

"Oh, no, I performed many times at Knossos. I cannot even remember how many – twenty at least. Crete, especially Knossos, was beyond my ken. Women participating alongside men, an open city without walls, the murals, markets, and exotic foods. The island was vibrant and cosmopolitan – so many cultures, trade goods, languages. That was something else I found I was good at – languages. I knew Lydian and had picked up a working knowledge of Trojan and Achaean. Minoan came easy to me – I guess because I was so anxious to learn it. I assumed I would always be there. I had found my home away from home.

"I performed for almost a year until the day when you saw me. It was a big festival, with a score of representatives from all over the seas. What a spectacle. I would have enjoyed it more, but the King had asked for a difficult performance, so I was serious about getting it right."

"The performance went as planned until the last run, when the bull 'took aim' as we say, and … yes … I got caught on the horn."

"A shame," said Arithon looking down at her thigh, though she had it covered.

"Yes, it was, but many have been hurt far worse – gored in the gut or lungs and many have died. They quit placating the bull toward the end of the performance, so he charges us. It is the most explosive time," she said.

"Yes, it was your final run, when you ended up at odds with the horns."

"I was at odds with them all right," she expressed. "I was hurt for months – the wound was deep and would not close. The nurses were skilled though, and I became interested in their craft while they attended me. They taught me about plants and ointments and how a wound can be healed."

She touched Arithon's chest scar with the tips of her fingers, sending shivers through him before she retracted.

"The King was moved by my injury and had his personal healers work with me. The King visited me many times. We became friends.

"He told you to prepare," she said with a sly smile.

"How could you know that?" he asked.

"Because I noticed you also, my worthy Minoan, someone my age sitting next to the King" she laughed, "And the King told me about you after I asked.

"From our conversations, I sensed you were on his mind," she added.

"Lucina, how can our lives be so … linked?"

"I feel it, too, Arithon," she said, looking off into the night sky. "Is it too precious to hold for fear of breaking?"

Arithon mulled this over for a long while. She was voicing what he knew to be true. What does one do with the most precious gift of their life? Seal it away for safe keeping, or risk it for the gain to be realized. He did not have the answer and wondered if he was mature enough to know. He shifted, look over to meet her eyes, took her hand and then leaned back with nothing to say.

She resumed as he relaxed. "I spent six months recuperating in Knossos, sometimes in the Palace, but mostly with the acrobats, who helped me recondition my muscles, so in time, I could do all I could before, and my only reminder of the incident was my ugly scar.

"I even started performing again and I was soon completing stunts no one had accomplished, like a double somersault, which many had thought impossible. I had a good build for it; I was light, but strong, and driven. I look back on it now, and wonder how I ever performed such feats, but at the time, it was my life, my worth; working until I was too tired to move. I used to have these huge calluses on my palms from all the repetitive routines, balancing and walking on my hands, and of course working with the horns. It lasted for two years."

"Two years?"

"Yes, then an odd thing began to happen – I started becoming a woman –"

"Good thing," he interrupted. Lucina released her hand and hit him.

"I began to put on weight on my hips and chest –"

"Better yet," Arithon interrupted and this time flinched before the blow could come.

"I was going through the changes and my balance shifted. The moves which had once been effortless, became labored. I could do all the stunts, but I sustained injuries like a sprained ankles and sore wrists. Even the Achaeans came to the point where they felt I had served my time in a dangerous sport and had earned the right to quit before I was killed, and so one day I was put on a ship bound for Athens.

"All in all, I had spent over four years on Crete and learned much of what the Minoans had to offer – and it is substantial. I participated in the festivals, visited every palace, and mastered the language."

"Your Minoan is flawless," he said,

"Not true of your Lydian," she replied.

"Four years in Athens, at the Temple of Athena," she began again. "I hated it. I had few outlets for my physical pursuits, though I was permitted to spend time with my old acrobatic school on days I was not required.

"And then three years ago something changed. The Achaeans were becoming bolder about their role in the Aegean, and they became intensely interested in Crete – all of Minoa for that matter. Someone found out I knew much about Crete and the language, so while I was left to live in the temple, I spent my days in the courts of power. There I learned much of the Achaean mind and its desires."

"What did you do for them?" he asked.

"Often I would serve as a translator – either directly or indirectly."

"Indirectly?"

"Yes – indirectly. They might have a meeting with a Minoan, and he may speak Achaean to the Achaeans present, but Minoan to his compatriots or he might bring his own interpreter. I would act as a servant, but later they would ask me what had been said in the background."

"Sounds like an awkward position?"

"Oh, it was! Often, I would not tell them all that was said, or how it was said, but I had to give them the general intent – otherwise I was at risk. Sometimes it was very portentous and sometimes it was funny or crude or insulting. I heard a few comments about me that would make a mariner blush."

Arithon laughed and asked, "Did you blush?"

Lucina smirked and then as if remembering said, "One time, I got mad and retorted and the whole meeting disintegrated – it was a big mess."

"Tell me," he said, "it sounds interesting."

"Oh, really it wasn't. A contingent from Melos was in Athens, and they were working on a large business arrangement, with many moving pieces – quite complicated. One of the principal traders was a crude bully – pushing everyone around and insulting everyone under his breath. I disliked him from the start, and then when I was bringing refreshments of wine and olives, he said in Minoan to one of his partners, 'I wouldn't mind fucking that little animal there,' referring to me. I lost my temper and replied in Minoan, 'Well, sir, I am a woman. We could find you a suitable animal to copulate if that is your wish. Do you have a preference – a goat perhaps?'"

Arithon laughed admiringly. "Oh my, what happened?" he asked recovering from his mirth.

"His jaw dropped and then his partners laughed, which made him mad and he tried to strike me, but I dodged his blow and slipped out in the turmoil which followed. You laugh, and I can too – now – but at the time I was reprimanded and locked up in the temple for weeks before they would use my services again."

"Lucina, I love you," he said, surprising even himself, as he turned to face her.

Lucina said nothing at first but picked up his hand and cupped it in both of hers, resting them on her lap.

"I know," she said, and began again.

"On the spring solstice this year, the Achaeans brought me to Limnos. I believe they were supposed to bring me to Troy, but they stopped short. I soon learned they had other plans for me.

"The Achaeans and the Trojans met in Limnos – halfway – to make an exchange. Lutea was to be my replacement."

"Is Lutea your sister?" he asked.

"Half-sister. The Trojan wife of my father," she answered. "If I had left her on Limnos the Achaeans would have killed her or enslaved her."

"Why?" he asked.

"Because at the exchange point, in a surprise move, the Achaeans did not want her and asked to purchase me," she explained.

"Buy? As a slave?"

"No, not as a slave, but it seems I was valuable to the Achaeans and they were willing to compensate. The Trojan delegation refused – it was not empowered to make that deal. Vorkoros sailed to Troy with them to negotiate a solution leaving Lutea and I on Limnos."

"Vorkoros," Arithon voiced and removed his hand from her lap.

Lucina shifted and pulled his hand back, slow but insistent.

"I have known him a long time. He is proud and arrogant, but he protected me in Athens and on Limnos – and –," she broke off, and started anew. "I have lived in four cultures, Arithon, and I have been afraid, I have been angry, I have been used and protected, and I have known love – in all of them. You have been secure all your life. Be careful. Not all danger is on the point of a sword. Do not lose yourself.

"Do you understand?"

He did not answer.

"I believe you do. I hope you do," she said as she stared at his unseeing eyes.

"After Vorkoros left, I knew I must escape. The Achaeans never capitulate – I know that about them. The Trojans will resist. I cannot discern all Vorkoros' plan, but on his return, he intended to take me back to Achaea with or without Troy's consent."

"Why would they risk a war over a woman?"

"Because her father has tin, she is fluent in Minoan and she knows the cities and geography of Crete."

371

"Invasion," Arithon whispered.

"Yes. They want Crete first, but they need to keep Troy at bay while they negotiate with my father for the tin. Once the Achaeans take over the Aegean, they will come for Troy."

Arithon paused for long while. "You are in great danger," he said.

"Yes, because I am a threat to all" she agreed. "For the Achaeans, I am the gambit which holds both danger and promise. They will kill me if they cannot have me because I know their true goals. If the Trojans find out, they will see this as treachery on my family's part, kill me, destroy Thyateira and possibly go to war with the Achaeans."

"And somehow it all centers on you," Arithon mused. "I see now why you have been so secretive."

"Forgive me," she said.

"I do," Arithon replied.

"I did not want to betray the Minoans. I needed to escape," she began again. "And I did for a brief time. I got away on a merchant ship – bribed the captain. But Vorkoros returned, gave chase, and caught us before we reached Thermi. My timing was bad."

"Was it?" Arithon asked.

She looked at him and he was staring at her.

"No," she smiled in realization. "It was not."

He pivoted the hand in her lap to hold hers. "Lucina. Come with me," he said.

She felt his crushing sincerity on her entire being.

"Arithon, you are dear to me," she said shifting to face him. "I love you for all you are and will be – a great king – I have no doubt. I love you because you have loved me all these years. Years when I was jostled from one place to the next, barely enough time to make friends before I was shuffled off again – no time to plan for or create a life." Tears were streaming down her face.

"And then you come along and tell me what I have always longed to hear – that there is someone who has loved me through it all, unabated and untouched by time. And loved me for what I was – or could become. This is more than I could have ever wished for," she said wiping the tears from her cheeks.

Arithon started to speak, but she gently lay her fingers across his lips. "Do not speak – I could not stand to have you object.

"Arithon, I have enjoyed every moment with you. I feel alive like I never have. I was able for a short time to play with makeup and fix my hair and dress to please someone I desired. I enjoyed our conversations, our shared wisdom, our runs, our fighting side by side and our lovemaking. I love the way you look at me. I love that you have loved me from first sight. I love that you love me. In every way you are my complement. But –" she hesitated, "this was our time. This was our precious gift. It will end tomorrow."

"I cannot accept that, Lucina. This was more than fate or chance meetings – those are only the tells – like the signs before a storm. And the tells are clear: it will be a great storm – our life. Maybe even a legendary storm. But that storm is you and I together. "

Arithon reached over and pulled her to him, her face against his chest, sobbing quietly while he held her tight.

"Though I cannot offer you the one thing you never had," he said.

"You offer me everything I want," she spoke into his chest.

He started to speak, but she again reached up and put her fingers to his lips, unable to discuss it anymore. She only wanted to be held.

And so there they sat, in the gathering cool of the night, the lamp flickering at their feet, she draped across his lap, while he cradled her.

Chapter 38 New Dawn

Himeros, God of uncontrollable desire, rejoiced and then wept for Artemis would soon tear down that which he had made.

He awoke slowly; the pale light of the approaching dawn was in the sky dimming the stars so only the brightest held forth. He was holding Lucina and he could feel her rhythmic breathing: she was not yet awake. Somehow, they had covered themselves in the night, and they now lay under the linen Po had sent. His arm had fallen asleep, and as he shifted to stir circulation, it unsettled her, and he felt her eyelashes brush his chest as she opened them. He pulled her tighter, not wanting to let her slip from his grasp, but she pushed away to sit up.

"How long have you been awake?" she asked.

"Not long."

"Shall we go?"

"No," he said pulling her down to spoon her. "Let me hold you but a while longer."

Comfort such as they seldom knew lay over them, but sleep was not to take them again, and the realization of what the day would bring began to sink in. Arithon was basking in her warmth, feeling the flow from her body to his, and it soothed him, but the thought of it passing, disturbed his tranquility.

"What are you thinking about?" she asked.

"You," he replied.

She was quiet and then said, "No matter what happens, think of me from time to time, Arithon. It will comfort me."

She kissed his hand and pulled it up under her chin, holding it like it belonged to her. She waited and then turned into him and pushing his hair back while caressing him brought her lips to meet his.

"It is dark for a short while," she murmured. "Let us get lost for this brief moment."

She reached down and pulled her tunic up to her waist and rolled over on her back pulling him over. She had not had his weight on her like this and she felt overpowered by the strength which pressed her into the sand.

She did not want to think – she wanted him to smother her in his grasp so she could think of nothing but now – with him. She reached down and tugged at his loincloth, and he rose up just enough to help, and then it was off and he lowered his warm body back onto hers and she spread her legs to allow him. The desire flushed her. She loved he wanted her so much and she wanted him. He rose and then they melted into each other, and for that moment in time they were one. And then he was insistent, and she held him even tighter, burying her face into his chest. He lowered his head and their lips met and she locked her hands around his neck, swinging beneath him as he balanced on his outstretched arms. And he stayed with her, pushing her rhythmically into the sand, a continuous and uninterrupted pounding which was taking her to someplace she had never been. It alarmed her and then took her and she went over the edge, a warm throbbing that she lost herself in and she cried out and pulled him to her tight, so she could feel his pleasure, just as she had felt her own.

And then he was quiet, and they held each other until they felt the need for air and pushed apart. He fell to the side but scooped her back into a spoon, panting in her ear.

She again pulled his hand up and kissed it and then nestled it back under her chin.

They lay quiet for a brief eternity, as the oncoming sun changed the sky from black to blue.

"Arithon, we must go," she said.

"I know," he whispered into her ear.

They rose, gathered what they had, and made their way back to the ship, Lucina knowing they had just spent their last moments alone.

CHAPTER 39 TROY

Hera watched with interest the mortals at the Spont, but not
was now the time to meddle, another day it would.

Po was waiting for them at the rail and helped them aboard. Lucina
retired to the cabin in a hurry, and Arithon moved unthinking to ready the
ship. The crew, hearing the activity, rose to assist, aware of the odd silence:
a backing wind on a troubled sea. Po caught Arithon's eye, causing him to
pause and look out over the water, dappled with the orange and pink of a
new sun.

"She has to return to her people," he said.

"As do you."

Po gathered containers to break their fast and sat down forward on the
ship away from the cabin. They ate and talked, Arithon relating all she had
told him.

"It is time for you to return to Knossos," Po said after his young
apprentice stopped talking and stared off into the bay.

"Yes, I have much to tell him."

"And he, you."

Arithon's eyes darted in thought and a slow realization began to
descend upon him.

"How long have I been involved?" he asked.

"Early. Your modesty protected you. Selleres has kept track of you more
than you know. He wants a mariner … and now I suspect a warrior."

"The Achaeans," said Arithon with resignation.

"There will be much killing, Arithon," said Po. You used to be the
reluctant warrior. You can choose not to go – you might like yourself better
in your old role."

Arithon shared a sad smile between friends and said, "I would. But it is
too late for that."

Po left Arithon considering and maneuvered the ship out of the narrow
slot and turned her north along the coast. The women remained in the
cabin, though Patara ventured out to gather food. Life was returning to her

eyes, and all around her were encouraged. She played word games with Sestos before she returned to the cabin, as she remembered her errand.

Arithon rowed for a while to loosen his limbs. The exercise always made him feel better and it helped him clear his head. There was something about having to keep the rhythm which prevented your mind from wandering too far, always bringing you back to the present; otherwise your oar would strike the one ahead or behind and the whole line would cascade out of position. It always drew a negative response from the rowers and you instantly became the butt of their verbal abuse. It happened every hour or so, but the crew prided itself on its efficiency through the water, as all mariners do, and upsetting forward momentum was considered unprofessional. The port and the starboard crews held contests to see who had the least oar crashes, with the losers providing the evening meal or after dinner song. Arithon was always conscious not to contribute to any one side's negative score and this required just enough concentration to prevent his thoughts from running away from him.

Lucina came out while he was rowing and he watched her find Sestos, who nodded in his direction. She located him, smiled, and waved, spoke to Sestos again, and then disappeared into the cabin.

After Arithon had calmed his racing mind, he rotated out and ended up at the rudder next to Po.

"It is time for us to head south."

Po nodded.

"One last try for Mara and then I will go see Selleres."

Po pushed over on the tiller to keep the ship from yawing as the starboard side experienced a massive oar crash.

"I will not be singing tonight," Arithon smiled. Po laughed aloud.

The door to the cabin opened and Lutea appeared and motioned for Arithon to come.

Po turned his attention to the ship and Arithon walked to the cabin door, where he knocked.

"Come in," she responded. "Always the gentleman."

Arithon stooped in and sat on his usual bench as the other two girls left.

The girls had been busy. Lucina was as beautiful as he had ever seen her, but more astounding was her transformation.

"You are Minoan again?"

"Everything but the tight open front bodice," she smiled.

"I like the bodice," he said. "Other cultures cover the breast, but I know not why. It is a lovely part of the woman."

"Would you like to see me with my breast exposed?" she asked.

"Of course – you especially."

"The Achaeans and the Trojans are not as keen on it as you Minoans. Only the slave women are bare-breasted – it is considered low. They want their wives and daughters to keep covered – stylishly, mind you – but covered.

"But I agree with you. I was bare breasted on Crete, though I cannot do it here. But I can go as Minoan in other ways, and I intend to. It was they who sent me away, so if I come back a Minoan, then so be it.

"But more than that, I wanted to please you –" and her voice broke, but she did not cry, though she wanted to. "And I like your culture, Arithon – I wish I were Minoan."

"Who knows how long anyone will be a Minoan."

"I wanted you to come here before we reach Troy, because I want to make you up as we did before. I want" – now her voice was cracking – … I want you to escort, me if you will?"

"Yes," he said, his own voice wavering. He thought if she cried, he may himself – something he could not remember doing for a long time.

"Then turn around and let me braid your hair," she said, gaining her composure.

He complied and she began to comb his hair.

"I like when you work with my hair," he said to the wall in front of him. "It makes me tingle – it gives me pleasure."

"I know," she said.

"And I will miss it."

"What if Mara is not in Troy?" she asked.

"Then we will leave for Rhodos," he said.

"But I thought –" she broke off.

"Mara is resourceful, and he knows where to find us."

"Where after Rhodos?" she asked.

"To war maybe. Or out of the Aegean. I do not know," he said pivoting his head to look at her. Tears were in her eyes, but she wiped them on the blanket.

"Turn around," she commanded. "I want to add the dolphin."

"The dolphin?"

"Yes, I think it protects you and I want to make sure you are safe when I am not here."

"A small one then – I have no plans to fight anyone."

"Of course – one here on your left side – does that meet with your approval?"

Arithon said nothing, but sat still and erect as she, on her knees, began her painting; except this time, she executed it with more care than before, working hard to create a work of art.

He watched her from above, his mind wrapped in the melancholy of something on the edge of greatness but lost in only a moment – like Thera, never to be fully achieved. She concentrated on the last dolphin she would paint, her eyelashes blinking down against her cheeks and her lips pursed in concentration – occasionally wetting them with her tongue. She felt his stare and cut her eyes up, her finger frozen in midair as they communicated their pain across the space which separated them.

"Don't," she said, and he said nothing.

She continued her work, while his body responded to her delicate touch, the waves of pleasure mixing with the agony in his mind, so that he thought he would go mad – and then she was done and she looked up at him again, but did not move.

Arithon, still sitting on the bed with her kneeling, fumbled under his bed and retrieved the Theran female ring, now tied on a cord, which he and Szaba had found in the cave on Thera. She watched, her large brown eyes tilted up, and wondered if he had been planning this gift. He reached up under her hair with both hands, tying the jewel around her neck. She tilted her head to one side to touch his beautiful hand and closed her eyes.

He finished, cupped her face, and pulled her up to meet his lips. They paused. Ever so delicate, he then kissed each closed eye and the center of her forehead, and then said, "I do not think I can do this – come with us. We are fated you and I. Have been our entire lives – we both know this now."

"Arithon, I will always be yours. I will always be that image – the one you have and will always have. Take that of me for now – it will not change."

Arithon said nothing but pulled her to him in a crushing embrace and spoke into her ear.

"I named you Swift for your soaring grace, but perhaps I was too prescient. My grandfather told me a swift seldom alights, but lives on the wing, always wandering."

There was a knock at the door and Sestos was speaking, "Arithon, Arithon, you are needed."

Arithon placed Lucina on the bench and opened the door.

"Sorry, Arithon, but we have turned into the harbor and –"

"No, you are right to come, Sestos – what is it?"

"Look, I believe that is a Phoenician ship on the beach. Zorkos I would wager."

Arithon did not follow his point but looked up instead at the massive walls of Troy. Lucina joined him, as his gaze dropped to the beach.

"Port turn," he cried over to Po at the steering oar. "Port reverse." The port crew reversed their direction and the ship turned.

"Have we been seen?" Lucina asked.

"Of course," Arithon answered, "but I am not going to risk seizure of this ship.

Po, bring her around to the point and I will take the tender on in."

"The skiff is bigger, if you would prefer."

"Oh, yes, that would be better for the four of us."

"Four of who?" questioned Sestos.

"The women and me," said Arithon.

"Arithon," Lucina said, pulling on his arm. "Patara wants to remain aboard."

"Patara?"

"Yes, she is afraid to go. She feels safe on board with you and Sestos. I do not think she would go without a fight."

"Then let it be," said Arithon, agitated Zorkos was here. He had still held out hope Mara could be purchased from the slavers.

"Sestos, would you grab my axe?"

"Wouldn't you rather have a – no wait, we don't want Zorkos to find out we have the swords."

"Now?" asked Po.

"Yes. I will be back before nightfall – if not, leave without me," he responded.

"But Arithon –"

"No, Po, look at this place. If things go bad, you cannot assail a walled city."

"Then do not go," Po began, but Lucina cut him off.

"He is right, Arithon. I have changed my mind. Do not accompany me. I do not –"

"I am going. I must see if it is possible to purchase Mara. Get ready!"

No one aboard approved of the plan, but not one could think of anything better, and so it was that Lutea, Lucina and Arithon climbed into the skiff and proceeded into the estuary of the Scamander River under the midday sun, the girls holding their few belongings on their lap while Arithon rowed. Scores of Trojan women could be seen washing clothes on the rocks of the shallow river.

They beached a short walk from the quay, and ignoring the Phoenician ship as if disinterested, walked up the hill, three unlikely figures: a tall Minoan with a double headed axe tucked in his belt; a lithe, and beautiful Minoan girl limping at his side; and a slight Trojan girl following behind.

At the gate, Arithon was reminded of the ramparts of Tiryns, and wondered at Lucina's fate inside a walled city. His heart beat, his body flushed in a rush of panic, and he quailed, unable to take her across the threshold. But then he heard Lucina's voice speaking in a strange language and the gatekeeper was ushering them under the massive lintel.

They were inside.

Lutea led them up the maze of streets, making their way to the most protected part of the city – the Citadel itself. They met another guard at the entrance, who repeated the behavior of the first and just as suddenly they were inside the palace; escorted by two armed men, who led them into an antechamber and remained on guard outside the door.

The three were quiet, until Lucina said to Arithon in Minoan, "Let me talk – I will try to find out about Mara."

A head appeared at the door – a young woman, who smiled at Lucina, hugged her, and spoke so rapidly Lucina had to slow her down. She motioned at Lutea, who left in a run.

"I know her," she said to Arithon as they were being led out of the room and down a hall. "I have not spoken Trojan in years, and I could barely keep up with her. Lutea is off to find her cousins."

In a room at the back of the Citadel, three men and a woman awaited them, sitting in a circle of eating lounges with short tables in front of them. Their guide retired, but the guards remained.

One of the gentlemen spoke to Lucina who nodded her head and said, "They want you to take the open lounge, and I will share with the Lady.

They want me to introduce the King – Simois, his wife Annytus, and the Prince Lysis."

"Arithon of Thera," he said, dipping his head.

Arithon sat stiffly erect on the lounge. The Trojans reclined on theirs. Lucina spoke at length, while Arithon remained attentive, but uninvolved with the conversation. He could pick up the gist: she was explaining her presence in Troy. Attendants brought in food and drink, and Arithon ate fresh fruit, nuts, a grain porridge, and diluted wine. He had not had such a meal since Akrotiri, and he had eaten much more than he realized, when he noticed they were looking at him.

"The King wants to know when was the last time you supped," said Lucina with a smile.

Embarrassed, Arithon, put down the pomegranate he was holding and said, "Your fare is excellent – I am sorry if I have been gluttonous. I have not had such a meal in many months."

"It is all right, Arithon," Lucina said. "They want to please you – a guest friend … for now," she added.

They began talking again and it became contentious immediately. Lucina's eyes were showing tears, but her speech was often defiant, sometimes negotiating. He watched her as a man who had often witnessed the nuance of trade and it came to him that she was bargaining for a stake much higher than commodities. He was both proud and fearful for her. But what was in the balance?

Finally, Lucina turned to Arithon and said, "My arrival is unexpected," she began. "They are grateful you have brought me here, and ask what they can give you in return?"

"Tell them I want you," he said.

"Arithon, hush, do not assume they do not understand you," she said. The woman, Annytus, perked up at his statement, and looked at him with renewed interest.

"I mean it," he said.

"Arithon, stop," she pleaded. "I cannot go with you and you must go to your people – they need you, and mine need me." She looked at him with such anguish that he relented.

"Ask of Mara, please," he said, almost as if he were apologizing.

Lucina spoke to the King, who with a nod redirected the statements to the Prince. Arithon heard the Prince mention Mara, Zorkos and Hittite, and his stomach went cold. The King did not appear pleased, and a conversation ensued, ending with a call to an attendant who received his instructions and disappeared at a brisk, official-acting walk.

"They have gone to get Zorkos," explained Lucina. "The King knows nothing of Mara, but the Prince seems to know something. I do not believe the King cares for Zorkos. He does not like the Hittites."

Neither did Arithon.

CHAPTER 40 A LIFE WORTH LIVING

*Pothos, god of longing, companion of Eros, floated slowly to
the earth like the feather of a great bird released on high.*

Arithon was as uncomfortable as he could ever remember; sitting in the palace of a people he knew nothing about, and listening to a conversation in a language he could not follow, while the lives of two people he cared about were in the balance. He wanted to stand, grab Lucina, and fight his way out of the city, and never return to the north Aegean.

But he did not have to wait long before Zorkos appeared at the door and was ushered in. He was not offered a seat but stood on the outside of the circle, his arms folded.

He was a squat, but impressively built man, with massive arms and legs and a protruding torso, which made him look deformed. He carried a large iron sword tucked into a scabbard attached to a massive belt of leather and bronze. He had a round shield with a point in the middle and wore a cone shaped hat of hardened leather. His face was grim, but he glanced at Arithon with an intelligent sneer.

"How can I assist?" he asked in Phoenician. Arithon could understand him, and so listened with his eyes cast downward, concentrating to translate.

"This Minoan, Arithon, is inquiring about a Phoenician called Mara. You made the same query yesterday," the Prince said.

"Yes, I did. But why would such esteemed Lords concern yourself with a renegade," he answered, stern but polite.

"It is no concern of ours – except this man has performed a service for us, and this is all he asks in return."

"He interferes with a matter related to the Hittite empire," he said. "I do not believe you would want to be involved – our kingdoms peacefully coexist."

The King was uncomfortable with this statement, but he was a proud Lord, and did not like the tone of this ugly man.

"In my house, I decide what concerns me," the King interjected, "but this matter is an unofficial one. My two guests are free to resolve it how they may. I can act as an arbiter if you both agree."

Arithon nodded. Zorkos squinted and then nodded with a cold stare.

"Arithon, then," the King said, "what do you want of this man?"

"I wish to purchase Mara's freedom – if he has him."

Zorkos chuckled and then said, "He is not for sale. I have sworn to bring him back to Hattusa."

"A difficult impasse," the Prince said.

"It is not," Zorkos offered. "I want what Mara stole from me – valuable weapons. And I believe they are in the possession of this Minoan."

Arithon said nothing.

"I will fight this man for what is mine. If I kill him, I want my weapons returned to me. If he kills me, then he can have Mara."

Everyone was silent; anguish flushed Lucina's face and it did not go unnoticed by the Queen.

Arithon said nothing. He had not come to fight – he did not want to fight.

Zorkos laughed out loud. "It seems the Minoan is not up to such a challenge. Mara may be worth a few specks of silver, but he is not worth a fight."

Arithon pursed his lips and his eyes narrowed. He stood and addressed the King. "I accept. If I win, then I ask you to assist me in attaining Mara's release from the Phoenician captain."

"That I can do," the King answered. "He is in my harbor."

"Arithon!" said Lucina.

Arithon looked at her and smiled. He had acted in anger, but for some reason he had no fear of this man, though he knew he should – remember lesson number four: underestimate no one.

"Where?" Zorkos asked.

"Not here – not in the Citadel – it is forbidden," the Prince replied. "We have a courtyard outside the Ilios."

Zorkos spun around and started out. The others looked at each other and then followed. Word spread through the palace and out onto the streets and a growing crowd was assembling before they could arrive. The King, his family, and attendants gathered on the steps of a building with Lucina standing next to the Queen, a look of dread on her face. But she realized her despondency might affect Arithon, and so she smiled and looked at him and mouthed in Minoan, "Dolphin."

Arithon smiled back.

"Arithon," the King said in Achaean, "I will have a shield brought for you."

Arithon smiled as if to himself and replied, "I never have one when I need it. It is a bad habit which I will not break if someone keeps giving me one. I will do without."

The King furrowed his brow, while Zorkos laughed aloud. Lucina looked on.

"Are you sure, young man?"

Arithon nodded.

"Prepare yourselves."

Arithon and Zorkos faced each other and stepped back a few paces. Arithon removed his belt and tunic, retaining only his kilt, then picked up his axe and held it in both hands.

"You have been in some trouble," said Zorkos with interest, looking at Arithon's many scars and unhealed wounds.

Arithon said nothing but stared across at his adversary: focused.

"Begin," said the King.

Zorkos waded in, confident of his weapons, and warrior mentality, even if his opponent was a head taller, and possibly stronger. He swung his sword with a practiced skill. Arithon countered with his bronze axe and the two weapons met with a numbing force that stung their grip. The noise and fury were so violent, that those gathered around in a tight ring anxious to have a close view, were now anxious to give ground: the circle expanded rapidly.

But Arithon saw none of this, concentrating only on his opponent. To his own startling surprise, he was beginning to think like a warrior and not a frightened madman. His mind was calm: there was no hate. He felt fear but no panic. He was doing what he must, because he could, like at Kamari, and, yes, because he was good at it. He accepted his warrior fate with some melancholy, but the hesitancy of reluctance was no more.

His dedication to practice and his earlier fights had seasoned him beyond what Zorkos was expecting. Arithon countered every move the Hittite could launch, and he anticipated every thrust and swing as if he could read the man's thoughts.

Arithon began to develop a strategy; he felt in control; and what a terribly odd sensation it was. He was looking for a weakness; a way to defeat this adversary. And then it was there – the answer was as clear as sky and water: his foe was frustrated by his inability to land a blow.

Arithon, without shield, could not allow contact except on his axe, and so dodged the sweeping arcs and thrusts of his sword, tiring them both. Zorkos, impatient to end it, stepped forward and raised his shield to obscure the view of Arithon, while bringing his sword from underneath. But Arithon met the shield with his left fist, unbalancing Zorkos, whose thrust he struck with his axe, knocking the sword out of his hand and across the courtyard.

Zorkos recovered from his teeter and darted over to regain the sword, but he stood there panting from his efforts.

"The dolphin tries to tire me," Zorkos laughed as they faced each other across the stone paved square.

Arithon said nothing, but maintained his concentration, knowing Zorkos would change his tactics. He did not have to wait long as the Hittite plowed in, only this time he sought to maim. He swung at Arithon's quarters – his arms and legs, trying to wound him deep enough to cripple.

But Mara had taught Arithon this very series of aggressions and their counter tactics on the beach. He felt as if he were sparring with Mara, except Zorkos was wholly intent on drawing blood.

But Arithon prevailed, dodging or springing from every assault, until they were both dripping sweat in the midday sun, only Zorkos was struggling for air to the point of dizziness, while Arithon, though winded, was fueling his body, primed with the strength of youth and a confidence previously unknown to him.

Seeing an advantage, Arithon attacked for the first time. Zorkos fell back, protecting himself well until Arithon landed a powerful blow, shattering his shield and slicing into his left shoulder, causing Zorkos to cry out.

Lucina, distressed to the point of bursting was unable to contain herself and screamed in Minoan, "Dolphin!"

The crowd took up her cry and chanted, "Dolphin! Dolphin! Dolphin!"

Arithon, on balance, both shieldless now, advanced with a series of deadly slices, but Zorkos, the seasoned warrior, was not yet done, and finally caught the haft of the axe with his sword, cracking it off and sending the blades spinning.

387

Remembering his training with Po, he first feigned to the left as Zorkos pushed in, buying enough time to run and retrieve the axe, which he picked up, just as Zorkos aimed a high, two-handed blow to Arithon's head.

Lucina screamed as the blade descended. But Arithon raised the double blades, using them as a shield. The sword struck home on the bronze with a chilling clang.

Arithon pivoted up on his left foot and with his right delivered a violent blow to Zorkos' ribs, sending him over backward – the sword, leaving his hand and spinning off into the crowd of spectators who made way for its trajectory with a collective, "Oooohhhhh."

Zorkos, sprung to his feet like a wild animal, and jumped full force at Arithon's head, causing him to topple over backward, taking the brunt of Zorkos' weight on his chest, knocking the wind from him. He next aimed his thumbs at Arithon's eyes, but Arithon caught both arms by the wrist and heaved enough to dislodge Zorkos from his perch.

This was now a wrestling contest – a test of strength for them both; and they were well matched, both surprised by the ferocity still available.

Arithon could feel the hate in Zorkos' grip as the Hittite managed to get both hands on his throat as they rolled on the stones. Arithon landed a vicious open palm blow to Zorkos' nose, breaking it – blood flowing down his face and dripping onto Arithon. In the scrambling which followed, Zorkos, an efficient killer, attained a superior position on Arithon's back and brought his arm under his chin, choking with all his strength. He put another hand on the side of Arithon's head to get the leverage he needed to break his neck, but Arithon grabbed that hand with both of his and twisted it with all of his strength, causing Zorkos to scream in agony as he wrenched the tendons. Arithon then heaved him over his head, Zorkos landing in a defeated crush.

He did not move but lay looking up at the Theran.

Arithon looked down on the Hittite and huffed, "Mara."

Zorkos rolled up on his side, spat blood and said, "You are too late, Minoan. His head hangs from my mast – go and look at it."

Arithon's eyes widened in horror, and Zorkos laughed aloud, "I killed him yesterday and –"

He did not finish his words, as Arithon kicked him under his chin with a blow that slammed his head back onto the stone with the thud of a dropped melon. Arithon stared at the heap of a man lying at his feet and then turned to look at Lucina on the steps with the other Trojans. She hobbled to him and started to hug him but thought better of it, pulled herself up close, and said, "Arithon, I am sorry."

He stared down, too exhausted to talk. He sank onto the steps and she sat down beside him.

A courtier brought him a drink of water and the gratitude of the King, who disappeared with his attendants, except Queen Annytus, who beckoned Lucina to follow her. Arithon listened to an exchange that was clearly a plea for time, which the Queen granted, but Arithon saw the guards move in closer.

"Arithon," she said in quiet Minoan, "I did not think it would end like this."

"Nor I," he responded, gathering himself, "but who can foresee any ending, especially their own."

"I cannot. I have misjudged many things. My Lutea gambit bought me little. My negotiations are not going well. I almost wish …"

"Come with me."

"Shhh. That is no longer possible, but you need to go before they reconsider you."

"Me?"

Arithon looked past Lucina and saw Annytus was still within earshot and watching them.

"They trust no one and they think you are dangerous. … And you are," she said, nodding over at the lifeless Zorkos.

"My father is in trouble, Arithon. I still think I can help, but I may have miscalculated. The Achaean's interest in me has placed me in danger."

"Can you get away?"

"Not today," she said, and her eyes darted.

"Lucina."

"Arithon. Go. I am a clever girl."

"I know," he said with quiet pride.

"Now go, while you still can. I know where to find you."

"And I, you," he said.

They stood and he reached for the blue stone ring around her neck and fingered it. At the same time, she picked up his hand and twirled its mate about his finger.

"We have said all we needed, Luci. You know all that I feel," he said with a gentle smile. "Hug me and let us part with the memories of our time together. Yes?"

"Yes," she said smiling. She rose on her tiptoes, put her arms around his neck and whispered, "goodbye Ari," into his ear, and then settled back to her feet, turned, and started away.

She could feel his gaze upon her, but she did not turn. She met Annytus and disappeared around the building. Arithon stayed and stared, unseeing, dispirited and broken. It was a long moment before his will returned and moved him from his stricken pose.

He picked up his discarded tunic, retrieved his axe blade and exited the walls of the city. As he approached the quay, he left the main road and angled off toward his skiff, picking his way through the fly covered rot and detritus ejected by a walled populous. He forced himself to take a glance at the Phoenician ship, to verify Zorkos' crushing words, and saw a human head, blackened by the sun, hanging from the mast.

He turned away too numb to feel any more.

Once in the skiff, he bent to the oars, watching the city on the hill recede as he moved out of the harbor. He stepped aboard his ship and Po looked into his eyes and knew the boy was no longer.

***

It was evening, and the *Dolphin* was flying south, her sail full of the north wind. Arithon stood alone at the bow, staring ahead. The crew noticed, as his usual spot was back by the steering oar, and they wondered at the look on his face – a grimness he had never shown.

Szaba was settled on the aft deck, building arrows from the raw materials he kept on hand. He did it often, and it seemed to relax him. Sestos had watched him do it a hundred times, fascinated by the skill and dexterity he showed creating the points from raw obsidian, and fitting them into rods he straightened with his scraping tool after rolling them on the deck to see how they wobbled. Sestos was watching him now, but his mind was on Arithon.

"Szaba."

Szaba looked up from his work.

Sestos continued, "I am worried about Ari. I have never seen him like this, and I have known him all my life."

Szaba looked at him but made no comment.

"Why don't you go talk to him?" Sestos suggested.

"You have known him all your life."

"Szaba, stop that! You would be better, I think. I joke too much, and this looks … well … serious – and you are always serious."

"And you are always joking."

"Szaba! Stop that I said! Would you go and talk to him? He loves you, Master Nubian."

"And he loves you too, Master Minoan," Szaba said with a smile, enjoying this spar with Sestos – the Sestos of many words. "But I will go and do as you ask."

"Good. Do it soon. He is making me crazy standing up there like a bowsprit. It is unsettling the crew."

"Yes."

Szaba finished the arrow point he was making, much to the consternation of Sestos, rolled his work back up into the skin with his tools, and rose stiffly to his feet.

He came up behind Arithon and was there for a few seconds before Arithon noticed him.

"Szaba," he said, "it is good to see you walking again."

"I am better. Lucina has magic."

Arithon started as if in pain and said, "I am glad."

"How is she?"

"In trouble, I think."

"I was once in trouble," said Szaba, staring south. "But you changed that. You are stronger than you know. My life is by your side, as long as you will have it so."

"We are going to war, my friend."

"Short or long, my choice is the same."

Arithon turned with a slow smile and their eyes met.

Arithon glanced back at Po, inhaled deep the sea air, felt the nimble role of his ship, and knew he was ready for Knossos – where it all began. But he was not whole.

Szaba remained with him, the spray in their faces and the wind at their back, the *Dolphin* gently bobbing at the bow as she pushed through the water – the fastest ship in the Aegean.

And so they stood until the sun set and Po called them back for a bite to eat and discuss the course they should take back to Minoa: the land of ancient mariners.

***

After full dark, the *Dolphin*, still plowing the waves, guided by the stars and anxious to make headway, pulled up as her sail dropped to the deck. Two figures climbed into the skiff and pushed off, while the *Dolphin* again hoisted her sail. It billowed full, straining the ship into motion, as she disappeared into the darkness heading south, the tiller vibrating the steersman's hands.

The End

ABOUT THE AUTHOR

Late one evening in the college years, alone in the attic apartment of an old Victorian home, David discovered a worn copy of *The Hobbit*. When he reached *The End* and looked up, daylight was breaking through the dormer window. Since that morning, stories rooted in history and myth have taken him on life's journey. On his den shelves, alongside his Tolkien collection, are scores of books on Ancient Greece, which taught him the veracity of the Mark Twain quote, "The ancients stole all our ideas from us."

When not reading, he explores the streets of Seattle on bike, hikes the Pacific Northwest, and marvels at the astonishing impossibility called birds.